I ACCIDENTALLY HOOKED UP WITH A VAMPIRE

USA TODAY BESTSELLING AUTHOR

JESSICA CAGE

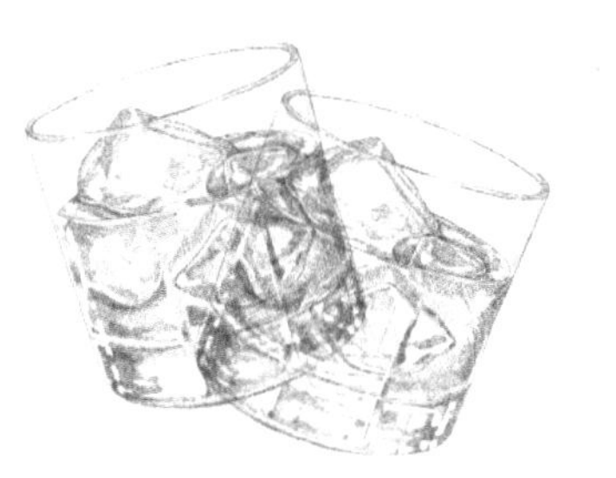

Contents

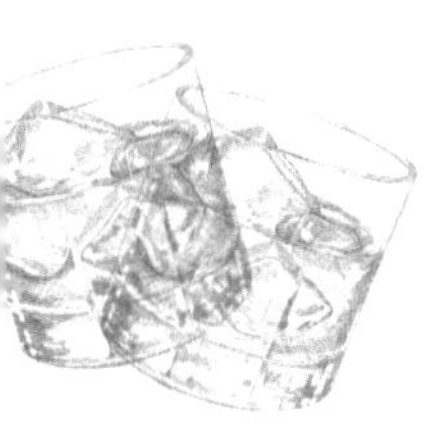

TRIGGER WARNING

This is a book with vampires.

This is a vampire book.

This is a spicy vampire book.

Vampire things happen.

Spicy vampire things.

Blood, boo, we talking about blood.

On things, in things, and being slurped from things.

Have you ever been swallowed up?

Well, not like this!

If bloody vampire play is a problem, this is your warning. This is a book with

vampires.

This is a vampire book. This is a spicy vampire book.

Vampire things happen.

Spicy vampire things.

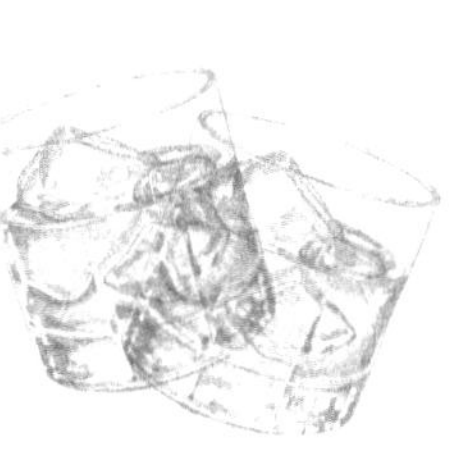

THIS ONE HAS NO BOOTY JUICE...

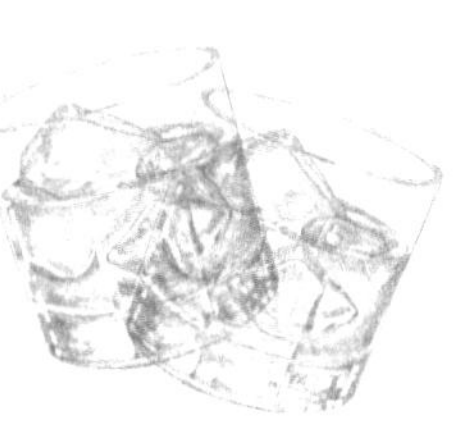

1

Boss Bitch?

"**C**ome sit on my face and nourish me."

I frowned at the text from the man labeled, "Shaky legs". The last time I saw him, he tried to pick me up and damn near dropped me on my head. They say the skinny ones have freakish strength. Yeah, well, he didn't get any of that. Instead of responding with a quip about how he needed to focus on leg day, I put the phone down. There were much more important things to focus on than a man whose legs trembled when he tried to carry me to the bed.

"Alright, bitch, you got this!" I pointed to myself in the mirror at my desk in the small office I'd soon be trading in for one with actual windows! "This is what you worked for. Five years in the making! Best buyer in the game! Of course they're promoting you! Who else would they choose? Walk in there with your head high, but not too cocky because, you know, melanin. And walk out on top of the world!" After I finished hyping myself up, I checked my edges, made sure my braided bun was secure, then headed out the door.

I walked into the large conference room with my head high and my acceptance speech ready to go. I'd worked my ass off, and it was finally happening. Management only used the big conference room for big announcements. It was my time to shine. As I closed the door to my small office, I imagined my name next to my new title. Whitney Harris, Senior Acquisitions Broker. This was a moment that would not only add more notoriety to my name, being in one of the top private brokerages in the world, but it would also more than double my salary!

I went over the list of my qualifications in my head. Tripled the profitability of my department in the last quarter? Check. Acquired four highly sought after pieces? Check. Landed a contract with an artist everyone was breaking their necks to get? Not an easy thing, considering the woman lived on the other side of the country and was never available for face-to-face meetings. Check! Though I worried that one could work against me because she vanished for months after we signed the contract and the higher ups chose not to work with her anymore, but that wasn't my fault. I did my job!

The hefty bonus check sitting in my bank account and encouraging words from upper management in our last meetings added to my confidence.

I caught my reflection in the window and straightened the collar of the new silk shirt I'd worn just for the occasion. The only thing hurting the moment was the fresh butt length braids in my hair. I had them pulled up into a bun that added at least six inches to my height.

I sat in the chair across from the managing partner of my department, my nails freshly manicured and ready to shake his hand as I accepted the offer.

"I'm sorry to have to tell you this, Whitney, but we have to let you go." Mr. Conrad, the managing partner for my department, sat across from me, coffee foam on his top lip and feigned pity in his eyes as he dropped the hammer.

When I tell you my jaw nearly hit the glass table in front of me. There I was, in my power suit, on cloud nine after just signing a mortgage for a new condo, and my history-making step up in the industry turned into a swift boot out the front door.

"Maybe I didn't hear you correctly. Did you say you're letting me go?" I leaned forward so I could better hear him. "After the year I've had, the raving quarterly review, and the multiple six figure contracts I've landed, you're letting me go?"

"As you know, the last quarter wasn't as strong as we had forecasted and, because of that, we have to make some cuts." Beads of sweat formed on his bald head as he gave me the form response. That was what they always said.

"John, please don't play in my face when you just gave me a bonus a month ago!" I sat back. "What's the real reason?"

"Whitney, you know what this is." He lowered his voice. "I don't want to do this, but they're forcing my hand on the matter. That contract that fell through, despite your other successes... It put a bad taste in the owners' mouths."

"How was I supposed to know she was going to drop off the face of the Earth? She never did anything like that before! And you were the one who told me to do anything it took to get Rayna to sign that contract!"

"Yes, I know, but you were the lead buyer on the deal." He lifted the cup of coffee and sipped from it, adding even more froth to his top lip. "And considering she had a perfect reputation, they think you're the reason she did what she did."

"You've got to be kidding me." It took everything in me not to reach across the table and slap the foam from his face. "So that's it?"

"We have a sizeable severance package here for you, and I've written out some great recommendations as well. I even pushed for them to give you more money in the deal, and you'll still get your pending commissions on the contracts being settled now." He slid the folder across the table to me. "Take your time and review the package. We're open to negotiations."

"Yeah. Right. Thanks." I took the folder but didn't open it. I would look it over when I didn't have his beady eyes staring at me.

"HR will reach out to you for your exit interview. Take the rest of the week to get your things in order. I've set your official last day as Friday." John stood from the table and awkwardly straightened his jacket before reaching out to shake my hand.

"Of course." I stood, holding all my rage inside, and walked out of the office. I wouldn't give them the satisfaction of seeing me upset, and I damn sure wouldn't sully my perfect manicure by touching his sweaty hand after he just fired me. Nope, I would paste a neutral expression on my face until I got out of the building and far away from any security cameras. Then, I would lose my shit!

John had to be out of his damn mind if he thought I would hang around after being let go. Within five minutes of returning to my office, I packed my stuff, including my portable vanity and pictures of my cat, and headed home. It didn't matter what the paperwork said. Was it professional? Maybe not, but professionalism went out the damn window with my hopes and dreams. I was done.

"Hey girl, are you okay?" Nina, the nosey woman who I knew had been gunning for my job, met me at the elevator.

"Perfect." I smiled and pressed the call button for the elevator. Of course she knew I was being let go. Hell, she was probably the one who pushed for it. The heffa had been lurking around the office, just waiting for me to mess up.

"I just heard the news." She flipped her stiff ass bob, shaking dandruff onto her pink top.

"Oh, is that so?" I tilted my head. "In the five minutes since it happened, the news made it across the office and into your ear?"

"Well…" She dropped her eyes.

"No worries. I'm good. But you may want to do something about that scalp situation." I pointed to her shoulder. "I hear a little rosemary oil works great for that."

Just then, a soft chime sounded in the hall as the elevator door opened. I stepped inside, proud of myself for not grabbing her by the neck and shaking her like a snow globe. Watching her expression drop didn't entirely make up for the shit storm that had become my day, but it damn sure put a smile on my face. Right as the doors closed, my phone buzzed with new notifications. I looked down to see supportive messages from my girls in the group chat.

"You got this, girl!" Lena messaged with six twerking emojis.

"Yes! Boss woman in the HOUSE!" Jackie followed up with a series of houses, airplanes, and martini glasses.

I read the messages, and my heart dropped—not only because my world was collapsing, but because I would have to feel that collapse alone. There was no way I was going to tell them about what happened, not with such a big night coming up. I would keep it to myself. That wouldn't be so hard to do for forty-eight hours.

"Thanks! See you girls tonight!" I replied simply and put the phone in my pocket as the elevator doors opened to the parking deck.

It was a twenty-two-minute drive home from my former job to my new condo. The condo I'd just closed on. The condo that was loaded with unopened boxes and gifts from friends and family.

Twenty-two minutes for me to dwell on the idea that my life had just imploded, just enough time for me to wonder if it was too late to back out on my mortgage. I could handle going back to a crappy one-bedroom apartment. I'd stayed in my last place, which was falling down around me, for years after I could afford to move out. Why? Well, this was why. My biggest fear: signing for a mortgage and then losing my income.

Granted, my savings were pretty stacked and my portfolio looked good, but in the current job market, I could be without a gig for a year or more. How would I keep it all together?

"Okay, one night to feel sorry for yourself, Whitney. That's all you get!" I stared at my expression in the rearview mirror of my car. I'd made it home and sat parked in the designated spot of the shared garage. Instead of jumping out and running to my lush new home, I sat there staring at the bag that had all the important things I grabbed from my desk.

WHITNEY HARRIS

I don't know why I took the name plate from my door. Maybe it was to remind myself that I'd made it far enough to have a private office. Maybe it would motivate me to kick my shit into gear and get back out there. Or maybe it would haunt me, a reminder of my failure.

Ten minutes later, I was standing outside my door and hyping myself up to walk inside. No, buying this condo wasn't the biggest mistake of my life. No, I wouldn't go into debt and end up homeless on the sidewalk. It was all going to be O-Kay!

After my weak ass pep talk, I opened the door and immediately received a smack in the face. So much for lifting my mood. The massive paw of my Maine Coon knocked against my cheek before Maverick jumped down from the ledge above the door. The twenty-seven-pound, nearly four-foot mass of black hair stood in front of me and rolled his eyes before he hissed and launched an attack on my legs with a series of smacks.

"Dammit! Stop it, Maverick!" I fussed at him. I knew it wasn't his fault. Maverick was particular about his lifestyle, and I'd moved him away from his comfort zone and had yet to unbox his new cat tower. The thing was a giant contraption that would cover half of a 20x15 wall in the front room. I promised him I would have it up so he could look out over the land like the king he was, and yet, it still sat in the box by the window.

To appease the massive beast, who had a natural white collar in his fur that made him look like a spy, I quickly went to grab his snacks. Once he had a handful placed neatly at his feet, he chilled out.

"I'll have plenty of time to put the damn thing together now." As soon as the words passed my lips, my heart dropped as my eyes found the one piece of art I'd put up.

I couldn't wait to get it on my wall, and the day I got the keys to the place, I hung it over the fireplace—a beautiful alien landscape that somehow felt familiar to me. It looked even more vibrant in contrast to the stone wall behind it. It was hard to deny her talent, but in that moment, if I could find the artist, Rayna, I would smash the damn thing over her head.

Whatever happened, I would make sure I kept my place. The condo featured high ceilings, hardwood flooring, and lots of natural lighting coming through the floor to ceiling windows. It had just enough space for me and my big ass cat. A great primary suite, a secondary room I would use for my office. This was my home now, and I wouldn't let a bald man and a bobble head bitch ruin that for me.

I turned my back on the painting and headed to my bedroom. There was still work to be done. I could busy myself with unpacking until it was time to head out to meet the girls. Did I want to have to pretend like I was okay? No. Would I ruin Lena's accomplishment with my shit? Hell, no. I'd still be out of a job after she made her big announcement to the world.

With my music blasting, I'd gotten most of my room done before it was time to go. I fed Maverick because I didn't want another attack when I got home and headed out with my best smile plastered on my face.

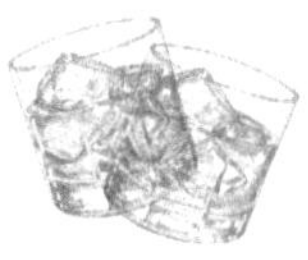

"Not all dick is created equal, that's all I'm saying!" Jackie clapped her hands as she fell on the small plush couch beside me. "You know damn well that some dick just changes your life. And others... Well, we pretend they never happened."

"Girl, what the hell?" I stared at my friend in disbelief as she dished about her latest venture into the world of dating.

The woman had no filter, even when we were in the middle of a bougie dress shop. Over her shoulder, the clerk gawked at her outburst, and her light brown face turned beet red. Jackie just kept on talking like nothing happened.

We sat in the waiting area outside of the dressing room as Lena tried on dresses for her big night. We were the judge and jury, only there to make sure she looked her absolute best for her party the next night. It was one of the few places in the area that made dresses for plus sized baddies that didn't add a touch of frumpiness to each design.

"Listen, there are classifications for dick, and you know I'm right!" She lowered her voice after I pointed out the woman behind her. "Honestly, there should be certified publications about this somewhere."

"Classifications?" I cackled. "Girl, I just cannot deal with you sometimes."

Jackie was the outspoken one in our trio. If something was on her mind, you were going to hear about it. It's what made her such a successful content creator; that, and her master's in marketing. She was a powerhouse and had built a brand that empowered women without sugar coating anything.

Around the corner, Lena's head poked out of the dressing room. "And what you would classify this one as?"

Jackie tapped her chin with her finger as she pondered the question then blurted out, "Relationship Dick!"

I couldn't help it. I fell out laughing and instantly regretted it as my freshly braided hair dropped out of the loose bun. Despite the pain spreading across my scalp, I kept on cackling. Maybe it was the complimentary wine, or maybe it was just that I always felt so much better when I was with my girls, but the weight of the world was slowly melting away.

"Please tell us: what is relationship dick?" I urged Jackie to continue.

"Relationship dick. You know, it's good enough if it comes with the benefit of commitment," Jackie explained her reasoning. "I mean, you get cuddles, food deliveries, and foot rubs. It's good, and it basically hits the spot and can be damn good with some guidance, but it better have some added perks to make it worth the ride." She rocked her hips like she was on a horse, holding her drink carefully so she didn't spill a drop.

"Wait a minute. Is this someone you would commit to?" I gasped, because I had never thought I would see the day when Jackie said she would settle down. "I don't know... Relationship dick doesn't sound too bad."

"Him? No. Girl, you know I don't make commitments. But that's his classification. Nothing I can do about it." She shrugged. "It's not *my* fault. And honestly, his morning breath is hell. I told him he should go see a doctor and recommended him to the guy up north."

"You did not recommend him to your ex!" I slapped her thigh.

"Why the hell not? He's a competent doctor and does great work. I'm not going to mess with his bag just because he was cursed with a little dick."

"And what about Scott?" Lena popped out of the dressing room and did a quick twirl in the pea green dress then frowned when we both gave her a thumbs down. The damn thing made her hips look wide and flattened out that plump ass. "He seemed nice enough."

She shrugged and headed back into the dressing room to change into the next look.

"Oh, Scott? Scott had that damn dickmatize dick." Jackie fanned herself with her hand. "No way I could keep his ass around. I love myself too much for that."

"Please explain this one." I lifted my glass while we waited for Lena to try on her next dress. This conversation was perfect. It was fun, lighthearted, and avoided the dreaded topic of my promotion.

"That's the dick you're supposed to run away from. It's so good that it makes you forget you're a grown woman with goals, responsibilities, hopes, and dreams of your own. One day, you're living your best life, and the next, you're calling out of work and skipping out on your girls." She sucked her teeth. "The problem with that kind of dick is, it tricks you into thinking you're in love. You completely forget that it's connected to a bum who can't do shit for you. And what's worse is, when you're selfish with that kind of dick, it turns on you!"

"Turns on you?" I leaned away from her and scrunched up my nose. "Does it bite you or something?"

"You know what I mean. Think about that girl, Ciara, from college. Home-girl had the brightest future. Then, she met Evan, and it was like she completely forgot who she was after he put it on her. Flunked out of her last damn class and dropped off the face of the Earth. Last I heard, she is struggling with his four kids by her damn self. And where is he? Out there, putting it down on another unsuspecting fool."

"Well damn. When you lay it out like that, I can think of a few others who fall into that category." I nodded. There were a few women I knew who let a man distract them from their goals. Every one of them was playing catch up to make up for the time they lost because of it.

"We all know at least one woman who let a man knock her off her path." She crossed her finger over her chest. "I pray I never fall down the path of the dickmatization."

"Stop it." I shook my head at her.

"Whatever. Y'all know I'm right." She pointed at me. "I hope you would slap some sense into me, just like I would for you."

"What kind of dick are you looking for?" I asked her as I struggled to put the bun back in my hair. After the second failed attempt, Jackie popped my hand with her bony finger and took over.

"Right now, I'm looking for that good comfort dick. You know, it hits the right spot and doesn't ruin your damn life. That's the dick we all should look for. It comes attached to a man who will take you out and not want to wife you up or fill you with babies. Just chill." She finished my bun then kissed my cheek. "There you go, babe."

"Thank you. You know, I can see this becoming a new series for you." I thought about her massive social media following. She had an army of women who would go to war for her. They would eat it up.

"I'm already working it out in my head. The girls will love it!" She nodded. "Maybe I'll write a book of my own. Lena can help me."

"Yes, our award-winning, bestselling, internationally known author bestie!" I cheered.

This was the reason I couldn't tell them about my job. Lena's dreams were coming true. The book she wrote, *To Conjure Love*, about a woman who read a spell and created her perfect man, had become an international sensation. In twenty-four hours, she would stand in front of an audience of her peers and her fans and announce that her book was not only becoming a series, but she'd signed a seven-figure deal for it to be turned into a major movie! I was so proud of her, my heart could explode, and I just didn't want to take away from her moment. I knew Lena; she was the mom of our group. The moment she learned about my termination, her focus would shift from celebrating herself to coddling me.

"I really can't believe this is happening." Lena stepped out of the room again, this time wearing a cute cream dress that complimented her dark brown skin and showed off just enough of her curves.

"Well, you better believe it. And while it's happening, you're going to look damn good!" Jackie stood and clapped for our girl.

After several twirls and a bow, she paid for the dress, and we all headed home. Lena had to rest up, Jackie had content to schedule, and I had a damn cat tower to put together.

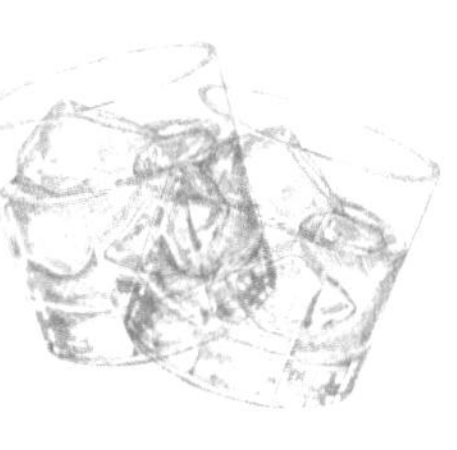

2

Baldy and the Big Mouth

"*You dirty skank!*" Maybe Maverick didn't say that, but I swear that's the look he shot me as he walked by.

It wasn't my fault I only got half the tower together. The shit was way more complicated than I thought. I stood in the mirror, checking myself and ignoring the cat.

"You're unemployed, but you sho' is fine!" I smacked my own ass because no one else was going to do it. The soft green dress made me feel powerful, and it also hid the bloating after a night of drinking and eating ice cream while I fought with the damn tower.

I'm not gonna lie, it took some time for me to get comfortable in my skin, and it wasn't because I was a plus sized queen. No, it was because my mental health was trash. You know how I learned that? I lost one hundred and six pounds and was still sobbing into my pillow every night. Six years of therapy and seventy-two of those lost pounds returned to my ass, and I was finally happy with who I was.

Just in time for a spiral of, "What do I do with my life now?"

I fed Maverick, who ignored his food and threw his ass in my face. "Get over yourself!" I fussed at him before I grabbed my purse, a small gold clutch with a claw clasp, and headed out the door.

I drove out of the city to the coast, where an exclusive gallery awaited. That's where Lena's party was happening, courtesy of my connections in the art world. It wasn't until I pulled up in front of the waterfront property that I remembered how I made that happen: John Conrad. It was his connection that secured the event space, and I'd invited him to join the celebration.

Just as I handed the valet my keys, John pulled up. The bright red sports car, signature of a man going through a mid-life crisis, roared as it drove up behind me. I wanted to do anything but talk to that man again, but it was satisfying watching him struggle to get out of the car only inches above the ground. He actually *rolled* out of the damn thing and had to push himself up from the ground.

"Pathetic," I muttered as I turned and headed inside. There was something else I would have to do all night: avoid that ridiculous man.

"Big money in the big money dress!" Jackie danced up to me as I walked through the large glass doors and into the gallery space.

The new construction was only a year old and had hosted some of the most elite events in the area. The massive glass windows at the back of the building overlooked the ocean, the highlight of the space for me. That was where I planned to spend most of my visit.

Prompted by Jackie's greeting, I twirled to give her every angle of the dress she helped me pick out and accepted her offer of a fresh martini. My girl knew me well.

"You look like a snack! Let me get a bite," she teased as we walked further into the space.

"Me? Girl, look at you!" I drew my finger up and down the length of the mini dress with pastel mosaic print and subtle beading. With her short pixie cut, she looked like a walking piece of art curated perfectly for the venue.

Jackie loved a strapless dress because it meant she could show off her tattoo that covered her from her neck down her left shoulder. It was an intricate floral piece she got as soon as she finished college. She said she had to wait because she wanted her father's checks to clear and cover her tuition before she pissed him off.

"Well, I couldn't let my besties outdo me. Besides, there are going to be some fancy art guys here. Gotta catch their eye some way!" She wiggled her narrow hips and sipped from her drink.

Where Lena and I were certified thickums, Jackie had a swimmer's build. If it weren't for her triple Ds, she might have taken up the sport. She said her breasts messed with her buoyancy.

"Where's Lena?" I scanned the large open space with art-lined walls. "Have you seen her yet?"

"Just briefly. They swept her into one of the back rooms to get ready for her speech."

"This is amazing. I mean, I remember those late calls with her talking about how much she wanted to give up on this dream. Now look at her."

"I'm glad we were there to help her through it." Jackie nodded. "I mean, look at all of us! We're doing the damn thing! Educated, sexy, and successful! It's what we planned."

"Yeah." I dropped my eyes and sipped my drink. "I need to find the restroom. Drank too much water before leaving the house."

"Okay, I'll—"

"Jackie, is that you?" a matronly voice called out, and we turned to see Agathine Bradley, one of our former professors and an editor at Lena's publisher.

"Damn. I guess I have to be cordial." Jackie took another swig from her glass. "At least this time, she can't ruin my life with that red ink of hers. The ladies' room is in the back corner by the big red painting that looks like day two of your worst period. I'll find you in a bit."

"Great descriptors." I waved her off, honestly grateful I didn't have to keep up the show. Besides, if she followed me to the toilet, there was no way I was going to avoid the topic of my job.

It was only by a miracle I skirted around it at the dress shop. The one time they asked me about it, I lied and told them the meeting had been delayed. I'd have to buy them sushi to make up for it—that was the rule. White lies in our friendship were okay, as long as they were followed up with a solid explanation, a week of groveling, and a sushi boat big enough to feed a sorority.

I spotted the sign for the ladies' room right where Jackie said it would be, next to a giant painting of what appeared to be the worst blood clot known to woman. The thing was nightmare inducing! I stopped to examine the painting and wondered why the hell they hadn't swapped it out for something more fitting for the event. If nothing else, it would be a conversation starter.

The door to the ladies' room was at the front of a long hall that stretched to the back offices where the staff worked. My hand was inches from the handle when the door to the office opened. Thank God I didn't actually have to pee, or it would have been a total embarrassment because I swear, every muscle in my body relaxed when I made eye contact with the man who stepped into the hall.

He was taller than me, a difficult thing to find at nearly six feet myself. He had a towering stature, wide shoulders, and a smooth brown complexion. This wasn't a man without a skincare routine. He wore a tailored suit with gold cufflinks that matched the round wireframes on his face.

I had no idea who he was, but the brain between my thighs was instantly intrigued.

"Mr. James." A short woman appeared by his side. "I'm sorry, there are two other contracts we need you to sign for the catering."

"Yes, of course," he spoke, and it was like he was whispering in my ear.

When he glanced down at the woman, I took that as my moment to dip inside the door. This night was about Lena, not my suddenly raging hormones.

"This is not the time. You know how you get when a man gets in your head. All your damn common sense goes out the window! The brain needs to be locked in right now," I fussed at my reflection in the bronze-framed mirror. "Celebrate Lena, dodge John, and take your ass home!"

Did I need to stay in there for twenty minutes? No, but I wasn't risking bumping into that man. I figured it gave him plenty of time to leave and was on point with the avoidant behavior I needed to make it through the night. And hell, if he noticed how long I was on the toilet, he might not want to approach me! Win, win! Sorta.

Twenty minutes wasn't long enough.

"Whitney, there you are." John came walking out of the men's room just as I stepped into the hall.

"Oh, hey." I nodded.

"You know, I wasn't sure if I should still come to this thing, considering everything that happened." He adjusted his belt buckle.

"You were invited." I couldn't even *pretend* to be nice to the guy. It was all too fresh. There he was, riding the success my hard work brought to the department, and there I was, unemployed.

"Yes, well, I wanted to tell you—"

"Girl, I feel like I just left the worst oral examination of my life!" Jackie walked up.

"That bad?" I turned away from John to address my friend and hoped he would take that as a message to leave me alone. You think he did? No!

He stood there lurking as I spoke to Jackie about her run-in with the professor, long enough for Jackie to frown at him.

"Can I help you?" She twisted her lips. "Is there a reason you're standing here staring at us?"

"Yes, I'm—" John started.

"Jackie, this is John Conrad. He's one of the managing partners at the brokerage company," I introduced him, hoping to avoid any words like "former" or "termination."

"Oh, it's nice to meet you." Her expression relaxed into mild disinterest.

"Yes, you as well." Jackie gave me a side eye, her expression screaming, *"Is this someone I need to kick in the nuts for you?"*

The answer was yes, but it wasn't the time for that.

"I was just telling Whitney how happy I am for the invite. My sister loves the book. I was hoping to get a signed copy for her," he lied. But why?

"John, there you are," a grating voice that perfectly matched her parmesan-producing scalp called out over the soft jazz music played by a band in the far corner of the space.

I know damn well he didn't ask her to come to this! The thought burned through my mind right as the stiff bob bubble head bitch walked up. Nina.

"Whitney, you're here too?" she asked, as if she didn't already know Lena was my best friend.

"Why wouldn't I be?" I spoke before I could temperature check her. Damn my hot head, because the next words out of her mouth ruined my plans for the night.

"Well, I just assumed since you don't work for the company anymore, you wouldn't want to be at a showing like this. I mean, everyone is already talking about how you got fired." She pursed her lips and adjusted the strap of her gold frock. "John thought it would be a good idea for me to come since I'm taking over some of your old accounts. I can network a little without the pressure of contracts and—"

Nina stopped talking as those bony fingers with the pink ballerina nails popped up in her face.

"Hold on, what?" Jackie looked at me.

"Excuse me. I was talking." Nina pushed Jackie's hand out of her face, and I had to grab my friend. I knew where this would go.

"Jackie, it's cool." I grabbed her by the waist and pulled her to my side.

"Is it?" Jackie looked through her long lashes at me. "What is she talking about?"

"John," I addressed the moron before I scowled at the big mouth next to him. "Nina. Enjoy the party."

It took two minutes to pull Jackie to a location where I could spill the tea without flooding the room.

"You got fired?" The moment we were out of earshot, she went in on me.

"Yeah, I did." It wasn't like I could deny it anymore. What would I do, claim two of my coworkers were bold-faced liars?

"When did this happen?" She looked over her shoulder.

"Yesterday. Actually, right before you guys texted me wishing me good luck."

"Yesterday? You told us they rescheduled the meeting. You said it was delayed."

"Yes, the meeting about my amazing promotion was delayed...indefinitely."

Jackie stepped away just long enough to grab two fresh drinks from the server passing us by. She handed one to me and took a sip from her own. "How did this happen?"

I pointed across the room at the two people we'd just left. John was grabbing a drink from a server who passed him, and Nina was talking his head off. The man already looked like he was regretting his choice. Good. "He hyped me up then knocked me down. I'm still trying to understand it myself."

"Why didn't you tell us?"

"You know damn well why I kept it to myself." I took a deep breath and sighed. "Lena. Come on, Jackie. You know how she is. One word of this, and this moment in her life becomes a footnote in her efforts to take care of me. I couldn't do that to her."

"Yeah, you're right." Jackie sucked her teeth. "Damn. Okay. Tonight, we keep this to ourselves, but tomorrow, we're telling her everything. And then, you're going to give me that busted Edna's information so I can find her and kick her ass. I don't know the details yet, but I know she has something to do with this. I can smell a pick me a mile away."

My laughter mixed with the taste of the drink on my lips.

"I ain't never seen a bob so damn stiff!" she cackled and lifted her finger, pointing at the short menace. "That's what happens when you're not a girl's girl! May her lace never melt and her scalp always itch!"

Lena wouldn't mother me that night, but Jackie would. She kept a drink in my hand and a smile on my face. Any time John or Nina came near me, she gave them the meanest death stare that had them running in the opposite direction.

We stood with our arms linked and our eyes teary when Lena came out to a loud round of applause, and we screamed to our hearts' content after she made the announcement! A movie was officially in the works! After that, it was a slew of drinks, bumping dance music, and continued celebration. We hoped we would get more face time with Lena, but every time we got near her, someone else was pulling her away. The last time we tried, Agathine appeared, and Jackie vanished like a phantom in the night.

An hour after I lost Jackie, I was standing by the window, looking out at the water. There was a small nook created by the massive poster boards of the book cover, the perfect place to hide and let my mind drift. There was something so calming about it; watching the waves crashing against the shore had me considering a stroll on the beach. I would have done it if I wasn't afraid of being posted on the nightly news.

Local woman loses job, gets drunk and swept out to sea!

What a terrible headline!

"I've been looking for you all night."

I scoffed before I turned around because I knew who it was. John stumbled over to me, face dripping sweat and breath smelling like ass. Great way to represent the company, John!

"We should keep in touch." He laid his sweaty palm on my arm and leaned in closer. "Just because we don't work together doesn't mean we can't be friends."

"That's exactly what it means." I pulled away from him and wiped my arm with the cocktail napkin from my drink. "Considering we were never friends before, why would we start now?"

"Exactly. This is our chance." He stepped closer to me. "We were professionals. Restrained. There's no need for that now."

"You need to find some coffee and sober up." I stepped away from him again and realized it was the wrong move. It put me further out of view of everyone at the party.

"What do you mean? I'm plenty sober." He moved in closer and again put his slimy hand on my arm.

I looked over my shoulder. No one noticed because no one could see us. I had to diffuse the situation without making a scene.

"Take your hands off me unless you want to lose one." I dropped my eyes to his hand and threatened his life.

"Whitney, don't be like that," John insisted. "You have no idea how long I've wanted you."

"It's not a mutual feeling, John," I scoffed.

"Is there a problem here?" The deep voice was like a jazz bass, cutting through the noise of the party with confidence and turning the expression on the sweaty face in front of me from a sad attempt at seduction to one of fear.

"Mr. James." John took several nervous steps away from me before he turned to look at the man who had joined us.

"Is there something I can help you with?"

"No, not at all. I was just speaking to a former employee." John, of course, said that for no reason other than to establish some form of dominance. He wanted to put me in my place.

"Whitney Harris?" Mr. James looked at me before holding his hand out.

"Yes," I said and placed my hand in his to shake. *Breathe, bitch, breathe!* My mind raced right along with my quickening pulse. How was it possible for a total stranger to make my entire body hum?

"It's great to finally meet you."

"Finally?" I pulled my hand from his because I wanted him to pull me in closer. If I didn't end the contact, I would find a way to embarrass myself.

"Yes. I've heard great things about your work in this art space." He paused and looked over his shoulder at John. "Is there a reason you're still here?"

"Oh, I, um, yes, I had more to say to Whitney," John shakily asserted.

"Right." Mr. James turned his deep brown eyes back to me. "Excuse us a moment."

He turned, placed his hand on John's shoulder, and pushed him far enough away from me so I couldn't hear what he whispered in his ear. I didn't need to hear it; I could see the result on the scummy guy's face. With an expression that said he was ready to vomit from fear, John nodded to Mr. James, waved at me, and then tucked his tail and ran.

"I don't know what you said to him, but thank you." I smiled at Mr. James when he returned to my side.

"You look upset." He shook his head.

"I am," I said honestly before I eyed the glass in my hand. Maybe it was time for me to stop drinking. I should have played it cool. No, that sweaty, ball-headed bastard hadn't upset me!

Mr. James tapped the frame of his glasses, nodded to the rest of the room, and then presented me with the one thing I wanted most: an escape. "If you'd like, I can offer you a better view of the water and a chance to get away from things."

"I don't know." My mind said no, but that smaller brain, the one squealing between my legs, said hell yes!

"There are also much stronger drinks available." I pointed to the nearly empty glass in my hand.

What was I saying about needing to stop drinking for the night?

I tossed one last look over my shoulder and then threw that thought out the window with my hopes of being the next Senior Acquisitions Broker.

"Lead the way."

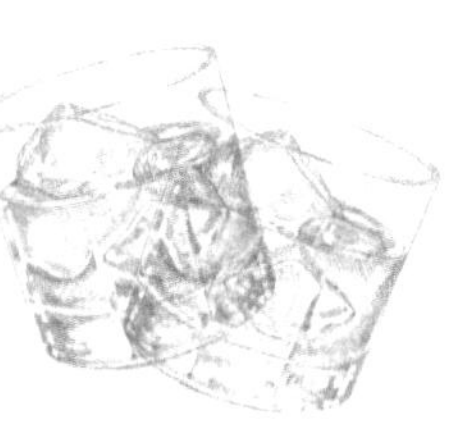

3

Domino Effect

I followed Mr. James along the edge of the party. What started off as a sophisticated affair had quickly become a dance party, Jacki and Lena at the heart of it. I smiled, watching my girls enjoying themselves. Then, I saw John and Nina at one of the high top tables. His shoulders slumped, and she was eyeing Luna Sky, the curator for another major gallery.

I only wished I could be in the room when she approached Luna. If there was ever a woman who hated a kiss ass, it was the woman who busted balls to get where she was! She was an example of how to play the game and not fuck up your moral compass trying to get to the top.

We walked away from the party, down the hall marked by the blood clot painting, and toward the private back offices. I thought he would lead me into the room I'd seen him come out of, but instead, it turned right down another hall that ended in a set of gold elevator doors.

"Fancy," I said.

He smiled over his shoulder before tapping a small screen where you'd expect the call button to be. It lit up, and he quickly entered a code before the doors slid open.

He stepped to the side, allowing me to enter ahead of him.

The ride was quick and quiet, and it opened to a massive private gallery.

Mr. James stepped out and waited for me to take in the amazing private collection of paintings and sculptures. The room was full of modern artists. I'd expected to see the classics like Rembrandt and Picasso, but he surprised me.

I admired the sculptures of an artist named Anak, who did the most intricate work with stone. Each sculpture was like a nesting egg. Inside it was a smaller, more complicated piece, the smallest of which you would need a magnifying glass to see.

"So, this is what happened to it." I chuckled. "You know I worked on getting this for months! One day, poof, it was no longer available."

"Sorry to snatch it from under you like that, but I couldn't let it get away." He joined me in admiring the piece. "You know he's working on another collection? If I have it my way, every piece will be mine."

"Trust me, I understand. I wouldn't want them to have it now anyway." Served those assholes right for firing me.

"What happened there, if you don't mind me asking?" he questioned.

"The job ended." I shrugged—what more was there to say? A lot more, actually, but I wasn't sure I wanted to get into all that.

"Fair enough." He slipped his finger under the perfectly tied knot at his neck to loosen his tie. "Can I get you something to drink?"

"You're hanging out with me?" I don't know why I expected the man to drop me off in the private space and leave me alone.

"Yes. I can't leave you alone up here." He winked at me. "For all I know, this is a cover so you can steal precious art."

"Ooh, do I look like an art thief?" I twirled to give him a better look at me. "I always wondered what a life of espionage would be like. Don't you think I would look great in a black jumpsuit, sneaking through corridors?"

"Right." He looked me up and down and then turned away. "I like you in green, to be honest."

There was a concealed door in the corner at the back of the room. It fit seamlessly with the dark wall. With a simple tap of his fingers, it opened to reveal a sleek office with custom leather furniture, more art, and large windows that overlooked the water. I entered behind him and let out a sigh when I looked out the window. He hadn't lied. This was a much better view than the one downstairs.

"Oh, this is beautiful." I went right over to the window. "You can see the skyline so much clearer up here."

"You like the water." He said it like it was fact, not a question.

"What makes you say that?"

"You were staring out the window before." He joined me. "Few people do that when they come here. They come, drink, party, and leave. We put the gallery here for the view, and very few people ever notice it. It's meant to compliment the space, add to the beauty of the art, not be ignored."

"You were watching me?" I raised a brow at him.

"I was doing my job, making sure things went well with the party. Of course, I noticed you." He headed to the bar at the back of the small room and made a drink. "Would you like one?"

"What are you drinking?" I asked.

"I'm having scotch, but I think water is best for you." He chuckled. "Your cheeks are red."

"You lure me up here with the promise of a stronger drink and then offer me water?" I put my hand on my hip. "I'm a big girl. I can handle myself."

"Whatever you say." He made the drinks and rejoined me at the window, where he handed one to me. I eyed it for a moment too long, and he grunted.

"There's nothing in it. We can switch if you want." He pulled back his offered hand and pushed the other drink at me. "I'll sip from both if you like to prove there's nothing in it."

"Sorry, I'm a little wary of the opposite sex right now." I grabbed the drink from his hand.

"Mr. Conrad?" He sipped from his glass.

"Yes. Because of him." I nodded. "You'd think after terminating someone, the last thing a man would try to do is get in their pants."

"Is that what happened?" Mr. James' jaw tightened with the question. It almost looked like he wanted to return to the party and continue his conversation with my former manager.

"He didn't come outright and say it, but all that talk about being friends made it clear enough." I sipped the drink. "I barely wanted to work with him to begin with. The only reason they put me on his team is because his department was struggling. Here comes Whitney to clean up the mess, and then I'm the one who gets the boot!"

"I'm sorry you had to deal with that." He sighed. "Would you like to talk about it?"

"You want to hear about that?" I frowned.

"Do you have anything else to do?" He narrowed his gaze at me. "I mean, we could stand here in silence until the party is over, but that sounds tedious. And it seems to me like you need to talk about it. If it just happened yesterday, I can't imagine you've had much time to process it."

"You're right about that. I kept it to myself because I didn't want to take away from Lena's moment. There will be plenty of time to tell her about it when this is over." I took a long sip from the drink. He was right; this was stronger.

"You're a good friend." He nodded. "Few would put their pain to the side like that."

"It's a job. A damn good one that I worked my ass off for, but it's just a job. I've had jobs before, and I'm sure I'll find another."

"Of course you will." He walked away and returned with two black chairs so we could sit and look at the water. "Like I told you, your reputation is great. I know that short woman with the stiff hair wants you to think people are talking about you being fired, but it's not for the reason you may think. Once the news broke that you were a free agent, a lot of firms started buzzing about the possibility of taking you on."

"Even though I lost a major contract?"

"The artist who went missing? They held that against you?" He scoffed.

"According to John, yes." I rolled my eyes. "To them, I lost the company millions. It would be a risk to keep me on."

"Well, they're morons if they think that." He tapped the gold band on his right ring finger against the glass. "Especially now that she resurfaced."

"She has?" I perked up; I had heard nothing about the woman being back on the scene.

"Just yesterday, actually. And rumor has it, she tried to reignite her old contracts a few months ago. I'm sure if she found out what they did to you, she'd refuse to work with them again."

"Wouldn't that be nice?" The scotch made its way through my veins as the music from below reached us. It was a slow jam. I swayed back and forth in my seat while he watched me.

"Would you like to dance?"

"What?"

He stood and held his hand out to me. "You're moving like you want to dance. So, let's."

"Um, okay." I put my hand in his, and he pulled me to my feet. "You know a lot about me. Here I am, ready to dance with you, and I don't even know your full name."

"Is that a requirement?" His brow furrowed.

"Dancing requires our bodies to press up against each other." I rubbed my palms over my chest and stomach then pointed at him. "I should know more about you if we're going to do that."

"Domino. Domino James." He chuckled and then pulled me into him.

"You sound like the spy now." I lowered my voice to mimic him. "Domino. Domino James."

He reacted by pulling me closer to him. He placed his hand on my back and spoke in a hushed tone as our bodies swayed to the music. "You're really intrigued by the spy thing, huh?"

"I am. It's sexy," I whispered, encouraged by the feeling of warmth spreading through my veins. "You would make a good spy. I'd hire you."

"Would you?" He lowered his face to mine, and it was then I realized I'd gone ahead and slipped into flirting again. Damn it. That happened way more often than I ever wanted to admit.

With his deep eyes locked on me, it was too late to turn back.

"The look, the voice, the hidden office. Oh, yeah." My eyes dropped to his lips. When I looked back up, he was staring at me. Those deep eyes looked hungry, like he would swallow me up if given the chance. I wanted to give him that chance.

"Kiss me." The words moved from my brain out of my mouth with no filter. Had Jackie taken over me?

"What?" He looked genuinely shocked by my order.

"Don't ruin it. This is sexy." I turned and slammed the rest of my drink before gently dropping the cup into the seat. "Kiss me."

Domino gave me what I asked for. He pulled me close and kissed me. It was a gentle invitation at first, but when I responded to the taste of his lips, he found new urgency.

I put my arms around his neck and lifted to my toes to better reach him. He leaned forward and moved his hands to cup my ass before pulling me into his arms. I wrapped my legs around his waist, and in the back of my mind, I dared his legs to tremble. They didn't. Domino held me up with confidence. One hand cupped my ass while the other caressed my back as our kiss grew deeper.

"Well, damn," I spoke against his lips.

"I got you," he said, understanding my thoughts before I could voice them.

"Do you?" I asked.

He moved his lips to my neck and answered me with a firm kiss right over my pulse. "Relax, Whitney. I'm not going to drop you."

"What are you going to do?" I knew what I wanted him to do. My panties were soaking wet, and my heart pounded in my chest. Was this what I thought would happen? Absolutely not, but damn it if it wasn't hot. I could deal with the consequences later.

"Whatever you want me to." He put the ball back in my court. If this was going to move forward, I'd have to make it happen.

"Undress me." I leaned back just enough to look into his eyes.

"Are you sure about that?" He asked for confirmation, but I could tell by the look he gave me, he was just as ready as I was to throw caution to the wind.

"Yes. I am."

Domino lowered me back to the floor and then took his time slowly removing my clothing. First, he pulled the straps from my shoulders one by one, letting them fall down my arms. The entire time, he kept his eyes locked on mine, searching for a hint of hesitancy, but there was none. I wanted this. I wanted this man I'd never met before, whose name I only learned just a few moments before, to undress me. I wanted his hands on my body and his lips to touch mine again and again.

As the dress fell to the floor, revealing my body, I didn't feel the usual anxiety. The first time naked in front of a new person was always nerve-racking, and not just because I'm a big girl. Hell, even when I was small, I was worried. Maybe they would hyper-focus on the fact that one boob was slightly bigger, or see the scar on my hip from when I fell off my bike as a kid.

Maybe it was because I didn't think I would ever see him again, but I didn't care what he thought of my body. We were spies, meeting in the night for one sexy moment, never to see each other again. This was for the plot! With that thought in mind, I went to work removing his clothes.

I undid the rest of the buttons on his shirt, revealing his firm body. Domino had what I called a borderline dad bod. He wasn't cut like he spent hours in the gym, but he was still solid to the touch, no jiggle. After I removed his shirt, my fingers lingered on the button of his pants. I looked up at him for confirmation, and this time, it was his turn to give me the go-ahead. He did so by grabbing the back of my head and pulling my lips back to his. When our lips parted, his pants were on the floor. We stood in front of each other in our underwear, just looking at each other.

Domino crossed the room and returned with a plush rug on the floor in front of a small fireplace. He set the rug down in front of the window before he took my hand and led me over to it. Carefully, he helped me lay down on the rug before he continued undressing me. He made quick work of removing the lacy red bra, then, with the help of me lifting my hips, he pulled away the matching panties.

His eyes didn't move from my body as he lay next to me. I waited for him to say something, but his hands did all the talking. And because I suddenly lost the nerve to look at him, I stared out the window at the moon above us as his fingertips traced a path across my body. They moved with gentle pressure up from my knee, across my belly, to my breast, where he drew circles around each nipple.

"Beautiful." He pressed his lips to my ear as he complimented me.

I smiled as he kissed my neck then gasped when his hand slipped between my thighs. His fingers gently danced across my clit as he played with varying levels of pressure. The alternation felt insane.

"Do you like that?" he asked as his lips moved from my neck to my collarbone.

"Yes," I moaned and squeezed my thighs around his hand.

He removed his hand from between my legs and pressed his fingers to my lips. "Taste yourself."

I locked eyes with him and slowly licked each finger clean, sucking the tips as I finished. There was a glint of something in his eyes, something that made my stomach tighten and my pussy drip. The corner of his full lips lifted as his fingers returned to my pussy. I expected him to continue the motion on my clit, but the tip of his finger slipped inside me instead. I lifted my hips just enough to let him know I wanted more, and he responded in kind. Domino slipped a second inside, then a third. His thumb joined the action and rubbed my clit as his fingers danced inside me, coaxing the first orgasm from me.

"Do you enjoy being tasted?" he asked, and this time, he put his fingers in his own mouth. My mouth watered as I watched him lick my juices from his fingertips.

"Hell yeah." I chuckled and squealed as he moved to replace his fingers with his mouth, cupping my ass to lift me into a better position. I rolled my hips again as he went to work with his tongue.

Domino brought me right to the edge of another orgasm then stopped.

"I want to feel what it's like to be inside you." He looked down at me expectantly.

It was my turn to take control. Encouraged by his hungry glare, I reached down and pulled his dick out of his boxers. He was larger than expected. I won't lie; the weight in my hand made me nervous!

"Do you have a condom?" I asked. Thrilled or not, I wasn't about to risk catching something or getting pregnant by a total stranger.

He left me for a moment, then returned with an unopened box. I took it from him. I wanted to do it myself. Domino locked eyes with me as I rolled the condom on him. Dick secure, I lay back and pulled him with me. He kissed me as I guided his dick inside me and moaned as my body stretched to fit him.

"Damn it," he said then buried his face in my neck. It was like he didn't want me to see him. I took it as a compliment. Pussy so good, he couldn't look me in the eye!

We started with slow, steady strokes. I hadn't fucked in a while, so it was a tight fit, but with each stroke, my walls relaxed, and when the tension left, Domino picked up the pace. He kissed my neck with more pressure, and his fingers found my clit again.

"Yes!" I cried out as he continued fucking me. "Harder."

Domino took the order and slammed into me. Each stroke came with more power, and I gripped his ass to encourage him to give me more.

"Shit," he said, and I knew that tone. He was about to come, but he didn't want to just yet, so he switched positions. He rolled me to my side and moved behind me, sliding into my pussy from behind. Those powerful strokes were slower this time.

As he fucked me and kissed the back of my neck, he grabbed my breast and teased my nipples. The sheer number of sensations hitting me all at once was overwhelming. I felt like I would lose it. I gripped the rug beneath us and pushed my ass back on him.

"Put your leg up." He spoke with his lips pressed against my neck.

"Huh?" I looked back at him and saw the strain in his eyes. It was like he was holding back from doing something more. I wondered what that was.

He didn't repeat himself. Instead, he grabbed my leg and lifted it in the air. "Keep it there."

I quickly wrapped my hand around my knee to hold my leg up.

"Damn, you feel amazing," he groaned.

"Shit," I gasped as he pulled out until he reached the tip, only to slam back into me.

"I could take you all night." He bit my shoulder a little harder.

"You really like to bite, huh?" I spoke between moans.

"Would you like me to stop?" he asked, pulling back so he could look me in the eye as he thrusted into me again.

"No, don't stop. Do it again," I encouraged him, and when I looked back, I could see that struggle in his expression again. This man had a kink, and I'd just found it.

Instead of biting me like I'd asked, he put his fingers in my mouth, encouraging me to suck them before he lowered his hand to my pussy. Two fingers slipped inside me, joining his dick and stretching me further as his thumb found my clit again. With a series of small circles, it wasn't long before my legs were shaking.

I struggled to hold my leg up. Just as I was about to drop it, he chuckled.

"Oh yeah, here it comes." He licked my shoulder. "Yes, give it to me, Whitney."

"What?" I gasped.

"Look at yourself," he ordered. "Look at that pretty pussy."

I looked down just in time to see it. My body tensed as I came, and for the first time in my life, I squirted. I watched as my orgasm erupted and sprayed out around his dick and fingers.

"Oh, shit!" I couldn't hold my leg up anymore, but it didn't matter. Domino flipped me over onto my knees and slid down to lie with his face right under my pussy. He caught the last drops of my cum in his mouth then slid his fingers inside of me to coax another eruption. And again, I squirted, this time all over his face.

"Yes!" he said proudly as my cum showered his face and my knees shook. "My turn."

He turned me around so I could look out at the water as he fucked me from behind. My titties bounced as the waves crashed and the music from the party below grew louder, just in time to mask the sound of my voice as I screamed out.

"Goddamn it!"

He lowered his chest to my back and put his mouth to my ear. "Thank you, Whitney," he said, smacked my ass, and then came.

I would never look at the water the same again.

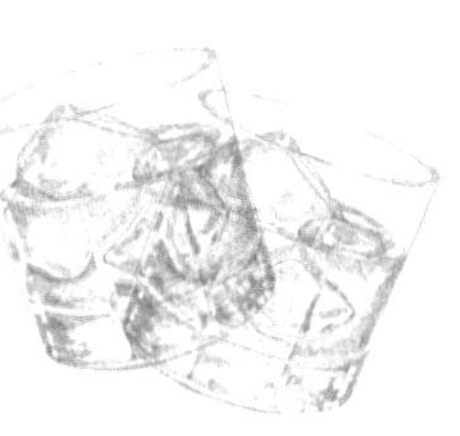

4

Maverick's Tower

Firm taps on my cheek pulled me from a fantasy about wrapping my lips around Domino's dick. Unfortunately for me, I didn't realize I was dreaming. I accepted the offer into my mouth and started sucking, but the sensation on my tongue was wrong...furry. I paused and opened my eyes to see Maverick staring at me in total disbelief. He looked genuinely disgusted! I looked down, and yes, his damn paw was in my mouth!

"UGH!" I spit and scratched my tongue as I jumped from the bed and ran to the bathroom to clean my mouth. As I scrubbed my tongue, Maverick stood in the doorway, both judging me and rolling his eyes because my chaotic start to the day was further delaying his meal.

"Raawr," he fussed as I started my third scrub.

"I'm coming!" I gargled then spit out the oral rinse and wished it was something stronger, like bleach. "This is why they warn women about getting cats!"

Maverick slapped the door with his tail, huffed, turned and walked away.

"Ugh, my head. How the hell did I get home?" The last thing I could remember was orgasms over the ocean. "Please tell me I didn't drive."

I stomped back to my bedroom and checked the app for my car. Luckily, it had a location tracker on it. The map showed it was still parked at the venue.

"I must have gotten a ride." I opened the rideshare app to check if I had tipped the driver. If they got me home safely, they deserved a big one. But there was no ride listed for the night before. "Huh?"

My next option was to check my security cameras. Maybe Jackie or Lena dropped me off. I expected to find an embarrassing clip of them dragging me to my door, but when I opened the app to view the recording, I saw myself walking down the hall at an odd angle, my arm dangling in the air, as if hooked around someone's neck, but I was alone. When I made it to the door, I struggled to put my key in the lock and swatted at something like it was distracting me, but there was nothing there.

Then, I checked the internal camera to see me standing in an open door and waving at the empty hallway.

"Damn, his scotch really was strong." I rubbed my head.

There was more to the video, but I closed it, opting to read the new message that popped up on the screen instead. I didn't need to watch any more embarrassing behavior.

Jackie: Get up and wash ya ass. We're on our way! I didn't tell her, but you will! Better order that sushi boat.

Me: Now?

Jackie: You got an hour to pretty up and get your story together.

"Damn it!" I tossed the phone on my bed.

Raawrar! Maverick fussed from the hall outside my bedroom.

"I'm coming!" I rolled my eyes.

After feeding Maverick, I hopped in the shower and scrubbed up. At least I'd be able to offer the girls a juicy story after I told them about how my life fell apart.

While I waited for the girls to arrive, I stood in my kitchen and placed an order for the largest sushi boat from our favorite spot and called the gallery.

"Hi, I left my car there last night. Is it possible to come pick it up?"

"I'm sorry, but the gallery is closed until Monday morning," the soft voice answered over the phone. "The valet team won't be back to access any stored keys, but your vehicle will be safe on site until then."

"Great. Well, I didn't have much to do this weekend anyway. Thanks." I ended the call and stared at the phone. It was true; I planned to spend the two days avoiding unpacking by scouting for new artists for the firm. I gave half a thought to pulling out my laptop to the job hunt then tossed that idea aside as well.

Across from the kitchen, freshly unboxed, was my new custom couch. The Chesterfield sofa with the distressed antique nail heads in custom dolphin fabric was the first thing I ordered for my new spot. It said sophisticated, established, and successful. It also came with a hefty price tag of well over three thousand dollars.

"I should send it back." I frowned. As if protesting the thought, Maverick jumped on to the couch and scowled at me. "Hey, it's either the couch or your tower."

He rolled his eyes and swatted his tail. After years of being berated by the fussy feline, I knew this was his sign that I was being overdramatic. I would have continued the one-sided argument, but the doorbell rang. It was time to face the music.

I had barely opened the door before the two women barged inside. Not only were they there to get information out of me, this was the first time they would get a look at the condo in person. I had refused to let them in before the deal was final, and then I wanted to wait until I was unpacked and had the space decorated.

"How are you not unpacked yet?" Lena pointed to the stacks of unopened boxes then turned on me with that angry mother glare. She didn't have kids yet, but when she did, they were in for some prime A guilt!

"I've been preoccupied with other things."

"Yes." Jackie stepped in between us. "Other things. Do tell." She threw the scarf I was sure she'd worn only for that moment over her shoulder and headed off to pet Maverick.

"Really?" I rolled my eyes at her. "Real subtle."

"Okay, what's going on?" Lena wagged her finger. "Jackie was acting really funny about getting over here, and now you're getting fidgety on me."

"Well, tell her." Jackie reappeared with the massive body of fur in her arms. Maverick stuck his tongue out at me and then nuzzled his face in her neck, just like a traitor.

"Fine." I took a deep breath, walked over to Lena, and took her hands in mine before blurting it out, "I lost my job."

"What? I thought you were being promoted." Lena looked over at Jackie, who shrugged.

"Yeah, so did I." I dropped her hands. "I don't know what happened. I was ready to accept this great new position, and now, I'm unemployed."

"When? I know they didn't call you on a Saturday morning to tell you this." Lena sucked her teeth. "That has to be illegal or something."

"No. They told me a couple of days ago."

"This happened days ago, and you didn't tell us?" Lena looked hurt. "Why would you do that?"

"I wanted to wait. It wasn't like I wouldn't still be unemployed after your big night." I looked Lena in the eye. "You needed to enjoy your moment. What kind of friend would I be if I took that away from you, knowing how you are?"

"How am I?" Lena tossed her hands on her hips, and the frame of big curls around her face bounced.

"Mother hen!" I laughed. "Lena, I love you, but you have a hard time celebrating yourself."

"She's right," Jackie chimed in between kissing Maverick. "You'll find any reason not to, and fussing over one of us is your top reason to disregard your own shit."

"Well, damn." Lena chewed her lip. "I guess I can't be mad at you for not telling me."

"Oh yeah, you can!" Jackie snapped. "I'm getting my sushi boat!"

"I already ordered it, but they won't deliver for another few hours, so in the meantime..." I trailed off and looked at the stacks of unopened boxes.

"Not this bitch lying to us and then putting us to work!" Jackie exclaimed as she put Maverick down. He immediately walked over to his half-assembled cat tower and purred. "And my baby's tower isn't even done yet?"

"Hey, I can't do this by myself." I pouted and fluttered my lashes at them. "I'm sad. Pity me, please. I have no job!"

"That better be the biggest damn sushi boat on the menu!" Lena rolled her eyes. "Where do we start?"

"You help the liar with the boxes. I'm gonna get Mr. Maverick right." Jackie issued the orders, and we went to work.

A few hours later, Maverick's cat tower was complete, and the boxes were half empty. I'd given the girls the total rundown of my firing and had to rein Jackie in. She was ready to march down to the office and raise hell.

While Lena and I struggled to stuff the broken-down boxes into the trash chute, Jackie played with Maverick, complaining I wasn't showing him enough love. We made it back from the trash chute just in time for the sushi boat to arrive.

As we sat on the floor of my new living room listening to lo-fi, Maverick took the chance to perch atop his tower and look out the window at the skyline.

"Look at him. Royalty!" Jackie praised him, and he lifted his head in acceptance of her fawning.

"I really love this view." I rolled my shoulders. "Never thought I would have a condo with a view of the ocean!"

"And now you do. Sitting on top of the world." Lena wiggled as she popped a roll into her mouth. "I'm so proud of you!"

"For now." I rolled my eyes.

"You'll get another job, Whit." Jackie smacked my leg.

"Yeah, I know. Just feeling a little deflated."

"I still can't believe that Conrad guy still showed up at the party. Did he chase you off? I mean, you disappeared. We were about to have a twerk-off, but you weren't there." Lena lifted to her knees and started bouncing her ass.

"Oh, just give me another reason to kick that guy's ass, please!" Jackie balled up her fist. "You know he had the nerve to come asking me where you were? Looked like he saw a damn ghost or something."

"Oh, about that." I lifted my beer to my lip and took a long sip.

"What?" they said in unison.

"So, John pushed up on me, as if the asshole really thought he could get with me after firing me," I started.

"Maybe he thought you would be desperate." Lena laughed. "He sounds like the type to prey on vulnerable women."

"Maybe. Honestly, I thought I would have to break his hand when he kept grabbing me."

"Alright, that's it. I'm whooping ass!" Jackie looked ready to bolt out the door and find John.

"No need. The owner stepped in and handled that." I offered the detail I knew would bring her focus back to the juicy details I was ready to share.

"The owner?" Lena leaned in. "What owner?"

"He owns the gallery. Apparently, he was John's contact who got us into the space. You know, that's the only reason I invited the moron. But anyway, this man was fine, and I don't know what he said to John after he caught him pushing up on me, but he got the hell out of there."

"Wait." Jackie leaned back, squinting her eyes before she wiggled her finger in my face. "That look on your face. What happened?"

"Long story short, I left the party with the owner." I took another sip and watched them lock eyes.

"You're boring us about losing your job when you left the party with some hot gallery owner?" Lena scoffed. "What the hell is going on with you?"

"It's like she wants us to smack her!" Jackie laughed. "Tell us everything."

"Yeah, so sexy gallery owner gets rid of the scum. Hot! You leave the party with him," Lena recapped. "What happened next?"

"He took me to see his private collection on the top floor. We had to use this fancy ass elevator with a passcode. While I was looking at the pieces, he accused me of being an art thief, and—"

"That was all it took!" Jackie screamed. "Kinky bitch!"

"What?" Lena rolled her eyes.

"Girl, you know how she has that thing about being a spy!" Jackie sipped her drink.

"You have a thing for spies?" Lena gasped. "I had no idea!"

"I never told her that." My face warmed.

"You bitches have a lot of secrets," Lena snipped.

"How did I get in trouble?" Jackie gasped and clutched her imaginary pearls. "It started in college after she worked on that double agent animation with that guy. She got it in her head about how sexy it would be to be a spy. It's why she made us watch all those movies!"

"You said it was for research!" Lena yelled and pointed at me.

"Oh, it was—for her fantasies!" Jackie laughed.

"Anyway," I continued the story. "Do you want to hear the rest of the story or not?"

"Sorry. Continue." Lena swallowed her laughter.

"We started talking about the job shit. Thanks to Dandruff Darla, everyone already knows."

"Who?!" Lena choked on the piece of fish she had just popped into her mouth.

"Nina. The trifling heffa, I'm sure, will end up with my job after this," I clarified.

"I gotta write that one down for my next book!" Lena laughed. "Continue."

"Well, work talk, scotch, spy stuff, and..." I trailed off.

"And what?" Jackie held her breath.

"I lost my favorite panties. Pretty sure they're still under that desk." I bit my lip and waited for the meaning to sink in for them.

"No!" Lena gasped. "In the office?"

"Y'all fucked?" Jackie asked. "I need to know for sure. What did you do?"

"Yes, we did." I dropped my head. "Right there on the floor."

"You didn't!" Lena smacked her hand over her mouth.

"Scotch. I'm blaming the scotch." I looked back up just in time for Maverick to come flying at me. He jumped off his perch, snatched a piece of sushi, and ran down the hall. "Damn cat."

"Scotch?" Lena asked. "Continue the story."

"Yes, it must have taken over my brain." I dropped my head again.

"Nah, sis, look up and face your whorish ways!" Jackie cackled.

"I can't believe you did that. Did you use protection?" Lena lowered her voice like one of our parents was listening.

"I've read those sex scenes you write. When do they ever reach for a condom?" Jackie snickered.

"Hey, that's fiction. STDs are real!" Lena corrected her. "Readers don't enjoy reading about sexual precautions, but this isn't one of my books."

"We used a condom!" My face was on fire. "I don't know how it happened. I didn't think I would be fucking anyone last night, but the drinks, the music, and something about that man..."

"What's his name?" Lena asked. "Please tell me you know his name."

"Domino."

"Domino? Oh, hell, that sounds like a damn sex god." Jackie sucked her teeth.

"Exactly!" I shook my head.

"Was it good?" Lena asked, whispering again.

"Best I've ever had." I nodded. "I mean, that man made me squirt!"

"You lucky bitch." Jackie slammed her drink down. "So he dicked you down real good and then what?"

"I don't know. I mean, after being picked up, flipped around, and having multiple orgasms, it's all kinda of hazy."

"Wait, weren't you still talking to that guy? What's his name?" Jackie snapped her fingers, trying to recall the name of the guy I'd gone out with exactly twice and never again.

"Patrick?" I scoffed.

"Yeah, the bookstore guy. I thought you liked him." Jackie looked at Lena, who nodded.

"Long story short, our second date was a disaster that ended with me running away from him and trying to hide my embarrassment until I made it to the safety of my car." I cringed. I still couldn't believe what started out as a sweet date had ended so terribly.

"Hold up, what?" Jackie straightened. "Why would you ever be running away from a man?"

"All I can say is that's the last time I let Lena hook me up with anybody." I pointed to my curly-headed friend, who dropped her head and pretended to be cleaning her glasses.

I'd met Patrick through Lena. They were both in the publishing industry. She'd met him on a trip to some literary event and said he would be perfect for me. He was, at first, but it wasn't long before I realized he'd been putting on his absolute best show for me. The man wore a mask of confidence and security when really, he was as about as confident as a toddler taking their first step. On our second date out, he showed me just how secure he was in his manhood.

"I'm being blamed for this?" Lena gasped. "Why?"

"You said the first date was good," Jackie pointed out. "How did he fuck it up?"

"Yeah." Lena tapped my leg. "What happened to roaming the bookstore, hand-holding, gaming together? That sounded so sweet."

"And it was sweet—for a first date." I inhaled deeply and let out a sigh. "I was really hoping this one would work out, but I should know better by now about getting my hopes up so early."

"What did you do? The second date was supposed to be a carnival, right?" Jackie nudged me to continue the story. "You ran away from him at a carnival?"

"Yes, I did. Everything was going well until we walk by this cute couple thing. Guys were carrying their ladies to win prizes. The further you make it, the better the prize," I explained the game that ruined the date. "Honestly, it looked fun, and we stood there watching as people tried to make it further. Soon, you could tell the men were competing with each other. The entire thing was funny as hell."

"Don't tell me. Please, don't tell me." Jackie put her hands together as if praying to the gods that my story wouldn't continue down the path she knew I was taking her down.

"You know exactly what happened. Little Patrick decided he wanted to participate in the game." I cracked open another beer; I was going to need it to finish the story. "Of course, when he asked, I told him no. I mean, you see me. I'm Miss Thickums over here. Ain't no way in hell that man was going to come anywhere near winning that game carrying me on his back."

"Is he really that small?" Jackie asked.

"Thin as a string bean," Lena laughed. "I mean, but skinny guys are strong sometimes. Sometimes, they surprise you. I know I've had my share of men come through and toss my ass around like I was nothing. Makes a big girl feel dainty!"

"Yeah, well, he wasn't one of those surprises. All I know is, he swore he could pick me up and carry me across the finish line. No matter how much I said I didn't want to, he just knew he could do it." I recalled the way he begged me to let him try. "It was like having a little kid pleading and tugging at the bottom of your shirt for candy or some shit."

"See, that right there is annoying as it is. You didn't want to. Why keep insisting?" Jackie rolled her eyes. "I would have left right then."

"I should have," I agreed with her. "Lord knows I should have, but no. I stayed because I really hoped he would drop it."

"Maybe he was trying to prove something?" Lena offered.

"To who?" I laughed. "Girl, I know what the scale says when I step on it. I'm big and proud of it. But what you're not about to do is embarrass my big, beautiful ass in public."

"How bad was it?" Lena asked and, in my peripherals, I could see Maverick stalking back up the hall, ready to snatch another piece of food. It was a game he played—the plate next to me was his, and he knew it. I think it kept his hunting skills sharp.

"Girl, his lil ass was grunting, sweating, and damn near dropped me! He made it three steps!" I held up three fingers. "Three shaky ass steps! I hopped off his back before we both face-planted in front of everyone. People were laughing. Women were trying to avert their eyes, but I caught a couple of those pity glances."

"Now *that* is embarrassing." Jackie put her arm around me. "I'm so sorry, friend."

"Tell me about it. So, I promptly walked my big, sexy black ass back to my car and drove away. He was running after me like a lost puppy, holding his back like he had hurt himself." I shook my head. "Second guy this year with wobbly knees trying to prove something by picking me up!"

"Doesn't sound like Domino had any trouble carrying you." Jackie shimmied her shoulders.

"Not a damn one!" I lifted my bottle, and we toasted to the triumph. "He would have won that race!"

"So, are you going to see him again?" Lena rubbed her belly, the surefire sign she had reached her max on the sushi.

"I highly doubt it, considering we didn't exchange information." Maverick purred nearby, as if he understood what I said. No new men for him to worry about. When I turned to look at him, he huffed and walked back down the hall. He would have to start his stealthy hunt all over.

"You had a damn one-night stand with a millionaire?" Jackie's look of pride turned into one of feigned disgust. "That's not one you catch and release, girl!"

"We don't know he's a millionaire," Lena corrected her.

"Hmm. Let's think about this. He owns the hottest gallery in the state and has a private collection inside a secret office only accessible by a special code," Jackie listed off the man's known attributes, which to her added up to a new sugar daddy. "You gotta go back there. Claim your man!"

"Jackie, I'm not doing that. I shouldn't have even been with him. I mean, he clearly has ties to my industry. If anyone found out what happened, it could ruin my reputation!" I rebuked her complaints. "That's the last thing I need happening right now."

"Where did I go wrong with you?" Jackie complained. "I knew it. I'm giving too much attention to my audience. That's why you're a lamb lost in a world of wolves."

"You're so damn dramatic!" I laughed.

"She is, but I need more details. I need positions, smells, textures," Lena refocused our conversation. "You'll never see him again, fine. Tell us everything about what happened last night."

"You going to use this for writing material?" I rolled my eyes. I knew it. Lena was always collecting material for her novels.

"Maybe." She winked. "Hey, I'm running out of my own source material to pull from."

"So you go out there and toss your ass in the air!" I joked with her. "I'm going to need a royalty share if you want to use this material."

"Oh, so the millionaire had your ass in the air?" Lena narrowed her eyes. "Interesting."

"This is getting juicy!" Jackie was seconds away from squealing. "How was it? You know... Was he big?"

"I'm not answering that question." I winked, and Lena laughed.

"That means he was!" Lena screamed.

"I still can't believe you fumbled the bag so hard. I thought I taught you better than that!" Jackie grabbed me by the shoulders and started shaking me. "We could have had paid vacations and spa days!"

"You just want more research for your dick classification." I rolled my eyes at her when she released me.

"Well, now that you mention it..." She winked. "Happy to swing back around to that question. What was it like?"

"Absolutely not!" I wouldn't admit anything to her about the classification of Domino's dick, even though I was sure it was the kind she'd tell me to run away from.

As our laughter died, my phone rang, and I looked down to see an unknown number on the screen.

"You know, if this was my book, that would be Domino calling you."

"Answer it!" Jackie shouted.

"No! I don't know the number."

Lena gave Jackie a look I hadn't seen since college. Faster than I thought possible, Lena wrapped her arms around me, and Jackie snatched the phone from my hand. She hit the answer button and put the phone to my ear.

I froze.

"Hello, is this Whitney?" the line crackled with the sound of a deep, commanding voice.

"Domino?"

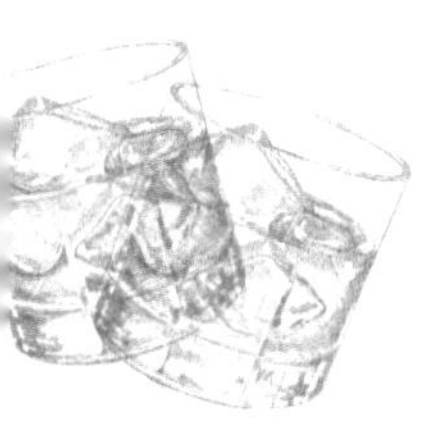

5

Unexpected Offer

"I hope it's okay I'm calling you now. I got your information from the registry at the gallery," Domino's deep voice reached through the phone and stroked me in places shielded by my clothes.

"Um, yeah, it's fine." I tried to keep my nerves from my voice, but from the look on my friends' faces, I knew I had failed.

"Tighten up!" Jackie whispered and flicked my knee with her finger.

"I wanted to make sure you were okay," Domino spoke. "You were out of it last night when I took you home."

"Oh, *you* took me home!" If nothing else, Domino had just provided me with a sense of relief. "That part was a little fuzzy."

"I didn't think you would remember." He chuckled. "I told you the drinks were strong. You know, you say some strange things when you're drunk."

"Oh no. What did I say?" I could feel my face warming.

"Nothing you need to know about now, though I am inclined to rent more spy movies now."

"Right." That was it. That was the embarrassment I felt climbing up my spine. "Well, thank you for making sure I got home safely. I appreciate it."

"Of course. You insisted on calling a ride, but I didn't trust it." He paused. "I had another reason for reaching out to you tonight."

"What's that?"

"I would like to take you out for dinner tonight—if you're available." He dropped the invitation in my lap with no hesitation.

"Tonight?" I looked at both Jackie and Lena, who could hear him through the phone. Both their eyes lit up.

"Yes. I understand if that's too soon. My schedule is clear, and I wanted to take advantage of that," Domino responded. "I understand if you're busy. If tonight doesn't work, we could schedule for another night."

Jackie pinched me as Lena put her finger in my face. It was their simultaneous warning not to drop the ball again. I wondered quickly how long they would badger me if I dared to say no to his offer. How many sushi boats would it cost me? Whatever the number, I knew I couldn't afford it.

"Ouch!"

"Is everything okay?"

"Yes, sorry. Just a little bug bite." I frowned at Jackie.

"Girl, you better say yes!" Lena whispered and mimed writing on a notepad. "Material!"

"Yes," I hesitated, but the two women in my face left me no choice. "I-I can make tonight work."

"Great." There was a slight lift in his voice that made me smile. Domino was excited to see me. "I'll pick you up at eight. Does that work for you?"

"Eight is fine," I confirmed the time and rolled my eyes when Lena pretended to cheer.

"See you then," Domino confirmed.

"Bye." I ended the call and stared at my friend.

"Yes!" Jackie jumped up and started pop-locking. "Millionaire zaddy!"

"You're ridiculous." I laughed at her.

"No, I'm not. Now," she clapped her hands, "we have an hour to get you ready."

"An hour?" I scoffed.

"Girl, it's seven! Or did you not notice the sunset?" Lena pointed out the window.

"Seriously? Why would you let me agree to this?" I struggled to get up from the floor and groaned when my knees popped. "How the hell am I going to be ready in an hour? I look and smell a mess!"

"Don't panic. You take your sweaty ass to the shower. Jackie will pick out your outfit, and I'll clean up this mess." Lena went into mothering mode then turned her finger on Jackie. "Nothing too provocative."

"Well, hell, he's already seen everything!" Jackie shouted before they fell out laughing and Maverick finally snatched his last piece of fish.

Exactly one hour later, I stood in front of the mirror in a little black dress that dipped just low enough in the front to give a little peek at the goods—not that it mattered, according to Jackie. I pulled my hair in a half-up style because I refused to fight with another bun and put on some simple diamond stud earrings.

"Oh yeah! Look at you." Jackie did a victory dance behind me. "He is going to feed you then eat you!"

"Jackie!" Lena gasped.

"Don't worry, I give you full right to use that line in your book." Jackie laughed. "No royalties required."

"You two are impossible." I turned from the mirror. "But I do look good, don't I?"

"A confident queen! Now, I want a full report as soon as the date is over." Jackie ordered as she nuzzled Maverick one more time before heading out of my bedroom toward the front door.

"Don't forget, it's all in the details!" Lena laughed as she followed her. "Paint me a picture!"

"Yeah, whatever!" I waved them out the door and shut it behind them after watching them dance down the hall.

After refilling Maverick's water bowl and making sure there were exactly two ice cubes included, I grabbed my purse and took my phone off the charger. And right on time—the doorbell rang.

I opened the door to find Domino standing there in a dark gray suit and holding a bouquet of lilies. My favorite flower.

"Lilies," I gasped. "How did you know I loved lilies?"

"In between your renditions of a song apparently called *Secret Agent Man*, you mentioned it." He handed the flowers to me.

"Will you ever tell me everything I said?" I took the flowers and inhaled the fragrance.

"Not a chance," Domino chuckled. "Are you ready to go?"

"Yes, one second." I took the flowers inside and quickly put them in a vase. I would cut the stems when I got home. One last eye roll from the cat drinking his fill, and I was out the door.

I try not to be impressed by the car he drove. I couldn't let him know how I enjoyed the sexy leather interior and the specialized seating that warmed and cupped my butt. The damn thing even had a massager built into it. Yes, I used it while he drove us to the small restaurant by the ocean, and any time I moaned in appreciation, he laughed at me.

Unfortunately, I also had to hide my excitement when he opened my door, both when I got in the car and when I got out. I couldn't let him know how I felt when I realized not only had he scheduled an entire date for us on short notice, but he had also reserved the best seat in the house with the best view of the water. The girls would think I was exaggerating. How truly sad to say those simple actions were miles above what most men were doing.

I just kept telling myself Domino wasn't supposed to be a permanent fixture in my life. He was supposed to be a fantasy. Something I could look back on in my old age and say, *I can't believe I did that.*

"Are you sure you don't want to eat?" I leaned across the table after Mika, our server, walked away from the table.

I had ordered the honey cajun salmon, but Domino only opted for a simple glass of whiskey.

"No, I'm not hungry, but I wanted to feed you." He smiled.

"It's kind of awkward to eat alone."

"I didn't think about that." He looked at me, and it felt like he was trying to read my mind to figure out what he should do next. Then, he waved down the server. "Actually, I'll have what she's having."

"Yes, sir." Mika smiled and walked away.

"I thought you weren't hungry." I narrowed my eyes at him.

"I'm not." He nodded. "But this way, it won't be as if you're eating alone."

"So you're just going to waste a meal?"

"It won't go to waste. I know you like it, so I'll have him pack it up and you can take it home with you. This way, I get to feed you twice." The corners of his lips lifted, and he winked at me. "Does that work for you, Whitney?"

"Clever. But thank you. I really do hate to eat alone, especially in a nice restaurant like this."

"I'll make a note of that." Domino sipped from the drink Mika had placed in front of him. "I thought a lot about your situation with the job."

"Well, damn!" I laughed nervously. I wasn't sure what to expect from the date, but thinking about my failed career wasn't in my top five guesses. "Just right to it, huh?"

"I'm sorry, it just—you seem very passionate about what you do," Domino spoke carefully.

"I am." I took a long sip of the wine in front of me. "Years of college, networking, building relationships, scouting artists. It's what I love, what I live for. I figured I would build a career and establish myself, then maybe even one day start something of my own. But getting fired just when I thought I was going to take a step up? That definitely wasn't on my plan."

"And what's your plan now? Are you going to let that passion go to waste because the owners of your last firm were morons?" Domino looked at me intently, and I couldn't take my eyes off him. He wouldn't let me escape the conversation. I could already tell Domino would be someone to challenge me, and I wasn't sure how I felt about that.

"Honestly, I'm afraid of sitting down to figure that out. I don't want to start all over, but I might have to. I love what I do, Domino. You know, I used to paint. I used to draw and sculpt and do all kinds of artsy things. I thought I was going to be the creator of those beautiful pieces I loved to stare at for hours on end." I played with the edge of the cloth napkin they had folded like origami. "Unfortunately for me, I didn't inherit any kind of artistic talent, but I had an expert eye for art. I was the absolute best at identifying young artists long before they ever blew up.

It was like I could see into their creative futures. I was even curating galleries in college just for fun. That's how I got started in this business."

"Everything they say about you is true," Domino said admiringly. I would have asked what people were saying, but his next words shifted my focus entirely. "This might be out of line, I'm not really sure, but would you consider working with me?"

"You're offering me a job?" I leaned back in my seat. "So this was a ploy to get me to come to work for you?"

"No, I'm not offering you a job. I'm asking you if you would like to start a partnership." Domino straightened, and he suddenly sounded a lot more official than before. "Whitney, there are going to be a lot of offers for jobs coming your way. Trust me."

"How do you know?" I tilted my head. "Did you hear something?"

"Yes. I've heard a lot. The moment word spread about your departure from your last company, others were buzzing about where you would go next. Everyone knows your last official day there was Friday. They'll give you the courtesy of a few days before they send the headhunters." He nodded. "Yeah, professional courtesy comes first."

"Well damn, I had no idea," I said honestly. "Of course, I have my own connections, and I intend to use them, but I never knew I was so sought after."

"I don't think you should be looking for another job. You're too good for that." Domino hyped me up, and I wasn't about to stop him. "You shouldn't be building wealth for someone else. You should build an empire for yourself."

"And you want to be a partner in my empire?" I couldn't help the flirtatious tone that slipped out. I tried to hold it back, but sometimes, it just happened—especially when I had just been sitting on the man's face the night before.

"Yes." He cleared his throat. Oh yeah, he recognized the shift in my tone. "More like an investor."

"This is an unexpected offer." I sipped my drink. "I didn't come here expecting a partnership."

"That's understandable." He licked his lips and smirked. "Especially after what happened between us last night. But I'm perfectly able to separate personal and professional desires. I can see the value in your work and admire the way that dress cups your ass when you walk. Still, I understand not everyone can do that. This isn't something you have to decide now. Take your time."

Our professional conversation ended there, and we finished the meal talking about art, music, life, and looking at each other like we couldn't wait to get away from the busy restaurant. Every time I lifted my food to my lips, he licked his lips like he wanted a bite. Whenever he ran his finger across the rim of his drink, I couldn't help but imagine him playing with my clit. By the time the waiter returned with the check and the packed meal Domino hadn't eaten, I was squirming in my seat. Thank God for panty liners, or I would have ruined my dress.

"The water smells so good." I sighed as we stepped outside. "Only a few good nights left before the temperature starts dropping again."

"You're right." Domino stepped away to speak to the valet and handed him the to-go bag. "Let's go."

"What?"

"You need to get closer to the water. You love it too much not to."

Domino took my hand and led me down the small path from the restaurant to the beach. When we made it to the sand, he kneeled in front of me and slipped my shoes off before tucking them under his arm.

We walked down the beach to the edge of the water, just close enough for me to get my toes wet.

"Okay, you were right. I needed this."

"Relaxing, isn't it?"

"It is. Lately, I've spent more time looking at the water through windows than actually going to the beach."

"That's something you should change." He turned to me and pushed a stray braid back over my shoulder.

"You're right again," I said breathlessly, and not because I was tired after what turned out to be a longer walk than expected. Domino took my breath away. Every time he looked at me, I felt like I would melt.

"You'll learn I'm often right." He smirked and glanced at my lips.

"Is this how all your partnerships go?" I looked up at him.

"No." He leaned closer, his lips just inches from mine. "This is how it's going with you. Would you like it to end now?"

My brain was screaming hell no, and so was my pussy. Too bad for her and me, someone interrupted what was turning out to be a real good moment!

"Domino James! Now, what are you doing out here?" the unrecognizable voice called out, and Domino visibly tensed up at the sound of the man's voice.

He stepped away from me and turned around, putting himself in between me and the approaching figures. There were only two people, a man and a woman, who both had that androgynous look. The man had deep brown skin, high cheekbones, and sunken eyes. The woman had dark brown skin and wore a gold hoop in her chunky nose with purple graphic makeup. Her vibrant eyeliner reached up into her temples and blended with the edges of her matching purple afro. They both wore all black from head to toe.

"Vance," Domino addressed the man.

"Oh, you give the warmest welcomes." Vance wrapped his long arms around himself.

"I guess I'm just invisible." The woman looked around Domino at me.

"What do you want?" Domino asked, ignoring both their comments.

"We're just out for a stroll, just like you and your friend here," the woman spoke and pointed her long nail at me. I noticed both her pinky fingers were sharpened and dipped in red polish. "Aren't you going to introduce us?"

"No." Again, he was short with them.

"Will we never be friends again?" Vance asked. "We were all so close at one point."

"What do you think?"

"Okay, I get it." Vance put his hands up. "I just came to share a message."

Domino glanced over his shoulder at me then pointed to Vance, who turned and walked away. The two men walked just out of earshot and spoke as the woman stayed near me and said nothing. I got the feeling she was afraid to speak to me.

What the hell is this man into? I wondered as I watched the tense exchange between him and the man called Vance. A few minutes later, Vance and his friend left, and Domino returned to me.

"Is everything okay?"

"Yes. We should go." Domino placed his hand on the small of my back, returning to his softer side. "I should get you home."

I didn't question him. Clearly, there was a problem, and I wasn't about to make it mine. Shit, I had enough to deal with.

Domino drove me home, food in hand, and insisted on walking me to my door. "Don't worry about your car," he said as the elevator opened.

"Huh?" I had been lost in my thoughts, considering the man I spent the night with. There was a lot to process—the offer, the tense interaction with his former friend, the way my body still wanted him.

"The valet? You left your car behind. I'll have them drop it off to you tomorrow."

"Oh, thank you I appreciate that," I spoke as we reached my door. After unlocking the door, I turned to him. "I had fun."

"I'm glad," he said, lingering as I opened the door.

I chewed my lip as the pause stretched on. What did he want me to do? Sex had to be off the table. I couldn't ride him while considering a partnership. Could I? No. I had to show some restraint and keep my hands to myself. Yep, I was ready to stand on business—until he took a step back then my ankles got weak and I came crashing down!

"Would you like to come in?" I blurted out, more eager than I ever wished to be.

"I—" Domino hesitated. "Are you sure?"

"It's still early." I looked into those deep eyes, and that was it. *Fuck it.* "Yes. Please come in, Domino."

I pushed the door open further and stepped inside, and after a flash of conflict in his expression, Domino followed me.

RAAARW!

And the second he did, the big mass of hair leaped through the air. Before I could respond, Maverick attacked, his claws ripping into Domino's face as the two tumbled out of the apartment and into the hallway.

"Maverick! No!"

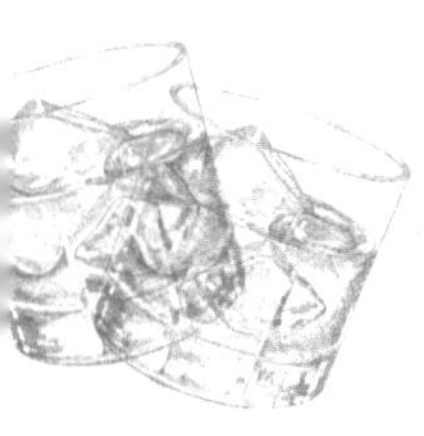

6

Domino's Kink

"Goddamn it! Stop it!" I screamed as the cat tried everything to get away from me.

It took all the strength I had to pull Maverick off Domino. With my arms wrapped around his core, I carried the big menace to my office, tossed him inside, and slammed the door shut. Maverick protested by running around the office and knocking everything off my desk before he returned to the door to stare at me through the glass.

"You are a nightmare, you know that?" I fussed at him before running back to the hallway to check on Domino. "Great, I go from getting offered my dream gig to getting sued because my cat is a demon."

"Whose suing you?" Domino stepped inside the door and closed it behind him.

"Are you okay?" I asked him and tried my best to assess his injuries.

"My shirt has seen better days," he flipped the shredded collar around his neck, "but other than that, I'm okay."

"I thought he ripped your damn face off." I moved closer to examine him.

"Luckily, that's not the case." He chuckled.

"I'm so sorry about that. He's always been a handful, but he's never attacked anyone before."

"It's me." He inhaled deeply. "Cats never like me. It's a shame because I used to love them as a child."

"Must be something in your blood," I joked.

"Yeah, must be." He lifted the bag of food still in his hand. "You might want to put this up before your cat goes for it too."

"Thanks." I took the bag from him and headed for the kitchen. Domino followed me down the hall. "Are you sure you're okay?"

"Yes, Whitney, I'm okay. I promise," he reassured me. "This is a really nice place."

"Thanks. I'm still getting settled in."

"And you have a great view of the water, just as I imagined," he continued his compliments.

"You imagined what my view would look like?"

"After I dropped you off last night," he reminded me.

"Oh, right. Sorry."

While he admired my home, I took care of the lilies. In between glances at the man in my home, I carefully cut the stems and added them to the vase of fresh water.

"They look beautiful," I said as he walked back over to the counter where I stood.

"Worthy of being in your home," Domino flirted.

"I—" When I looked up at him, I missed the stem and instead cut my finger. "Fuck!"

I quickly grabbed the towel hanging on the stove behind me to wrap it around my finger before peeking at the wound. When I saw the small cut, my shoulders relaxed; it wasn't as bad as it felt. I opened the drawer where I stored a first aid kit. I always kept one in the kitchen, just like my mom taught me. We could cook, but we weren't the best with knives.

As I pulled the box from the drawer, I couldn't help but notice the tense expression on Domino's face.

"Queasy around blood?" I pulled my finger out of view. I didn't need him puking in my kitchen after being attacked by my cat. Did someone say *best date ever*?

"Not exactly." He helped me open the box and took a sharp inhale when he handed me a Band-Aid.

"It's really not that bad." I winked at him, and we both flinched when Maverick hissed and smacked my office door.

"He really doesn't want me here." Domino chuckled. "Maybe I should leave."

"That fool will be fine." I brushed off the thought and wrapped the bandage around my finger. "I'm sorry. He's usually a jerk, but it's never this bad."

"It's fine." His jaw tightened as he stepped closer to me. "I'm willing to deal with an insane cat to be with you."

"Would you like a drink?" I cleared my throat and pointed to the simple collection on the counter. "My bar isn't as good as yours, but it gets the job done."

"No." Domino grabbed my arm and pulled me closer to him. "I need to kiss you now, Whitney."

"Need?" My heart raced as his hands gripped my waist.

"Yes." Domino snatched me up, burying his face against my neck as he sat me on the counter. He pressed his lips against my pulse and inhaled.

He said he needed to kiss me, but he didn't. I waited until I couldn't take it anymore. Being that close to him, smelling the cool scent that lifted from his skin... I had to take matters into my own hands. I grabbed his face and pulled his lips from my neck. We locked eyes in some unspoken agreement before our lips met.

I wrapped my legs around his waist, using them to pull him closer to me as we kissed. Domino pressed his hips into me so I could feel the bulge in his pants. We stayed there on the counter, kissing and dry humping until I was out of breath.

Domino dropped his head to my chest like he was hiding from me. "I'm sorry. I shouldn't have done that."

"Don't apologize now." I lifted my chest and felt his lips near my nipple. I wanted to rip my shirt off and put one in his mouth. "Kiss me, Domino."

He looked up at me and kissed me again. His hunger moved from my lips to my chin, my neck, then my shoulder. And then, he bit me. It was a gentle pressure, but it was enough to make me wince.

"Did that hurt?" He pulled back. "I'm sorry."

"No, it's fine." I bit my lip, and when he focused on my mouth, I realized I'd leaned into Domino's kink. "Do it again."

The corner of his mouth twitched. He liked my encouragement.

"Where is your bedroom?" he asked.

I turned and pointed to the door to the right of the kitchen that led to my bedroom, opposite where I had locked up Maverick.

With little effort, he picked my ass up, cupping each cheek as he kissed me and carried me to my room. He kicked the door closed, the sound echoing in the silence of the room, before taking me to the bed. I felt his teeth sink into my flesh once more, a gentler bite than before, but I understood him. Domino was a biter.

As we undressed each other, I tested my theory and bit his shoulder. He tensed for a moment, but then he relaxed, and a deep moan slipped through his lips. He wrapped his arm around my middle and held me against him, encouraging me to sink my teeth further into him—and I did.

While I nibbled his neck, Domino's fingers found my pussy. With each gentle stroke, I became more turned on, and soon his fingers were slick with my excitement. Still holding me close, he lowered my back to the bed. I dropped my head and moaned before returning to biting his neck.

He smacked the pillow next to my head. "*Fuck*!" Domino groaned as my teeth pressed into his flesh.

"You like biting, don't you?" I said playfully. "What else do you like, Domino?"

"I like to eat!" His eyes darkened as he moved. He made me stand on the bed, ass on the headboard as he ate me. With one leg on his shoulder, I gripped the headboard and pushed my hips forward so he could get to every bit of me.

"Oh! Yes!" I cried as he slipped his tongue in and out of me. "Eat that pussy!"

Domino scooped my other leg up, and there I was, back against the wall, legs on his shoulders, ass in his hands. I didn't think it could get any better, but I was wrong. He lifted me entirely, taking all my weight onto his shoulders as he carried me over to the window. Not once did he stop enjoying his meal. I gripped the sides of his head for dear life as he brought me closer to orgasm.

Before I came, he lowered me to my feet, turned me around, and fucked me up against the window. The cool glass on my tits and stomach combined with the pressure of his dick pounding into me made my head spin. What was this man doing to me?

He pushed my braids away from my neck and bit me again, this time with more pressure. It hurt, but damn it, if it didn't make me scream with pleasure.

He kept me there up against the window, biting my shoulder until my legs shook from my orgasm.

Then, with my nipples pinched together in one hand and his other wrapped around my stomach, he fuck-walked me back to the bed, a powerful thrust accompanying each step we took.

"Dammit!" I cried out before turning around and pulling him back on top of me as we collapsed onto the bed.

Again, I bit him, and he responded with more urgency.

"Harder! Fuck me!" I smacked his ass and bit his nipple.

His hand twisted into my braids as his lips pressed against my forehead. Domino gave me every bit of pounding I wanted, each stroke going deeper, pushing me further across the bed until we lay in the center of the tousled sheets. My legs were tangled in the bedding as I tried not to run away from what I'd asked for.

When my mouth met his again, I decided to really lean into the bite thing. I sunk my teeth into his lip, but my excitement came with more pressure than I intended. My body froze beneath his as the metallic tang of blood flooded my mouth.

"Shit." Domino stopped and licked his lip. Red coated the tip of his tongue.

"Oh, damn." I touched my hand to my mouth when I saw the blood on his lip. "I'm sorry."

"It's okay," he said, but I could see he was struggling.

"Are you sure?" Don't ask what took over me; I couldn't help it. I looked that man in the eye, tightened my pussy around his dick, and licked the blood from my lip. "We can stop if you'd like."

"Hell no." Domino gripped the back of my neck and lifted me to him.

"Great answer." I rocked my hips, encouraging him to continue fucking me as I started kissing him again. The coppery taste of his blood filled my mouth, and the passion between us grew. His lip only bled for a few moments longer, and by the time the taste faded, we both came again.

With that second orgasm, I felt high, like I was floating outside of myself and watching the scene play out. I wished I had some popcorn to enjoy with the show as Domino fucked me two more times. The man had me all over the bedroom, and at one point, I swore we were floating over the bed! After the last orgasm, I lay next to him as he rubbed my ass and kissed my forehead while I fell asleep on his chest.

When I woke up, I was alone. The sun warmed my flesh and highlighted the bite mark he left on my hip. He hadn't broken the skin, but it was deep enough for me to see in the impression that one of his teeth was slightly crooked.

"Damn, it feels like I've been branded." I shook my head. "Well, this will give Lena something to add to her notes."

I stretched and got up from the bed. I would have to let Maverick out of the office. The cat was going to make my life a living hell for leaving him in there all night. As I went to let Maverick out, I checked my phone to find a motion alert notice from the security camera.

"It must have caught Domino as he left." I smiled and tapped the notification to watch the recording.

The video loaded just as Maverick walked out of the office and smacked my legs with his tail. I almost dropped the phone on his head because the video showed the door opening and closing, but there was no one there.

I assumed it was a glitch in the recording, so I scrolled down to open one of the other videos—only to watch Maverick flying through the air and clawing at nothing. I watched myself pulling the cat off the invisible prey and dragging him back into the house.

That video ended, and I tapped a later recording, only to watch myself dry-humping air and floating from my kitchen to my bedroom. I could see myself, I could see Maverick, but there was no Domino.

"What the fuck?"

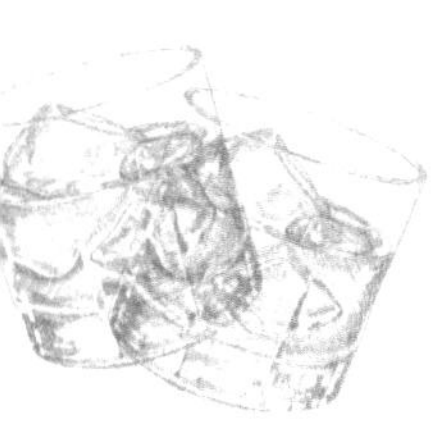

7

A visit from Nyesha

I restarted the video over ten times, hoping it would just fix itself. Something must have corrupted the recording, or maybe there was a glitch I just didn't have an explanation for yet. No matter how many times it looped, the image was the same. I was alone, fighting with my cat and floating across the room from the kitchen counter into the bedroom.

All I could see were bits of images through the open door because I'd never put a camera in my room. There were way too many reports about scuzzy companies peeking in on their users. Last thing I needed was images of my bare ass on the dark web. I watched the last glimpses of myself inside the room from when Domino had me pressed up against the window.

Instead of watching it again, I checked the other videos. The camera had also recorded when the girls came over; it was possible the glitch affected other recordings. They were there, on screen, so it wasn't my eyes. It wasn't the camera. What was happening?

I thought about going online to search if anyone else had their security cameras do the same thing. Before I could figure out what to type into the search bar, my phone rang. It was the doorman.

"Hello?" I tried to keep the budding paranoia from shaking my voice.

"Ms. Harris? This is the front desk. You have a valet here to drop off your car," he informed me.

"Oh, yes. Thank you. I'll be right down." I'd been so freaked out about the video that I forgot about my car. Domino had said he would have it dropped off for me.

I fed Maverick and offered him an extra treat as an apology for keeping him locked up. He must have forgiven me, because he allowed me to pet him. After promising him a good brushing, I grabbed my wallet and keys and headed down.

The elevator ride felt twice as long, which didn't help my overthinking. I opened the video and played it again. Why couldn't I see Domino on the camera? Of course, my mind started going down a laundry list of reasonings, all of which seemed more improbable than the last. Maybe he was really a ghost. Maybe I'd made him up. I mean, apparently, I was the only one who saw him at the party, and Jackie had said John looked like he'd seen a ghost. Was that why he was so freaked out?

DING.

The elevator reached ground level, and I put my thoughts of phantoms to the side.

"Ms. Harris," the young guy who worked the front desk of the building greeted me when I stepped off the elevator.

"Good morning, Cordell." I smiled at him, hoping to appear as if my mind wasn't just on a supernatural spiral. He had one of his textbooks open on the desk in front of him. He was in law school and very close to graduating. "How are your studies going?"

"Great. I'm so ready to be done." He laughed. "Only a few more tests before the big one."

"I know you're ready to be out of here, but I'll be sad to see you go." It was true. In the short time since I moved in, I came to look forward to seeing him. He was young and had an optimism about life that most of the people I spent my days working with seemed to have lost.

He stood and handed me the key fob for my car. "The valet couldn't hang around, but here is your key. It's parked right outside. I checked it out for you. Not a scratch in sight."

I chuckled nervously. "Thank you."

I exited the building; parked just to the left of the door was my car. Just like Cordell said, it looked in perfect condition. I only wished I could see the guy who dropped it off. I would ask Cordell to show me the security tapes, but what if that guy didn't show up either? No sense pulling him into the psychosis when he was so close to graduating law school. It would be a guaranteed mental breakdown. When I got in the car, I had every intention of driving it around the building and pulling into the parking deck. I was going to return to my home and continue trying to figure out what the hell was happening. That was until I saw the black envelope on the passenger seat.

My name was written in gold ink on the front of it. It had to be from Domino.

Okay, I need to talk to someone about this, I thought to myself as I put the car in gear and drove away from my home. I could only think of one person to talk to. Lena. She would help me work through the nonsense, and I could convince her to open the letter, since I was clearly too chickenshit to do it myself.

"Hell, she writes about freaky shit like this. Maybe she can help me wrap my mind around what is happening to me now," I reasoned as I drove the twenty minutes to her home. She had a beautiful house surrounded by wildflowers. It was exactly the way I imagined her living. Pulling up to the house, you would think it was owned by fairies. In a way, it was, because Lena was all sorts of magical.

And I don't just mean the fantasy stories she wrote. Lena came from magic. Her grandmother was a witch. She even told us she pulled some of the spells in her books from her grandmother's notes. We often joked about someone being dumb enough to perform a spell from a novel and it working, but she said she had modified them enough that they would never work.

It wasn't until I brought the car to a stop in front of her place that I realized I hadn't called ahead. Big mistake, because she didn't answer the door.

Me: Hey girl, where are you?

I sent her a text and headed for the porch swing. Like always, I paused and looked at the ridiculous contraption. It was a hammock-style swing. Every time I tried to get in it, I nearly lost my life. This time, when I carefully squatted and scooched my ass back into the net, I slipped! My foot went out, and the entire thing tilted back and smashed against the wall.

"Dammit!" I fussed as I struggled to get up and examine the wall. Luckily, there was no damage I'd have to pay for—not that I could afford it after losing my damn job.

After readjusting once again, I eased my ass back, and this time, I landed safely in the swing. I'd worry about the exit strategy later. Usually, I needed Lena to help me, but there had to be a way.

Colorful vines wrapped around the chains that secured it in place and gave off the sweetest scent. The cool breeze flowed in, and I dropped my head back and started swinging. I could just sit there and wait for her to come home. It was much more relaxing than being in my own home would be.

My phone finally buzzed with the response from Lena.

Lena: Out of town, remember? I'll be back later tonight. I can see you on the security camera. Are you okay? I saw you just bust ya ass!

I frowned at the series of laughing emojis and then looked up at the camera.

Me: Yeah. My bad. I forgot. Hit me up when you get back?

Lena: Of course. Be careful getting out of that thing!

I waved at the camera and, after a few careful thrusts and a grip on the porch railing, I made it out of the swing.

I should have remembered that she was on a day trip as part of the press tour for the movie. Instead of blowing up her phone with my nonsense, I headed back to my car and called Jackie. She lived even further away. I wasn't about to drive another thirty minutes unless I was sure she would be there. She didn't answer.

"Damn." I sent her a quick message to call me when she got a chance then sat in the car.

What was I going to do?

Going home was completely out of the question. I couldn't do that. I didn't want to be there. Instead, I drove to the beach, craving the salty smell of the ocean.

It didn't take long to make it there, and I was relieved to find it wasn't overly crowded for a Sunday afternoon. I took my shoes off and stuffed them in the knapsack I kept in the trunk of my car. The netted bag swung over my shoulder while I walked along the shore. Every few minutes, I lost the urge to rewatch the videos from the night before. Each time, the queasiness in my stomach worsened, and a wave of cold dread washed over me.

When I tapped the live feed, I could see Maverick in the apartment. He was on his cat tower, looking out at the water and licking his paw. Then, I had the feeling someone could be in my home and I couldn't see them. What the hell was the point of having a camera if there were invisible people?

"He was not invisible," I said aloud and stuffed the phone in my pocket. "This shit is crazy."

I spent the day on the beach, having the same conversation with myself over and over. Every time I thought about going home, I remembered that invisible man on the recording. How could I go back there? How could I ever feel safe in that space again? So instead, I strolled the beach for most of the day, until my legs were tired, sweat-drenched the back of my shirt, and my stomach was growling.

No matter how conflicted I felt about it, I had to take my ass back, if only to keep myself from starving. Besides, the sun was setting, and for the first time since I was a freshman in college, I didn't feel comfortable being out by myself. When I got back in my car, I saw I had a message from Lena.

Lena: Flight delayed. I won't be back until the morning. Are you okay?

Me: Yes.

Lena: Talked to Jackie. We'll come over tomorrow. Brunch?

Me: Yes please!

This was perfect. One more night to deal with the issue, and then I could talk to my girls. They would help me make sense of it. The last thing I wanted to do was cook. I've been through enough. I didn't deserve to have to work my ass off in a hot kitchen. Instead, I went to my favorite fusion restaurant. They made a mix of Asian and Mexican cuisine and had the best Korean tacos.

After I placed my order, I stood in the restaurant, looking at the pictures on the wall. The owners left a Polaroid on the counter that people could use to take pictures of themselves and tape to the wall. People got real creative, and there was even a picture of a group of friends dressed up as cartoon characters. It took a while, but I finally spotted the one Lena, Jackie, and I had taken. It was simple:

we all blew kisses at the camera. I snapped a picture of it with my phone and sent it to them in the group chat.

That was when I felt the prickles on the back of my neck.

It was the same feeling I got whenever someone was looking at me. I could just feel their eyes on me. And then, out of the corner of my eyes, I saw the top of the purple afro. It bounced happily across the top of the sign on the window until it reached the door. When the door opened, the woman I'd only seen once before entered. She had a wide smile plastered across her face, and she looked at me like she was bumping into an old friend.

"Oh wow, you're Dom's friend, aren't you?" She said with fake surprise. I didn't know what she was trying to pull, but I had a feeling she meant to run into me.

"Yes. I'm sorry, but I don't think he ever said your name." I matched her fake energy with my own. Whatever issues she had with Domino, I refused to let her pull me into it.

"Nyesha." She held her hand out to me. "Sorry, I saw you from outside and I just had to come in. Domino has the worst manners when it comes to introducing people. I don't think he told me your name either."

"Whitney." My gut told me not to tell her, but I did. I shook her hand.

"Whitney. Such a beautiful name." She looked me up and down. "Matches the woman."

"Thank you." I stepped aside. "I'm not in line if you need to order."

"It has been so long since I've seen him with someone." She completely ignored my comment. "I was beginning to think he would spend eternity alone."

"Eternity?" I laughed. Whatever the man was, he was fine. If he wanted to be with someone, he could. "That's a little dramatic, isn't it?"

"Maybe." She shrugged. "But I take it you don't know him that well, huh? He's really quite stubborn. Though, he may still be putting his best foot forward. Trying to impress you, you know?"

"No, I'm not sure what you mean." I smiled. "Besides, it's not like that between us. We have a professional relationship."

"Hmm." The way she looked at me was like she could see a replay of the unprofessional things I'd done with Domino all over my face. "I doubt that." She stepped closer.

"How do you know him?" I tried to change the subject.

"We go way back," she said wistfully. "We were all real close at one point, and then things fell apart. Dom and Vance fought like crazy, and it broke us up. I miss those days."

"They used to fight? It did seem like there was tension between them, but I couldn't imagine them actually fighting." I thought back to the man who had spoken to Domino the night before. No, I couldn't see them being close friends, but fighting sounded over the top.

"Well, we're older now. More mature. That was more of a business conversation than anything."

"I see. Well—" I froze as Nyesha walked over to me, titled her head, and sniffed me like a damn animal.

"Definitely not professional." She winked. "I can smell him all over you."

"What?" I stepped back from her. "Okay, I don't know what you have going on with Domino, but I want nothing to do with you or him, and I damn sure don't want some random woman sniffing me!"

She narrowed her eyes, and the biggest, shit-eating grin stretched across her face. "You don't know, do you? How fun."

"Know what?" That was when my intuition kicked in. Granted, that ho was late to the party, but my internal voice was yelling for me to get the hell away from Nyesha.

"Miss, your food is ready." The raspy voice of the worker tickled my ear.

I turned to see the woman standing with my bag held out.

"Thanks." I grabbed it and headed for the door, but Nyesha blocked my way. She backed me up against the wall and sniffed me again.

"He's claimed you." She licked her lips. "They will never believe this!"

"What the hell are you talking about?" I pushed her away from me, and her smile turned into a frightening scowl. She was smaller than me. I figured I could take her in a fight if I needed to, but you could never be too sure. Those little girls were always so scary. They had tiny dog syndrome.

"Nyesha, what are you doing?"

Both our heads snapped toward the door. Domino stood there with his eyes locked on Nyesha. As soon as she saw him, she backed away from me.

"Domino. Fancy seeing you here." She waved at him. "I was just talking to our new friend."

"What do you want?" He took a protective step toward me, but I couldn't help it. I backed away from him, and they both looked at me suspiciously.

"I was just checking out the menu." She licked her lips. "You know, they say this area has some delicious treats."

"Since when are you into," he paused to look at the menu then turned back to her with the same look of disgust, "fusion tacos?"

"Since when do you care about what I'm into?" She fluffed her afro.

"I don't," he answered.

"Good." She stepped closer to me. "I was just chatting with Whitney, getting to know her. Learning all the things she knows about you—and the things she doesn't."

"I should go," I said, feeling the tension between them, but again, when I moved to leave, Nyesha stepped in my way.

"Oh, no. Don't go. Stay." She leaned against the wall in front of me. "How about the three of us eat together?"

"I really need to get back home to my cat."

"Cat?" She laughed and clapped her hands like a kid in a toy store. "How precious! Domino, did you tell Whitney how much you love cats?"

"Nyesha..." Domino's voice was tight, like he was holding back something.

"Fine, fine. Don't get your panties twisted. I'll back off." Nyesha straightened herself and headed out the door. She paused and looked at me over her shoulder. "You take good care of yourself, Whitney. Stay out of trouble."

I watched her until I could no longer see her purple afro bouncing down the street. It wasn't long enough for Domino to leave.

"Are you okay?" he asked.

"I'm fine. Why wouldn't I be?" I headed out the door.

He moved closer to me, like he was going to take the bag, but I stepped back from him.

"What did she say to you?" He frowned. "Are you afraid of me?"

"Should I be?" I paused, giving him time to answer. When he didn't, I continued, "She didn't say anything except you used to be friends and now you aren't."

"That's it?" he asked.

"Look, I don't know what kind of drama you have going on, but keep me out of it." I looked around him. "I should go."

"Okay." He turned and opened the door. "I respect that."

"Thank you." I walked through but kept from touching him. What I wanted was for us to go our separate ways, but as I walked to my car, I could feel him behind me. I turned on him. "Why are you following me?"

He lifted his finger. I looked to where he pointed to see his car parked just behind mine.

"Oh, sorry. I guess I'm a little paranoid."

"Why are you paranoid?"

I considered telling him about the video, but how smart would it be to confront a potential monster alone in the middle of the street? Nyesha hadn't said anything to make me afraid of Domino, but I *was* afraid.

"I'm going to follow you home," he said when I didn't answer his question. "I just want to make sure you get there safely."

"You don't have to do that." I shook my head no.

"I would prefer it, if you don't mind." He took a deep breath. "If you're feeling paranoid, you shouldn't be driving. I understand you don't want me to drive you, so this is the next best thing. Please."

"Fine," I said. "But you're not coming in."

"Okay, whatever you want."

Domino followed me closely as I drove from the beachside restaurant back to my place. Twice, I considered trying to ditch him, but that made no sense; he knew where I lived. I also thought about the job offer. I needed the income. Could I ignore what I'd seen and have a professional relationship? Hell no! The man vanished on camera! What the actual fuck?!

"Shit, he said there would be countless offers coming. I can just take one of those," I spoke to myself as I pulled into the parking deck.

"What are you doing?" I asked when I got out of my car and noticed he had also parked. "I said you can't come in."

"I wanted to make sure you were safe." He walked over to me.

"Domino, I am safe." I pointed around us. "I'm home. Why wouldn't I be safe here? Is there something you need to tell me?"

"Whitney—"

"Domino, this is too much." I stopped him; I had a feeling he was about to be way too fucking honest with me. Whatever it was he had to say, I suddenly was a thousand percent sure I didn't want to hear it. "I don't want you here. I don't want you in my home right now. There is a lot I need to process."

"Are you saying I can't come in?" he asked. "Are you taking back your invitation?"

"That's a weird fucking way to say it, but yes, that's what I'm saying." Maybe he was the crazy one, not me.

"Okay. I understand." He said it like he was happy about it.

I almost called him back to ask him why, but then once again, I decided I didn't give a fuck. I could be done with Domino and his fucked-up friends.

"Bitch, you got bills to pay and no job to pay them with," I cursed out myself as I stepped into the elevator. "Get your shit together. You had a couple of good nights, some real good dick, and now it's time to move on. Jackie warned you about this shit."

When I stepped off the elevator, I had a sudden thought of checking the camera. I opened the app and watched the live feed as I walked to my door. The elevator slid shut, and I watched myself walking. Just as I was about to close the feed, the elevator doors slid open again.

I froze; I knew there was only one other person who lived on my floor, and she was out of town for the next six months. For a good five seconds, I waited for someone to step out, but there was no one there.

"What?" I turned around, and my heart started racing. I couldn't see her on the camera, but she was standing there, grinning under her purple afro. Nyesha.

She waved at me, and then, like a menacing little chihuahua, she started running at me.

I turned to run, but the bitch was faster than I thought. She grabbed me by my butt-length braids and pulled. The swift motion sent me to the floor, and my bag of fresh Korean tacos flew out of my hand, knocking against the door.

As I tried to get up, she kicked me back down and stood over me, grinning like a lunatic.

"I smell him all over you." She pointed at me. "Professional, my ass."

"What the hell is your problem?" I asked as I scooted back from her.

"Oh, I don't have a problem." She bent down to look at me. "It's more like a curiosity. I want to know what you taste like."

"Bitch what?" I scrambled to get away from her; I was not into that shit. But she grabbed me by my ankle. Even though I had to be twice her size, I couldn't get away. "How the fuck are you so strong? Are you a crackhead or something?"

She climbed on top of me and pinned me down. "Come on, Whitney. Just a little taste." She stuck her tongue out at me, twirled it in the air, and then the bitch licked me! She ran her tongue down my neck.

I did everything I could to get her off me, but nothing worked. It was like my struggle was adding to the fun. Each time I lifted my hips, trying to knock her off, she giggled.

Then, she did it. She lifted her head, flashed her hungriest smile, and her goddamn canines extended! It was something out of a horror movie. Her lips curled back, giving more room for the protrusions. I screamed and pulled away, but again, this only made her more excited. Then, she narrowed her gaze until it was like the realization hit her.

"You really didn't know!" She laughed maniacally. "Even better!"

She opened her mouth wide, fangs bared and ready to bite into me. I braced myself, because what the hell else was I supposed to do? Clearly, she was stronger than me, and apparently, she was a motherfucking vampire! Just before her teeth reached my neck, something powerful knocked her little ass off me. I looked to where she slammed against the wall and then up at the man standing over me. Domino.

"Get inside. Close the door," Domino said as he lifted me from the floor and pushed me back toward my apartment.

He didn't have to tell me twice. I bolted for the door. It took me no time to open it and step inside. When I looked back, I saw Domino standing over Nyesha and the elevator door sliding open. *DING!*

When the doors opened, Vance stepped out. He took one look at Nyesha on the floor and attacked Domino. I could barely see what happened. It was a blur of fists flying and, after one loud smack, they landed on opposite ends of the hall. Domino stood just outside my door.

"That's it. It's time for you to die." Vance took out a knife and lifted it like he was going to throw it.

I don't know what the hell came over me, because I reached out, grabbed Domino's collar, and pulled...him right into an invisible fucking wall! There was a loud, powerful shock like electricity that flashed between us that sent Domino flying into the opposite wall.

"Holy shit!" I said.

"Oh, Domino, did she take your invite away? How sad," Nyesha said and then pulled a knife from her back. "Guess there is nowhere for you to go. She'll have to watch you die before we eat her!"

"Oh, fuck this." I couldn't let them get into a damn knife fight in my hallway, and I damn sure wasn't about to be eaten. "Domino, please come in!"

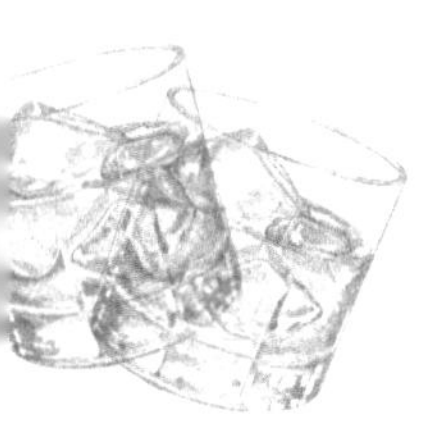

8

The Truth about Domino

I didn't hear what Domino said to Vance before he closed the door, but I did hear Maverick's battle cry as he ran down the hall and positioned himself between us. He hissed at Domino, as if daring him to take one step closer to me. I looked down at the massive cat and realized he looked even bigger than before.

"No. Stay back. What the hell was that?" I shouted when Domino tried to navigate around the cat. "What are you? Why can't I see your ass on the security camera? Is that bitch a damn vampire? Are you? I mean, she had fucking fangs! What the actual fuck is happening?"

"What question would you like me to answer first?" As he spoke, the cut I hadn't realized was on his lip moved. The blood sucked back into the open wound, and it sealed shut like a zipper being closed. Within a few moments, the mark was completely gone.

"Oh, hell no! See, that's fucked up!" When I stepped back, Maverick took that as his permission to attack. He pounced at Domino, once again digging his claws into his face, and reopened the wound that had just healed.

I could have helped, but I didn't. This man knew he wasn't human, and he still let me fuck him. As far as I was concerned, Maverick was doing me a favor. I stepped back and fixed my braids while they struggled. It took a minute, but eventually, Domino grabbed Maverick by the collar. He held him at an arm's length and tossed him into the office.

"Were you even going to help me?" Domino slammed the door and turned to me. "Were you just going to stand there and let your cat maul me?"

"Were you going to tell me you were a fucking vampire?" I pointed at him. "That's what you are, right?"

"No, I wasn't going to tell you because I didn't want to involve you in this."

"Right, and that's why you fucked me twice and offered me a job?" I slapped my hand over my mouth. "Oh shit, I bit you. I fucking bit you! Your blood. It got in my mouth!"

Of course, that little piece of information slipped out of my head until I was facing down the vamp. I bit him and I swallowed his blood. I should have known something was up with his ass when I did that. What the fuck was I thinking? "Does that mean I'm going to become a fucking vampire? I don't want to be a vampire. I'm not trying to live forever!"

"Were you able to go out into the sun today?" He rolled his eyes. "Don't be dramatic."

"Don't come at me like that! Thanks to Lena's spooky loving ass, I've watched the movies and I read the books, but vampires aren't supposed to be real. They sure as hell ain't supposed to be doing the freaky shit we did together!" I suddenly felt nauseous. Nothing about living forever sounded appealing! "I'm going to be sick."

"No, Whitney." He held his hand up to me. "You're not a vampire. Calm down."

"What about your blood? It's in me now. Does it do anything?" I touched my stomach. "I think I feel different. Am I different? I mean, is that how vampire babies are made or something?"

"Vampire babies?" he scoffed. "No, that's not a thing. You're the same as you ever were, only I can feel you now. It's the start of the process to making a familiar. You drink my blood and I drink yours. Only, I haven't had your blood, so it will fade in time. But for now, when you're in danger, I'll know it. I'll know how to find you."

"And if you drink my blood?" I didn't know why the hell I asked. Why did it matter? I wasn't letting his ass drink my blood.

"The bond becomes permanent." I could hear the hope in his voice. He wanted it to happen! Domino wanted to do some freaky blood bond with me.

"So I'm basically your temporary familiar now?" I started pacing the room. "Great. This is just great!"

"Something like that, except you don't work for me." He shrugged. "Usually, familiars end up working in the vampire system, hoping to one day become immortal. Most never do. They die serving their vampires."

"But you offered me a job!" That was it. The panic kicked in. The deep breaths I took to combat the tightening feeling in my chest did absolutely nothing to help. "This was your plan all along, wasn't it? But the purple afro bitch ruined it for you."

"Whitney, you need to slow down. You're going to pass out if you keep breathing like that." He stepped closer to me, and I held my hand out to stop him.

"Of course, I'm going to pass out! You do realize my entire frame of thinking is crashing and burning right now, right? I mean vampires are real, and I let one eat me out!"

"Whitney..." he said my name.

"Nope!" I put my hand in his face to silence him. "On second thought, get out. I don't want you here." I pointed to the door.

"Aaaaahhhhh!" Domino screamed, because the moment the words left my mouth, it was like I'd hit a magical ejection button. An invisible force lifted him into the air and carried him away from me. As Domino went flying down the hall, the door swung open, seemingly of its own accord, adding to the chaotic scene. The force dropped him outside the door, and he stumbled back, his body crashing against the wall with a thud.

"Holy shit!" I ran to the door and looked out at him. "Are you okay?"

"Really?" he grunted and rubbed the back of his head.

"Sorry." I paused then stepped back and crossed my arms. This was actually good for me. "You know what? No, actually. I'm not sorry. This is better. You stand there and tell me what the hell is going on."

"This is how you want to do this?" He took a step closer to the door.

"Yes, actually." I nodded. "Tell me everything from right there. Start with the obvious. Are you really a vampire?"

"We've covered that, but yes, I am." He spoke through a tightened jaw, clearly not happy with the position he was in, but I didn't give a fuck. At any point, he could just walk away and leave me the hell alone.

"Shit, you were supposed to say no!" I pointed at him.

"Whitney, a magical force just kicked me out of your home because you told me to leave. How would me lying to you about what I am account for that?" I could see the frustration building in his expression.

"You were supposed to say whatever the hell you needed to say for me to go back to a normal fucking life." I dropped my head back. "I know what this means,

Domino. You being here means my life is going to be a nightmare now. And it's already not on the best path as it is."

"Would you like me to also apologize for that?" He tilted his head.

"I can't believe this shit. No. Actually, I don't believe it. You're not a vampire. I'm choosing delusion!" I waved my hands in front of me, as if the motion would erase everything that had just happened. "None of this is real. I don't care. It's fiction because I say it is. I don't believe it. I refuse."

"Alright, that's how you want to do this." Domino grinned and stepped as close to the door as he could without getting another shock from the barrier. He looked me in the eyes and then slowly let his fangs extend. The sharp points rested against his bottom lip, and my pussy actually quivered. This was not supposed to be sexy!

"You couldn't just let me live in the delusion?" I pointed at him but kept my hand on my side of the barrier. "You had to go and put your fangs out there?"

"How else would I get you to believe me?" He looked up at the door frame. "I'm not about to take another shock to prove my point. That shit hurts. And that's saying something, because very little actually hurts a vampire."

"You're a vampire." I took a deep breath.

"I am." He nodded. "Will you let your delusion go now so we can talk?"

"Damn it. I'm too old for this shit! Hot young girls get the vampires. I'm in my thirties. My back hurts if I sneeze without bracing for impact!"

Domino slowly inhaled as I tested his patience. "What are you talking about?"

"Nothing. Damn." I threw my hands up in defeat.

"Whitney, please let me in." He said calmly. "I need to talk to you, and I would prefer it if I didn't have to stand in the hall. As you can see, all you have to do is say you want me to leave, and I will. I can't hurt you."

"You know what else I saw? I saw how fucking fast you are." I narrowed my eyes. "What's stopping you from taping my mouth shut so I can't say the words?"

"Do you think I would violate your trust like that?" he asked. "If you do, I will leave."

"Yep!" I slammed the door in his shocked face so hard, the wall still trembled as I marched down the hall.

"Seriously, Whitney?" he called from the other side of the door.

"Damn right! You got me fucked up!" Despite how boastful I was, I didn't make it far before my damn heart started pounding in my chest like I was about to have a panic attack. "Fuck!" I frowned and turned back to the door. "This is such a stupid idea!"

"Come on!" he continued. "Let me in."

When I reached the door, I swung it open. "Fine, maybe I don't think you would hurt me. Which makes no fucking sense, because you're a literal monster. But that's probably because your weird ass vampire blood is messing with my head."

"I am one. And I promised you, I don't plan on ever hurting you, but they do." He pointed to the closed elevator door. "They know where you are now. They will come back."

"Damn it." I looked at the elevator then back at him. "Okay, but I swear, one bad move, and I'm kicking your ass back out."

"I understand." He nodded in agreement before I stepped back and waved him forward. When he didn't move, I frowned.

"What's the problem? You don't want to come in now?"

"You actually have to say the words." He looked at me like I was a toddler learning to walk. I could just hear his thoughts. *How foolish this silly little human is!*

"Oh, okay. Domino, please come in."

Domino smiled, picked up the bag of food I'd forgotten about from the floor outside my door, and came inside.

I took the food to the kitchen counter, sat down, and busted the bag open so fast, I almost got a paper cut. It took years to overcome being an emotional binger. This seemed like the perfect time to resurrect that old side of myself.

"Alright, give me your vampy history." I pointed at him as I laid the food out in front of me. "What do I need to know so I don't get eaten by one of your buddies out there?"

He chuckled. "Very well." Domino stood across from me and watched me dig into my food. "We've established that I'm a vampire. Nyesha and Vance are vampires as well, and there is a whole world out there full of them. We are the creatures of the night. We can't go in the sun, and we drink blood to survive."

"Human blood?" I gawked and slid the red sauce that came with my food to the side.

"Yes." He smirked. "Human blood."

"You're supposed to tell me that you only drink dogs, wolves, and lions, and you don't need to drink that often," I corrected him. "Tell me you have to run off to the woods to catch a meal."

"Once again, you're asking me to lie to you. I'm a monster. A reluctant monster, but nonetheless, I enjoy the feed. And I'm telling you the truth so you can understand what is really happening." No longer hiding his enhanced abilities, he moved so quickly around the table, he brought a gust of air with him. He leaned into me and was so close, I could feel his breath on my cheek. "You are a part of this world now. My world. You are a part of my monstrosities, and there is no going back. I won't pretend that there it is. All I can do now is try my best to protect you for as long as possible."

"Alright, turn down the brooding vampire shit." I hesitated then put my hand on his chest. He looked down at it and licked his lips before I pushed him to the other side of the counter and returned to my food. "So I'm like a walking snack bag to you?"

"Yes." His eyes dropped to my breasts. "But not for those reasons."

"Hey, eyes on my face, sir! This is not the time to flirt. You're a vampire. I'm a human who should be having a mental breakdown about all this, but I think I'm in shock." I pulled the first taco out and took a bite. "Pretty sure you just said I'm a monster or some shit."

"You're right. I'm sorry. It just happens sometimes." He shrugged. "Look, long story short, I've spent most of my time as a vampire alone. Nyesha and Vance were my friends at a time, but they changed. It happens. The longer you're a vampire, the less you care about humanity."

"How long have you been a vampire?" I asked around a mouthful of food. "And don't just say something vague, like 'a long time'. How old are you?

"I'm one hundred and forty-seven years old."

"Get the fuck out of here!" I smacked my hand over my mouth when the front door opened, and Domino lifted from the ground. "Oh shit, no. I invite you in!" The door slammed shut, and he fell on his ass.

I lifted from my seat and peered over the edge of the counter at him. "My bad."

"It's fine." He huffed as he stood again. "As I was saying, I was forty at the time my brother made me vampire, and I have been a vampire for one hundred and seven years."

"You've looked like this for over a hundred years. That's impressive."

"Not so difficult to do when magic is the reason behind it."

"Magic. So magic is real too? Is everything real?"

"I'm not exactly sure what you mean by everything." He leaned back against the counter. "But there are many unexplained things in the world. Humans make them fictional because they can't fathom not having an understanding of how something came to be."

"Wait, you said your brother made you a vampire? How?"

"Yes. He left our home as human one day and returned as vampire. He didn't want to suffer eternity alone. So, he made me join him. It hasn't been the best for our relationship."

"He's still alive?" I asked.

"Yes," Domino forced the answer out of his mouth.

"Why did you say it like that?" I peered at him. "Like you wish he wasn't."

"Because as long as he is alive, those nutcases won't leave me alone." Domino glanced toward the window. "I'll never know peace."

"What nutcases?"

"Nyesha and Vance. They work for him." Domino looked at the door. "And now, he undoubtedly knows all about you. They would have told him the night they first saw us together."

"Seriously?" I dropped the taco on the plate. "What the hell do I have to do with any of this?"

"It's their job to report everything to him. He's the king of this region," Domino explained. "I'm a loner, so seeing me with anyone is something worthy of reporting."

"I'm sorry your brother is the vampire king. There's a vampire king?"

"Yes, and now that he knows about you, you can't stay here."

"What do you mean, I can't stay here? This is my home. Hell, I just signed a mortgage!" I defended. "Besides, I am safe. They can't come in here, right?"

"Are you planning to never leave your home?" He laughed. "You think you can manage to be inside every night before the sun sets?"

"Well…" I thought about it. "No. I guess not."

"Finally you agree with me. How long will it take you to pack your bag so we can get out of here?" He left me in the kitchen and headed for my bedroom.

"What the hell do you think you're doing?" I followed him. "Look, I don't know what makes you think I would just pack up my stuff and waltz out of here with you, but I don't know you like that, freaky shit or not."

"I'm trying to keep you safe." He looked back at me as he opened the doors to my walk-in closet. "I thought you were on board with that."

"Funny, as far as I can tell, you're the only reason I'm not safe right now." I pointed out. "Wouldn't hanging with you mean more danger?"

"That's not entirely true."

"Oh? Then what is the truth?

"We don't have time for this now." He looked around the closet. "Where do you keep your luggage?"

"I have the time. You need to make it. And keep your hands off my stuff!" I grabbed his arm and pulled him out of my closet before I shut the door.

My head was spinning. There I was, standing in my home, talking to a man who had revealed he was a vampire. A vampire who I had fucked, twice! A vampire who I wanted to fuck again, despite knowing how completely ridiculous it was to want to do so. Maybe it was the blood. Yeah, it had to be. I wasn't a horny nutcase who didn't care about the fact that her life was in danger!

"What are you thinking?" Domino asked after I'd gone silent.

"I'm thinking about how insane this is. And how I want to make all this go away, but I don't have time to sit here trying to debunk the logic of the moment.

I need to look beyond that, and you need to tell me everything I need to know about this vampire king and his lackeys he might try to send after me."

"What do you want to know?" Domino walked back out of my bedroom and headed for that custom couch I didn't want to sit on.

"So the king, do you work for him too?" I stood as he sat, asking the first thing that came to mind.

"In a sense, yes. I do. Every vampire in the region does." He looked up at me. "We have to report in about our businesses, pay taxes, and stay in line. Honestly, it's not that different from being a human."

"Great. Just my luck to get hooked up with an immortal who has a damn day job."

"Funny." He winked. "I don't have a day job, to be clear. I cut a check twice a year, and for the most part, he leaves me alone."

"If he leaves you alone, why is it a problem now?" I crossed my arms over my chest because I knew the answer to the question. It was the most obvious thing.

"Because you exist now." He said it. Damn it, he said it! I was the reason this shit was happening now.

"So this is one of those things where siblings have an issue with keeping their hands off each other's things? Am I like a toy you two are fighting over now?"

"To put it in the simplest of terms, yes. But there is something more."

"Let me guess: my blood is special and you both need it to unlock some secret hidden magical properties?" I laughed, but he didn't, and I stopped. "Wait, no, you gotta be kidding me. I was joking."

"Joke or not, it is the truth. There *is* something special about your blood. I haven't even tasted you, but I know it. I can smell it and so can the others. It's why Nyesha lost her shit. Believe it or not, she's usually more composed than that. You're enticing."

"You know, typically, an attractive man telling me I'm enticing would be a good thing. But in this case, it's disturbing. I mean, you and your brother only want me because of the blood that's in my veins. Here I thought I was going to have some sexy sibling rivalry going on." I tried to joke to ease the tension.

"Is that another one of your fantasies?" He raised a brow and stretched his arm along the back of the couch. "I'm enjoying my dive into spy fiction, you know."

"Maybe, but this is one I think we can avoid acting out, especially since I'm pretty sure it wouldn't end in orgasms, but in death."

"That's a smart choice." He looked at the empty space next to him then back at me.

I wasn't ready to join him.

"What's the plan, vampire man? You clearly have enemies, and as a result of that, I have enemies. How do we deal with this?"

"First, as I said before, we need to find a new place for you to go."

"Why do I have to go somewhere else?"

"I think it would be obvious that you're not safe here now."

"I have Maverick. Clearly, he's like a vampire detection system, right? That's why he doesn't like you!"

"About him. You may want to look into that cat. I'm not sure he's one hundred percent feline."

"What?"

"It's a joke." He laughed, but I got the feeling there was some truth to his comment.

"Regardless, he can detect you. And as long as I don't invite them inside of my house, what's the problem?"

"Vance and Nyesha have become my brother's favorite pets. They were among the first vampires to join his territories. They do whatever he wants without question." He looked at the door. "But they aren't the only people on his payroll. He has humans, familiars, who work for him. They won't have any problem walking through that door with or without your invitation."

"What makes your brother king?" I didn't want to think about the second part of his statement. Living alone was scary enough without thinking about human threats who could potentially break in.

"Vampire politics. He's only king of this region. There are more. Every region has a king or queen, and under them are other rankings that I won't go into right now. Just know that in this region, there are thousands of vampires who have pledged their loyalty to him."

"Have you ever tried to usurp your brother?" I thought about what would make them hate each other so much. It would be stupid of me to automatically assume Domino was the good brother. He could have been the asshole who tried to take everything and failed.

"No, I don't want to be king. I didn't even want to be immortal. Why would I want to be the leader of the immortals? Vampires are annoying and selfish and entitled."

"And you're so above the rest of them, huh?" I pointed at him. "You have your ass on my brand new couch and are trying to force me to leave my home just because you said so."

Domino looked me in the eye then took his hand to rub it across the seat next to him. "It's a really nice couch. You should join me."

"Thanks." I rolled my eyes. "I feel better standing right now."

"Whitney, I'm a monster. I'm not trying to convince you I'm not. There's no point in pretending I'm good. I've done terrible things in my life and I don't regret them. This isn't the case of the tortured soul." He stood and stepped close to me again, leaving little space to breathe. "I kill humans often. I drink their blood and I love it. The taste, the smell, the feel of the kill. It's amazing to me. Right now, I would love nothing more than to sink my teeth into your neck and taste what has been tempting me since I first laid eyes on you."

"Why don't you?" I challenged him. "Wouldn't that be easier? Then you wouldn't have to deal with your brother."

"Because I like you and I want to keep you alive. I want to enjoy you, Whitney." He placed his hand on the small of my back and pulled me closer to him. I should have pulled away, but I didn't want to. "I plan to taste you, but I want to take my time with you. Savor you. No one else will have you. Do you understand?"

"Well damn."

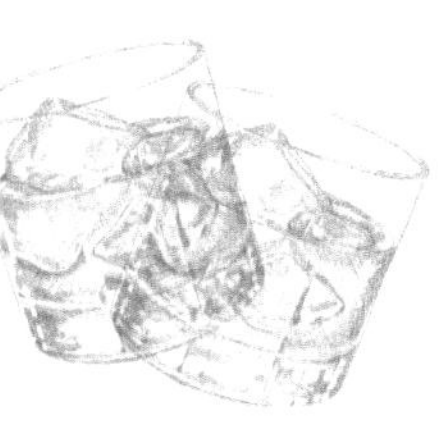

9

Sleepover

"I'm going to need you to give me some space." I fought the urge to lick my lips, because I didn't want him to think I wanted to kiss him, even though I *seriously* wanted him to kiss me.

"Are you okay?" He furrowed his brow.

"No, clearly, I'm not, because I found that attractive when I should have just run to my room and slammed the door in your face while rescinding your invitation to my home."

"Another kink?" Domino chuckled. "You like when I tell you I want to drink your blood?"

"I'm starting to question everything about myself right now."

"Interesting." Domino removed his hand and took two exaggerated steps back. "We need to get you somewhere safe. They know where you live now, which means they know where you work. They will be tracking all your habits."

"You know, when you saved me from that scuzzy ass John, I thought it was a good thing. But instead, I've gone from dodging slimy men to dodging vampires."

"I know this is a lot, I don't discredit that. So I'll give you some time to process it." He sat back down on the couch. "There are a few places we can go, unfortunately none my brother won't eventually find, but it will buy us some time. We can stay here tonight, but we'll need to move soon."

"You want to stay here with me?" I felt my face flush and my heart rate quicken. Why the hell was I excited about the idea of him staying over again?

"Yes, is that a problem?" His eyes dragged across the length of my body before he looked me in the eye.

Hell yeah, it was a problem. If he stayed over, I was damn sure going to fuck him again. *Blame the blood, girl! Blame the blood!* I chose to lie and looked at the door to my office. Maverick still watched us, only now, he looked disappointed. *I know damn well this cat ain't in there judging me!*

"You're worried about the cat?" Domino sounded as annoyed as Maverick looked. "Seriously?"

"I'm not going to leave him locked up in there all night!" I fussed. Not because I really cared about Maverick being locked up, but it gave me something to deflect from my real concerns.

"I'll go." He stood from the couch and suddenly, my heart was racing for a different reason. Fear.

"No." I stepped in his path. "You can't leave."

"You don't want me to stay, but you also don't want me to leave." He glanced at the door then back at me. "How exactly does that work in your mind?"

"You said it yourself; your vampire buddies may come back. They could be standing outside waiting for you to leave." I flipped the focus from my safety to his. "What if they attack you?"

"What do you suggest?" He sighed. Maybe that was how I solved my vampire problem: annoy them all to the point of abandonment.

"You can take the bedroom. I'll keep Maverick out here. He usually passes out on the cat tower after he's fed anyway."

"You want me to hide in your bedroom?" Domino chuckled. "I can't believe this is what I've been reduced to."

"I'm not the one who made cats hate you!" I shrugged.

"Fine." He looked at me like he wanted to pick me up and take me with him. "I'll wait for you in the bedroom."

Wait for me. He would wait, meaning he wanted me to join him at some point. "Okay," I said but wondered if I would be able to avoid spending the night in bed with him.

It took me two hours to get Maverick settled. The first half hour was me trying to keep him away from the bedroom door. Eventually, my offer of Korean tacos was enough to appease him. After he ate, Maverick became more affectionate towards me than he had ever been before. He cuddled my legs and pushed me onto the couch so he could jump into my lap.

"Oh, you're being friendly now. Is it because of the vampire?" I scooted from the couch to the floor, and Maverick rumbled in my lap.

"Look, I don't know the best way to deal with this. Apparently, you knew about vampires, but I didn't. If this is the time when you turn out to be a magical cat who can actually talk to me, go ahead. Because I don't know what to do."

I wish he did talk. I wish he opened his mouth. It would scare the living hell out of me, but then, he could give me the road map to peace. Instead, he put his paw over my mouth, telling me to shut up, and curled up tighter in my lap. I rubbed his back as he relaxed and drifted off to sleep.

Long after my leg fell asleep from the weight of his body, I rubbed his fur. But my eyes kept drifting to the door. I knew Domino was still inside, and I knew he was awake. It didn't make sense to keep avoiding him. So, I pushed the weight of the cat to the side and joined the vampire in my bedroom.

"Did you really expect the cat to have a solution for you?"

"Did you really sit in here all this time waiting to ask me that question?"

"Got me there."

"Look, nothing's going to happen tonight. You're here to keep me safe from the crazy vampires and to stop yourself from getting attacked when you leave. We're just gonna lay here and go to sleep."

"You're going to sleep. I don't sleep at night." He pulled out a phone from his pocket and started tapping on the screen.

"What are you doing?"

"Outside of taking care of you, I have a business to run. Just making sure everything's in order."

"Perfect." I left the room, walked to my office, and returned with my laptop in hand. "We can both get some work done."

Our silence filled with the sound of my laptop keys clicking while his gaze fixed on the world outside the window. He'd already finished his tasks on his phone and slipped the device back into his pocket.

"I don't want this, you know." I looked up from my laptop. It had been at least twenty minutes since I'd done anything of value. There were very few emails for the unemployed.

"I know." He reached over and closed the laptop.

I shifted to look at him, crossing my legs as a safety line. "But you don't care, do you?"

"That's not true at all." He smirked. "I care about your love of art, your passion for beauty, and your dreams of a creative future, but I want you. And I told you, I'm a monster and I'm selfish like that."

"So you're a man." I stuck my tongue out at him.

"Yes. I'm a man who needs to get some rest now. The sun will be rising soon." He looked at the bathroom door. "I suppose I can stay in your tub. If there is no direct sunlight, I should be okay."

"What happened to you not sleeping?"

"I don't sleep at night. I'm a vampire." He tapped his temple with his finger.

"Don't get cute." I thought about letting him curl up in the tub. It was big enough, but he wouldn't be comfortable. "Okay, have at it."

He nodded and stood to walk away, but before he made it to the door, I flipped the switch on the nightstand that controlled the automatic curtains.

"You couldn't mention that before?" He pointed at the moving track above the window.

"Yes, but I also could have let you sleep in the tub." I winked.

Domino narrowed his gaze at me. "You just wanted to look at my ass." He undid the top button on his shirt.

"What are you doing?" My eyes tracked his fingers as he adjusted his shirt, undoing another button.

"Am I supposed to sleep fully clothed?"

"You want to take your clothes off?" My face warmed at the thought.

"Calm down. Nothing is going to happen. Besides, in a few minutes, I'll be in a frozen state. That doesn't give me much time, and you know I like to take my time with you."

"You're going to freeze?" As hot as what he said was, I couldn't focus on that. There were more important things at hand. "Freeze like turn to ice? Become a statue? Can I watch?"

"You're a freaky little voyeur, aren't you?" He pulled this shirt off and folded it neatly before placing it on the chair next to the bathroom door.

"I am not!" My face felt red hot. "I mean, I'm curious. You would be too if you were in my position!"

"This is your bed. So, I can't stop you from staying and performing your perversions." He nodded at the door with a teasing expression. "Unless you're worried about your cat again."

"Maverick will be just fine." I waved my hand dismissively as I readjusted on the bed. "Okay, do it."

"It doesn't work like that." He chuckled and finished undressing. Domino carefully laid his pants across the armchair. Then, he returned to the bed wearing nothing but the black boxers that lifted and showed off his toned thighs when he climbed in the bed. When he pulled the cover over himself, I felt a wave of subtle disappointment. "You don't have to stare at me. It takes some time."

"Oh." My shoulders slumped. I didn't know why I thought it would be an instant transition.

"Lay with me." He patted the bed beside him. "You should get some rest as well."

"What?" I glanced at the covered window.

"You're entering the world of vampires now. You need to get on my sleep schedule." I could tell by the lift at the corner of his lips that he knew what he was doing by saying that.

"Oh, so I have to adjust my life to accommodate you and not the other way around? You're such a–,"

"Monster? Yes." He ran his tongue across his lips. "Don't just sit there gawking at me."

Dammit, why is that so hot?

"Does it make you uncomfortable?" I opened my eyes wider and leaned closer to his face. "Does this weird you out, Domino?"

"Yes." He flicked my nose. "You're like a child sometimes."

"Fine. But if I'm like a child and you want to be around me so much, what does that say about you?" I moved to lie beside him, remaining on top of the cover and happy for the added space the king-sized mattress allowed. "Is that better?"

"Moderately, yes." He turned his head to the side to look at me. "I'm trusting you with my life right now, Whitney."

What the hell was I supposed to say to that? I understood what he meant. If he really did freeze when he slept, he would be in a vulnerable state. He had to trust that I wouldn't hurt him while he couldn't protect himself. Something about that made my heart race, and not because I was worried he would wake up and decide I was better for a snack than a companion.

He looked at me for a few moments longer before his eyes closed. My mouth fell open as I watched him. He didn't turn to stone, but the life seemed to drain from him, leaving him empty and lifeless, right before my eyes. His life ebbed away, leaving behind a woody scent that seemed to embody the very essence of him. His rich brown skin turned a dull gray, and his breathing stopped. I couldn't help myself. I poked him. He was stiff as a board and cold to the touch.

"Holy shit," I whispered. "He really is a vampire."

I couldn't sleep. I just watched him for hours. And it wasn't until Maverick scratched at the door that I realized just how long I'd been staring at the man. I stretched and grabbed my phone from the nightstand and headed out of the room to deal with the cat and to make a call to the one person I thought would believe any of what was happening.

"Lena?" I said as Maverick jumped at me, nearly knocking the water from my hand.

"Girl, your timing is perfect. I just stepped off the plane!" Lena sounded elated. Too bad I would have to ruin her day with vampire madness.

"Great, now get your ass over here! You're never going to believe this shit!"

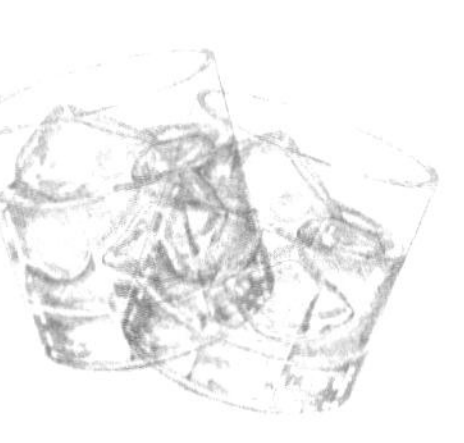

10

Call in the Girls

"**W**hat the hell took you so long?" I swung the door open.

"Girl. I got here as soon as I could." Lena stumbled into my door. "I didn't even stop to get Jackie. She's going to be pissed. You know she hates driving near the water."

"Yeah, I'll get her some sushi to shut her up." I poked my head out of the door to make sure she hadn't been followed and shut it. "Shit got real weird last night, and you're the only person I think would even come close to believing me right now."

"Okay, I'm all ears, but can this story come with some coffee?" She stretched her arms over her head and went to pet Maverick. "I had the longest night, and they didn't even have coffee on the plane. How do they expect people to function like that?"

"Damn the coffee," I fussed but headed straight to the counter to start the grinder because I honestly needed a healthy dose of caffeine my damn self. "You know Domino?"

"Yes, what about him?" She smacked her head. "Wait, how was the date? I can't believe we didn't get the details. Sorry, girl, it's been so busy."

"Don't worry about it. I know you've been on the move, and we both know how Jackie vanishes for days when she's in her creative bag." I leaned on the counter. "The date was okay. We had good food, a weird interaction with one of his friends, came back here, fucked, and oh, he offered me a job. But that's not the point right now. That's not why I asked you to come over."

"I'm sorry. What could possibly be more important than all that? What friends? Where did you go to eat? How was the sex? What's the job?" She abandoned her efforts to pet Maverick, who refused to come down from his tower. "Remember, I said details, not bullet points!"

"Lena, please, focus!" I snapped my fingers in her face.

"You're telling me to focus, but you're all over the place, dropping bombs in my lap like I'm supposed to ignore them." Lena peered at me over her glasses. "Remember, I haven't had coffee yet."

"Okay, you're right. I'm sorry." I took a deep breath and pinched the bridge of my nose to help calm myself. "This is just some freaky shit, and honestly, I thought you would be the only one to believe me."

"I'm listening." She sat at the counter. "Freaky is the cornerstone of my world. Lay it on me!"

The grinder chimed to remind me of the beans I'd been preparing. I transferred the fresh grounds to the brewer, checked the water levels, and started the machine before answering her question.

"Okay, so it started after our date. The next morning, to be exact. I wanted to watch the security recordings because Maverick attacked him when he came in. Only when I watched them... Wait, it's better if I show you."

I picked up my phone and opened the app where the videos were stored. After opening the recording of Maverick's attack, I handed the phone to her. "Look!"

"What am I looking at?" She frowned as the video continued playing. "Hold up. Why is Maverick attacking the wall?"

"He's not!" I pointed at the screen. "Look closer."

"It looks like he's floating in the air." Lena squinted. "What the hell?"

"He wasn't floating. He was attacking Domino, only you can't see Domino there, can you?" I tapped the screen. "I'm not crazy. He's not there!"

Lena's eyes shifted between the phone screen and me. Her face turned red, as if she already knew what I was going to say. But I highly doubted she could ever figure it out, so I blurted it out.

"Lena, believe me. What I'm going to say sounds insane. I know it, but trust me, I'm not losing my mind." I grabbed her by the shoulders because I was sure she would fall out. "Domino is a vampire."

"Vampire." Lena took a deep breath before putting my phone down on the counter.

"Yes." I glanced at the bedroom door. "He's a vampire, and he's in my room."

She put her hands on her hips and paced the floor. "You have a vampire in your room?"

"The man is cold as ice. Frozen solid and sleeping," I explained. "The sun came up, and he went down."

She pointed to my bedroom door. "In there?"

"Yes." I sighed. "Lena, please trust me."

"Whitney, I trust you." Lena glanced at Maverick, who huffed and jumped on the couch. "If you say there is a vampire in there, then there is."

"I called you because I thought you could... I don't know. Help me figure out what to do."

"Why would you think I can help you figure out what to do about a vampire?" She let out a shaky laugh and looked at Maverick again.

"You write about this shit." I narrowed my eyes at her, only to notice how fidgety she was becoming. She started fluttering her eyes, which was something she only did when she lied. The girl could never play poker, because her eyes always told when she was trying to bluff.

"Meaning what?" She looked away from me. "Girl, it's made up!"

"Clearly not, because there is a damn vampire in my bed!" I threw my hand on my hip and tapped my foot. "Okay, something's up. Why are you blinking so much?"

"I don't know what you mean." She pointed to the coffeemaker. "Is that ready yet?"

"Lena, you only blink like that when you're hiding something."

"Or maybe I blink a lot when my friend says she has a vampire in her room." Her hands flew up, her curls bouncing wildly around her face, making her gesture seem even more dramatic. "I don't know. It's never happened before."

"Right." I moved closer to the door. "You want to see him? Maybe that will help you believe me."

"I don't know if that's a good idea." She stepped back. "I mean, I trust you, girl. If you say it's a vampire, then it's a vampire."

"Well, I don't know what to do. He's not the only one."

"Of course not." She nodded slowly. "Because one vampire isn't enough, right?"

"Two others showed up here last night," I reported the incident as Maverick yawned with boredom. "He fought them off, but apparently, I'm in trouble now."

"What, do you have special blood or something?" Lena laughed. "That's always the trope."

I said nothing.

"Did he really say that to you?" Suddenly, the nervous edge disappeared from her voice, and she looked afraid.

"You have to see him." I yanked her arm, pulling her along with me, and raced towards the bedroom door.

I opened the door and pushed her inside, shutting it quickly behind me. The sun was out, and I didn't want to risk it affecting him. Domino was exactly as I left him: fast asleep, under the cover, and looking dead as a damn doorknob.

"Holy shit." Lena put her hand over her mouth. "He's a vampire."

"See!" I pointed. "I know this is fucked up, but now that you see him, I feel so much better."

"I- Whit, this is bad." Lena looked at me. "He shouldn't be here."

"You believe they're real now, right?"

"Well, duh, bitch." She ran her hands over her forehead, pushing the curls out of her face. "I've always known they were real. They just weren't supposed to end up in my best friend's bed."

"Hold on" I pushed her back out of the room. I didn't know if Domino could hear us, but it felt weird standing over the bed and talking about him like he wasn't there. "What the hell do you mean? You always knew they were real?"

"Whit, I come from a magical family. Just because I didn't practice doesn't mean I don't know about the shit." She pushed Maverick aside on the couch and sat down. "Vampires are one of the first things they teach us about."

"So why act like you didn't know?"

"Because we're supposed to deny the shit. How do you think these secrets are kept? We deny, erase memories, and in extreme cases, commit people to psych wards."

"You can erase my memory?" I pointed at my head. "Bibbity boppity make Whitney forget this shit?"

"Not me. I don't practice magic," Lena snapped at me. "I told you that. But there are people who could make you forget any of this exists."

"Okay, so we do that. Simple enough. Sign me up!"

"Yeah, except then you'll be walking out there unaware that there are vampires who know you have special blood and are out there hunting your silly ass down," she shot down my idea.

"Shit, you're right." I rolled my shoulders as she knocked down my option for a peaceful escape. "OK, so all this supernatural magical shit is real. Now what do I do?"

"The hell if I know. I told you, girl; I don't deal with any of this stuff," Lena brushed me off.

"Maybe not, but you know a lot more than I do." I narrowed my eyes at her, because she started that rapid blinking bullshit again.

"True, but I'm still not trying to get involved." She looked out the window and fixed herself as if someone was watching. Unless they had a powerful pair of binoculars, they couldn't see her.

"I'm sorry, but at this point, you're involved. You held your party at a venue run by vampires. I then fucked one of those vampires. The vampires know about me, which means they know about you. And if they're digging into my past, maybe they're digging into yours. And soon enough, they're going to find out about your witchy bloodline."

"Damn it, I don't want to be the sacrifice or magical best friend in this shit." Lena paused. "Wait, you're the one who booked the venue! Don't put that shit on me."

"Okay, you weren't supposed to pick up on that. But it doesn't matter, my witchy friend. I suggest you help me find a way to deal with all of this."

"We need Jackie." Lena nodded.

"Why?"

"Because we're a trio, and if I gotta deal with this fuck shit, so does she." She reached into the pocket of the plaid vest she wore over a tight black shirt.

"Girl, that's just petty." I laughed. "But do it."

"It is." She pulled out her phone, dialed Jackie's number, then waited for our friend to answer. "You need to get your ass to Whitney's house now. How fast can you get here? There's a problem with the crazy man."

Lena hung up the line.

"She's on her way."

"She's going to kick your ass." I laughed as the coffee maker chimed.

"Good thing I got so much of it. Maybe it won't hurt as much." Lena stood and smacked her ass. "Now make my coffee wench!"

It took Jackie exactly thirty-seven minutes to get to my place, which meant she'd broken more than a few traffic laws to make it to me.

Jackie pounded on the door, and as soon as I opened it, she came storming inside. "Where's the asshole?"

"See, I told you she would come ready to fight," I yelled at Lena, who sipped her coffee.

"Shit, we might need a fighter." Lena put her cup down. "Hey, Jackie, good to see you."

"What's going on?" Jackie adjusted the bonnet on her head. "You bitches got me out the house looking a fool. It better be worth it."

"You want to tell her or should I?" I looked around Jackie at Lena.

"It's your twisted love life!" Lena laughed. "You do the honors."

"Bitches." Jackie smacked her hands together in our faces. "I barely brushed my teeth and I'm still wearing a bonnet. What the hell is going on?"

"Quick rundown, Domino's a vampire with enemies who want to drain my blood, and he's in my bed, currently in a frozen sleep state," I spit out the most ridiculous explanation I could fathom.

I expected her to threaten our lives for playing a joke on her and head out the door with a promise of another sushi boat. But she didn't. Jackie turned to look at Lena with a serious expression on her face. She then spoke with an air of disgust she'd reserved for the scummiest of men. "Vampire?"

"Yep." Lena sighed. "He's in the bedroom."

"How?" Jackie balled her fist at her side.

"I wish I knew." Lena sighed. "These things happen."

"They aren't supposed to happen to her, Lena!" Jackie scowled.

"Hold up. Why are you not freaking out?" I looked between the two of them. "You *both* knew about this?"

Jackie held her hand up to silence me then stomped over to the bedroom door. With no fear, she walked into the room.

"Vampire, huh? Only one way to be sure." She walked over to the window and pulled the curtain back just enough to let a small beam of sunlight enter. The light hit Domino's forehead, and his skin instantly sizzled.

"What are you doing?" I ran over and shielded Domino's face with the cover. "Close it!"

"Yep, he's a vampire." She dropped the curtain and headed back out of the room.

I pulled the cover back to see the minor injury had already healed. Once I was sure he wouldn't burst into flames, I followed Jackie back out of the bedroom, but she had already left the apartment.

"Where did she go?" I asked Lena, who had returned to her coffee.

"Oh, she'll be back." She pointed at the door. "Just wait."

"Right." I sighed. "Are you going to explain any of this?"

"Yeah, yeah. After my coffee." Lena looked at her phone. "I probably need to have them reschedule my next few weeks. This is going to be a problem."

Twenty minutes later, the door swung open, and Jackie stood there with a black duffel bag in one hand and a damn stake in the other.

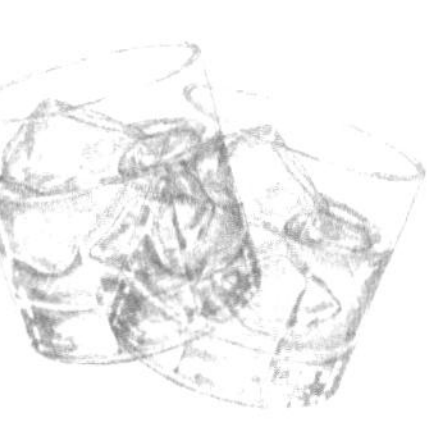

11

Jackie's Bag

Jackie stood in my doorway, head cocked to the side, bonnet sliding down her twists as she dropped the bag. It fell to her feet with a thud. She'd also changed out of her 'ass whooping' sneakers and instead had on a pair of combat boots.

"Jackie, what the hell?" I pointed to the weapon in her hand. "Is that a damn stake?"

"You know anything better for killing vampires?" She twirled it around her hand like a skilled assassin. "If you do, I would love to know what it is."

"Okay, clearly, there are some things we need to tell you." Lena stood. "Is it okay if I get another cup of coffee before we start? Girl, this new blend is amazing."

"That's it. I'm not the one who lost my mind. It's you two bitches." I pointed at Jackie. "You're standing over here like some black vampire slayer." I pointed at Lena. "And you're over here acting like it's no big deal that our friend apparently drives around with a vampire killing kit complete with combat boots!"

"The jeans and jacket are at the cleaners." Jackie winked and kicked the door closed behind her.

"Whitney, the truth is out there now. There's no going back. The only thing we can do now is lay it all out." Lena poured another cup. "I'm a witch, you know this. I never practiced, but it's in my blood. And Jackie, well, she is, in fact, a vampire slayer. Only, she hunts all kinds of shit, not just vamps. You should see the jacket. It has the cutest logo on it."

"Logo? You have a monster-slaying logo?"

"What business doesn't have a logo?" Jackie huffed.

"Business?" I sat on the chair next to the counter and rolled my eyes at Lena, who headed for the couch with her coffee in hand. "You're running a business?

"It's the family biz. I only recently took over. That's why I've been so busy. Sorry I didn't call you back, but I was actually out on a mission to deal with some nasty werewolves. They can be the worst!"

"Remember that guy in college? What was his name?" Lena snapped her fingers.

"Matt!" they yelled in unison.

"The football player?" I scoffed. "He was a werewolf?"

"The one who smelled like ass all the time? Yes, him. Don't get me wrong, they don't all smell like that, but he liked to go get freaky with the actual wolves. The ones that don't turn into humans. They say that's what makes them stink like that." Jackie flopped down on the couch next to Lena, and Maverick jumped into her lap. "Still, it's a nasty practice."

"There were werewolf football players at our college." I dropped my head in my hands. "I'm going to throw up. Wait, is that bestiality?"

"Depends on who you ask." Jackie ran her hand along Maverick's back then twirled her fingers in his tail.

"Look, we didn't want to keep this from you, but we didn't have a choice," Lena explained. "You know back in college how there was a mix-up and the dumbasses in administration assigned you to our dorm instead of that girl Penelope?"

"Yeah." I remember being so nervous to meet my first college roommates, but when I opened the door to find the two of them decorating the room, that all melted away. It crushed me when the woman came by just a few hours later to tell us they had made the mistake.

"Well, you were in a magical dorm. Everyone in that building was, in some way, supernatural," Lena continued. "You weren't supposed to be there."

"So why did they let me stay?" I asked.

"Two reasons. One, I really liked you," Jackie boasted. "And two, we realized there was something special about you. We didn't know what it was exactly, but we could just feel it."

"So we petitioned for you to stay with us and promised to protect you," Lena added. "They came back a few times offering to fix things. But by then, I had got a taste for the real Penelope and wanted nothing to do with her uppity ass. It's also why we had to move off campus after the first year. But it was worth it. I mean, you remember how dope that apartment was!"

"Why would you do that? Fight to keep me around only to hide all this from me. It couldn't have been easy to keep this a secret for the last sixteen years!"

"It wasn't. And it took a lot of work to shield you," Lena said. "I don't do magic, but I did for you."

"You did?" I looked at her.

"Happiest day of my grandmother's life was when I went to her asking her to teach me how to put a protection spell over you." Lena smiled the way she always had when she spoke of her late grandmother. The woman was truly her best friend. "She was so happy telling me the things I needed to gather, including a lock of your hair."

"Good thing she used to shed so much!" Jackie laughed. "Like a damn German Shephard!"

"I did not!" I touched the braids in my head. "I mean I had breakage, but it wasn't that bad."

"Whitney, you left enough hair to make a damn stuffed animal in the shower every time you washed your head!" Jackie pointed at me. "But that didn't matter to us. You were adorable, and we wanted to keep you around."

"So you just voluntarily became my protectors?" I narrowed my eyes at them expecting another secret to drop on my overly shedding head. "No one made you do it?"

"Of course no one made us! The only other person who knows about you is my grandmother," Lena said. "We'd already made up our mind before we talked to her. If you were going to be our friend, you wouldn't be exposed to the freaky shit by association. That way, we could keep the other supernatural beings from knowing about you while not having to drag you into our world. That didn't seem fair to you."

"I told her it was a bad idea." Jackie checked her nails. "I said we should have told you everything from the jump. This way, you would be prepared when this all inevitably fell into your lap."

"Jackie, you protested for half a second." Lena threw her finger in Jackie's face. "And when she showed up with those cheesecake brownies with the caramel syrup, you stopped!"

"They were good, weren't they?" Jackie grinned as she looked at me. "You think you can whip up some of those now?"

"Excuse me! Existential crisis here!" I waved my hands in the air and started pacing, because the cute little bar stool I bought for my counter was starting to hurt my ass.

"Oh, yeah, sorry." Jackie chuckled. "They were good, though."

"What does this mean?" I asked.

"Let's start with the most important thing." Lena sipped her coffee. "Domino said your blood is special, right?"

"Yea, so?" I glanced at the door. Would the vampire emerge at the very mention of blood? No. No, he wouldn't.

"Did he explain why?" Jackie stroked Maverick, and the big guy purred in her lap.

"No," I answered.

"We should do that, right?" Lena looked at Jackie, who dropped her head back dramatically.

"You want to let the vampire guy, do it?" she laughed. "He'll try to make it all sexy and shit. That's how the vampires are. *Oh, your blood, it calls to me.*"

"You're right." Lena's eyes snapped to me with glaring suspicion. "And she's already falling for him."

"I am not!" I held my hand up. "Who said anything about falling for him?"

"Whitney, please." Jackie scoffed. "Lie to your mama, not me! There is a man in your bed who you know for a fact is a vampire. If you weren't falling for him, he wouldn't be here. All you have to do is tell him to go, and his ass would go flying out the door."

"Anyway..." I rolled my eyes.

"Delusional ass," Jackie muttered.

"Can I finish?" Lena waited.

"Oh, yeah. Sorry." Jackie snickered. "Not my fault. She enjoys lying to herself."

"Okay, don't freak out, but Domino told the truth." Lena held her hand up. "And before you go off, the only reason we know about this is because of the initial spell we had to do to protect you. Your hair reacted funny, so she had to adjust it and, in doing that, she figured out what you are."

"What am I?" I leaned forward. "What do you mean, she figured out *what* I am?"

"Whitney, you are a descendent of aliens." Lena glanced at Jackie and back at me. "They were magical beings from another world who came here to live."

"I'm just going to nod and accept this as a fact so you can continue your story." My hands gripped the edge of the counter. "I will *not* panic about being told that my family were aliens. I'm going to get through this moment." After a deep breath, I waved at Lena for her to continue.

"Good enough for me." Lena took another sip of coffee. "Your bloodline is rare. I mean, over the years, their genetics were either killed off or so diluted by the human gene pool, it's pretty much undetectable. But there are a few of their descendants who, for some strange reason, still have heavy traces of that original DNA, and you are one of them. I mean, it doesn't mean you have any of their abilities, but it means you are special."

"Why is my blood so special for vampires?" I focused on the facts and not the tightening feeling in my chest or the way my stomach twisted in knots.

"They drink it and they change. The outcome varies. Either they become day walkers, an evolved form of vampire, or they devolve into something so disgusting, they literally eat themselves alive." Jackie provided the answer. "So there were vampires who hunted your people down, some to drink and some to kill. I guess they figured it was worth the risk to be able to walk in the sun again."

"How is that possible?"

"From what I could tell in my research, it has something to do with human DNA. There are different strands, and those strands react differently to being mixed with alien DNA. Some mixed and became miracle juice while others became toxins," Jackie said. "I still have the research papers if you want to read them."

"And how do you know what will happen?" There it was again, that strange concern for a vampire's well-being. What if my blood was toxic to vampires? That would mean Domino would be at risk simply for being around me.

"There are a few ways to find out. We can draw your blood and run a series of tests. We can take you to a more powerful witch and let them work their magic. Or, we can just let a vampire bite you and see what happens."

"You think Domino wants to risk it?"

"Funny." I chewed my lip. "Is there anything else I should know? I mean, any other freaky secrets you've been keeping from me? Lay it out there now, because I don't want any more surprises."

Just then, Maverick jumped down from Jackie's lap. He strutted across the room, as if making a show of himself.

"Um..." Lena looked over her shoulder at the cat, who had climbed to the top of his tower.

"Maverick?" I pointed at him.

"Yeah, so, about the cat."

"Don't tell me my cat is really some dude who can change shape and has been watching me get undressed for ten years!"

"Do you really think we would let some creepy dude do that to you?" Jackie ripped the bonnet from her head and threw it at me.

"Well, you let me walk around being vampire bait and you said nothing about that!"

"We did a protection spell!" Lena threw her hand up in the air. "It's like that counts for nothing."

"A spell that failed!" I pointed at the bedroom door. "Or is this what you intended?"

"Back to Maverick." Lena pointed at Jackie. "It's her fault."

"How is it her fault?" I looked at Jackie. "What's up with my cat?"

"He's a demon."

"WHAT?!"

"Yeah, he's not from Earth. I mean, he's adorable, just slightly modified." She looked up at him. "I met a witch who needed help. I solved her problem, and she gifted me with a cat. The thing is, he's actually fantastic at detecting creatures we don't want around you, so I gave him to you as a gift."

"You have *got* to be shitting me!" I looked at Maverick. "You're a demon?"

Maverick stretched his body across the top platform of the tower and let his paw drop. It was as if he was bored with the topic.

"There are actually a lot of them around Earth now. They really hate vampires!"

"She said he tried to rip Domino's face off!" Lena giggled. "Man, I wish they showed up on cameras. I would have loved to see that!"

"What is it about the cameras? I mean, I've seen Domino's reflection," I paused to think, "at least I think I have. Why can't I see him in the video?"

"It's not all vampires, only the really old ones, which means your guy is ancient," Jackie explained. "Mirrors aren't the same as they used to be. They don't use silver to back them, so you can see their reflections, but there is something about the old ones. After a while, they emit these electromagnetic fields. It's a part of the magic that keeps them alive. I don't know all the science behind it, but it messes with the functions of most cameras."

"They sell special ones now for that, but they are really expensive," Lena added.

Jackie squinted her eyes at me. "Do you need us to slow down? I mean, if you need time to process, let us know."

"No, don't slow down, because there is a damn vampire in my bed that's going to wake up when the sun goes down and there are other vampires out there who know where I live and want to drain my blood." I paused. "Wait, Nyesha. She tried to drink my blood."

"What?" Lena straightened in her seat, and Jackie hopped up. "Someone tried to bite you?"

"Yeah, you said my blood could either fix them or fuck them up, right?"

"Yes," Jackie said.

"So why would she take the risk unless she absolutely knew it wouldn't hurt her?" I glanced at the door. Nyesha wouldn't be there, not while the sun was up. I was safe.

"She wouldn't." Jackie looked at Lena.

"Unless she knows for sure." Lena looked at me. "Did you leave anything out? Anything at all. I mean something had to have happened. Maybe her blood got on you while you were fighting?"

"What would that do?" I frowned.

"It's like an early detection thing. They figured out a while ago that if your blood is toxic to them, theirs is toxic to you. If even a drop of vampire blood got on you, you would have an instant reaction, like the ugliest rash you have ever seen in your life!" Lena explained. "But on the other hand, if your blood makes them better, their blood strengthens you. Think temporary Wonder Woman-level strength."

"Shit." I paced the floor, fanning my face, which was warming with each passing second.

"What?" Jackie asked. "What's wrong?"

"Domino." I pointed at the door. "Nyesha said she could smell him on me."

"What about him?" Lena asked.

"Um. Well." I was on the verge of hyperventilating. "Kinky sex shit. It was an accident at first. I bit him too hard but, it was weird—I liked it."

"Slow down and explain what that weird ass sentence means," Jackie said.

"While we were having sex, there was some playful biting. And then, I bit his lip a little hard, and his blood got in my mouth." I dropped my head. "I sucked the blood from his lip."

"Gross!" Jackie screamed.

"You sucked his vampire blood?" Lena gasped. "You freaky bitch! First the spy thing, now this? What else is there?"

"I don't know what took over me! It just happened."

"Well, that's how they know. She could probably smell his blood on you." Lena looked at Jackie. "And if she went to the king to tell him about it, that's going to be a big problem."

"Which means we have to work twice as hard to protect you from them now." Jackie looked around. "Good thing you lost your job."

"Hey!"

"What?" She shrugged. "It's one less thing for us to worry about."

"I know, but dang." I looked at the couch where Lena sat then out the window. "It's not fair. I just got it all, and now I have to lose it."

"We'll have to gather your things. Pack up what's important to you so we can get out of here." Jackie scanned the space then landed on the office door. "I'll check the office for anything. Your laptop in there?"

"What about Domino?" I asked, halting my friend's movement toward the office door.

"What about him?" Jackie turned on her heel to face me.

"We can't just leave him here." I looked at Lena, who shook her head no. She wouldn't help me reason with Jackie.

"We can, and we will." Jackie crossed her arms over her chest. "What about a vampire who wants to suck you dry says bring him along for the ride?"

"Jackie..." Lena spoke her name with the gentle touch of a mother trying to stop her child from having a tantrum.

"You expect me to play nice with a vampire?" Jackie looked at Lena just as Maverick jumped from his tower, landing next to Jackie. I guess he was on her side.

"Until we figure this out, yes," I answered. "Look, I love you guys, but you kept all of this away from me for years. As far as I can see, having a vampire on my side is a good thing. He protected me last night."

"My family has been taking down vampires for years. I don't need to partner up with one to keep you safe."

"He said he can find me now. I mean, I've had his blood." I took another route. "Do you think he will stay away from me just because you said so?"

"She's right. It's like a tracking system, and the shit is going to last longer because of what she is." Lena frowned at her cup, which was empty again.

"Fine." Jackie shook her head. "Order food. If she has one more cup of coffee, she's going to be useless to us. I want pancakes. I deserve pancakes!"

"You do that, and I'll make some phone calls." Lena took her phone and headed out the front door.

"Great. Pancakes." I pulled out my phone and opened the food delivery app.

I spent the day watching my friends eat and make phone calls while I packed my bags with what I thought I couldn't live without. Nothing felt too important to leave behind when my life was on the line. I packed my devices and chargers, a few changes of clothing, and my skincare routine. I'd just gotten my late-stage acne under control, and I wasn't going back to pimple patches.

The last few hours of the day were the worst, waiting for the sun to set so we could talk to Domino again. At least *he* would be well-rested. I'd dozed off on the floor twice but woke up at the slightest noise. Just as my head fell back against the wall next to Maverick's tower, he jumped on me.

"What the heck, Maverick?" I groaned. "Why did you do that?"

"The vampire is waking up." Jackie bit into one of the burgers we'd ordered for dinner. "He can feel his presence again."

"Oh." I glanced out the window, and the sun was almost out of the sky. "I should go in first. Talk to him before he comes out here."

"Yeah, let him know he has visitors." Jackie winked.

"Play nice," Lena said.

"I said I would, didn't I?" Jackie took another bite and waved at me. "Go on, let's get this over with."

I left my friends in the living room, joking about Jackie's reaction to Domino. When I closed the door, he was still sleeping. I'd been in a few times while packing my bags, and he hadn't changed before. But as I approached the bed, I could see the color was returning to his flesh and his chest moved with slow intakes of air.

I climbed into bed next to him and lay down just as I was when he went to sleep. The woodsy scent filled the room again as Domino took a deep breath, and then his eyes opened.

"Whitney..." he spoke my name.

"I'm here." My hand moved toward him, but I stopped myself. Was it smart to touch a vampire just as he woke up? What if he was hungry?

Domino looked over at me with a smile that quickly vanished. He sat up and looked at the door. "Someone's here."

"It's okay. They're my friends." I sat up next to him.

"You invited friends over?" He frowned at me. "Why would you do that?"

"Because I wasn't going to deal with this on my own," I answered.

"And they're okay with this?" He raised a brow. "You must have really great friends."

"I do." I smiled. "But apparently, they knew you existed — vampires, I mean."

"Alright. That's opening a lot of questions, but I'm sure I'll get the answers I need faster by going out there." Domino stood from the bed.

"Wait." I held my hands up as he started dressing. "You're not going to eat them, are you?"

He laughed and patted his stomach. "No, Whitney. I will not eat your friends. I'm good. Besides, I won't need to feed for another few days."

"Oh. Okay, good." I waited for him to dress, and when he finished buttoning his shirt, he joined me at the door. "Ready?"

"Yes," he said. "Open it."

The moment I crossed the threshold, the piercing sound of metal screeching through the air filled the room. A second later, Domino dodged the dagger sent flying at his head. It landed, blade first, in the door frame.

Instinctively, Domino pulled me behind him and prepared to defend me. Then, he paused and looked at me with what seemed like disgust. "You're friends with a hunter?"

"That's right, vamp, so you better watch your ass!" Jackie held a stake in her hand and pointed at him.

"Seriously, Jackie?" I asked. "You're paying to repair my wall."

"Worth it to see the look on his face!" She sucked her teeth. "Chill, my aim is better than that. If I wanted to hurt him, I would have."

RAWARRR!

"Maverick, no!" I held my hands up, but the massive feline pushed right by me.

Once again, the cat attacked, and all Lena and Jackie did was laugh. It took some doing, but we got Maverick off Domino's face and into his carrying case.

"So you're the vampire fucking up our friend's life?" Jackie kicked her duffel bag full of weapons.

Domino's jaw tightened. "And you're the hunter who couldn't detect a vampire?" He chuckled. "What are the odds of that? I knew about the witch, but you caught me off guard."

"Excuse me?" Lena stood from the couch. She'd made it her home for the day. "What do you mean you knew about the witch?"

"You're the author, right?" Domino nodded. "I looked into your history."

"You did?" Lena asked. "Why?"

"It's standard business practice." Domino sat on the stool next to the counter. "I do the same for everyone who has an event in the space. We make sure there are no conflicts. Your family, while full of witches, has had no issues with vampires in the last four decades, so I let it slide. I have plenty of allies who are witches. I actually considered feeling you out for it, but I realized you're not that connected to your magic."

"I don't even know how to process that last line." Lena looked hurt. Despite being so adamant that she wasn't a practicing witch, it was like Domino having said it upset her.

"Are you going to help me convince her she needs to leave?" Domino didn't address Lena's statement and pointed at me. "She thinks she can stay here."

"Her bags are packed," Jackie said. "We realized there is another level to the threat."

"Her blood." He nodded.

"Yes. And apparently, your little friends have figured out how special she is." Jackie said. "So we're moving her to somewhere safer. If I had my way, we'd already be gone, but she insisted on waiting for you to wake up."

"I would have found you."

Jackie huffed. "That's what she said."

"Excuse me?" I stepped in between the hunter and the vampire. "Can you not stand here talking about me like I'm not right here?"

"My bad." Jackie shrugged.

"I thought you were supposed to hate vampires!" I pointed at her.

"Hey, this one was talking some sense." She crossed her arms over her chest. "That doesn't happen that often."

"We still don't know where we're going," I pointed out.

"Yes, we do. We're going to going to my place." Jackie glanced at Lena, and Lena nodded in agreement. "It's the best option. Safe and warded against vampires."

"I'd prefer somewhere else, but it sounds like the best place. There aren't too many vampires who would be eager to go knocking on a hunter's door," Domino agreed. "You'll have to adjust the wards."

"Why the hell would I do that?" Jackie snapped.

Domino's brow lifted. "How do you expect me to be there if you don't?"

"I never said you could come with us. I agreed to let you wake up and know where we're headed, but I'm not letting a vampire kick it at my place."

"Jackie." I stepped closer to her. "What happened to playing nice?"

"I *am* playing nice. Whitney, I love you, but you don't know what you're asking me to do here. If I let him into my home, he gets access to all my information. I'm not doing that."

"What about the guest house?" Lena asked from the couch. "He could be there, but he wouldn't be in the main house, which means no access to your secrets. I'm sure there is a spell we could do to grant him limited access to that area only."

"Why?" Jackie rolled her eyes at Lena, sending a silent curse at her for opening her mouth. "Now she wants to talk about modifying spells after dodging her abilities for years."

"Just trying to be helpful. Though I'm not sure how much help I can give you, considering I'm apparently disconnected from my magic." Lena rolled her eyes at Domino, who either didn't notice or didn't give a damn.

"Great." Domino stood. "Sounds like we have a plan. Are we ready to leave now?"

"No sense in putting it off, I guess." Jackie pointed at Domino. "You're not riding with me."

"I wouldn't dream of it. Wait." Domino suddenly reached for me, causing Jackie to pounce and pull me to her side. "We aren't alone."

"What?" Lena stood. "What is it?"

"There are vampires here," Domino announced.

"Seriously, Lena?" Jackie snapped. "I thought you reinforced the wards."

"I did!" Lena said. "I don't know what's wrong."

"Now is not the time to figure it out. We need to get her out of here!" Domino looked at Jackie's hands on my shoulders. "The wards at your place better be a whole lot better than this."

"They are, trust me."

"I'll distract them. Is there another way out?" Domino asked me.

"Service elevator." I nodded. "It takes us down the back and out to the parking deck."

"Go," Domino ordered. "Hurry, I'll hold them off long enough for you to get out. They're in the stairwell. Sounds like they sent someone up the elevator as well."

"Are you going to be okay?" I looked at him, worry twisting a knot in my stomach.

"Are you more concerned with the vampire's life than your own? Because I swear to God, Whitney, I will whoop your ass when we get home!" Jackie fussed.

"Jackie." Lena picked up one of the bags I packed. "Chill."

"I'll be fine." Domino smiled at me. "Go."

"Why do you care so much?" Jackie picked up the cat carrier in one hand and her duffel bag full of weapons in the other.

"I don't know. Can we just blame it on the blood thing and drop it?" I grabbed the last of my things and we all headed out the door. While Domino went to the left down the hall to face off against the vampires, we headed right. Luckily, the service elevator came as soon as we hit the button.

My heart pounded as we rode down. Each floor we passed felt like a new threat. They could have realized what we did and cut us off.

That's exactly what happened. When we stepped off the elevator exiting into the parking garage, we came face to face with two vampires stalking my car.

"Shit." Jackie handed Maverick to Lena. "Get her to the car. Now!"

"Let's go." Lena pointed to her Jeep, which was parked on the opposite side of the deck in one of the visitor's spots.

"Wait, we can't leave her!" I looked back at Jackie. "There are two of them."

"Trust me." Lena pushed me forward. "She's got it."

We made it to the car, and by the time Lena opened the door, Jackie had staked the first vampire. As she pulled the weapon from the chest of the woman, who turned to ash and blew away on the night breeze, the other vampire attacked her.

I watched in awe as Jackie dodged a fast punch, dipped to the right, and punched the vampire in the throat. He choked on the impact, holding his neck and leaving his chest wide open. Jackie was faster than I thought she could be.

With the second vampire down, Jackie tossed her bag over her shoulder and jogged over to Lena's ride.

"Watch out!" I yelled as I saw the man appear behind Jackie. He sneered, revealing his fangs, and ran at her.

The blood-covered hand came out of nowhere, crushing his windpipe and sending him hurtling over the parking deck's edge before he could reach Jackie.

"Go!" Domino yelled.

Jackie jumped into the back seat, and Lena sped off. When I looked back, Domino was gone.

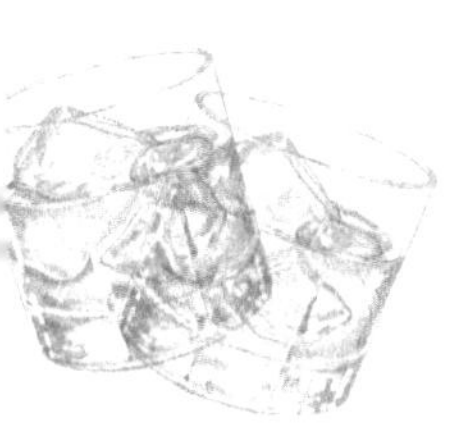

12

Hunters History

"Jackie, I need you to take over." Lena pulled the Jeep off the main road onto a side street. She checked the mirrors to make sure we weren't being tailed. "You drive. I'll cloak us so they can't follow."

I'd never seen my friends move so fast. Lena hopped out of the driver's seat as Jackie climbed over from the back seat to the front. It was like they'd practiced the move a hundred times. By the time Lena's door closed, Jackie was already pulling off. I gripped the door handle for dear life, because even when we weren't running for our lives, Jackie drove like a madwoman.

I looked to the back seat to see Lena pulling a small black case from under the seat and opening it to reveal a collection of magical charms and potions. It was a mobile apothecary.

"Since when do you keep that on you?" I gawked at the items. "I thought you weren't a practicing witch."

"Is this the time when I confess my secret?" Lena spoke while her hands worked effortlessly to craft the spell she needed to cast.

"Another one?" I narrowed my eyes, and she peered at me over her glasses with that 'try me' look.

"We've already established that we kept some things from you for your own good," Lena said. "I think we can move past that point now. Just to save time."

"And your magical practices had to be one of those things?" I asked. "I already knew you came from a family who practiced."

"Yes, you knew, but you also think magic is leaving stones in the moonlight and writing repetitive manifestations. While that is a part of it, what I do is so much more intense. It's dangerous work, Whitney." Lena lit a match and tossed it into the bowl where she'd combined a slew of other ingredients. The concoction went up in flame, and a cool green smoke spread through the car. When it reached me, it caused a prickly sensation that stretched the length of my body.

As the tingles subsided on my skin, I looked at her with a new sense of wonder. "Okay. Tell me."

"I've been using magic for a few years now," Lena admitted. "It's not like I didn't know how. I just was always reluctant. Using magic makes me feel sick sometimes, and I thought it meant something bad about me, so I rebelled against it. However, a time came when I had to put that aside for the good of myself and my family. I could take a little nausea if it means protecting the people I love."

"And Jackie knows all about this?" I glanced at our ass-kicking friend, who kept her eyes on the road ahead. Of course, she knew.

"Yes." Lena peeked in on Maverick. "She was the one who convinced me it would be a good idea. Things are getting more tense in our world, and anyone who doesn't take measures to defend themselves is going to be in big trouble."

"And now I'm a part of that world." I turned around and looked out the window. "I'm not supposed to be, but I am."

"You are!" Jackie smacked the steering wheel, causing my head to snap back to her. "Isn't it great!"

"Ask me when we're not on the run from vampires." I rolled my eyes and turned to look out the back window. I didn't see anyone behind us.

"But that's the exciting part of our world. The thrill. You don't know how many times I wished I could tell you about our adventures." Jackie sounded like she was ready to burst. "But now, I can tell you everything!"

"Your adventures?"

"Yes!" Jackie looked over her shoulder at Lena. "And now, you get to join us. I mean, there is no way you're going back to pretending none of this exists. And if we can tap into whatever powers you inherited from your alien ancestors, we'll be an ass-kicking trio!"

"Jackie, ease up." Lena's mothering voice came out.

"Yes, Jackie. Ease up." I pointed to the road. "On the power thing and the gas pedal. I don't want to die in a fiery car crash either."

"Don't be such a baby. I'm not going to kill you on the road." She winked at me then frowned when Maverick fussed in his case on the back seat.

"I don't think he wants you to slow down." Lena laughed. "You know how much he hates being in this thing."

"He'll be fine." I waved her concern off.

"Why do you act like that toward my baby?" Jackie snapped her fingers.

"Maybe because he beats on me." I turned and pointed at the cat. "Little menace!"

"He would never!" Jackie shouted. "And ain't nothing little about our boy. He barely fits in that carrier you got him stuffed into."

Maverick hit the case with his tail in protest.

"It's not my fault he grows so fast!" I laughed. "Besides, I have his abuse on my security camera. You want to see it?"

"It's edited," Jackie quickly dismissed me. "I don't want to see your propaganda!"

"Whatever." I rolled my eyes and straightened in my seat. "Your baby? You can have him."

"You know you'd be lost without Mav in your life!" Lena popped my shoulder. "Don't be like that."

After more talk of the life of my oversized cat who I'd just learned was actually a demon, I felt the weight of my body double. Exhausted from a sleepless night, I drifted off to sleep, lulled by the rumble of the car on the highway.

"We're here." Jackie tapped me on the shoulder to wake me.

"Oh." I sat up and rubbed the sleep from my eyes. "Sorry, I didn't mean to pass out like that."

"Girl, you needed the rest. Chill." Jackie jumped out of the car. Lena was already unloading things from the back seat. She sat the cat carrier down and opened it. Maverick took off running.

I watched him like a shadow crossing the ground as he ran from the Jeep up the stairs to Jackie's massive front doors.

Where Lena's house was a quaint little fairy nook, Jackie's was a fortress. She lived over an hour away from my beachside condo, closer to the hilly country. It was a home she inherited from her grandmother and, with the money from her father and her own business, she'd built it out. When she first got the home, it was a nice colonial-style mansion, bigger than anything I'd ever lived in. But over the years, she'd remodeled it with more contemporary finishes and even purchased more of the surrounding land to extend her perimeter.

I remember asking her what war she was preparing for when she told me about the stone barrier wall she was having installed. It wrapped around the acres of land and opened in the front, which was a five-minute drive from the nearest road.

"You know, this house makes a lot more sense now." I scanned the massive front entrance.

"Does it?" Jackie asked and handed me one of my bags.

"You fight monsters for a living. Of course, you need a house built for battle." I nodded. "You've made even more changes since I last came over."

"Yeah, it's a work in progress. Almost exactly how I want it." Jackie grinned and headed for the entrance where Maverick still waited to be let inside.

My phone buzzed in my pocket. When I pulled it out, I found a message from Domino.

Domino: Whitney, are you okay? Why aren't you answering?

I glanced up at the notification bar and saw three missed calls from him.

Me: Yes. I'm okay. We just got to Jackie's place. Are you okay?

Domino: Good. I'll be there as soon as I can. I'm fine.

Me: Do you know how to get here?

Domino: Yes, because you're there.

"Right." I locked the phone screen and slipped it back into my pocket.

"Domino is good. He's going to come here when he can," I announced to the others.

"Oh, that's right. The vampire is coming over." Jackie pointed at me. "You better be glad I love your ass."

"She's never going to let you live this down, you know that, right?" Lena nudged my shoulder with hers.

"Seriously?" I threw my hand up. "I didn't ask for this."

"Well, while you two work that out, I'm going to start working on the guest house." Lena pulled out her travel case full of spells and potions. "This is delicate work, and if I don't do it right, your little vampire boo is going to go boom!"

"Only the guest house!" Jackie yelled. "I don't want that thing roaming around my property!"

"He'll have to come over the wall to get to it, but I'm sure he won't have any trouble with that." Lena turned to me. "You should probably tell him that."

"You really want me to text him the secret vampire path to the property?" I frowned.

"No, don't do that," Jackie agreed. "He's smart. He'll figure it out. I don't want him losing the damn phone and there being an open invite to vampires that gets out. We have enough to deal with!"

The contemporary touches to the house continued on the inside. Just in the entrance were large, white marble walls that reached up to a high ceiling. Soft wood flooring went throughout the home, with carpets in all shades of beige and wood tones. She had soft blue accents everywhere. Honestly, Jackie's home felt like the two sides of her that those close to her knew best. The exterior was hard and imposing, but inside, she was soft, fluffy, and cozy. It was why I loved her so much.

Maverick turned into a different cat when he stepped inside. Where he was lord of terror at my place, he was a big silly fool at her place. He bounced around, swatting at the feathered plant, and then rushed to the kitchen, looking for food.

"So, we've agreed. That's your cat now?" I pointed at his tail as it disappeared around the corner.

"Don't be like that." Jackie pet Maverick when he returned to her. "So, what do you want to know?"

"Everything you think I should know." That was like Jackie, straight to the point.

"Right, start with the important stuff. Follow me." She fluffed his head one more time then turned to head down the hall to the right of the entrance. This, as far as I knew, was her work wing. It was where she created content and built all the great plans for her business. I peeked inside the content room, which had at least four more cameras set up than the last time I'd been there.

"You know, it's really impressive that you've managed to keep all this growing while dealing with the monster hunter stuff," I complimented her.

"Thanks! It's all about balance!" Jackie beamed. "Also, I'm not the only one out there doing this job, you know?"

"Of course, there are others."

"Tony from college? She's a total badass. I wish you could see her in action, but she sticks to Brazil these days. They have some wild creatures down there!"

"Have you ever gone?"

"Yeah, a couple times when they had to call in the reserves. But we can get into that later." Her eyes widened when she looked back at me. "I have pictures!"

I couldn't help but laugh at the way she danced down the hall. It had been a long time since I saw her that excited. The image took my mind back to the first time she convinced me to go out with them at school. I was determined to be a bookworm, but Jackie had other plans. After a week of particularly grueling tests and learning that my crush had dicked-down damn near every freshman on campus, I caved. That was the night I learned how many shots it took to convince me to try a keg stand. The number wasn't nearly high enough.

"Alright, this is where you learn all there is to know about me and a lot of the creatures you didn't know existed." Jackie stopped in front of an unassuming door. "Are you ready?"

"If I say no, does this all go away?" I asked with feigned hope.

"No." She blew me a kiss and opened the door.

It led to the basement, a part of her house I'd never seen because, as far as I knew, it was a place for storage. That wasn't too far off the mark, because the lights turned on to reveal a massive library. Soft lights illuminated rows of shelves full of books on one side of the basement, and on the other sat a more technical layout, with computers and massive monitors.

"When the hell did you put this in?" I looked around. "This is amazing."

"It's always been here. I've upgraded things, but this is my family's history. It goes back for centuries," Jackie said proudly. "There are other historical texts here as well. I've spent so many hours down here."

"Are you human?" I asked. "I mean, if your family has been a part of this for so long, what makes you all so special?"

"I am human, for the most part. Like you, there is something that makes me special." Jackie smiled. "There are some extra perks that come with my bloodline."

"What does that mean?" I walked over to the first shelf and ran my fingers along the spine of a massive book with text I couldn't read.

"My ancestors were one of the first human families to learn about the supernatural world. Unlike so many others, they didn't tuck tail and run. They stood and fought and they were rewarded. A coven, thankful for the help of my family and two others, offered them a reward. They would make them, in a sense, superhuman in exchange for their help in policing the supernatural community.

"The spell would work not only on them, but their entire bloodline," Jackie continued. "We're human, but we live a little longer than average. I've recently hit the age where my aging will slow down. Where a normal human is expected to live around eighty to ninety years, I'll last closer to two hundred and fifty. It's not an eternity, but it's long enough to do some damage and train the next generation. My grandmother was closer to three hundred years old when she passed away."

"Holy shit! You might as well be immortal." I walked over to her and poked her cheek. "How old are you now?"

"You know how old I am. We went to school together." She frowned and slapped my hand away. "Same age as you, fool!"

"Sorry, this is a lot to process." I sucked my teeth. "Lena's an actual witch and, apparently, a lot more powerful than I thought, and you're a pseudo-immortal."

"I get it. You know, we don't have to do all this right now." Jackie led me to sit at the large table in the center of the basement. It was covered in stacks of books and scribbled notes, all in Jackie's writing. "You look exhausted, and I know those little catnaps you took weren't enough. You should shower and rest."

"I can't yet." I pulled out my phone and looked at the notification bar. Nothing new.

Jackie rolled her eyes. "The vampire?"

"Jackie." I placed the phone down on the table. "Please."

"I'm trying." She flopped down in one of the chairs then kicked the one next to me out so I could sit down.

"Are you?" I tapped my nail against the white surface of the table. "Because it really doesn't feel like it."

"No, not really, but I will." Jackie winked. "It's hard to go from completely hating something to tolerating it in less than a day. My family didn't have the best history with vampires. We were all taught to stay the hell away from them. It's been ingrained in me since I was a kid, so you're going to have to give me some time."

"Thanks. I really do appreciate your trying and letting us stay here." I reached over to touch her knee. "Can you forgive me for not taking your personal history into consideration?"

"Of course I can. I know this is all a lot for you, and besides, you're not usually that selfish. I wouldn't be friends with you if I thought you were." Jackie blew me another kiss then cocked her head to the side. "What's wrong?"

My shoulders dropped. "Nothing."

"Whitney, be real with me." She narrowed her eyes at me.

"I feel like I don't know you or Lena. Not really. You've hidden so much from me. I get you had to, but all I can wonder now is how much about you don't I know. How much have I missed out on? It's hard to process that."

"We're still the same people," she said softly. "Are you telling me you don't have any secrets?"

"Of course I do, but they aren't world-shattering ones."

"World-shattering?" Jackie sighed. "Look, I'm sorry this happened like this, and had either of us had our way, you would have known in college. But we had rules to follow. And we had to protect you because we love you so much. You don't know how hard it has been to do that."

"I wish I did. I mean, thank you. But I wish all these years, I could have known."

"You know now. That's what matters. You get to be a part of all this!" She clapped and gestured at the stacks of books on the table. "I get to pull you into my world even more. It's everything I've ever wanted!"

"You're really excited about that." I smirked. "What about your family's secrets?"

"I am excited! And I know you can keep a secret!" She laughed. "Do you know the last trip we took together, to the islands? I had to dip off and pretend I was sick, but really, there was a damn vamp fight nearby. I had to step in and stop things from getting bloody."

"You fought vampires in Honolulu?" I gasped.

"Yes, and I ruined my favorite swimsuit. I mean, I don't even know what they were doing out there. It's not like vamps to frequent the such sunny places, but like we said, things are changing." She shrugged. "We have to adjust."

"That was a cute suit." I thought back on the black strappy number that took way too long to get into but was worth it just for how amazing she looked in it.

"Only wore it once and couldn't even replace it because it was a limited edition!" Jackie slapped the table. "I thought about reaching out to the designer, but she's a witch who would have me bargain my life away for some cute threads."

"Found you." Lena bounced down the stairs. "It's done."

"Will it work?" I turned to ask her.

"Yeah." Lena shrugged. "I mean, we'll know for sure when he gets here, but it should do the job. He can go to the guest house, that's it."

"Good." Jackie nodded. "Damn well better be it."

"Maybe I should go there and wait for him?" I grabbed my phone from the table. "Just in case."

"You like him, don't you?" Lena looked at me over her glasses, and her mouth dropped open. "That's it!"

"What?" I felt my face flush with heat. "What are you talking about?"

"Come on, be real with us." Lena leaned in. "I've been trying to figure out what's different. You actually like him, like as a person. That's new for you!"

"I don't know." I took a step back from her and hit the chair behind me. "It's not like I've had the time to figure out what I think about him. So much has happened in just a few days. I mean, we haven't even really had any time to really get to know each other."

"Just enough time for passionate sex and blood sucking?" Lena gawked.

"Lena!" I reached out and smacked her shoulder. "Damn, girl."

"Sorry," Lena said. "Maybe you can get to know him now."

"Ma'am. We're supposed to be keeping her away from vampires," Jackie said disapprovingly.

"Please, you know how this goes." Lena waved her off. "That vampire is not about to leave her alone. Not after all this. As far as he's concerned, she belongs to him, and I get a feeling it's a mutual connection."

"I'm sorry, what? I belong to him?" I shook my head, disagreeing with her comment. "Are you kidding me?"

"It's not like that," Lena explained. "Vampire pairing is an intense thing. They get real territorial and protective. He may not admit it, but I think Domino has given you his heart."

"It's been like four days, chill!" I laughed. "No one is giving anyone their heart!"

"That's all it takes for them. For such gruesome creatures, they really buy into that romantic love at first sight thing. I think it has something to do with being alive for so long." Lena tapped her chin. "You just learn how to spot it after a while."

"Let's not freak her out." Jackie stood from her seat, placed her hands on my shoulders, and ushered me toward the steps leading out of the basement. "Whitney, go rest please. The vampire might not make it here tonight. You haven't slept. If you're going to deal with this shit, you need to be rested."

The guest house was a miniature replica of the main house. It had modern finishes and airy décor that felt more like a vacation home. I'd spent many a drunken night in the place because it was easier to leave in the morning without disturbing Jackie. Lucky for us, it also had a mechanical blind system. I'd purchased mine after being spoiled by hers. Domino would be safe inside.

Jackie was right. As soon as I pulled the clothes from my body, the ache of exhaustion kicked in. I considered skipping the shower, but I knew it would make me feel much better in the morning if I didn't. Besides, her shower came equipped with those head-to-toe pulsating shower heads. It was like getting a full body massage.

A half hour later, I was wrapped in the plushest of robes and stumbling to the massive bed. I checked my phone again to see if Domino had responded. Nothing.

"I hope he's okay," I muttered as I put my phone on the charger and climbed into bed.

My eyes closed to the flickering light from the lamp on the small nightstand and opened to the blood-covered face of a vampire.

"Aaaah!" I screamed and jumped from the bed.

"Whitney, it's okay, it's me." Domino grabbed my arm just before I punched him in the face.

"Dammit! Don't do that." I smacked his arm then looked at the red liquid that transferred to my hand. "Why are you covered in blood?"

"You left me in the middle of a vampire fight. Those tend to get bloody." He started unbuttoning his shirt. "I had to run and grab a few things before coming here, but I didn't have much time to clean up. They knew where I was, and I had to get out of there before they could follow me here."

"Oh, yeah. Sorry." I pointed to the door to the bathroom. "The shower is through there."

"Thanks. Looks like your friend's ward trick worked."

"Yeah, I guess so." I frowned at the blood I could see glistening in his hair. "Shower, please. And be thorough."

"Yes, ma'am." Domino left me alone with his blood-covered shirt. I picked it up by the one spot that didn't look to be soaked in blood and threw it in the trashcan.

When Domino returned to me, he was clean of the blood and wore a pair of red silk pajama pants.

"Whitney, are you okay? Really?" he asked when I stared at him.

"Yes, I think so." I pointed at his pants. "Enough time to grab those but not to clean up?"

"It was a prepacked bag." He chuckled and sat on the bed. When I flinched, he frowned. "You don't sound certain. Are you afraid of me?"

"Yes," I said honestly. "How can I not be?"

"I understand." Domino smiled. "It will take you some time to adjust. I'll wait for that."

"You sound so sure."

"I am. Oh, I drove your car here. I was careful not to get any blood on the inside." He stood and walked to his pants before pulling out the envelope. "You left this in there."

"Oh, your letter!" I pointed at the black envelope with the gold lettering.

"My letter?" His brow furrowed.

"Didn't you send this?" I straightened. "It was in my car the morning you had it dropped off to me. With everything going on, I forgot about it."

"No. I didn't." Domino tensed and flipped the letter open. His expression turned hard as he read the folded paper inside. "Damn it."

"What is it?" I pulled the cover from my legs.

Domino let out a deep sigh. "It's from Reddick."

"Who the hell is Reddick?" I peered at the paper.

His words were clipped and tense as he said, "My brother."

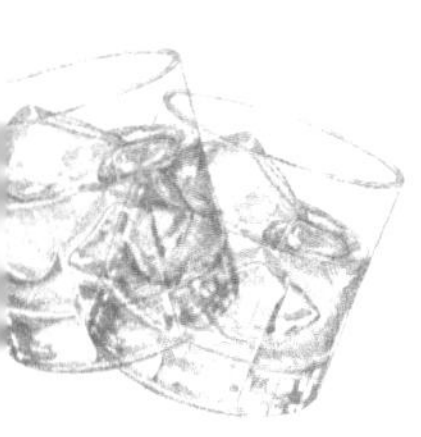

13

The Letter

"What do you mean it's from your brother?" I jumped from the bed and snatched the letter from his hand. "As in your crazy king of vampires brother?"

"That's the only one I have." He nodded.

My hands shook as I read the message on the page.

Ms. Harris,

I will make this short. My brother has taken an interest in you; therefore, I have taken an interest in you. Leave him, or I will make everyone you love suffer. I'll start with that beautiful friend of yours.

~Reddick

"He's going to hurt my friends. Why?" My voice trembled. "They have nothing to do with this."

"It's the way he works. It doesn't matter to him, just as long as it hurts." Domino paused then took the letter from me. "When did you get this?"

"The day you had my car returned to me." I pointed to the paper. "It was sitting on the passenger seat. I thought it was from you. I couldn't bring myself to open it."

"That means we have a much bigger problem than I thought. If someone working for me is also performing tasks for my brother..." He stopped and pulled his phone from his pocket. "I have to make some calls."

BOOM!

I nearly jumped out of my skin when the bedroom door swung open and hit the wall. Jackie had kicked the damn thing in and stood there, weapon in hand, in her, 'I'm ready to kick some ass' pose.

"Jackie, what the hell?" I yelled. "Why would you do that?"

"I heard you scream." She huffed when she saw Domino standing next to me. "I guess it was a false alarm."

Lena ran up behind her, pressing her hand to her chest. The woman looked like she was going to pass out. Her cheeks were red, and I could already see the sweat forming on her forehead.

"Damnit. I need my inhaler," she fussed. "Is everything okay? Are you okay?"

"Yes." I shook my head. "Yes, I'm fine. Domino just scared me, that's all."

"Hey, vampire, how about not making her scream like that?" Jackie pointed the dagger she held in her hand at him.

"Hey, monster hunter, how about not taking two years to get to her after hearing her scream?" Domino lowered the phone from his ear. "I thought you were supposed to be better than that."

"I'm not used to having threats coming to my home. Remember?" Jackie defended herself.

"Excuses." Domino flicked her off. "Maybe I would be better off taking her somewhere she could be better protected."

"I can protect her just fine!" Jackie stomped forward, but I moved between them and held my hand up to her.

"This is not the time for you two to start bickering." I looked back at him, and when he nodded in agreement, I turned to Jackie. "It's good you're here. I'm not in danger, but we do have a problem."

"What?" Lena stepped forward. "I thought you said everything was okay."

I took the letter from Domino and handed it to Jackie. She took a step back and read it, Lena peering over her shoulder. Their expressions were mirrored as their jaws dropped and they looked up from the page to me.

"Why is he coming after me?" Lena asked.

"Excuse me?" Jackie scoffed. "How do you know he isn't talking about me?"

"Beautiful friend!" Lena tapped the paper with her finger. "Clearly, he meant me. It was my party where they met."

"So you're saying he researched Whitney enough to send this letter out and never saw that I was her friend?" Jackie sucked her teeth.

"Are you two seriously fussing over which one of you the vampire wants to kill?" I threw my hand on my hip.

"I volunteer to kill both of you if that's what you want," Domino smirked.

"Real funny." Jackie side-eyed him and tapped the stake against her thigh as a warning before looking at me. "He says, 'beautiful friend'. I'm just saying, it's rude to assume he couldn't be talking about me."

"Anyway." I snatched the letter. "Regardless of whose life he was threatening, this is a problem. I thought this letter was from Domino. It was in my car!"

"Let's think about this," Lena said. "He knows where you live, but he can't get here. So for now, you are safe."

"This threat isn't just limited to the three of us," Jackie said. "We aren't the only people Whitney loves."

"So, we can't just stay here and hope it will blow over." My heart raced in my chest. What if Reddick went after my family? I thought of my little sister. She lived in another country, alone and unprotected. How would we ever be able to get to her before Reddick?

"No, we can't," Domino said. "And I'm not planning on waiting for my brother to strike first. That's not how I do things."

"What do we do?" I looked at him for answers.

"I—" Domino started but was cut off by Lena.

"You still need to lay your ass down and rest. And I need to reach out to someone." Her momma-brain was in hyper-drive. "She's a witch, a lot more powerful than I am. She can help us. We need to fortify our barriers and make sure Domino is the only vampire who can get through!"

"Agreed." Jackie dropped the letter on the table near the door. "While you do that, I'll work on beefing up our security measures. We need to get some more hunters here. Even if the vampires can't get on this property, they'll figure out where we are soon enough. And we know how much they like to use humans to do their bidding."

"Hey, I employ humans. I don't have familiars."

"Oh, so you're the only vampire who never created zombies to do your dirty work?" Jackie twisted her lips at him. "I don't buy it."

Domino shrugged. "I didn't say never. I just don't do it anymore."

"Guys..." Lena pulled Jackie's arm. "We don't have time for another round of shit-talking. Jackie, let's go."

"Yes, please go work on your response time." Domino threw the last jab at Jackie.

"You know what?" Jackie started, but her words were immediately muffled when Lena smacked her hand over Jackie's mouth. She wrapped her arm around our friend's waist and dragged her out of the room.

"Really?" I walked over to the door and closed it. "You just had to get in one more dig?"

"What? It's fun." Domino fiddled with the phone in his hand. "I find her amusing."

"I don't think it's a mutual enjoyment." I pointed at him. "You don't know Jackie; she might actually try to kill you!"

"Makes it all the more fun for me." Domino flexed. "She's not the first hunter I've met. I can take her."

"You two are a lot more alike than you think." I picked up the letter Jackie had dropped. "This is scary, Domino."

He sighed and dropped the show of arrogance. "I apologize. I know this is hard for you. Over the years, I've become desensitized to my brother's bullshit. It's not the first time he's done something like this, and unless I cut his head off, it won't be the last time."

"Yeah, well, unlike you, I care about my family. I have a sister out there." I balled the letter in my hand. "And she's going to be in trouble because of this. My parents, my loved ones, they're all over the place. How am I supposed to protect any of them?"

"You're right. Stay here. I need to take care of something." Domino tapped the screen of his phone and then headed out the bedroom door.

I sat on the bed, waiting for Domino to return, and looked at my phone. Should I call them? Should I let them know their lives were in danger? Would that do anything besides make them panic? Would I want to know, or would I want to live my life oblivious to the monstrosities of the world for as long as possible?

While I waited for Domino, my thoughts spiraled out of control, leaving me paralyzed with fear. Because what was I really supposed to do?

"What did you do?" I asked when Domino walked back into the room.

"My brother isn't the only powerful vampire. Just because I don't want to be king doesn't mean I haven't spent my time forming alliances. I have people all over the world, and I'm sending them to look after your family."

"Oh." I knew he wanted the admission to bring me a sense of comfort, but it had another effect. All I could think of was the letter and how it got in my car to begin with. "What if they are the ones working for your brother?"

"Whitney, I sent only the best." Domino sat on the bed beside me. "And your other family will be taken care of, I promise you. Though I've already received reports of hunters in the areas where they live, so I'm assuming Jackie alerted her people the second she found out about me. I'm impressed and yet annoyed that she beat me to it at the same time."

"Speaking of Jackie, what does she mean about the zombies?" I looked at him. "Can vampires do that?"

"They're not actual zombies. They are familiars, but the comparison is not that far off, to be honest." He chuckled.

"Do I want to know what that means?" My skin prickled at the idea that Domino could turn someone into the mindless beings depicted in movies.

"When true familiars are made, a blood swap is done. The vampire drinks the human's blood, and the human drinks the vampire's blood. This creates a bond of imbalance. The human becomes a familiar, someone obedient to the point of obsession. They will do whatever the vampire wants, even if it means ending their own life."

"You said you used to do it, but you don't anymore. Why?"

"It was hard to continue the practice. I couldn't do it anymore." His jaw tightened as he spoke. "Not after someone I loved dearly was used against me."

"What happened? I mean, if you're okay with talking about it." I wanted to know because I wanted to know what he cared about, what mattered to him so much that it would make him change himself like that.

"Reddick happened." Domino's expression changed. "Julia was my first love. I knew her before he turned me. I'd planned to marry her. But as the years went on, and I refused to become the monster my brother wanted me to be, he lashed out. He made threats on my life, but we both knew he would never end it. When I refused to comply, he made her his familiar. And then, after torturing her, he made her come to me covered in bruises. I was chained down; I couldn't get to her, but he made me watch it as he ordered her to drive a knife through her chest."

"Oh my God." I wanted to hold him, but I remained frozen by his side.

"After that, I couldn't see myself controlling another person. When he released me, I ordered the familiars I had to leave me. They were to go away and live their lives as if I never existed."

"I'm sorry you had to go through that." I looked at him. "That couldn't have been easy."

"Be sorry for her, not for me." Domino looked back at me. "Had it not been for me, she would have lived a full life. She would have had a family, children. She would have known love."

There was something in his eyes that told me the concern he spoke for his former love was really for me. Would I miss out on all those things because of him?

"I'm not your familiar, but does it feel the same?" My voice sounded small. Maybe I was afraid of the answer. "I mean, you have a connection to me that I don't have to you."

"No. This is different, somehow more intense." He dropped his eyes to my lips. "Which is why most vampires don't allow humans to drink from them if they aren't planning to make them a familiar."

"How does it feel?" I asked.

"How do I explain that?" The corner of his mouth lifted. "Whitney, my brain has been muddied with thoughts of you even before you had my blood. I won't lie, I've been with plenty of women in my time, all of whom I've been able to walk away from without a second thought. But not with you. You've consumed me from the moment I first saw you standing beneath that horrible painting. I wanted to take you then. I wanted to steal you away and keep you for myself. The more I learned about you, the more intense that feeling became. And now that you've had my blood, I feel as though I belong to you. My heart doesn't beat the same. My breathing has changed. Even the way my thoughts flow through my mind. All parts of myself have been modified by your existence. I would do anything you asked of me."

"Well, damn." I gasped. "I don't know how to feel about that. You know, people don't talk like that."

"I understand if it's overwhelming. It will wear off with time." He grabbed my hand. "In a few days, maybe a week or two, I'll go back to just thinking about you a lot. I won't be able to feel you or find you anymore."

"You won't?" Again, I knew Domino meant to make me feel better, but his words sent me into another panic. "What if something happens to me?"

"Nothing is going to happen. We'll handle my brother."

"Give me your blood." I flipped his hand over in mine. "Do it."

"What?" he smirked. "Why?"

"I don't want it to wear off." I came up with a logical reason, since I wasn't ready to face the illogical one. "You see how slowly they got here. And Lena's ass could barely breathe. No, it can't wear off. I need someone faster, because I sure as hell can't fight off a vampire on my own."

"Are you sure?" Domino shifted his weight. "Whitney, I didn't tell you that to make you panic. Know your friends and I will do everything to keep you safe."

"Is there any danger in it for me?" I asked, because that was the only thing that mattered. "If I keep drinking your blood, will it hurt me?"

"No, it won't hurt you physically, but the more you have, the more addictive it becomes," he explained cautiously. "The last time, you felt different, right? In any other scenario, you wouldn't have eagerly sucked my blood from my lip. You would have panicked and probably asked me about my sexual history. Instead, you pulled more of me into you."

"Yes, that has been bothering me." I chewed my lip. "I mean, I wouldn't have done that with anyone else, I know it, but the thought of your blood didn't freak me out. It actually excited me."

"It's like a drug, Whitney." He put my fingers to his lips. "The more you have, the more you want."

"So I drink your blood and I get high?" I laughed. "You're a literal drug?"

"Something like that." He smiled. "But my blood isn't the only reason women find themselves obsessed with me."

"Oh, really?" I popped his shoulder. "Will I lose myself? If I continue to drink from you, is that a possibility?"

"I'd never let you lose yourself, Whitney," Domino promised me, and I believed him.

"Okay, do it." I nodded. "Please."

Domino looked me in the eye and lifted his wrist to his lips. He watched me closely as he bared his teeth and let his fangs drop. I flinched, but he continued.

The sharp point of his fang punctured his wrist right on top of a vein, and the blood flowed down his arm.

With the same intense eye contact, he offered the opening to me. I grabbed his arm with both hands, my lips hovering above the wound. When he nodded, I pulled his wrist to my lips and drank from him. The first taste was what I expected, the strong coppery taste like pennies, but then, it changed. It turned sweet like honey. Each swallow left my throat warm, and that spread through my body like fizz. I felt tingly all over, and when those tingles reached my pussy, I could only think of one thing.

I dropped his wrist from my mouth and placed my hands on either side of his face. He didn't move or speak; he waited. Domino waited for my lips to reach his. He waited for my gentle kiss to grow in urgency and for my leg to drape across his lap. He waited for me to unwrap the white robe, now speckled with his blood, from around my body. When it hit the floor, Domino stopped waiting.

He grabbed my ass and encouraged my kiss to deepen. I groaned and reached down to pull his dick from the pajama pants. Foreplay was a foreign word that meant nothing to me. My body was ready for him. I slid his dick inside my pussy and started rocking my hips.

"Mmm," Domino moaned against my lips as his grip tightened on my ass.

Everything he did felt so much more intense with his blood in my body. I'd only been high a few times in my life, but weed didn't have shit on Domino's blood. It was like an out-of-body experience. My heart raced, and I felt like I was watching myself from above. I sat back, cheering myself on as I rocked my hips and pushed him back onto the bed. My head dropped, and the braids swung across my back.

"Yes," I moaned as butterflies circled my head.

Domino lifted his head, pulling my breast to his lips, and as he sucked my nipples, my pussy tightened around his dick. He thrust his hips up, digging deeper as I came down on him.

"Fuck." He lifted once again, but this time, he wrapped his arm around my back and picked me up. Domino shifted our position on the bed, bringing me to the edge as he lifted my legs in the air and fucked me, watching each time his dick slid in and out of my pussy.

"Touch yourself," he demanded.

I did as he asked and rolled my fingers over my clit while he fucked me.

"Yes!" I screamed, and he slapped his hand over my mouth.

Domino smiled. "We don't want your friends running back over here."

"Oh, shit," I giggled as he picked me up again. I wrapped my arms around his neck and held on as he continued to fuck me, holding me up in the air. "You're so strong."

"You're impressed by that?" Domino growled. "Watch this."

He leaned back, and I held my breath, waiting for the impact as we crashed to the bed. It never came. We floated in the air, our bodies suspended by an invisible force.

"What is this?" I looked over his shoulder at the mess of covers and tossed pillows.

"One of those freaky vampire things." He kissed my neck. "Ride me."

"This didn't happen before." I moaned as his tongue swirled against my flesh.

"I had to hold back before."

Domino peeled my arms from around his neck and pinched my nipples as he pushed me upright. I braced myself on his chest. When I looked at him, he gave me an encouraging nod, and I started rocking my hips again. With each push, I gained more confidence. His hands moved to my hips and added more stability to my motion.

We lifted higher in the air until my hands, thrown over my head, gripped the exposed beam above the bed. Domino shifted his hips and turned me around. My breast and stomach pressed against the wood as he fucked me from behind. He kissed my shoulder and licked the sweat from my flesh.

I laughed again and realized I was much more intoxicated than I thought. I should have been afraid of splinters or worse, falling on my ass, but I didn't care. Instead of worrying about the logistics, I pushed my ass back against him and took every stroke like a champ.

Domino kept fucking me until my orgasm dripped down his dick. After I came, the magic faded, and we dropped from the ceiling, landing gently on the bed. I don't know what he intended to do next, but I saw his dick glistening with my cum, and I had to taste it. When I grabbed him by the ass and took his dick into my mouth, Domino gasped.

"Shit!" he called out and wrapped his hands in my braids.

I turned and pushed him down on the bed then went right back to sucking his dick while I sat on his face. He didn't need instructions. Domino's tongue slid in and out of my pussy as I sucked his dick, keeping my eye on his feet. I waited for the moment. Just when his toes curled, I shifted my hips forward, replacing my mouth with my pussy and started riding him. Reverse cowgirl.

"Damn it!" He smacked my ass, and I fucked him harder. "I'm about to come!"

Domino lifted his hips once more and twisted, knocking me off him. I popped my ass up in the air and looked back at him. "Do it."

Two strokes of his hand around his dick, and Domino came all over my ass.

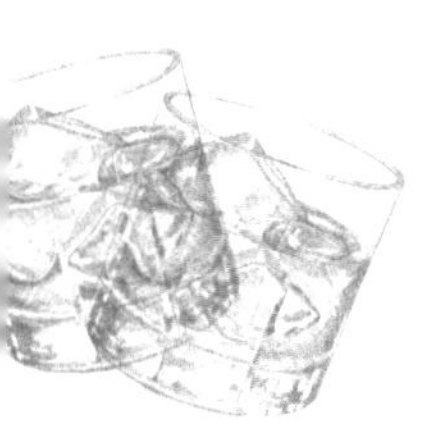

14

Oh, hey, Likosa!

I didn't know if it was the sex, the blood, the fatigue, or a combination of all three, but I slept through the day. As Domino's eyes fluttered closed and his breathing slowed, I knew it was time to rest too. I snuggled close to him and let sleep overtake me. I had dreams of butterflies and blood and woke up when the woodsy smell pulled me back to consciousness. When I opened my eyes, Domino was already awake and watching me.

"You're awake?" I squinted.

"Yes, the sun has set." Domino pointed to the window. He'd opened the curtains to let the moon illuminate the space.

"Oh, I slept all day?" I groaned and stretched out next to him. "Damn."

"How do you feel?"

"Honestly? A lot better than I did yesterday." I sat up and climbed out of the bed. "Is that another effect of your blood?"

"Yes, it is." He watched me pull the robe around my naked body. "Where are you going?"

"To brush my teeth!" I frowned. "I'm not about to sit here talking to you with yuck mouth."

"Yuck mouth?" He laughed. "Whatever you say."

"Don't you brush your teeth?"

"Only after a feed. Sometimes, it gets a little messy, and I get flesh stuck in my teeth," he said too honestly.

"I'm going to act like I didn't hear that, because I spent the night with my tongue in your mouth."

"I was joking!" he called out after me.

"Sure!" I waved him off. "I hope you know this means I'm going to monitor your oral hygiene now."

I followed up a thorough scrub of my mouth with another shower. Part of me expected Domino to join me, but he didn't, even though I stayed in there long enough to give him ample opportunity. Dissatisfied with the otherwise wonderful shower, I dried, dressed, and headed back out, expecting him to be sitting in bed. He wasn't.

"Where'd he go?" I muttered before I heard dishes clinking together. I left the bedroom to find Domino standing in the kitchen with an apron around his waist and a mess on the counter. "What are you doing?"

"I—" He looked up at me. "Making you something to eat."

"Oh?" I couldn't help but laugh at the disaster in front of me. "What exactly are you making that requires four pans and a sink full of dirty dishes?"

"Sit." He pointed to the small dining table.

"So, was that like a unique ability for you, or can all vampires do that?" I asked him as I adjusted my braids and headed for the table.

"What?" He looked up at me from the plate he worked on.

"The floating sex thing." I reminisced about our activities from the night before. "That was wild."

"Older vampires can do it, not the young ones." He winked at me. "The older we get, the more inherent abilities we gain access to due to the magic that made us."

"So there are things you can't do because you're not old enough? Like what?"

"Eventually, I won't have to be sexually aroused to float or fly." Domino tossed a kitchen towel over his shoulder like a proud chef.

"No shit! Really? There are vampires who can fly?"

"Only a few are old enough, but yes."

I sat down and waited as he finished whipping up his concoction. It was hard enough to hold back my laughter as he continued his destruction, but when he put the plate in front of me fixed with runny eggs, undercooked sausage, and the scariest biscuits I think I'd ever seen, I fell out laughing.

"What?" He frowned. "You don't like it?"

"I'm sorry, but what is this?" I looked up at him as I sucked my lips in to stop myself from laughing.

"Food," he said proudly. "You need to eat."

"Someone might call it food."

"What do you call it?" He looked offended.

"Confusion." I snickered. "As in, I'm confused why the kitchen looks the way it does when there is so little on this plate."

"Excuse me for doing something nice for you." Domino reached for the plate and, for a moment, I thought the man would actually start pouting.

"I'm sorry, I am." I poked at the meat with my fork. "And I appreciate the effort, but I don't feel safe eating this. I'm not even sure it's done."

"Well, I tried. Maybe we can just order out." Just as he snatched the plate from me, my phone rang. I ran to the bedroom to grab it while he cleaned up the disaster he made.

Lena: Heads up, we're on our way.

Jackie: Yeah, so put some clothes on. I know that vampire kept you up all night.

Me: I don't know what you're talking about.

Jackie: I was on patrol last night....

"Oh, crap." I stared at the message, complete with a winking emoji at the end. My mind flashed back to Domino covering my mouth. Had she really heard us?

I'd find out soon enough, because two minutes later, they were knocking on the door.

"Everyone decent in there?" Jackie called out from the other side.

"Come in!" I called as I walked back out of the bedroom and into the open area.

Jackie tiptoed through the door with her hand over her eyes.

"Whatever!" I said and picked up a pillow from the sofa to toss at her. Even though she didn't see me toss it, she caught it and winked at me before she turned to her left and saw Domino standing in the kitchen, surrounded by his mess.

"Yo!" Jackie threw her hands up and stomped over to him. "What did you do in here?"

"I tried to cook for her." Domino pointed at me. "She didn't like it."

"And you had to demolish my kitchen to do it?" She pointed at him. "You're cleaning this up."

"I thought hunters had better eyesight than that?" He stretched his hands out to his sides. "Can't you see that's what I'm doing?"

"My eyes work well enough to see that you shouldn't be anywhere near a kitchen."

"You want to come give me some lessons?"

"I knew it!" She looked at me. "Are you hearing this sexist bullshit?"

"I'm hearing something, but it's more like an overreaction." Lena laughed and lifted the small brown basket she had in her hand. "I brought you something to eat, girl. I figured you'd be starving after everything that happened yesterday."

"Thank you." I smiled and joined her at the table.

Lena laid out the meal and joined me, and we ate the food while Jackie and Domino continued poking at each other in the kitchen.

"Do you think that will ever end?"

"Yeah right!" Lena laughed. "Jackie loves messing with vampires. It's her favorite pastime. And now you've gone and given her extended access to one."

"Great." I chuckled and bit into the sandwich. "Mmm, what is this?"

"Roast beef. I made it in the slow cooker and used my grandmother's special seasoning."

I stopped chewing and looked at her. "You used magic on this?"

"If magic is a mixture of spices from the grocery store and herbs from my garden, then yes." She laughed. "Eat your food, girl, and be thankful you know at least one person who can cook."

I glanced at Domino, who put the last of the dishes in the dishwasher. She was right. I reached over and grabbed her arm. "Thank you so much!"

We laughed until Domino and Jackie joined us at the table.

"Now that my kitchen is clean..." Jackie shot Domino another signature side-eye. "We need to go over our plan."

"Yes." Lena smiled. "We made a lot of progress while you were sleeping."

"Yes, we did. I've already reached out to the other hunters. They are coming here to help. The first of them should arrive in a few hours." Jackie pointed her thumb at Domino. "I told them about this guy so they won't try to take his head off if they see him. I still suggest keeping a distance."

"Thanks," Domino muttered.

"We need to figure out what we can do to make Reddick stop," Lena spoke. "So I reached out to someone who I think can help us with that. She's the reason my magic has progressed so quickly over the last few years. Think of her as my magical mentor."

"You have a mentor?" I grabbed her hand. "That's so cool!"

"Thanks. I wish it could have been my grandmother, but she used to be friends with her, so it works out." Lena smiled. "I think you will really like her. She'll be here soon."

"Jackie, your hunters are also watching over Whitney's family, correct?" Domino asked.

"Yes, why?"

"I asked some of my contacts to monitor Whitney's loved ones. It might be a good idea if you let them know about it. I don't want there to be any issue if they cross paths."

"You're right." Jackie pulled out her phone and started typing on the screen. "While I do that, is there anything we should know about your brother?"

"Like what?"

"What makes him tick?" Jackie clarified. "I found a general history on him, but it looks like no other hunters have been able to get close enough to this region's king to find out anything substantial."

"And you want me to hand over my brother's secrets?"

"I want you to tell us what it will take to keep *my* best friend alive."

Domino looked at me and sighed. "Right."

"I know this has to be difficult for you," Lena interjected with a softer approach.

"It really isn't." Domino raised his hand to stop her. "I hate my brother. He's a monster who uses his power for terrible things. But when you consider what he is, it's not too far from the expected. Reddick is selfish, and even before we were vampires, he found joy in torturing me. The only way to get him to stop is for Whitney to cease to exist. By now, he understands how much she's come to mean to me."

"How would he know that?" I asked.

"He sent me an ultimatum as well. Leave her alone or he would take everything away from me. Soon, he will begin dismantling everything I've built for myself over the last century."

"And you're just going to sit here and let him do that?" Jackie looked disgusted.

"I'm going to sit here and let him think he can." Domino took a deep breath. "My brother is vain. He thinks true power comes with a title. It doesn't. The vampire kings are nothing but pawns being moved around by a higher power."

"Are you that higher power?" Lena leaned forward with wide eyes.

Domino laughed. "If I was, we wouldn't be hiding out here."

"Oh, I guess that makes sense." She deflated back into her seat.

"All I mean to say is that while he spent years playing politics, I spent my time working on things that mattered far more. My brother thinks he knows everything there is to know about me. He does not."

The knock on the door drew all our attention to the front of the guest house. Jackie hopped up from her seat, drawing two knives from hidden pockets, and Domino grabbed my chair and pulled it to him so fast, I almost got whiplash.

He put me behind him and turned back toward the door, his fangs ready for the attack.

"It's okay!" Lena hopped up from her seat with her hands held out to Jackie and Domino. "Remember I said someone was coming? It's her."

"Are you sure?" Jackie asked.

"Did either of you sense her presence before she knocked on the door?" Lena asked as she walked over to it.

Jackie and Domino looked at each other and shrugged. Clearly, neither of them had noticed anyone was nearby.

"I'm so glad you could make it here today," Lena spoke around the door, and when she pulled it open, the woman who entered looked nothing like I imagined she would.

I thought it would be someone old and wrinkled by time, but she looked maybe ten years older than us. There was a glow about her as she moved beneath the intricate headpiece. I would have thought she was royalty, and I gasped when her eyes opened to reveal irises that glowed a soft shade of pink.

"Lena..." Her voice felt like a melody she'd taken years to perfect. And then, the woman attacked.

She lifted her hand, and her lips moved, but I couldn't hear her words. The next thing I knew, Domino went flying back across the room. His foot hit me in the shoulder as he passed me. He clawed the air, reaching for anything that would stop his momentum. The wall did the job.

"Stop!" I jumped up and ran over to Domino, who looked like he was being smashed by an iron. The sickening crack of his bones rang out around us.

"Likosa, no!" Lena stepped in the way as well, and the woman stopped her assault. "He's on our side."

"Oh." Likosa dropped her hand. "My apologies. You said it was an urgent matter. I only assumed."

"Girl, you didn't tell her he was here?" Jackie, who hadn't moved a muscle to help, laughed. "She could have killed him."

"I did." Lena looked back at Likosa. "This is Domino."

"Well," Likosa narrowed her gaze at me, and my stomach knotted. There was something there that didn't sit right with me. "It must have slipped my mind. You know I'm much older than I look."

"It's alright." Jackie waved off her apology. "He's a vampire, he'll heal."

"Domino, are you okay?" I kneeled over him.

"No, but I'll be fine." He coughed, and I flinched when another one of his bones snapped back in place. "Damn it, that hurts."

"He's fine. See!" Jackie finally approached the newcomer. "Likosa, right? That's such a unique name. Thank you for coming."

"Thank you. And it's my pleasure. Anything for Lena." She looked at my friend with loving eyes. "Her grandmother was one of my favorite people."

"Do you think you can help us out here?" Lena closed the door. "As you can see, we have a tricky situation."

"The vampire and the untapped witchling." Likosa pointed at me.

"Witchling?" I stood, rubbing my shoulder, which stung from the impact of Domino's foot. "Me?"

"Don't get too excited. It's the best name I can come up with for someone with your unique situation." She glided over to the table where we were all sitting and took a seat. "Descendant of the aliens who landed on your world. You know, oddly enough, you're the second one I've met recently. I'd say your situation is a little better than hers. Nasty work dealing with demons."

"There are others?" I asked, and something inside me perked up. If there were others, maybe they could help me understand everything.

"Yes." Likosa paused and looked at Lena. "Remind me to talk to you about that later."

"Me?" Lena pointed to herself.

"Yes, that's a private matter. Nothing to do with all this." She waved her hand as if batting away bugs.

"Okay..." Lena glanced at me, and I shrugged. If she didn't know what the woman was talking about, there was no way I was going to decipher it.

"Now, on to the reason you've called me here." Likosa turned her pink eyes back to me. "Whitney and the vampire."

"Yes." I looked back at Domino, who still looked out of it. I was expecting him to bounce back sooner, but his eyelids fluttered sluggishly, and the pallor of his skin made it clear he was far from healing.

"I—we—wanted to find the best way to protect Whitney from his brother, the king of this region." Lena was the one to explain the situation. "As I suggested in my message, this is a much bigger problem than we imagined it would be. He's vindictive and is going to come after Whitney and anyone she loves to hurt his brother."

"So predictable." Likosa looked downright bored, as if the threat placed on my life wasn't entertaining enough. "It's as if, in all those years they spent roaming the world, they couldn't get a little more creative."

"How do we protect her?" Jackie asked, picking up on my frustration. She looked at me and gave me the 'this will be over soon' look.

"You don't, but she can." Likosa nodded at me. "This isn't a damsel in distress story. She is more than capable of handling this on her own."

"I can?" I scoffed. "Not the witch, the vampire, or the hunter? The *human*?"

"Human?" She slapped the table, and we all jumped. "Sorry, I just hate when people don't know their own potential. I'm sure Lena has explained to you that you're not a simple human. Whitney, you must tap into that bloodline of yours. Your people were powerful, and they passed on amazing talents hidden in your genetics. If you unlock it, it could potentially save you."

"So, this isn't a guarantee?" I asked. "What's the point then?"

"What in life is guaranteed?" Likosa poked at the half-eaten sandwich still on Lena's plate. "I'm sure, a few days ago, you probably had a well-thought-out plan of what you would do with your years in this world. How's that working out?"

"So to save my life, I have to change?"

"And everyone you love, yes. It's either that or die; it's really up to you." Likosa pointed at Domino. "Doesn't look like he is all that great at protecting you."

"I doubt his brother could do what you just did," I defended him.

"True." Likosa did a half-bow. "I am quite a phenomenal entity, aren't I?"

"This isn't right. I don't want to change who I am." I ignored what felt like an ego trip coming from the woman. "What would I even become?"

"You would still be the same, just enhanced by something that already exists within you," Lena said.

"Whitney," Jackie started, but I held my hand up.

"No. This is too much." I sighed. "All this is happening too fast. I still haven't wrapped my mind around how everything I thought I knew is wrong. People I thought I knew aren't who they said they were. I don't want that to be true about myself. I know who I am and I'm not some alien being."

"Just—" Jackie took a step toward me, but before she could take another, a force pushed her across the room and into the wall.

BOOM!

The walls shook and the window exploded, sending glass flying through the air like projectiles. Lena screamed as a piece of wood knocked her over, and in the midst of the chaos, Likosa was calm. She stood and sighed before working magic to defend herself.

The door behind her swung open, and men all dressed in black rushed in. There were dozens of them, and even more came through the window where the explosion happened.

Everything happened in a rush. Jackie was back on her feet, fighting. Lena and Likosa worked together, using their magic to subdue as many as they could, but they just kept coming.

"They're human!" Lena called out just as Jackie was about to take the head off a guy.

"Damnit!" she fussed and instead of beheading him, knocked him in the back of the head, and he passed out at her feet.

I froze. Domino was still down, but I could see him trying to fight through his pain. His hands balled into tight fists at his sides, and his legs and arms twitched like he was trying to get up from the ground.

BOOM!

Another explosion sounded, this time accompanied by a white-hot blinding light.

I quickly lifted my hands to shield my eyes when a solid object suddenly clasped around my waist. I looked down and saw a sharp, menacing claw. Metal teeth clamped into my flesh. Despite my efforts, I couldn't get the thing from around me.

"Whitney!" Jackie ran for me, and I held my hands out to her.

Just before she reached me, four attack dogs piled on top of her and the damn thing pulled me out of the room.

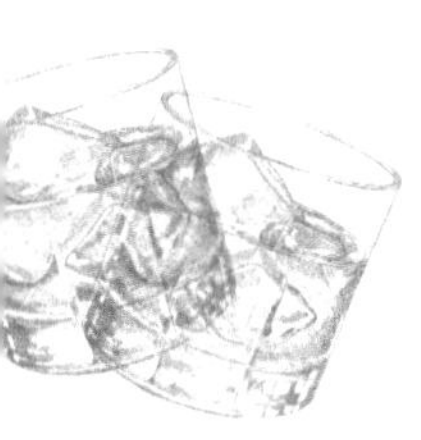

15

Vampire E.D.

The pain from the clamp around my stomach didn't stop. It dragged me at least thirty feet before three masked men stuffed me into a van and drove me away from safety. They left the damn thing wrapped around me, crushing my rib cage, until we reached the new destination.

We were back near the water. The salty tang of the ocean hung heavy in the air, and the wind, now carrying the scent of brine, whipped against my skin through the open windows. Any other time, I would have been happy to be there, but now, I only felt terror. I was supposed to be safe in Jackie's compound, but the wards Lena and Jackie had put in place hadn't accounted for anyone who wasn't a deadly supernatural being.

We were in one of the richest areas of our seaside town. The minions said no words as they dragged me from the back of the van and up to the tall, dark mansion. It was constructed of gray brick and looked more like a crypt than an ocean front oasis. Knowing who owned the place, it seemed fitting.

"Let me go!" I struggled as the large man lifted me over his shoulder and carried me up the steps into the home. As he walked, his shoulder pressed into my stomach and made the pain in my ribs even worse. "Put me down!" I tried my best to kick off his shoulder. Nothing worked.

The man, flanked by two other silent companions, took me into the home, down a long hall lined with archaic-looking paintings, and dropped me in a small sitting room. There were several love seats and a bar along the back wall. They said nothing before they left me in the room alone. The click after the door closed thwarted any hope of trying to escape. The zombies had locked me inside.

"Great, guess I'm not walking out of here." I felt around for my phone but realized I didn't have it. "Shit!"

I refused to panic. One way or another, I was making it out of there. After looking around the room, I spotted the window to the left of the bar. Heavy curtains covered it, but they easily slid to the side. Just outside the window was a small ledge, but nothing else. Even if I could get it open—which I couldn't, I tried—I would likely plummet to a messy death on the beach below.

"Son of a bitch." I smacked the window seal and dropped the curtain.

"Are you trying to leave already?" a deep voice said, and I froze. "And without even talking to the host? I would say I'm offended, but humans have lost their manners over the last few decades."

"And this is when I meet the sadistic brother?" I turned on my heel to spot the man who stood just inside the open door.

I was right. He was definitely Domino's brother. They shared the same wide nose, dark eyes, and upturn at the corner of the mouth. He was slightly taller, with a slimmer frame, and where Domino wore business casual, he was in a surprisingly relaxed look: black jeans and a gray t-shirt. Despite the attire, Reddick felt menacing. His presence made the hairs on the back of my neck stand and my stomach hurt, and not because of the bruises left behind from the claw.

"It's nice to meet you too, Ms. Harris." He smiled, and my skin prickled as he held his hand out to me. When I didn't accept his handshake, the uneven grin fell from his face. "Is this really how you want to behave?"

"Considering you just had your zombies rip me out of my friend's place with a fucking claw, yes!" I couldn't believe the man had the nerve to stand there talking about my poor manners after literally abducting me.

"I just want to talk." He dropped his hand to his side. "How else do you suggest that happen with my brother and your ambitious friends keeping you locked away?"

"You could have called. I mean, you left a note in my car." I took a step back and realized there wasn't much space between me and the crimson-colored wall. "Clearly, you have my information."

"Hmm, that may have worked." He moved closer to me in response to my movement. "But this is a topic best handled with a face-to-face discussion. Not everything can be done over the phone. I'm sure you understand that."

"What do you want from me?" I scanned the room. There wasn't anywhere for me to go. Even if I wanted to run, he could catch me. It'd only make killing me more entertaining for the vampire.

"When I first heard about you, I wanted to kill you. I can't have you making my brother happy." He let out a quick chuckle then paused, slowly revealing his fangs. His tongue rested against a point as he stared down at me. "But then, I found out more about you, about what you can offer me."

"I can't offer you a damn thing," I boasted, trying to mask my growing fear.

"Oh, but I know you've learned by now that isn't true." He smiled, flashing his fangs. "There's something special about you, and I want it for myself."

"I don't know what you're talking about." That's right, play dumb. It was the best I could think of to buy myself even a few more minutes of time—not that I thought it would do much. Still, if my friends were coming, and I hoped like hell they were, it could be the difference between them finding me alive or without a drop of blood left in me.

"Your blood, Whitney." He spoke with slow intention. "Your blood is what every vampire wants, and once word gets out about you, I won't be the only one dying to sink my fangs into your pretty neck. Do you think it will be difficult? There are vampires out there who are far more powerful than I am. They are older, stronger, and won't hesitate to snap your head off. You already see my brother can't protect you. Where is he now?"

"Domino will find me." I wanted to sound brave, confident in what I said, but my voice trembled. This wasn't the worst of it. Reddick wasn't my worst nightmare; he was the prelude to something far more terrifying.

"Oh, I'm sure he will." He clapped, took three steps back and sat down on the blue loveseat with white feathers printed all over it. "And it will be the battle of the ages! I look forward to it. I haven't been able to get under his skin in nearly four decades. So, I thank you. You know, he really has kept to himself, and I've missed playing with him."

"You're sick." I remained still.

"Yes, living well over a century has that effect." He nodded quickly and looked at the floor. "You have to find new ways to entertain yourself. I thought it would take a lot longer for me to become bored with the thought of eternity, but you start to see it a lot faster than you think. The cycles. The way humanity just does the same thing, time and time again. It's the little things. It's maddening."

"Maybe you should just end it. There's nothing saying you *have* to live forever."

"I've considered it. I don't have to, but I'm addicted to it. Waking up, feeling the world shifting around me, filling myself with the blood of others; I want more of it. I want all of it." He inhaled deeply and looked at me with a grin that stretched across his face like a maniac. "And now, because of you, I can have it all! I'll be changed into something new, something powerful!"

"You can't have my blood." I shook my head. "I won't allow it."

"Allow it?" Reddick sneered, and then in a movement so fast, I couldn't remember blinking, he was on top of me. My back smashed against the wall, causing pain to ripple through my core. "How exactly do you plan on stopping me?"

"What happened to waiting for Domino?" I choked through the pain that already had my head spinning.

"Who said I was going to wait?" Reddick dropped his head back and laughed. His entire body shook with each boisterous trumpet of the humor he found in my question. "I'm not that stupid. Wait for him to come and ruin my plans? No. Domino will come, and when he does, your blood will have made me even stronger. My dear brother won't stand a chance, and he'll have you to thank for it."

Reddick rolled his neck and let his fangs further descend.

"Wait, no!" I squirmed, but there was no use.

With his teeth bared, he grabbed my head and forced it to the side, and then, the vampire bit me—or at least he tried. Honestly, I'm not sure what he was doing. I could feel his breath on my neck, and he did a lot of grunting and pressing his body against mine. It was almost like he was trying to dry-hump me. My fear eased into an annoyed state of confusion. Was he playing with me?

"Aaah!" he screamed in frustration and backed away from me. "What is this?"

"Performance anxiety?" I shrugged. "You tell me. I don't know what happens when a vampire can't bite! Is this like vampire E.D.?"

"I can bite just fine!" The man looked like he wanted to stomp his foot like a little kid.

"You say that, but I'm standing here." I put my hand to my neck and then checked for blood. There was none. "...unbitten."

A gush of air hit my face and, a moment later, the door stood open, revealing Reddick with a dazed man in his arms. He looked me in the eye, grinned, and bit into the man. Blood spilled everywhere. This wasn't a feed for preservation; this was him showing off because he couldn't get it up with me. When he was done with the disgusting display, he let the man drop to the floor.

"I can bite just fine," he repeated and wiped his mouth.

"So maybe I'm not the right person." I pointed to the man he dropped at his feet. "Maybe you're not into women. Have you explored that?"

I may have gone too far with that one, because Reddick darted across the room and punched the wall next to my face. I froze as the drywall crumbled around his fist and pieces fell onto my shoulder.

"What have you done?" He leaned in, putting his lips next to my ear. "Why can't I bite you? What spell is this?"

"I don't know what you're talking about." Again, my voice trembled with the fear I didn't want him to know I felt. So what if he couldn't bite me? That didn't mean he couldn't use other methods to get to my blood. "I didn't do anything. But whatever it is, I doubt you'll figure it out before my friends get here. I'm sure they know where I am by now."

"They are more than welcome to come. They won't get in." He sniffed my neck. "But I need a contingency plan while I figure out this issue with your flesh. I don't want to kill you. I need you alive and producing that wonderful blood so I can sell it to the highest bidders. Until then, I need to make sure I can always find you."

"What?" Okay, this was the time to panic. The vampire wanted to pimp me out for my blood.

He didn't say anything else. Fingers gripped the back of my head, his nails digging into my scalp as he held me in place. Reddick bit his wrist sloppily, letting the blood spill down his arm. He pressed his wrist against my lips, and when I refused to drink from him, he pulled me to his chest.

My back pressed against him, one hand covering my nose while he still pressed his wrist to my mouth. Eventually, I had to breathe. I opened my mouth, gasping for air, and with the flow of oxygen came his blood. Once my mouth was full, he covered both my nose and mouth with his hands, forcing me to swallow. It wasn't until I gulped down the blood that he let me go.

"No!" I cried out as he released me. I tried to spit up the blood, but it was too late. I could already feel the effects of it moving through my body.

"How do I taste? I've always wondered." He looked me up and down as I struggled to catch my breath. "Would you say my blood is better than my brother's?"

"You're sick!" I spit the remnants of his blood from my mouth at him.

"Then why are you looking at me like that?" He grabbed my arm and pulled me to his chest. "Why is your pulse quickening? I can smell your arousal, sweet like plums in the summer. You're ripe."

Reddick slid his hand around my waist, and I hated that he was right. His blood worked through my body just like Domino's had. Not only did it spark my arousal, but it also healed me. The pain in my chest where I knew I had at least one broken rib subsided.

I looked up into his face, and though my mind said absolutely not, my body said...well, maybe.

I had to look away from him, because the more the feeling spread, the more he looked like his brother, and it was as if his blood was a drug working to convince me he was exactly the man I wanted.

The pressure in the room changed, pulsating like waves of the ocean crashing against the shore. I squinted as I looked at the doorway, just beyond where the limp body of the man he'd fed off. Those ripples moved through the air, and I gasped as a woman dressed in a beautiful peach dress with a soft cape appeared. She looked like she was ready for a wedding.

Then, I recognized her and choked out her name—the artist who had cost me everything.

"Rayna?"

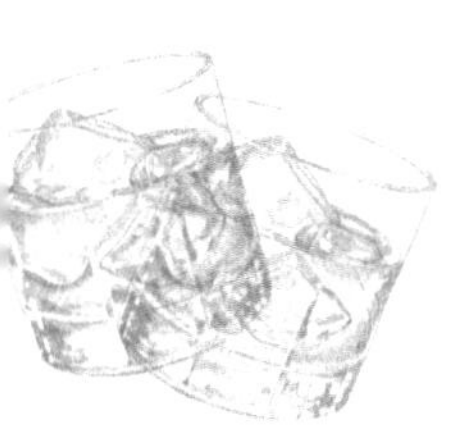

16

Take me to the Bane

"You must be Whitney." She lifted the bottom of her dress and took a careful step over the blood of the man on the floor, frowning at the spot that got on the heel of her shoe. "Oh, that's disgusting!"

"What the..." Reddick turned on her, and while he was quick, he wasn't quick enough. Rayna flicked her wrist, and a gust of power slammed into the vampire. The sound of his neck snapping as he hit the wall brought a smile to my face. *That's exactly what his ass gets.*

"Oh, crap." She pursed her lips and pointed at Reddick's limp body. "Still haven't figured out how to adjust the strength on that one. It has something to do with the atmosphere. Each world is different. Anyway, it should be fine. That one's a vampire, right? He'll heal. I think."

"If I'm lucky, he won't." I straightened my shirt. "I'm sorry, but what the hell are you doing here?"

"Oh, sorry. Right. I'm here to save you." She posed like a superhero, fists to hips and chest high, then laughed again. "Sorry, I couldn't help myself. This is technically my first rescue mission on Earth."

"Yeah, and that answer doesn't only add to my confusion." I stuck my neck out. What the hell did she mean by *on Earth*? "You just appeared out of thin air!"

"Right. Um, Likosa!" She pointed at me, as if saying the name of the witch would put all the pieces of the puzzle together. "You know her, right? She called me and said you would need my help. I was a little late, but she told me exactly where I could find you and asked me to scoop you up. When I first got here, I was outside, but when I saw what was going on through the window, I figured I better get in here. Are you okay? Did he hurt you?"

"I'm fine, I think. Wait, Likosa asked a famous artist to magically scoop me up from a crazy vampire." I leaned against the wall behind me to catch my breath. "How is any of this supposed to make sense?"

"When you say it that way, it doesn't sound any more logical, does it?" Rayna rubbed the back of her neck and looked around the room. "I don't know how to make this make sense to you. I think you just eventually learn to accept that it won't always make sense. That's what I did."

"I—" The sound of Reddick's bones snapping drew my attention to him. I waited for him to move. Had he healed that fast? When he didn't move from his crumpled position, I addressed Rayna again. "You're a witch?"

"Not exactly, no. I don't think that's what they would call me." Rayna pointed at the vampire then back at me. "Hold up. I didn't interrupt anything here, did I? It looked like you two were about to—"

"No!" I put my hand up to stop her. "You came just in time."

"Perfect." She laughed nervously. "It's funny how intimate a threatening situation can look from outside."

"You bitch!" Both our heads snapped toward the vampire. Reddick was back on his feet. He bared his teeth and charged at Rayna.

The woman barely flinched when he attacked. She flicked her wrist once again, and this time, the force that hit him seemed much more powerful than the last. Reddick's body slammed into the bar and broke through the top of the case that held several bottles of whiskey. The sound of glass shattering echoed through the room as expensive liquor splattered across the floor. Once again, he was limp, broken, and unmoving. Rayna peered at him, and when the sound of a bone moving back in place rang out, she smiled.

"Oh, great. I didn't kill him!" Rayna clapped. "The maid of honor murdering someone the night before the wedding can't be good luck, right? I'm not trying to do anything to ruin my friend's special day."

"Um, I wouldn't think so." I couldn't believe how nonchalant the woman was being. This wasn't the Rayna I remembered talking to before. She seemed more reserved and a lot more careful with her words. Was that just her professional side? Talk about a code switch.

"Well, let's go. I don't have much time. Like I said, I have a wedding to attend. My best friend is finally tying the knot tomorrow! I was doing a last-minute fitting just to be sure the dress would still wrap around my ass. You wouldn't believe how much your size is affected by moving between worlds. In some places, I'm thin as a string bean, but here on Earth, ass is wide as all get out!"

"Yep. I'm just going to pretend that makes sense. Anything to get me out of here before his ass wakes up again." Sure, it made sense that the woman kept talking about going to other worlds and how she felt different while on Earth. Nope, there wasn't a damn thing weird about it.

"You think someone would have come to check on him?" Rayna held her hand out to me and beckoned me towards her. "I guess he's not that loved. Some king, huh?"

"I sure as hell don't like him." Just as I placed my hand in hers, I saw a flash of purple. Large hair bounced across the room with the chaotic movement. The last time I'd seen the face beneath the hair, the bitch was trying to sink her teeth into me. Nyesha huddled over Reddick's broken body.

"Reddick!" She turned to me and bared her teeth. "What did you do to him?"

"Um, it was me." Rayna waved, calling the vampire's attention to her. Then, she leaned toward me and whispered, "Guess I spoke too soon, huh? This one looks pretty angry about him being hurt."

"I'll kill you!" Nyesha hissed, and with her hands poised to rip out Rayna's throat, she leaped through the air.

Rayna repeated her same magical blow. It didn't feel as powerful, but it still knocked the vampire to the other side of the room. Nyesha was far more agile than Reddick. She flipped through the air, bounced off the wall, and landed on her feet. As she shook off the effects of the impact, Rayna leaned closer to me.

"You might want to hold your breath." Her hand tightened around mine. "It helps."

"What?" My eyes widened as Nyesha charged us again, but she never made contact.

The air grew heavy with pressure, creating a surreal sensation of time standing still. Once again, I saw the shimmering ripples in the air, only this time, they encircled us. Nyesha's expression turned more vicious as the ripples moved faster, and then, along with everything else in the room, she faded into nothingness.

My ears popped and my eyes lost all focus as the pressure snapped around me like a rubber band.

That was it. One minute, we were standing near a bloody mess of a man, and then the next, we weren't. Darkness swallowed us for a few minutes, and I wondered if I'd died. Then, light trickled in as my vision cleared. It was just a few moments, but somehow, I felt like much more time had gone by. I could still feel Rayna's hand in mine, and I gripped it tighter.

When the shadowed edges faded and my eyesight fully returned, I saw Rayna standing in a massive cave next to a pool of glowing water. She lifted our joined hands up and winked at me.

"See, that wasn't so bad, was it?" She chuckled.

There wasn't nothing to laugh about. A wave of nausea swept over me, and my stomach twisted and turned like a storm. The soil became the target of my forceful vomit as I doubled over in agony.

"Oh!" Rayna jumped back, narrowly missing the splashes of my vomit. "Watch the dress, please. Keri will kill me if I get anything on it!"

"Sorry," I wiped my mouth and kept the thought to myself that she shouldn't have worn the damn dress to a rescue mission. "What the hell was that? Where are we? How did you do that?"

"We left Earth. I told you to hold your breath." Rayna looked around the cave with a nostalgic expression. "It gets better the more you do it, but the first few shifts are a bitch!"

"You gave me exactly one second!" I huffed, holding my chest, which burned from the forced evacuation of my stomach contents. "And it wasn't exactly like you explained what was going to happen. I should expect as much from someone so selfish."

"Selfish?" Rayna looked insulted. "How am I selfish? I just saved you from becoming a vampire's midnight snack."

"You know I lost everything because of you?" That was it. I couldn't hold it in anymore. "I would have never worked with you if I knew they would take everything away from me."

"Maybe the shift between worlds scrambled your brains." Rayna twirled her finger next to her head. "Girl, I don't even know you."

"You don't know me?" I gasped. "Wow! We corresponded for weeks on a multi-million-dollar deal that you flaked on, and now you don't know me?"

"Wait, Whitney Harris?" She had that, *oh shit, I fucked up*, look on her face. "The art broker?"

"Yes!" I threw my hands up. "The art broker who is no longer an art broker because you dropped off the face of the Earth, which now I see was a *literal* thing. I worked years to get where I was, and I lost it because of you! Girl, I just signed a damn mortgage!"

"They let you go because of that?" Rayna sucked her teeth. "I'm so sorry. I tried to make things better with the firm when I got back. They told me you had already moved on and weren't interested in reactivating the deal. I understood, nothing waits for me. And you probably don't want to hear this from me, especially since you're blaming me for your current situation, but I think you're better off. What kind of shitty employer does that?"

"Of course I'm blaming you. Had I not lost my job, I would have never messed with Domino and been pulled into this vampire drama."

"You can tell yourself that all you want." She shrugged. "I'm just here to drop you off so Likosa can do what she needs to do."

"Excuse me?" I snapped. "How can you be so insensitive?"

"Tell me something, Whitney. Where did you meet the vampire? Was it right after you got fired? Did your former boss push you into his arms as he kicked your ass out of the job? Or was it a neutral place where you would have met him anyway?"

"Well…" I paused as the water in the pool moved, creating small waves. The sound echoed around me as I accepted what she said. With or without my job, I would have met Domino. But would I have drunkenly fallen into his arms?

"You're looking for someone else to take the blame for how your life is going right now. I get it, but I'm not responsible for any of the choices you made," Rayna spoke with the careful tone I remembered her having. "And I'm sorry I didn't recognize you. Honestly, in the last year, I've been to so many worlds, faces and places are blending together. I should probably slow down, but I'm enjoying it."

"Happy to hear that." I rolled my eyes.

"Well, as you can see, life got a little strange," Rayna continued. "Not that I owe you an explanation, but I had to woman up and make some tough choices, my damn self. A month after I signed that contract, I fell into this world, and it was stay and take care of the commission or run from the demons who were chasing me."

"Demons?" I gawked. "You mean actual demons?"

"Are you not dealing with actual vampires?" Rayna tapped her temple with her finger. "Yes, girl. One day, I was a normal, albeit borderline depressed, woman. The next I am living with a demonic soul-tie and trying to figure out how to save myself. It wasn't like I asked for any of this. But I wasn't going to lay down and let this shit walk all over me. I had to fight. I'm sure you know what I mean."

"Do I?" I searched the space for somewhere to sit. To the left of the pool were racks full of various jars and parchment-wrapped boxes. Behind it was what looked like a doorway to another part of the cave. To the right, an ornate clawfoot throne covered in jewels. Was it meant for me? Probably not. Did I care? No!

"Likosa will be here in a few minutes. This is her place." Rayna looked at me plop my ass on the throne and smirked. "Sorry, I can't stay long. Time in this place works a lot differently than Earth, and I'm on a time crunch. I'm assuming she wanted us to talk because she could have gotten you out of there a lot faster than I did."

"Why would she want us to talk?" I turned my face away from her. My stomach was doing a two-step, and I was afraid I was going to puke again.

"Because we're alike." She pointed to me then back to herself. "I'm sure someone has mentioned the bloodline to you. We're kind of like cousins. The alien magical bloodline? We share that."

"We do?" I leaned back in the chair. What were the odds I would be related to her?

"Yes. Likosa explained it to me. I don't think our abilities are the same, but we come from the same people. I've been searching the universe for more information about them. So far, all I know is that there were seven distinct tribes in their world. Each tribe had different power sets. I think the people who landed on Earth were from different tribes."

"You keep talking about new worlds and speaking about Earth as if we aren't there now." I huffed. "What is wrong with you?"

"We aren't on Earth." She pointed to the water. "I thought that was clear by the spooky pool of water with crashing waves when there ain't a lick of wind in here."

That time, I laughed. "You really want me to believe you snatched me up and took me off the planet?"

"Whitney, when I vanished, it was because all this shit was revealed to me and I got snatched up and dragged to hell." She pointed to the ground. "That's where we are now."

"Right." I rolled my eyes. "Okay, I think I'm ready to go home. I know my girls are worried about me."

"Don't twist your face at me like that." Rayna put her finger in my face. "Where do you think you are now? Likosa's crib is smack dab in the heart of the Bane aka hell."

While I gave her the same 'this bitch done lost her mind' glare, Rayna chose to show me what she was talking about. The woman grabbed my hand, yanked me from the throne, and dragged me down the long passage that led out of the cavern. We tumbled outside, and I gasped at the view. It wasn't the majestic land or the weird mountains in the distance that did it for me. There were plenty of places on Earth that had that.

I could even deny the weird ass plants popping up from the ground. I was no botanist, I didn't know everything about plant life, but the damn creature flying through the sky with two sets of wings and screeching did it. That creature turned and revealed a matching one flying beside him. Then, as if that weren't enough, a damn gremlin-looking animal ran across the field and leaped into the air to attack the flying beast.

"What the fuck?" I screamed.

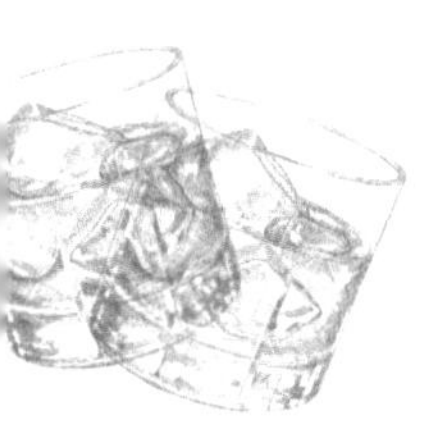

17

The Agreement

Rayna stood beside me with a weird look of pride on her face. "This is the bane."

"You—I—" I heaved. "This isn't real. This can't be."

"It is. And there is so much more. Wait." Rayna put her fingers between her lips and whistled. A moment later, a little blue monster jumped into her arms. "This is Piko. He's my baby. Usually, he lives with us, but when we have to go to Earth for too long, we drop him off here."

"That's it." I backed up from her as the wide eyes of the creature settled on me. "You might want to back up, because I think I'm going to puke again!"

Rayna hopped back and held Piko to shield it from me. "You good?"

"Yes, I think so." I looked at her top. "I think the thing got mud on you."

"Crap!" She dropped the pet and dusted off the dirt. When it fell away easily, she sighed in relief. "Look, I know the feeling." She took a deep breath, checking the top once again. "I never thought hell would be so pretty. Not at all what they told us it would look like, right?"

"Clearly, you changed." I didn't care about hell or even the creature she had. Rayna was different from everything I knew about the woman. I needed to know why. "Right?"

"What do you mean?" She reached down to pet the dog just before he ran off to join the other creatures in battle.

"You made the change, tapped into your powers. That's what Likosa told me I would have to do if I wanted to survive this. I would have to unlock whatever magic lingers in my blood."

"Oh, I did. When faced with a life or death situation, I chose life." She nodded. "It wasn't the easiest choice, though."

"How do you feel now?" I asked as the breeze picked up around us and moved the layers of her dress. She looked like she was about to say some profound shit.

"Sane." She chuckled. "Strange, but I feel like it all makes sense now."

"What do you mean? What makes sense?"

"Girl, my mind was fighting me for years." Rayna looked me in the eye. "I didn't publicize it, but I struggled with my mental health. I thought I was broken. Turns out, I was, just not in the way I thought. Something was missing deep inside me. And now, I feel better, stronger, and I get to do some really exciting things."

"So it was a good change?"

"Have you ever felt like you didn't belong? I mean, you look out in the world, and everyone seems to have it all figured out, but you don't. You check the boxes, achieve those worldly successes, and yet you still feel like it's not enough."

"Yeah, I do." I thought about the career I'd worked so hard for. No matter how much I achieved, it never felt as fulfilling as everyone said it should. "Your work, oddly enough, makes me feel less like that."

"I learned it's because I was depicting things in my work that were tied to our history." She looked out at the landscape in front of us. "Isn't it funny how we both end up working in the arts, looking for more beauty in the world, hoping it will fill that void inside of us?"

"I never thought about it like that."

"Whitney, I can't make the decision for you, but I was also hesitant. I thought if I did it, I wouldn't feel like myself anymore, but I feel more centered than I ever have. I also feel stronger and safer than I did before. You've opened a bag of bullshit you can't close, and even if you do, that smell is still gone get your ass, so you might as well do whatever you can to protect yourself."

"How did it change you?" I narrowed my eyes. "Are you immortal now?"

Rayna explained her circumstances with a sigh. "I am, but as far as I can tell, it's not because of the bloodline. It's because of my soulmate. He's immortal. To save my life, we did the marriage of souls, which means our souls are literally one now. Because of that, I am now immortal."

"So I won't live forever?" That thought brought me some relief. "I don't want to do that. That sounds exhausting."

"No, not as far as I know." She shook her head. "And yes, immortality sounds absolutely exhausting. I don't know how I'll deal with it."

"You didn't think about that before you agreed to do this?" I frowned at her as the two demonic beasts took flight again.

"You know, you'd be surprised at how few questions you ask when you're clinging to life." She narrowed her eyes, relaxing when the little blue pet took off running toward the gremlin's body, which lay limp in the field.

"I didn't really consider that." And then, it was all I could think about. I'd already faced the possibility of my own death more times than I cared to count since meeting Domino. That wasn't going to end overnight. What would I do if my life was really hanging in the balance?

"You're going to be okay, you know, with whatever decision you make. I don't want you to think I'm pushing you to do anything you feel isn't right for you. Just don't let fear make the choice for you."

"Thank you." I looked up at the odd sky. "For getting me out of there."

"Of course," Rayna turned and walked back into the cavern. "Not that I really had that much of a choice. I kinda owe Likosa for saving my life multiple times."

"So you trust her?" I trailed behind her.

"For an ageless witch who can cross universes?" Rayna paused and shrugged. "Yeah. I guess I do. Just be aware that she tends to get a little freaky with her magic."

"Very encouraging." I laughed. "What do you mean by freaky?"

"The first time I met her, she may or may not have made me come and then dropped me at the feet of my man like it was nothing," Rayna reported like it meant nothing, but there was something wistful about her expression that told me she enjoyed whatever Likosa did.

"I'm sorry, what did you just say?" I picked up a jog to catch up with Rayna.

"There you two are," Likosa's melodic voice chimed as we reached the magical waters. "Did you two make friends?"

"Is that what you wanted?" Rayna pointed at the woman. "What kind of games are you playing here?"

"I'm not playing any games. I just figured you two are going through the same things. It would be good if you bonded." Likosa examined Rayna's dress. "I see you managed to keep your dress clean."

"I had to; you know how Keri is." Rayna looked down at the spot where the dirt was before, and I could see her shoulders relax again. Her friend must have been a real gem!

"Yes, a spitfire. Unfortunately, she didn't invite me to the wedding." Likosa looked hurt, and I wondered how close she was to the human to expect an invitation to her wedding. "I would love to get to know her better."

Ah, so not close at all.

"Would you have come?" Rayna challenged the thought.

"Likely not. That world stinks." Likosa turned her nose up. "I don't know how they deal with it. All the pollution—you can smell the world rotting from the inside out!"

Suddenly, it felt like the cave had squeezed in on itself as the pressure changed. The surrounding air warped and shifted, and through that same rippling haze, a man stepped into view. He stood tall, with a dark complexion, a perfectly fitted black suit, and a massive pair of horns sticking out of his head.

"Oh, Metice!" Likosa sounded like she would break out into cheers. "You're here!"

"Yeah, not for long," he spoke with a deeply annoyed voice as he walked over to Rayna and grabbed her hand. "We need to get out of here. If not, your friend is going to hurt me. She's already threatened my life twice. It's almost time for you to meet up with her."

"Oh, damn, you're right." Rayna looked at me. "Keep in mind, if you go to new worlds, time moves differently. You have my email, right? Hit me up when things settle down, and I can help you through more of this."

"Um, thanks." I couldn't take my eyes off the man.

"Rayna, please," he urged her.

"Did you bring the horns out for a dramatic entrance?" Rayna pointed at his head, and after a cool smirk, the horns receded into his forehead. She looked at her demon man then back at me. "See? Totally worth it."

She winked at me and waved at Likosa, and the two vanished, hand in hand.

"Well, they have really become one of my favorite couples!" Likosa sounded downright giddy. "She brings him joy. Never thought I would see the day."

"He's an actual demon, right?" I pointed to the space where the couple had previously stood.

"Did the horns not give it away?" Likosa half-rolled her eyes.

"I'm sorry I'm having a hard time processing that I'm in hell!"

"Why does it take humans so long to grasp these things? It's like you're all sheltered little babies. Vampires are real, so are demons, and you're in hell now. Can we move on, please?"

"You're not as nice as you put on, are you?"

"I'm as nice as the moment warrants." She adjusted her headpiece. "Are you ready?"

"For what?" Just then, Rayna's warning about Likosa's brand of magic repeated in my mind. Did she expect me to get freaky with her?

"Didn't Rayna do her job?" Likosa sounded frustrated. "She was supposed to convince you to go through the process."

I raised a brow. "Was she?"

"Yes," Likosa huffed. "I swear, I asked her to do one thing."

My suspicion bubbled to the top, and I pointed at the woman. "This is all your doing, isn't it?"

"I'm not sure what you mean." Likosa slapped an innocent expression over her face, complete with wide doll eyes.

"Why did you send Rayna to me instead of just coming to get me yourself? She said you would have been faster. She also made it seem like you spoke to her before any of this happened, which means you knew about me before Lena called you."

"Lena had mentioned you in the past. I am someone who likes to be prepared."

"Being prepared meant getting Rayna ready to convince me to do something you had no idea I would ever need to do?"

"Your best friends are a witch and a monster hunter." Likosa threw her head back, laughing so hard, her chest heaved, and she instinctively covered her breast with her hand. "How exactly do you see that working out without you eventually being pulled into this world? I warned Lena about this the first time she mentioned you to me. It's not my fault she didn't listen."

"Are you behind this?" I stepped closer to her. "Did you plan this? I don't know your powers, but I feel like you are more than just well-prepared."

"Look, when Lena reached out to me, I knew what would have to be done. I knew you wouldn't take my word on such short notice." Likosa moved closer to the edge of the pool, and the waves stirred up even faster, slamming against the edge. "You don't know me, and I understand you are paranoid about things now. Because I understand that, I realized you would need to talk to someone who'd been through it. I didn't think you would get snatched up. Like I said, I just planned for what I saw was an inevitability."

"You're saying it was inevitable that all this happened?"

"Maybe not exactly as it has, but yes. Your entire life, you've been tiptoeing on the edge of a dangerous new world. You just didn't know it." Likosa bent over and ran her finger through the water. The rush of dangerous waves stilled. "I get it if you don't trust me. Most people don't when they first meet me. I'm a hard pill to swallow. It comes with the territory. It took a lot for Rayna to not look at me just like you are right now."

I glanced at the water. "What will happen to me?"

"You'll transform into someone who can protect herself." Likosa softened. "Someone who doesn't need a hunter, a witch, and a vampire to keep them safe. Not that any of them succeeded."

"Rayna said I won't be immortal, right?"

"No, you'll be like your friend Jackie. She lives longer than most humans, but she won't live forever."

I thought about it. I wanted to protect myself. There were vampires, demons, and I didn't know what else out there. Everyone was right; there was no turning back. I liked to believe what I saw, to trust the evidence in front of my eyes, and what was in front of me was a changed world, something I needed to be prepared to handle.

"Okay." I nodded. "As much as I wish I could just act like this isn't real, I can't, and I don't want to have you or anyone else running to my rescue anymore."

Likosa stood, head high and shoulders back like a proud parent. "Great. You need to undress for the next part."

"Why?" I looked around the cave and thought again about what Rayna said.

"I use the water as a conduit for my magic." Likosa waved her hand, and soft spirals danced across the water behind her.

"And I have to be naked?" Yeah, freaky shit was incoming.

"Unless you want your clothing to be ruined in the process," she said with no further explanation, only to drop the robe from her shoulders, revealing her naked body. Big breasts, fat ass, snatched waist—Likosa had the kind of body women were trying to pay for on Earth.

The brick house song played in my mind as I tried not to gawk at the perfection in front of me. "I'm no better than a man."

"I'm sorry?" Her expression turned inquisitive.

"Oh, nothing," I said as, without further debate, I undressed.

Likosa walked into the pool first, the water gently caressing her skin. I followed her and trembled as soon as the water touched my bare flesh. It was cold as ice, and I damn near jumped back out, but she tapped the surface with her fingers, and it quickly warmed in response.

She reached the center of the pool and waved me forward. It wasn't too deep. My toes touched the bottom, and the surface stopped just at the top of my breasts.

"Just relax." Likosa wrapped her hand around my waist to pull me closer to her.

Her hand moved up and down my back in slow caresses, and it felt like the same heat she used to warm the water raced through my body. I looked up at her as the combination of her touch and the lingering effect of the vampire's blood made my pulse quicken.

She gently touched my chin, lifting my lips before she leaned down and kissed me. This wasn't my first kiss with a woman, and I didn't plan on it being my last, but it was far more intense than any kiss I'd ever had. When her lips moved against mine, I heard whispers of a strange language in the back of my mind.

I wasn't sure if we dropped beneath the water or if she raised the water around us, but within moments, we were floating. Our kiss quickened, and Likosa parted just for a moment to look into my eyes. Whatever she saw, it brought a smile to her face before she kissed me again. The whispers returned, now louder and in English. *By the blood*, it repeated, taking on the deep bass of drums each time.

I braced myself, assuming the kiss would go further, something along the lines of an orgasm-producing experience, but it didn't. Likosa stopped and swam away from me.

"I thought..." I spoke through heavy breaths.

"What?" She looked back at me with a wink.

"Nothing." It wasn't like I could tell her I was expecting her to get me off.

"Wait for it," she said as she climbed out of the water.

Then, the water took on a new life. It raged around me, flipping me in every direction before it stilled. I looked out through the barrier at Likosa, who stood at the edge of the pool. Five heartbeats later, and lightning struck. The power ripped through the cave and passed through the water, landing right in my stomach. It burned for a moment before it cooled like ice.

The water raged again as more lightning continued to pulse through the cave and hit me. Each time, it hurt less until the last. There was no burning then, only a chilled acceptance from my body to this power. And then, it stopped. The water lowered, and I floated over to Likosa.

She reached down and pulled me out of the water.

"Hmm." Likosa looked me up and down. "Are you ready to go home now?"

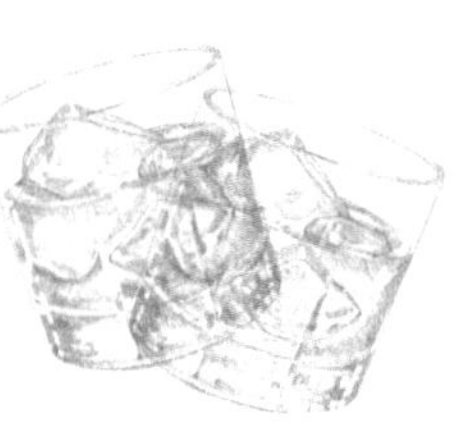

18

Maverick's Trick

I stood there, ass out, staring at the witch like she had lost her mind. She handed me a towel and watched me as I struggled to dress.

"Go home? What do you mean, *am I ready to go home*? What the hell was that?" I looked at my hands, and my fingertips sparked with energy. Tiny lightning bolts danced around my hands then absorbed into my skin. "What happened to me?"

"Oh, you want more explanations?" Likosa looked around me at the shelf full of potions. "Do you really need them? I have other appointments I need to get to."

"Well, yeah!" I threw my hands up, and a spark of light shot from my fingertips, blasting the ceiling. Chips of rock fell around us. I jumped back to avoid getting hit in the head. "See! What the hell was that? I feel different but the same. I know you unlocked something in me. Are you even going to tell me how to use it?"

"I could, but what would be the joy in that?" Likosa hadn't even flinched. Instead, she stood there, looking impressed by the destruction I caused. "The fun is in the discovery!"

"Excuse me?" I twisted the ends of my braids around my hand to wring out the water trapped within them. The weight was already pissing me off, and I just knew it was going to take forever for them to dry.

"Don't you want to stumble through it and figure it out?" She smiled. "Imagine how exciting that would be."

"Who the hell would choose that over having explicit instructions? If you know, just tell me!" I insisted.

"Fine, but I can only do so much." She hooked her finger towards her, telling me to come closer. "You'll still need to work on refining things."

"Thank you." I moved toward her, and when I got within arm's reach, Likosa reached out and flicked me on the forehead.

I wanted to fight her, but I couldn't. Before I could ball my fist to punch her in that pretty face, I went flying back into the pool, this time fully clothed. The water rushed into my mouth, nose, and ears and blinded my eyes.

A cacophony of sounds raced through my mind before the varying noises settled into one voice, one which told me, in simple terms, what my magic was.

Yours is a power that reaches the sun, channeling its energy in expressions of light and force. It is our gift to harness one of the purest representations. Look within, find your light, and shine. Four beats of your heart. Quiet the mind and direct the energy through your core and out.

That was it. The voice ended, and the water dumped me back at Likosa's feet.

I coughed and struggled to get back to my feet. "You know, you could warn a girl before you do that!"

She shrugged, unbothered by my choking. "I thought you understood my magic now. Did you get what you needed?" Likosa was suddenly holding several of the small vials in her hands. She held one up to the light and smiled.

"It was more a riddle than instructions." I stood, wringing out my hair once again. "But it's somewhere to start."

"Glad to hear it," she said without looking at me. "Well, have a nice trip."

"What?"

Likosa waved her hand and the ripples began.

"Wait, I—" I reached out to her because I had more questions, but an invisible force pushed me further from her. The last thing I saw was her waving her fingers and turning her back to me as she walked away.

That was it. She left me no more time for questions. The woman was done with me. The vacuum snapped around me, and I was in darkness for a moment before I was standing in Jackie's kitchen, dripping all over her fresh floors.

"Damnit." I slapped my hand over my mouth as the contents in my stomach stirred.

"Whitney!" Lena jumped up and ran over to me, but she stopped when I held my hand out to her.

"I think I'm gonna puke."

"No, the hell you're not!" Jackie hopped out of her seat. "You're already getting my floors wet."

"Jackie!" Lena fussed. "Seriously? She just popped in here from nowhere, and you're worried about your floors?"

"I just had these floors refinished! Are you going to pay for them?" Jackie ran out of the room and returned with several towels. One, she wrapped around me, and the others, she laid out on the floor and pulled me to stand on top of them. "Now, are you okay?"

"I—"

RAWWARR!

Maverick pounced, jumping into my arms. His massive body knocked me backward and into the wall. His body hummed as he purred and licked my face.

"Not my wall!" Jackie pulled me off the wall. "You're trying to ruin my house, aren't you? Is this some kind of payback?"

"You need help." Lena smacked her shoulder.

"Maverick, buddy." I tried to pull the cat away from me. He wrapped his paws around my head, refusing to let me go. "What is going on here?"

"He misses you!" Jackie was suddenly unconcerned with her ruined floors and walls. "Look at him. He was so worried about you."

"Since when?" I frowned and tried again to remove the cat. "Maverick, please, ease up!"

"Don't be like that. I told you, this cat loves you." Jackie rubbed his head, only encouraging his behavior.

"He loves when I feed him." I squinted at him, and there was something different there in his eyes. They flickered with a weird light, and then his body shuddered.

"Did you see that?" I looked at Jackie.

"What?" She shrugged and continued petting him.

"Maverick. He looks...different." I narrowed my eyes at him. "Lena?"

"He looks the same to me." Lena also rubbed him. "A little skittish but still the same Maverick. I really think he missed you. Where were you? You know, it's been a full day since you vanished! Likosa told us to stay here, and you would return. That's the only reason we weren't out there, hunting you down."

"You know damn well I was ready to go kick some vampire ass!" Jackie slammed a fist into her palm.

"I can imagine." I laughed.

"Especially since you won't let me hit the one you have stashed here!"

"Domino!" I gasped. How could I forget to check on him? "Is he okay?"

Rrrmmmmhhh

Maverick fussed in my arms.

"What is your problem?" I sucked my teeth at him. "Ow!"

The cat slapped me with his paw then gripped each side of my head and pulled my face to his. Everything slowed as he pressed his paws against my temples. A feeling like a sheet of ice spread across my skull, and my eyes rolled into the back of my head.

When I looked back at the cat, sparks of energy flowed from my fingertips, stabbing into his side. He didn't shriek from the pain and claw the side of my head like I would have expected. No, the maniac cat purred, as if the pulses of energy were no more than a gentle massage. And then, with Jackie and Lena still moving at half speed, Maverick changed!

His body expanded in size and changed shape. What was once an oversized cat turned into a small, Chinese dragon! His body wrapped around the length of me like a boa constrictor without the strangling hold. Long whiskers on his new face tickled my chin as his weight settled on me. First, it felt like a thousand tons pulling me down to the floor, but in seconds, my companion felt more like a second skin. Maverick was a part of me.

"Holy shit!" Lena jumped back, and her ass hit the table, sending drinks flying to the floor.

"Mav!" Jackie clapped her hands. "I knew you were special, buddy, but this is beyond anything I could have imagined."

"So you see it now?" I stood frozen, terrified that if I moved, Maverick would devour me.

"Of course, we see it!" Lena pointed her finger at us. "What did he just do?"

"Shit!" Jackie jumped around like a cocaine addicted rabbit. "That's what she was talking about!"

"Who?" Lena asked.

"The witch who gave him to me! She said he would do something like this if paired with the right person."

"And you gave him to me?" I spoke through tight lips. "You really are insane."

"I didn't think it would happen, but if anyone could use a protective, form-shifting guard cat, I figured it would be you. I just never thought it would happen. I mean, you've had him for years! What's different now?"

Energy crackled at my fingertips, and I lifted my hand to show them. "Me. I'm different now."

While Jackie and Lena stared at me, their brains trying to make sense of things, I rubbed Maverick's head. Instinct told me this was the best way to calm him. I spoke to him in a gentle tone. "Okay, Maverick, you can go back now."

His tiger cat roar sounded more intense, and it resonated from my head to my toes. He let out a powerful cry, and then his body unraveled from around me as he returned to the big cat I was used to. He licked my face once more before he jumped from my arms.

"What happened? Likosa told us not to worry, but I tried to do a location spell and couldn't find you." Lena watched Maverick with more trepidation.

"I doubt it would have worked, considering I wasn't on Earth," I answered her, still eyeing the cat who left the kitchen, swinging his tail.

"What do you mean *you weren't on Earth*?" Lena asked.

"Exactly what I said. It's a long story, but a friend of Likosa snatched me up from that vampire's crib and took me to another world."

"Another world? Why? What did she do to you?" Lena rambled off her questions.

"She—well, Likosa—unlocked whatever was in me. She did something to help me understand how to use the power, but honestly, it's a riddle that maybe we can solve later?"

"That's helpful," Jackie huffed. "Why not just tell you exactly what to do?"

"That's what I said!" I threw my hands up. "There was something else."

"What? Tell us everything!" Jackie insisted and grabbed my arm, pulling me to the kitchen table to join them.

"I will, but I really should check on Domino. Is he okay? Where is he?"

"He's sleeping. Sun's up for a little while longer." Lena pointed to the window, where I could see the last rays of sunlight.

"Oh." I looked at the fading sky. "That's right."

"So, what happened?" Jackie asked. "Don't make us wait for him!"

"His brother tried to bite me but couldn't," I reported. "It was like his teeth just wouldn't penetrate. Honestly, it was a little embarrassing. The man went and snatched up some poor guy to bite him in front of me, as if he had to prove a point."

"Of course he did. Vamp couldn't get it up for you?" Jackie laughed. "I'm telling everyone about that."

"Maybe we should keep that a secret," I stopped her.

"Why? That's a good thing, right?" She slipped the phone she'd already pulled out back into her pocket.

"Maybe." I nodded. "And maybe it's something we don't want to risk other vampires finding out about."

"Smart. What else?" Jackie asked.

"Well, he fed me his blood."

"Shit. So he can track you now?" she muttered. "As soon as that sun goes down, he's going to be here."

"I don't know. Maybe. What happens when two vampires give you their blood?" I asked. "Does one cancel out the other?"

"The most recent blood takes over," Lena answered. "Anyone before that will be cut off."

"So in order to stop him from finding me, I need to drink Domino's blood again?"

"Yes." Lena winked. "You like it, don't you?"

"I'm not answering that." I put my hand in her face. "Where is he?"

Annoyed, Jackie pointed to the stairs. "He's upstairs. Not that I wanted him in my house, but we couldn't leave him where he was after those morons busted up the place with that modified crane thing. I have the other hunters looking at it now. It was like some precision tool made for fishing humans. Those damn vampires are getting real creative."

"That's what snatched me up?" I rubbed my sides, remembering the pain it left behind. "Hurt like a bitch."

"Yeah, it had multiple clamp attachments, so they're able to use it a few times. After they grabbed you, the clamp detached while still restraining you, and they just threw you in the back of some van. I tried to get to you, but I was outnumbered." Jackie looked disappointed. "Next time, I'm killing the familiars. Subduing them takes too long."

"You can't do that." Lena pointed at her. "It's in your oath. You know you'll get booted from being a hunter if you do."

"What?"

"Whatever Likosa did to him, he's not healing. We even have donor blood here to give to him." She rolled her eyes. "Hard explaining what I needed that for. I had to pretend I was torturing a vampire for intel."

"Had to save face, huh?" Lena laughed.

"Damn right." Jackie pumped her fist. "I'm a warrior, not a caretaker for creatures."

'Thank you," I said. "I really appreciate this. I don't fully understand what doing this means for you, but I know it can't be easy."

"Yeah, yeah, best friends... What else are they there for?" Lena waved off my show of gratitude.

"Apparently dealing with vampires." Jackie sucked her teeth.

"Jackie..." Lena fussed.

"Look, I'm chill, but that vampire can't stay here forever." Jackie sat down and frowned at the mess Lena had created when she bumped the table. "My ancestors are probably rolling over in their graves right now."

"Would they be as dramatic?" Lena asked.

"If they are anything like her?" I pointed at the scrunched expression on Jackie's face. "Yes."

Lena and I laughed while Jackie ripped the towel from around my shoulders and wiped up Lena's mess.

"Anyway, your vampire is in the third guest bedroom. It's the one with the best curtains so he won't burn up in the sun."

"You're the best." I hugged her.

"Hurry up." She smacked my butt. "And find some damn dry clothes to wear!"

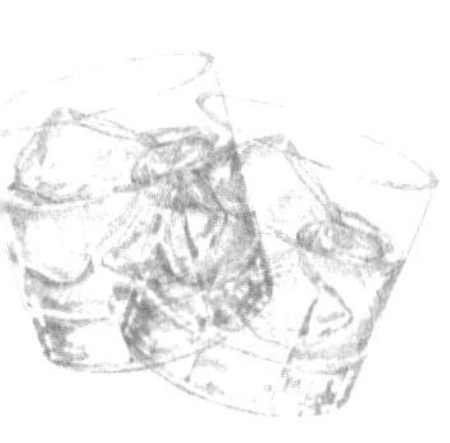

19

Domino's Dominance

I thought about going to change out of my wet clothes before I went to see Domino, but that thought made my stomach hurt. I couldn't delay it any longer. Not just because I didn't want Reddick to find me, but because I didn't want to be away from him any longer. Each step I took up the stairs and down the hall to where he slept solidified that feeling. Domino was a part of me, and I didn't want to be separated from him anymore.

Would I tell my friends about this development? Probably not.

When I stepped into the room, it was complete darkness. Only the soft flickers of a fake candle bounced off the walls. Though there was no sunlight in the hall, I quickly closed the door behind me to make sure I didn't disturb him. There was still some time before the sun completely set, and Domino was still sleeping. He lay in the bed, his shirt torn and his chest showing. To the right of his bed was a small cooler, several bags of blood inside—the supplies Jackie had called in a favor for.

I undressed from the wet clothing and wrapped my braids in the towel. After searching through the closet, I found a sheet to wrap around my body, toga style, and sat at the foot of the bed. I pulled the small cooler into my lap and held on to it. Maybe it was creepy, sitting there watching him, but I found it fascinating. Just like before, when he began to unthaw, that woodsy scent filled the air.

"Domino?" I whispered his name as the color returned to his face.

"Whitney." Domino sat up, teeth bared and eyes dark with hunger.

"Don't move." I took a bag of blood out of the box and frowned at it. Then, with his eyes carefully watching my every movement, I put the bag to his lips. "Drink."

He licked his lips, looked me in the eye, and bit into the bag. Once he'd drained it, I dropped the empty bag back into the cooler. Before retrieving another, I grabbed his hand and pressed his own wrist to his lips.

"Bite," I urged him.

"What?" He looked confused, his eyes darting between me and the cooler.

"Please." I nodded. "I need you to bite. Trust me."

"Of course." He opened his own vein as I asked.

When the blood flowed from his arm, I took another bag of the prepared blood and put it to his lips. He lifted his wrist to mine and waited. Four heartbeats, and I wrapped my mouth around the open wound and sucked. Domino moaned with pleasure as I drank from him. Then, he bit into the bag and continued his feed.

Three bags later, Domino looked healthy again, and my head was spinning from the effects of his blood.

"Why?" he asked as I lay on the blood-splattered sheet covering his chest. He drew lazy circles across my back with his fingers.

"Reddick." I sighed. "He gave me his blood."

"Shit." Domino tensed beneath me, and I looked up at his face.

"I'm sorry. He forced me to drink his blood. Jackie said the last vampire who gives you their blood can find you; it overrides the others? Please tell me that's true." I inhaled deeply as I waited for his response.

"You don't need to apologize to me, Whitney." His hand stopped on my back. "But unfortunately, that's not true. It's a rumor some vampires spread to give people a false sense of safety. Once we saw it was actually beneficial, we all just kind of unofficially agreed to stick to it."

"Dammit. So he can still find me?" I held his wrist up. "I made you waste your blood for nothing?"

"I wouldn't say it was for nothing." Domino winked and reached into the cooler, grabbing the last bag of blood.

"Do you like it? When I drink from you?"

"Do you?" He licked his lips and dropped his fangs again.

I stared at his teeth for a moment then opted to change the topic. "When will he come?"

"I don't know." He bit into the bag, and within seconds, he'd emptied it of its contents. Drops of blood trickled down his chin, and he slowly licked his lips, trying to catch them.

At first, watching him sink his teeth into the blood bag made me a little queasy. Crazy to think a few sips of his blood made the act look so much more seductive. Maybe it was the extra blood in my system that made me feel that way. I wanted him to bite me. I wouldn't let him, but I would settle for his tongue in my pussy.

"Domino..." I ran my fingers across the bare flesh of his chest.

"Yes, Whitney?"

"I need you," I whispered nervously. Would he judge me for the way his blood had me ready to jump him? Did I really care? No. Not really.

"What?" He looked at me with that hungry smile returned to his lips. "Oh. Do you?"

"I've had a lot of vampire blood." The devious smile that spread across my face mirrored his as I lifted to my knees beside him. "I feel like I might explode if I don't find relief soon."

"Can't let that happen, now, can we?" He licked his lips and retracted his teeth.

Domino moved almost too quickly for me to see. He lifted to his knees, pushed me back on the bed, and ripped the sheet I had wrapped around me. The fabric gave way easily. I gasped and pointed to the shredded ends.

"Jackie is going to make you pay for that," I laughed.

"I can afford it," he growled and grabbed my tits. "Damnit."

I moaned as his fingers rolled my nipples before he bent down to kiss each one, replacing his fingers with his tongue. Domino shifted from one boob to the other, sucking and kissing my nipples as his hands danced across my body. He gripped my stomach, hips, and ass before spreading my legs wider to slip his fingers into my pussy.

He abandoned my nipples to kiss me. The taste of blood still lingered on his lips, but I didn't care. I wrapped my arms around his neck and pulled him closer to me. His glasses fell from his face, and I tossed them aside as he continued to finger me. I lifted my hips, begging for the tease of his fingers to become something more. I wanted his dick instead. Domino smiled against my lips.

He pulled back, bit his wrist, and let a few drops fall onto my lips. Then, he sat up and dripped his blood over my breast, down my body until, finally, the warm drops hit my clit. I shivered, shocked by the sensation it caused. He put two pillows behind my head so I could see what he was doing, and I watched, licking my lips as his blood coated my lower lips.

Then, Domino followed the trail of his blood from my lips down my chest to my core. And then, this man sucked his blood from my pussy. His fangs dropped, but he never tried to bite me. Instead, he licked me clean, and when there were no more marks of crimson left, he lifted my hips with his hands beneath my ass and devoured my pussy. I gripped the sheets, preparing for the first of what I hoped would be many orgasms.

"Yes. Please. Don't stop," I moaned. "I'm coming!"

And for the first time, Domino disobeyed me.

He abruptly ended his meal and pushed to his feet to stand over me.

"What? Why?" I huffed. "Why would you stop?"

"Patience."

He unbuttoned the pants he wore and stepped out of them until he stood in front of me in only a pair of black boxer briefs.

"Watch me," he said. Then, he pulled his dick out and started stroking himself. After four of the slowest strokes I'd ever seen, Domino ran his fingernail over the tip of his dick. Blood dripped from the head and onto the floor.

"You want my blood?" he asked me as I licked my lips. "Come and get it."

If I ever denied the freak allegations, that moment proved me a liar, because I scooted to the edge of the bed and took his dick into my mouth. I sucked him so well, I could see his toes curling. His hands wrapped in my braids as he urged me to take him deeper. When his cheeks tightened in my hands, a sign he was ready to cum, he pulled me away from him.

I licked my lips as I watched him, slipping my fingers between my thighs, but Domino grabbed my wrist and pushed my hand above my head.

"Do not touch yourself," he ordered through heavy breaths.

This was a side of him I hadn't seen before, far more dominant. I chose to test the order given as I slipped my other hand between my thighs. Again, he pushed my hand away.

"One more time," he said, his voice a low rumble, "and you'll be punished."

"Oh yeah?" I narrowed my eyes and then slowly moved my hand to my pussy.

Fast as lightning, Domino picked me up from the bed and threw me across his knee.

"What did I tell you?" he growled.

"I would get punished?" I looked back at him.

"Exactly." Domino lifted his hand and grinned.

Smack!

"Oh!" I slapped my hand over my mouth as the sting of the impact spread across my ass.

"Are you sorry for disobeying me?" he asked.

"If I'm not?" I bit my lip.

Smack!

"Damn!" I cried out.

"Apologize, Whitney," he ordered.

"No," I refused.

Smack!

"You want another?" His voice had a dark edge that made my stomach tighten.

"What do you think?" I gripped his thigh and waited for another.

"Brat," he complained, but he gave me exactly what I wanted.

Smack!

Domino placed his lips near my ear. "Apologize, or I won't fuck you."

"Damnit," I muttered. "I'm sorry."

"For what?" He rubbed his hand in firm circles over my stinging cheek to soothe the sting.

I pursed my lips. "For disobeying you."

"Will you do it again?" He lifted his hand, a warning for me to comply.

"No."

"Address me when you answer me."

"No, Domino. I won't disobey you again," I said. It was what he wanted, but I knew that was a lie.

"Good girl." Domino flipped me over to the bed and onto my back, but before I could take another breath, his dick slid into my pussy.

He slammed into me four times, four powerful thrusts that left my legs shaking and my pussy pulsating. Then, he stopped.

"Why," I whined. "Don't stop."

"You're mine, Whitney." He twisted his hands in my braids and pulled my head back.

"Yes," I groaned.

"Don't ever let another vampire give you their blood." He tugged again, and my chin lifted, further exposing my neck.

Domino lowered his head and bit me, but not with his fangs. He pressed his teeth into me and then rubbed his finger across the mark left behind.

Oh, he was mad. Not because I disobeyed him—no, my Domino was possessive, and I loved it. Had it been any other man, I would have told him to kiss the ass he wanted to smack, but with Domino, something inside me screamed for him to show me more of his darker side.

"I won't." I lifted my hips to him and gripped his ass. "Fuck me, Domino."

And Domino obeyed.

Time and time again, he pushed me to the edge, but the vampire wouldn't let me finish. He was on top of me, then behind me. Then he had me hanging over the edge of the bed with my own titties damn near suffocating me, and every time I felt that orgasm ready to rip through my body, he stopped. It was when he stood, fucking me while holding me like I weighed nothing, that I lost it.

I shifted my weight in his arms to push him back onto the bed. When he was beneath me, I tightened my thighs around his and stuck my finger in his face.

"Have I angered you?" he teased with a laugh.

"Don't move!" I ordered and reached to put his dick back inside me.

"Your wish is my command." Domino folded his hands beneath his head and let me do my thing.

I rocked my hips and bounced my ass on his dick as Domino lifted his hips just right to hit that perfect spot. As I neared the peak of my orgasm, I felt him flinch and feared he would try to stop me. So, I wrapped my hands around his throat, a threat to stop him from interrupting me.

I kept riding—I wanted to taste him again. I pulled his right hand from behind his head and pressed his wrist to his lips. Domino growled and bit himself, causing the vein to open again. I pulled his arm to my lips and sloppily drank from him. His blood dripped down my chin and onto my breast, my hand moving to rub it into my flesh as I moaned. Domino's fangs dropped as he watched me, but he hid them again. He gritted his teeth and punched the nightstand, and it flew across the room, smashing into the wall.

"Let me see them," I ordered as I drank more of him.

He growled, and his fangs appeared again. Domino sat up, grabbing me with his free hand and licking the blood from my breast.

The energy continued to build inside me as I rocked my hips. I could hear my heart beating in my ears. *One.* I slammed down on his dick. *Two.* He licked my breast. *Three.* I kissed him with a mouthful of his own blood. *Four.* He smacked my ass and dropped his head back, fangs bared.

And that was it. That building heat ripped through me.

"Yes! God, yes!" I shouted and finally came. I threw my hands up in the air, and lightning shot from my fingertips, blasting the walls at my sides. I heard the shatter of the window pane just before a loud bang behind me.

"What the hell was that?" Jackie burst into the room, Lena following.

I slapped my hands over my tits as the curtain went up in flames.

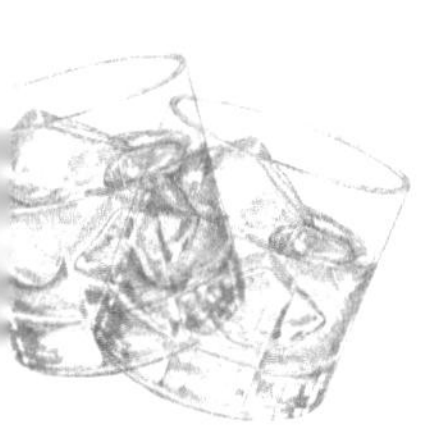

20

Twenty-Six Heartbeats

"Jackie!" I squealed.

"Oh shit, sorry!" Lena covered her eyes and turned away, but Jackie didn't.

"Don't you know how to knock?" Domino wrapped the ripped sheet around my body to shield me from their eyes.

"I'm sorry, but when I hear furniture being knocked around and then a damn explosion, knocking is the last thing on my mind. Coming up in here, busting up my place." She paused when her eyes landed on the burning fabric by the window. "My solstice curtains!!!"

"Oh, crap." I slapped my hand over my mouth, and Domino jumped from the bed completely nude, ripped the curtain from the wall, and stomped out the flame, which left a huge burn mark on the floor.

"Son of a bitch!" Jackie stomped her foot.

When he was done, he looked up to see Jackie staring at him with fury in her eyes. He grabbed the pillow and covered himself.

225

RAAWRR!

Maverick, still in his cat form, pounced through the opened door and attacked Domino. The massive body of black hair flew through the air, claws aimed at Domino's face.

"Shit!" Domino dropped the pillow to fend off his attacker. There he was, dick slapping his thighs as he fought off my cat.

Jackie laughed. Lena kept her eyes averted, and I hopped up to wrap a sheet around his waist before pulling the cat from him.

"Maverick, stop!" I fussed at the cat, who hissed at Domino again before jumping from my arms into Jackie's.

"I'm starting to take this personally!" Domino pointed at the cat, and Maverick made a ticking noise, like a bomb counting down to another explosive episode.

"You should!" Jackie laughed and carried the cat away. "You're paying for all the damages, vampire!"

Lena stumbled out the door with her hand still over her eyes. She bumped into the doorframe, only to run out of the room giggling like a child who'd just gotten away with stealing her mom's favorite snack.

"That was embarrassing." I walked over to the door and closed it.

"You covered my dick before you got the cat off me?" He laughed. "Why?"

"Hey, they've already seen the cat attack you. They don't need to see your dick too!"

"I'm not embarrassed about my dick." He looked down. "I have a nice dick."

"Of course, you're not embarrassed. You have no reason to be." I looked back at the closed door and then sat on the bed. "But my friends don't need to know *everything*!"

The sheet moved just above his dick, and I couldn't help but stare. He noticed where my attention was, and the sheet lifted with his arousal.

"Keep looking at me like that, and they're going to come back in here after I make you scream again," he growled.

"I..." The energy rippled at my fingertips, and I lifted my hands to show him. "That might not be a great idea."

"Okay, so I didn't imagine that. That came from you." Domino moved to sit beside me and get a closer look at my hand.

"Yes." I nodded. "Whitney, now with lightning strike! That's a cute name for it, don't you think?"

"How?"

"That alien bloodline everyone was talking about?" I dropped my hand. "After your brother attacked, Likosa had someone rescue me. They took me back to her place, where she unlocked something inside me. Now, I have this power I'm not sure how to control."

"Right."

I looked around the room at my wet clothes on the floor and the tattered sheet that covered half my body. "I don't have anything to wear."

"Hold on." He held a finger up, stepped back into his pants, and then vanished. I stayed there in bed, wondering what my friends could have possibly been thinking. Jackie had seen all of Domino, and if Lena hadn't gotten at least a glance, she'd surely be filled in on the details.

When Domino returned a few minutes later, he had my bag in his hand—the duffel I'd brought from home. He handed it to me. "Let me know if there is something missing."

I dug around in the bag for a few minutes and put together a suitable fit. "Thank you. This will work."

"Good. Now get dressed so we can face your friends. They're down there snickering like little girls."

"Yeah, I figured they would be." I looked at the blood still covering parts of my body. *Did they see that too?* "We really should shower."

"Or I could lick the rest of it off." Domino followed my eyes and grinned. "It would take a lot longer to accomplish, but it would be a lot more fun for me."

"You need to settle down, sir." I held my hand up to him. "They already walked in on us once. I don't need it happening again!"

With Domino standing there looking at me like he wanted to risk taking a bite out of me, I pulled the sheet tighter around me and escaped to the bathroom across the hall from the guest room. I wasn't in the shower but ten seconds before the vampire appeared behind me.

"Domino!" I whispered. "What are you doing in here?"

"I'm covered in blood too." He winked. "Sharing a shower not only saves us on time but is also eco-friendly."

"Yeah, I'm sure that's why you're here. To save water."

"And other things." He pulled me into his arms and cupped my ass.

His dick grew against me, and I couldn't help myself. I reached down to stroke him.

Domino turned me around, pressing me up against the glass. The water ran down my back as he slowly slipped inside my body. It wasn't long before I felt that energy building inside me. I turned and pushed him away.

"Wait." I held him back.

"Are you okay? What's wrong?" Domino asked with genuine concern.

I held up my hand to show him the small sparks at the tips of my fingers. "I don't think we should do this. Not here."

"Damn." He looked closer but jumped back when a spark lifted from my hand.

"Yeah, Jackie is already pissed. Destroying her bathroom would push her over the edge," I said, as if my friend wouldn't already be seething.

"Fuck." He took several deep breaths, pushed me to the side, and washed up at hyper-speed before he disappeared from the shower.

I could still hear him cursing in the other room as I finished my shower. I laughed until I looked down and saw the blood circling the drain. His blood. I wanted to be disgusted by the sight, but I wasn't. *What the hell was happening to me?* When I finished showering, I returned to the bedroom, where Domino sat, fully clothed.

"Does this mean we can't..." He eyed me as I dried off and pulled the shea butter from my bag to moisturize my skin.

"Not until I learn how to control this." I looked at the butter and then back at him. "Do you want me to do this somewhere else?"

"I know I can't touch you, but you will not stop me from watching." He waved his hand for me to continue.

I rubbed the butter across my leg and looked up at him. The man looked like he was starving, and not for blood. I almost joked about how he was being greedy, but I came, he didn't. If I thought I could finish him off without triggering that power within, I would have.

"Slower." His voice deepened.

"Seriously?" I chuckled. "This doing it for you?"

"Yes."

"Okay," I hummed and continued moisturizing my body, avoiding looking at him, since it was actually turning me on to have him watch me.

As I finished dressing, I could feel Domino's intense gaze fixed on me. After I adjusted my shirt, I glanced at him and saw the disappointment in his expression.

"Cheer up. It won't be like this forever." I walked over and patted his cheek. "Now, let's go face my friends."

"Oh, right," he grunted. "The friends again. You know there are more people down there, right?"

"What?" I stuffed my stuff back into the duffel bag and started making the bed, only to realize there was blood on the sheets. Pulling them back, I hoped like hell it hadn't soaked through to the mattress. The relief I felt when I saw the mattress was clean of the mess was insane. I already knew Jackie was waiting to cut into me, and she would be completely valid.

"I count twenty-six hearts beating. Some of them are outside, but most are downstairs right now," he said calmly.

"You can hear the heartbeats?"

"I'm a vampire. Yes, I can hear heartbeats. Luckily, I've fed, and I have control of my impulses right now."

"And if you hadn't?"

"Your friend would be a lot more upset with us."

"Twenty-six. Why are there so many?" I thought about it. "The other hunters. Are you going to be okay?"

"It's not my ideal way to spend the night, but I can handle myself." He nodded and grabbed the duffel bag from my hand.

"I'm sure Jackie told them not to try anything." I headed for the door.

"Doesn't mean they'll listen." Domino followed.

We headed downstairs to find a house full of people. Jackie stood in the center of the open space, surrounded by men and women dressed like they were ready for combat. Domino stiffened by my side, and just as he did, all eyes turned toward us.

A moment later, a dagger flew, landing blade first in the wall just behind Domino. Had he not moved, it would have gone right through his heart.

"Hey!" Jackie called out. "I told you guys this vampire is off limits. Who threw that?"

When no one fessed up, Domino pointed to the guy who did it.

"Miguel, really?" Jackie walked over to the man.

"Hey, it's a reflex now." The short guy with dark, wavy hair shrugged and pointed at Domino. "Not cool, ratting me out."

"Reflex my ass!" Jackie stomped over to him. "This is my house. I don't need you fucking up the place."

"Hey, I'm here to do you a favor. Chill." He winked at her. "Besides, what do you want me to do when a random vampire shows up?"

"Keep your daggers in your belt and off my damn walls." She paused. "That's it. Listen up. The next person to cause any destruction to my home is going to get my foot shoved so far up their ass, they'll be tasting the vegan nail polish on my toes. Got it?"

"Okay." Lena stepped up to Jackie and put her hands on her shoulder. "Let's bring this back to focus."

"You're right." Jackie pumped her hands by her side, as if pushing down her growing temper, then looked at the two of us still standing on the steps.

"Come with me. Now." She turned and stomped out of her home, and we followed her. Jackie led Lena, Domino, and me from the main house over to the guest house. Just as Domino said, there were hunters hanging around the perimeter of the property. They watched us carefully as we moved across the grounds.

Jackie dramatically entered the guest house, pushing the door so hard, it knocked against the wall. She pranced inside, holding her hands in an obvious display of the destruction. There was a large hole in the wall where a beautiful bay window once stood, surrounded by abstract paintings. I cringed at the sight, knowing Domino would be paying for it. I sure as hell wouldn't be. Hello—unemployed!

"Now," Jackie said once we were alone. "Talk."

"About?" Domino asked, clearly goading her.

"I can make a list." Jackie started counting off her fingers. "A vampire sent his zombies here to attack us. They destroyed my property. Whitney's ass vanished and apparently went to another planet then had the nerve to come back here, only to have bloody sex before lighting a damn fire in my guest room. Is that enough, or do you need more? I can go into having a vampire on my property with a house full of hunters!"

"Jackie, I'm sorry about all of that. You're right." I stepped closer to her. "I—"

"Whitney, I know all this is new to you, and I get how jarring this can be, but damn. Common courtesy isn't a new concept. What is going on with you?" she asserted. "I love you, but really, get your shit together."

"I don't have an excuse." I didn't try to make any reasoning for what happened. Everything happened so fast, and whether or not I meant to cause harm, I had. "I'm sorry, Jackie. Really."

"Jackie, it's not like she planned for your house to get attacked. Your people found the tracker in the car. That's how Reddick knew where she was," Lena offered.

"Okay, so I'll take that one off the list, but my guestroom is on you!" Jackie pointed at me then swung her finger toward Domino. "And you, vampire."

"I'll pay for everything." Domino nodded. "Send me the bill."

"And you'll promise to keep your blood play off my property." Jackie scowled. "I know how you vampires are."

"Sure." He smirked then threw a side glance at me.

"What's that look about?" Jackie narrowed her eyes.

"Nothing!" I panicked because I didn't want my friends to know I was the reason things got so bloody. "We really should start figuring out how to fix this place up."

"Yeah, we should, because Lena is sealing my house back off. You're up and moving again, so your all-access pass has been revoked."

"Oh, however will I go on?" Domino said dramatically.

"This is what your life will be like from now on," Lena snickered.

Simultaneously, Domino and Jackie's phones sounded off. They both threw up a finger and walked off in different directions to take the call.

"For two people who can't stand each other..." I looked at Lena to make sure she got my meaning. Even standing on opposite sides of the house, they held the same serious posture as they spoke into their phones.

"Yeah, I know." She shook her head. "It's spooky, isn't it?"

"We have a problem," Jackie stated as she returned.

"What is it?" I asked.

"I take it you got the same call?" She looked at Domino, who also rejoined us.

"Yes." He gave a tight nod.

"Okay, you're scaring me." I looked at Jackie. "Tell us what's happening."

"They have Jai." Jackie's words made my heart feel like it would explode in my chest. "The vampire has your sister."

21

Make the plan.

"What? Who has her?" I asked, even though I already knew who she was talking about.

"Reddick's men. I have confirmation they are on a plane headed here," Domino answered.

"How did this happen?" A mixture of rage and disappointment boiled in my belly as I pointed at him. "You said this couldn't happen. You both said she was safe."

"I don't know. With all our people watching, there is no way they should have gotten to her," Domino answered.

"It doesn't matter how it happened." Lena stepped forward. "What matters is that we know, and now we need to make sure when that plane lands, we're there to intercept."

"Why would Reddick want my sister? Is this just to hurt us?" My mind raced—I already knew the man was sadistic. There was no telling what he would do to Jai.

"Maybe he thinks taking Jai kills two birds with one stone," Jackie offered.

I turned to look at her. "How?"

"He hopes taking your sister will make us act recklessly," Domino explained. "It gives him what he wants and makes it easier to take us out. He'll also have her blood. If you're a descendant, then so is your sister. He will test her blood, and if it works, he doesn't need you."

"But we don't have the same blood. I'm adopted!" I panicked. "Domino, he was talking about making me a blood whore and selling me off to the highest bidder! We can't let that happen to Jai! She is innocent. She doesn't deserve this.

"You'd think he'd look into that before snatching her up," Lena said. "What happens when he figures that out?"

"We have to get to her; she won't be able to protect herself like I did," I urged them.

"What do you mean?" Domino asked.

"That's why Reddick fed me his blood. When he tried to bite me, he couldn't."

"I've been thinking about that," Lena said. "I made a few calls, and I think it might have something to do with your powers. Even before you unlocked your abilities, something protected you from him. It looks like this has happened before. The person had to basically give consent in order for the vampire to bite them."

"Meaning if I don't want to be bitten, I can't be?" I don't know why I glanced at Domino, but I did, and I could see him tense.

"Basically." She nodded.

"What if they get her blood without consent?" Domino asked. "There are other ways to spill blood."

"Hopefully, it kills them," Jackie said and winked at Domino.

"I would never do that," he responded sternly to the insinuation.

"Sure. I'm sure you ask all your victims for their permission before you feed. Give me a break." Jackie rolled her eyes.

"Sure. Do you have a preferred bone?" Domino threatened.

"Guys!" Lena snapped her fingers in between their challenging gazes. "We need to focus!"

"Thank you." I nodded at Lena before addressing the bickering babies. "Look, I know that, between the two of you, there are a lot of resources at our disposal. How do we get my sister back? She doesn't need to be pulled into all this."

"You're right." Jackie took a deep breath. "I apologize for letting my hatred distract me. We'll work together to plan an interception. We know they're still in the air; we have about six hours until they land at a private airstrip."

"That will only give us roughly two hours to do this before the sun rises again," Domino added. "After that, my people will have to retreat."

"You think that's enough time?" I asked.

"If we plan it right and can convince the hunters and vampires not to kill each other." Domino pointed back toward the main house. "You already have one dagger-loving hunter we have to worry about."

"Miguel won't mess this up. None of the hunters will," Jackie defended her group. "And if he really wanted to kill you, he wouldn't have missed."

"So," Lena said to interrupt another potential bickering session, "do we know exactly where the airstrip is?"

"Yes, it's the only one here equipped to deal with special cargo. It's roughly an hour away," Domino said. "Reddick wouldn't risk using another one. We've intercepted their flight plan, and that's where they're going."

"Good. That means we have four hours to prep before we need to leave." Lena chewed her lip. "Is that enough time?"

"What are the known threats?" Jackie asked Domino. "You know your brother better than anyone, right? What do we need to know about how he's going to move?"

"Don't overthink things. Reddick still likes to act in simplistic ways. He's cocky. He'll send in a slew of mediocre vampires, ones easily disposable, to assist his top guys. Those are the ones you have to worry about."

"Nyesha and Vance." I thought of the two vampires who had already tried to snatch me up.

"And others," Domino agreed. "He has seven in total who are his front runners."

Jackie held her hand up. "Who the hell are Nyesha and Vance?"

"They're my brother's special pets," Domino explained. "With the others, they run things for him."

"Nyesha is the one who tried to bite me," I added.

"Do they have special powers or anything we should be aware of?" Lena asked.

"Powers? Vampires have powers?" I asked and looked at Domino, who had displayed no powers to me.

"If they had them before they were turned, yes. If a witch became a vampire, she would still have access to whatever abilities she had prior to being turned." Domino nodded. "Most don't; some magic fights the turn, and it ends up killing the person."

"Do they have anyone?" I asked.

"No. Fortunately for us, my brother hasn't found anyone like that to add to his team. At least, no one I've heard of. It's the only reason he hasn't made a move to expand his territory."

"Explains why he is so adamant about getting your blood," Jackie added. "It's not just about pissing off his little brother. That kind of power would rocket him to the top of the food chain."

"Guess I'm really not that important to him." Domino dramatically stomped his foot. "Damn it."

"Oh, are you hurt to find that out?" Jackie poked her lips out. "You need a tissue to wipe away your tears?"

"Not gonna lie, it stings." He sniffled.

"Anyway!" Lena poked me before pointing at the vampire and the huntress. "I'm not sure this is any better than the bickering."

"Me either." I frowned. "I don't think I like this. Go back to fighting."

"Make up your mind, woman!" Jackie snapped at me before her serious tone returned and she addressed Domino again. "I'll talk to my people, you rally yours. I think we let the vampires make the first run. They'll be expecting it. They won't be expecting hunters to be there helping."

"Smart," Domino said. "We'll try to keep the casualties low."

"You might want to have all your vampires wear some kind of special color or something. That way, they don't get caught in any accidental crosshairs."

"Accidental?" He snorted. "I'm sure it will be an accident."

"Hey, I'm trying to eliminate the possibility." Jackie shrugged.

"Actually, I can help with that. I'll create some temporary charms." Lena perked up. "They'll protect the vampires from the hunter's weapons."

"Uh-uh." Jackie rejected the idea with a finger wag in Lena's face. "I don't need vampires running around immune to our weapons!"

"Chill." Lena stopped our friend from going off on another rant. "It will only last one night. When the sun rises, they'll deactivate."

"You can do that?" I asked, proud of her.

"I've been putting in a lot of work to improve my craft. You know, to be connected with my magic." She rolled her eyes at Domino, clearly not having forgotten his previous comment about her abilities. "When this is all over, I'll show you!"

"We need to map out our movement." Jackie left and returned with a large pad and pen, handing them to Domino. "Give us the layout."

Domino took the pad, and we all headed over to the kitchen counter since the table was smashed up. He quickly sketched out a map of the private terminal, complete with a line of trees and several markings for roads.

"This is the airport," he explained, pointing to his drawing. "The terminal isn't that big, and there are only a handful of familiars who work there. Most never last longer than a few months before they find themselves on a meal plan. To the east are the Blight Woods, and to the west is a private access road blocked by a massive stone wall. It runs about four miles, covered by another line of trees on the opposite side."

"How high is the wall?" Jackie peered at the drawing.

"Around forty-five feet," Domino answered.

"Blight Woods? I've never seen this place." Lena whipped out her phone and tried to look it up on a digital map of the area. "There's nothing there."

"That's because someone pays a lot of money for it not to be," Domino explained. "It's also a private territory. It's used as a feeding ground for arriving vampires."

"I thought you said vampires couldn't drink from animals..." I focused on that last statement.

"They can't," Jackie said through a tight jaw.

"So how can it be a feeding ground?" I asked.

"They release humans into the woods," Domino said with a straight face.

"Oh, my God," I gasped. "Are you serious?"

"That's terrible." Lena looked sick.

"Yes, well, I think that's the best entry point for the Hunters." Domino refused to address the atrocious nature of what he'd just told us. "They won't expect humans to come that way."

"What about the vampires?" I looked at Jackie. "What if they mistake you for food?"

"Then they'll die." Jackie smirked. "Besides, we have methods for fooling vampires. Most never see us coming."

"Reddick will be expecting an attack from us. He knows I won't sit back and let him do this. If we're lucky, he won't be ready for the hunters." Domino looked at his drawing again. "The plane coming in isn't full of vampires, and it's not a place where a lot of vampires just hang out. The only ones there will be Reddick's men."

"How do we access the woods?" Jackie pointed to the edge of the drawing, where Domino had sketched a series of trees. "Is there a way in?"

"There is a path with very little surveillance. You should be able to get through there without issue," he answered. "But you're going to have to use the river to get to it and then walk."

"How far is the hike?" Jackie asked.

"Roughly five miles," Domino estimated.

"Five miles!" I gawked. "Is there a quicker route?"

"That's nothing for us." Jackie brushed off my concern.

"Maybe not for you, but my ass ain't walking five miles." I crossed my arms. "Not unless one of your hunters is strong enough to strap me to his back."

"Who said you were going?" Domino and Jackie asked at the same time. They shared a look of disgust at their simultaneous expression.

"Of course, I'm going," I insisted. "Why wouldn't I?

"Whitney…" Jackie said my name in that 'oh you poor baby' tone.

"You think I'm going to sit here and wait for you to get my sister? Hell no." I held my hand up. "I'm going. This isn't up for debate."

"You don't even know how to control your powers," Domino added and held his hands up in defense when I side-eyed him.

"I'll figure it out." I sucked my teeth. "It can't be that hard, right? And we knew this was coming. That's why I did all this to begin with, so I could protect myself against threats."

"Yeah, protect yourself. Don't run into battle with hunters and vampires. You could get killed out there. And if we are too concerned with protecting you, they might get away with your sister."

"She's right," Domino agreed, and I felt like I would fall over.

"Now is not the time for you two to start agreeing." I pointed at him.

"When it comes to your safety, yes, it is," Domino insisted. "How do you intend to learn how to use your power effectively and in such a short time?"

"I—" For a moment, I hesitated because I really didn't know. But then, the answer hit me. "I do know someone I can call. She can help me."

"Who?" Jackie asked.

"Likosa's friend," I explained. "The one who got me out of Reddick's place. She's like me, and she said I could call her if I needed her."

"And you think she can help you understand this in such a short time?" Domino asked.

"I mean, it's the only option I have right now, and I'm going to take it." My eyes darted between them. Lena stood at my side, keeping her opinion to herself. When I glanced at her, I couldn't tell if she agreed with me or not. "I don't want to be in your way when it comes to saving Jai, but I'm not okay with sitting here helpless while you do it either."

"Okay, I think that's a great idea. If you can get her stamp of approval, you can come. But if she says you aren't ready, promise me you will sit this one out. Is that fair?" Domino offered the compromise.

"I think it is," Jackie answered for me.

"I don't think he was asking you." I rolled my eyes at her.

"Whitney," Domino said my name, snapping my attention back to the serious look on his face.

"Yes, okay. I promise." I gave in because what else was I supposed to do?

"While you work on that, I need to get my people together." Domino looked at me like he wanted to say more, but he didn't. Whatever thoughts he had floating around his mind, he kept them to himself. Instead, he pulled me into his arms and kissed me like we were alone. When our lips parted, he looked me in the eye, tightened his hold on me. "Stay safe."

"Of course." I looked up at him. "I promise."

"Good." He kissed my forehead, and then Domino was gone.

"Say what you want about vampires. That intense vibe is sexy as hell!" Lena clapped her hands and mimicked Domino. "Stay safe. With command, he said it!"

"You're ridiculous." I brushed off her teasing.

"Yes, you really are," Jackie said with much less amusement in her tone.

"Oh, shut up. You know it was hot." Lena mimed writing in a notebook. "I gotta capture that for my next novel!"

"I'll keep my opinions to myself." Jackie winked and rolled up the map Domino had drawn. "I need to take this to the other hunters."

"Oh yeah, and I need to get those charms ready for the vampires. Damn, I really should have asked him how many we need." Lena pointed at me. "Do send your lover a note and ask him for me?"

"Yeah, yeah." I pulled out my phone, first sending Domino the question for Lena and then emailing Rayna.

Domino responded within seconds, confirming he would need no less than thirty charms.

"He says thirty, maybe a few more."

"Thirty. Right, okay. I better get to work." Lena took a step toward the door but paused. "Are you going to be okay here by yourself?"

"Uh, yeah. Actually, I think some alone time will be good for me. There are plenty of hunters here now, so I should be safe from any attack."

"Yes, they will keep you safe. I'll send a few more over to hang outside and make sure nothing happens."

"Thanks."

Lena pulled me into her arms and gave me her best mama bear hug. "It's going to be alright. We'll get her back."

"Thank you." I hugged her back. "I'm sorry for all this."

"I'm not Jackie. I don't need an apology from you. And honestly, I don't think she does either. The thing is, hunters get a little testy when they're around creatures they're meant to kill."

"Really?" I chewed my lip. "I never considered this could be affecting her like that."

"Yeah, it's like a built-in fail-safe to make sure they don't get too buddy-buddy with the enemy. That's why she wants to get this over with as fast as possible. All those hunters out there," she pointed at the door that led outside, "they're basically ticking time bombs with Domino being around."

"Okay, so wrap this up and get him far away. Got it." I nodded.

"I don't know how you're going to manage this moving forward, but it will be fun to figure out."

"Maybe you can whip some magic up to help."

"I doubt it," she laughed. "But for you, I would sure as hell try!"

I sat alone in the destroyed guest house, waiting for a response from Rayna. Would she be able to help me on such short notice? For all I knew, she was on another world without access to email. I balanced my weight on the edge of the couch and tapped my phone screen, as if that would make her response come through any faster.

"Come on, please." I muttered. Even with feeling the strange pressure change and the ripple in the air, the woman still scared the shit out of me.

"Hey, girl." Rayna popped into the room in front of me.

"Holy shit!" I fell back off the edge of the couch and onto my ass.

22

TRAINING DUH!

"**Y**ou must have been lost in thought to not feel me coming." Rayna held out her hand to help me up.

"There's a lot on my mind." I accepted her help. "I don't think I'll ever get used to that. People can just pop up on you whenever they want."

"That's what I thought at first. There is a way to block your energy so no one can track you and do that. I'll show you how." She looked around and frowned at the destruction, kicking a piece of rubble near her. "This place looks terrible. Is this why you asked me to come? I got your email just as we were about to leave."

"Oh yeah, how was the wedding?" I asked. I figured I could sprinkle a little small talk in there to kick things off. Who wanted to deal with someone who only hit you up when they needed something? We could pretend for a moment that wasn't why I emailed her.

"Good. I cried more than I thought I would." Rayna smiled and her face lit up. "I mean, my girl looked so beautiful, even with the family drama. I don't know how she turned out so well adjusted despite being a part of that family."

"That's good. Not the family drama, but that it turned out well."

"Yeah, and now she's headed off to some tropical island." She sighed. "Oh, your email said you needed help. What's going on? Because again, I'm not a clean-up crew." She pointed to the mess on the floor.

"Oh no, I wouldn't ask you to do anything like that." I laughed at her twisted expression. "But I do need you to help me learn to control my powers. I have about two hours to do it."

"My ears must be clogged?" She rubbed her ear and leaned forward. "Say that again. You need to master your power in two hours?"

"I understand how ridiculous that sounds. Trust me, I do. But my sister is in trouble. If I don't learn how to at least control this thing, I have to sit on the sideline. I'm not looking to be a seasoned professional. I just don't want to accidentally shoot my best friend in the ass."

"Shoot her?" She looked around. "You got a gun on you? What is it with women and guns? Do you know my best friend made me go back to hell to get her gun?"

"You had a gun in hell?" I held my hand up. "How does that even happen?

"Long story, but..." she tapped her chin, then pointed at me. "By the way you're looking at me, I assume you didn't mean a gun?"

"No, I didn't mean a gun." I scratched my head suddenly, considering if Rayna was the right person to help me with my issue.

"Right..." She squinted at me. "So, what did you mean?"

"Apparently, my power is not the same as yours." I shook my hand in between us, hoping something would happen. It didn't. "I shoot electricity from my fingers or something."

"Right." She trailed off. "And Likosa didn't help you figure all this out?"

"Not really." I shook my head.

"That woman is up to something." Rayna sucked her teeth. "When I needed to understand my power, she unlocked a damn internal instruction manual with a simple spell. She could have done the same thing with you."

"You think so too?" I lowered my voice into my conspiracy theorist tone. "All that stuff about wanting us to be friends. It feels like she has other motives."

"It's likely, but whatever she does or doesn't have up her sleeve doesn't matter now." Rayna sucked her teeth and looked around us. "Well, we're going to need a lot more than two hours. We're not going to get that on Earth."

"Vomit-inducing shift?" I took a deep breath, hoping she would tell me I was wrong.

"Yep!" Rayna cheered. "Brace yourself."

This time, I didn't feel as much change in the pressure as I did the tightening around my brain. And then, my ears popped repeatedly and my vision blurred. When the overstimulation ended, we were standing in an extensive field of grass.

"Is this hell again?"

"No, in hell, you would lose time," Rayna explained. "This is a world I found a few months ago, another place from one of my paintings. Apparently, a lot of them are depictions of new worlds. Anyway, here, time slows down. An hour on Earth is about three here. It's not much, but it gives us more time to lock in some basic skills for you."

"Okay, good." I took a deep breath and noticed how heavy my chest felt. "It's kind of hard to breathe here."

"Oh yeah, you'll acclimate soon. This is a human-compatible planet; not that we're exactly human, but you know what I mean. I actually brought Keri here for an extended break from the wedding stuff." Rayna looked around. "There's a hot spring not far from here. I could hardly get the girl out the damn thing."

"A hot spring sounds relaxing right now."

"We can come back after you're done with your vampire problem. I'm sure you'll need it." Rayna clapped. "Alright, we're in a safe space. Show me what you got."

"I'm not really sure how to make it happen." I flexed my fingers. "Both times, it wasn't something I controlled. It just happened on its own."

"Let's troubleshoot this," Rayna suggested as a flock of birds flew over us. "When did it happen? What were you doing?"

"Um…" Of course, I hesitated. I was supposed to hate this woman's guts. She was the reason I lost my job. No, I didn't want to tell her about how an orgasm triggered the explosive showing of my power.

"What?" Rayna raised a brow. "Is something wrong?"

"Well, it happened with Likosa," I started. "And then once again when I was with Domino."

That should have been more than enough for her to understand where I was coming from. She knew firsthand what kind of magic the witch worked. *Come on, girl. Two plus two, you can do this!"*

"The vampire?" She tilted her head.

"Yes." I nodded slowly and widened my eyes, hoping she would catch my meaning and I wouldn't have to paint her a picture.

"You were…" Rayna pursed her lips then nodded slowly as the understanding hit her. "Well, I won't be doing that."

"Obviously." I looked away from her. "But that's the only time it happened. I haven't had time to try to make it happen on my own."

"Try it now." Rayna stepped to the side and pointed out into the distance. "Pick a target and blast it!"

"Just like that?" I looked around the calm landscape. "What if I cause some natural disaster?"

"I hardly think you're that powerful, especially now." She shook her head and scanned the horizon. "How else do you think this starts?"

"Right. Okay, I'll try."

After Rayna walked away to what she thought was a safe distance, I took a deep breath, lifted my hand, and chose a target. It was a blue tree stump. The thing looked dead, or what I imagined a dead tree to look like in an alien world. What more harm could I do? I aimed and pushed my hand toward the stump. Nothing happened.

"Anytime now," Rayna called out. "Just make it happen."

"And what if I already tried and failed?"

"Did you?" she called back.

I opened my eyes and turned to look at her. "Are you saying I always have a strained expression on my face?"

"Well, you were pretty angry at me when we first met. Some people just look like they have to poop. I wasn't going to judge you for that," she joked.

"Hilarious." I couldn't believe it, but I was starting to like Rayna, and that somehow pissed me off.

"Look, you need to visualize what you want to happen. It's the most basic instruction I can give you and it feels like complete bullshit, but that's where it all starts. Remember how it felt for your power to move through you before? Focus on that feeling. Pretend like you're back in that moment."

"Okay." I did it again, this time taking her advice, and it worked. Well, kind of. My fingertips sparked like the sparklers parents give their children for their first fireworks. Exciting to watch, but ultimately harmless.

"Well…" Rayna walked over and leaned in to get a closer look at my hand. She squinted as she examined the pathetic display. "I really hope you're a quick study, because this isn't giving us much to work with. Maybe we should take a step back. You said Likosa did something?"

"Yes. To be precise, she flicked me in the forehead and knocked me into that weird water. Once I was inside, I heard a voice in my head telling me what to do, but it spoke in riddle."

"What did it say?" she asked.

"It said my power reaches to the sun and channels its energy. I'm supposed to look inside myself and find the light." I paused, recalling the message. "Oh, and something about four beats of my heart and keeping my mind quiet."

"The quiet mind thing makes sense. You need to have a clear head, especially in the beginning." Rayna caught sight of something in the distance. "Trust me, I had a few accidents. Some caused me pain; one put me in a very embarrassing situation. You don't want that."

"How does it work for you?" I asked her. "What do you do to make your power work? Maybe I can use the same principles."

"I channel the energy, pull it through my body, and target it. It must be the same for you, except where my powers affect space, yours affect light."

"Channel the light?" I looked around us; the sky above was illuminated by the sun, but it was fading.

"The message said the energy of the sun? So, you pull from light around you."

"What if it's night?" I pointed out. "I'm dealing with vampires. Very few of my problems will happen during the day."

"Reach further; it's not night everywhere. And I think it is bigger than that. Think cosmic. The sun, the moon, the stars. Any source of light, even the light that isn't literal. There is a light inside of others, though I think that might lead you down a darker path, so let's not do that."

"Right. Okay, I have to think bigger."

"Focus on channeling the energy first." Rayna reeled me in. "Feel the energy around you and pull it to you."

"Feel the energy?"

"I visualize it like light sonic waves I can touch. Picture water crashing along the surface of the ocean. Pull those waves to you."

"Okay." I nodded. "I can do this."

I closed my eyes and focused on clearing my mind. Years of meditation had helped me with that. I pictured myself standing on the beach, slowly walking into the ocean. There were few waves to begin with, but the more focused I became, the stronger they grew. I reached out and grabbed the ridge of a wave and pulled it to me. When it crashed against my chest, I felt the charge of energy flow through my physical self. I did it again, and then I opened my eyes. Just as I did, a bolt of light shot out of my hand.

It darted across the grass but didn't quite reach my target.

"Well damn, you are a quick study." Rayna clapped.

"You're a good teacher. I can't believe I did that."

"Okay, now that you have it, the next time, try to actually hit the target. Before you release the energy, picture it bursting out of you like a bullet or a missile."

"I'm a weapon." My chest tightened with panic as the words slipped through my lips. What if that was what Reddick really wanted? I shook the thought from my mind; Reddick didn't know enough about me to think I could be his weapon. "I can do this."

I did what she said, repeating the visualization but adding the missile launch to the end. I pushed the energy out of me with everything I had, and that time, it landed. It hit the stump, but it didn't do a damn thing except spark at the edge and fizzle out.

"How is it possible? I damn near set my friend's house on fire last time," I complained. "That's not going to do much against vampires."

"No, but it's a start. Now, the fun part begins. This is when you do it over and over again until you feel more confident—or until we run out of time and I have to drop you back off in the middle of a vamp battle."

"Bootcamp?"

"Pretty much." She patted my shoulder. "Cheer up. At least you're still likely to survive."

In what felt like the blink of an eye, the hours disappeared. And in that short time, my abilities surprised both of us. While I focused time and time again to channel my energy, Rayna left me alone in the strange world and came back with a lawn chair, umbrella, and snacks. She cheered me on, and I took her encouragement and kept pushing. Hours later, I wasn't a professional magic wielder, but I was damn confident I could hold my own. Only once had I somehow pushed the energy backward and knocked myself to the ground.

"Listen, whatever happens, you are not to tell Metice about this." Rayna folded up her chair.

"Why?" I wiped the sweat from my forehead.

"Let's just say my intro training took a lot longer and was far more embarrassing." She sucked her teeth. "The man still pokes at me about it."

"It will be our little secret." I mimed zipping my lip.

"I hate to say it, but we're pretty much out of time here. I have to take you back now," Rayna said. "You ready?"

The nerves bubbled in my stomach as I considered her question. "Do you think I can handle myself with the vampires?"

"Yes, I think so. You won't be alone, and if you stay calm, you can take a vampire or two, no problem."

"Good. Then, yeah. I'm ready to go."

Rayna held her hand out to me and then pulled back. "Wait, why did you ask that?"

"Domino made me promise I wouldn't join them unless you said I could handle it."

"Oh, so if you die, it's on me?" She crossed her arms. "I'm not sure if I like that."

"Yeah, pretty much." I shrugged. "Good thing the vampire can't chase you to new universes."

Her lips turned up toward the strange sky. "Does this make us even about the job loss thing?"

"Um…" I thought about it. "No, I don't think it does."

"You're a tough one." Rayna held her hand out to me. "Keri would like you."

When we popped back into Jackie's guest house, it was quiet. I expected my friends to be there, waiting to curse my ass out for vanishing without a word, but they weren't. I headed outside, and Rayna followed me. Were there any hunters to greet us? No. If they were still there, protecting the property, they didn't make themselves known.

"Damnit. I'm too late." I stomped my foot. "How could they just up and leave me like that?"

"Well, you were kind of on another planet for several hours," Rayna justified. "Were they supposed to wait around and risk losing your sister?"

"I know you're speaking logically right now, but I would prefer it if you kept it to yourself."

Rayna chuckled and held her hands up in defense. "Do you know where they are? Maybe I can take you there."

"I... There was a map." I pictured Domino's drawing. "It's a private airport, but it's next to a place called the Blight Woods."

"Oh, I know that place!" Rayna pointed to the sky. "I was there recently."

"Do I want to know why?"

"No, actually, I don't think you do."

"Great, I won't ask."

"Well, let's go. Don't want to miss all the action!"

"You really enjoy this, don't you?"

"It took some time, but yes. I sure as hell wouldn't go back to my life of swiping through men on dating apps and watching bad TV!" Rayna held her hand out to me.

Just as I was about to accept her offered hand so she could pull me through time and space again, the menace roared. I looked over just in time to see Maverick leaping through the air. He landed in my arms, and I stumbled back.

"Maverick, you have got to stop doing that." I struggled. "You're too big!"

"Oh, he is handsome!" Rayna squealed. "I wanted a cat, but my mom had allergies. Then, I didn't want to be the crazy cat lady, so I never got one."

"Don't encourage him." I tried to put the cat down, but he clung to me. "Come on, Maverick. I have to go!"

"Looks like he's coming with us." Rayna wiggled her nose at him.

"Is that smart?" I frowned. "I'm supposed to avoid being a liability, remember? If I'm running after my cat, that could be a problem."

Maverick purred, and his form shifted slightly before returning to normal. His nose elongated, and his whiskers tickled my neck.

"I'm guessing that's not a normal cat?" Rayna pointed and stepped back. "What the hell was that?"

"No, actually. I recently found out he's a demon—and not just figuratively." I looked at her.

"Oh, yeah, he's coming with us," she said. "You have a demon pet. Trust me, you're going to want him there. Is he bonded to you?"

"According to Jackie, yes."

"Damn, I wish I could stick around to watch all this pay off, but Metice is waiting for me."

Rayna slapped her hand on my shoulder, and we were off.

Moments later, we stood at the edge of the tree line to the east of the landing strip. I watched as a small plane rolled to a stop. For a moment, it was silent. The engine of the plane whirred, and Rayna and I stood in the shadows, waiting for something to happen.

BOOM!

The right wing of the plane blew up! Fragments of the wing came hurling at us, and we dodged a flaming piece just in time. When I looked back up, I could see them. Vampires. They ran out of the terminal to check on the explosion, and just as they did, Domino and his men came jumping over the stone wall opposite where we stood.

"Well, boo, this is when I bounce." Rayna suddenly looked like she was happy to be missing out on all the fun. "Good luck!"

"I—"

Rayna disappeared. Maverick roared. And the other wing of the plane blew up!

23

That bitch is strong!

"Jai!" I said my sister's name. She was on the plane, and it had just exploded. I was supposed to be there to save her. Had I already failed? Instinct said run to her, run to my sister despite the vampires who would surely attack me. I had to make sure she was okay.

Before I could take a step, a hand clamped down on my shoulder. *Oh shit, it's a vampire!* That was my only thought before I lifted my hand from my side and turned. I was going to blow the bastard's head off its shoulders. Luckily, Jackie's reflexes were better than my own. My hand lit up, charged with energy, and just as I aimed, she dipped down, slapping my hand away from her face.

"Holy shit, girl!" Jackie said as the power around my hand fizzled out. "Watch where you aim that!" She grabbed my other hand and dragged me deeper into the cover of the trees.

"Sorry, I thought you were one of them." I pulled her into my arms. "Are you okay?"

"I'm good. How did you get here?"

"That friend I told you about. When we made it back to the house, you were all gone." I looked back at the plane. "Jai. We have to save Jai."

"I know what it looks like, but she's okay. Trust me." Jackie tugged me further away from the air strip. "We have it all under control."

"You intentionally blew up the plane my sister is on, and you're telling me you have it all under control?" I shook my head. "You expect me to believe that? I have to get to Jai."

"It's a controlled explosion. We had to find some way to get the vampires out here." She pointed to the plane. "Look closely. The plane isn't actually on fire. It's a decoy."

"How?" I didn't know what she was talking about, but it eased the pain in my chest.

"Lena is a lot more powerful than we thought, and she's getting stronger," Jackie said proudly. "It's her magic doing this."

"Lena? Really?" I looked closer, expecting to see my friend near the plane, but she wasn't there. "So, Jai is okay?"

"Jai is currently under a sleep spell; we figured it would be best if we could avoid having her witness this. It will give us a better chance of wiping her memory of everything. The less she sees, the less there is to remove."

"Right, Lena did say that was a thing." I took a deep breath. "Okay, so what do we do now?"

"We wait. Domino and his men are doing their job." She pointed out where the two groups of vampires fought. Some moved so fast, all I could see was the blur of hair and fabric. "The hunters are still in the trees. We'll wait here for our signal to join the fight. Trust me, the hunters are eager to get out there. It's been a long time since we've had a fight like this."

"I'll take that as a good thing."

"It is." She winked and then wiggled her fingers in my face. "What about you, sparkle fingers?"

"I'm okay," I confirmed.

"Okay is good, but are you ready for a fight?" She held up a fist.

"I'm ready for whatever it takes to save my sister." I looked back at the plane.

"Good." Jackie looked at me. "What exactly did your magical friend do?"

"The short story is, she took me to a world where time moves slower so I could have more time to train. For you, I've been away for a couple hours, but for me, it was half a day. I'm not going to pretend like I'm the best, but," I lifted my hand and pulled the light to my fingers, "I can control it now. I can target it. With more time, I'll get better at it, but for now, this is enough to help save my sister."

"Damn, you even sound like a different person." Jackie smacked my shoulder. "Perfect, because this world needs warriors, people ready for the battle."

"You really do enjoy this, don't you?"

"Hell yeah, I was born for it." Jackie smiled, and then another explosion sounded. She perked up even more as the flames spread. Less than a second later, the other hunters ran out of the woods. "That's our mark! Let's go!"

"What should I do?"

"Keep up and aim your sparkle power at anyone who gets near you!" Jackie took off running.

Now, this woman knew damn well I couldn't keep up with her. Jackie was at least seven paces ahead of me before I even took my first step, but it didn't matter. I was going to make it. Maverick kept an even pace with me as I ran, and at first, nothing happened. I watched the hunters and vampires collide and paid as close attention to my surroundings as I could. After a while, it was hard to hear much over my own heavy breathing, but I kept going.

"Got one!" A vampire with a bald head and wearing a small pink skirt dropped in front of me. He paired the skirt with a purple tank top and a long tie that tucked into the top of his skirt.

I skid to a stop, feeling the sting in my ankle when I did.

"Pretty and plump. What are you doing out here?"

"Rude!" I snapped, ready to defend myself, but I didn't have to.

Just then, Maverick jumped through the air over my shoulder. I saw his fluffy underbelly pass by me, and then, his claws ripped through the tank top and tore the flesh beneath it.

"Ah!" the vampire screamed and swiped at Maverick, but the cat moved faster than ever. He dropped to the ground, ran around the vampire, and tore through his ankles before hitting the back of his knees. The vampire fell to the ground and placed his hands over the wounds as they healed. Maverick then jumped on his chest and started ripping through him.

It all happened so fast, I could hardly believe my annoying cat had done it. When he was done, he waddled back to my side.

"That's for calling me plump," I said, and we started running again.

I couldn't see Jackie anymore, but I knew what I had to do. Get to the plane. Get to Jai. Get her the hell out of there. My heart raced as I ran through the chaos. Maverick was my shield and weapon, attacking any vampire who dared to make me a target. Each time the cat came into view, he was larger, as if the kills were fueling his growth. By the time we made it to the heart of the battle, Maverick's head was waist-high as he stood on all fours.

"Jackie!" I saw my friend again, battling the vampires. She was amazing, cutting down one vampire while simultaneously dodging another.

"Whit!" she called my name and threw a stake at me. It whizzed by me, creating a whistle in my ear before landing in the chest of the vampire behind me.

I underestimated how quickly my friend could move, because the woman made it to my side before the vampire hit the ground.

"Another point for me!" Jackie smacked her own ass in celebration of her kill.

"Are you honestly keeping score?" I frowned at her.

"Hell yeah. Miguel thinks he can outdo me." She flexed her muscles. "He's never beat me, not once."

"Right." This woman was actually enjoying herself, having fun in the middle of a battle. Not twenty feet from us, a vampire's head went flying into the grass, and Jackie looked moments away from calling for a twerk battle with the other hunters.

Maverick must have believed I was safe with Jackie, because he threw his head back and let out a noise that sounded like the howl of a wolf before he ran off. It wasn't long before the mass of black hair disappeared into the trees.

"Damn, he's gotten big," Jackie said as she threw out another stake. She tapped her waistband, and another one appeared.

"How?" I pointed at the band.

"I'm going to tell you this now: any question of 'how' is answered with one word. Magic. We don't have time for lengthy explanations." She winked and grabbed my arm, pulling me toward the plane. "Let's go. Stick close to me."

I struggled to keep up with Jackie, even though I could tell she'd reduced her speed to accommodate my slower pace. As I struggled to breathe and run at the same time, I wanted to tell her to go ahead without me. I would catch up eventually, and she wouldn't lose time getting to my sister.

Before I could say anything, something or someone slammed into Jackie. I didn't see what it was, but I watched my friend fly away from me. Her body moved through the air like a doll tossed aside in favor of a new toy before her back slammed to the ground with a loud thud.

"Jackie!" I screamed her name and ran over to her.

"Nuh-uh." Sharp nails dug into my scalp as someone pulled me away from my friend. "You're not going anywhere."

"Let me go." I struggled, clawing at the faceless person behind me.

"I don't think I will. You think you can bust up into our home, hurt our king, and walk away without consequence?" The woman pushed me further away from Jackie, and I looked up to find a purple afro above a pissed-off Nyesha.

"Are we forgetting the part when your people came and snatched me up?" I rubbed the back of my head where my scalp stung from her nails. "It's not my fault your leader made a fool of himself."

"I don't care. You need to pay for hurting our king. Now is when that happens."

Nyesha flashed forward, coming just a foot away from me, and then slammed her hand into my chest. I fell back and hit the ground. Suddenly, the woman was on top of me, straddling my hips to keep me down.

"I know we're not supposed to taste, but how can I not?" She quickly dropped her fangs and tried to bite me, but the invisible barrier over my skin that kept Reddick away did the same for her. Nyesha struggled for a moment, pressing herself harder into me, but nothing happened.

"What the hell?" She lifted and frowned at me. "What is this?"

"I didn't say you could bite me, bitch." I called the energy to my palm just as I had practiced with Rayna and shoved my palm into her forehead with all I the strength had. The explosion of power knocked her off me, and she flew back just like Jackie had when she was hit, only the vampire landed on her feet.

"Ahhhh!" she screamed. "It burns. Why does it burn?" She clawed at her face, but I couldn't see her with her head down. I got up from the ground and moved closer to Jackie, just in case the skank tried to attack again.

"My face!" Nyesha finally looked up, and I gagged at the sight of her. Her skin had melted, dripping from her face like ice cream left out on a hot day.

"That's nasty." Jackie appeared at my side again.

"Yes, it is." I put my hand over my nose, fearful of whatever smell melted flesh would produce.

Nyesha touched her face and cried. "What is this? No. No, no. Not my face! You ruined my face, you fat bitch!"

"Who you calling fat, bitch?" Jackie snatched a stake from her side and threw it at Nyesha. Even with her face melting, she was fast enough to dodge it.

"You'll pay for this." She pointed at me, tears running down the unmarred side of her face, and ran into the trees.

"Good job. I mean, she's definitely going to hold a grudge, but problem solved for now," Jackie complimented me. "Now, let's go. We're getting out of here."

Maybe it was the fat comment from the melting vampire, but I found the energy to keep up with Jackie as we circled to the other side of the plane. If I thought the fight was bad before, now, it was worse. I quickly spotted Domino. He looked like a warrior—still wearing his glasses, but his shirt was torn, revealing his chest, and blood covered him. My concern for him vanished, though, the moment he ripped a vampire's neck open with his bare hand. Blood sprayed across the scene, coating his face.

He wiped it away and looked up at me, and my heart raced even more. *Now is not the time!* I fussed at myself for being turned on by his savagery.

Domino took one step toward me then veered left to snatch a vampire off the back of a hunter. The man swung at Domino, but he grabbed him by the shoulder and pulled, ripping his arm straight from the socket. The vampire cried out as the hunter drove a stake through his heart. Domino locked his gaze on me, dropped the arm, and ran off to continue the fight.

"Damn," I muttered. Part of me wished I could continue watching him fight, but I had to focus.

"The veil will drop soon. We have to move," Jackie called out.

"Veil, what veil?" I looked around, as if I would see a piece of fabric draped over the area.

"The one keeping your sister safe." She pointed to the door of the plane, and I could see a fuzzy haze over the front of it. "Once it's down, we won't have long. I'll run in and grab her. You use your fancy light hands to cover me and melt any vamp who dares come near those steps."

"I can do that." I charged my fingertips and wiggled them in front of me.

Jackie led the way, and when we reached the steps, she darted up them. I wanted to follow her, to make sure my sister was okay, but I knew the part I had to play. I turned my back to the door and kept my eye on the battling vampires. They moved so fast, I could hardly keep up with them.

"Alright, Lena!" Jackie shouted. "Any time now!"

I glanced back at Jackie moments before the strange sensation passed over me. The veil in front of the plane pulled back, and instead of being in front of the door, it was between me and the rest of the battle. I placed my hand against the sheer surface, and it felt like tapping the top of still water. "Did Lena do this on her own?"

As soon as the veil moved, Jackie darted inside the plane. I turned my attention back to the vampires just as one approached me. He was big, with a long scar across his neck, like someone had tried to rip his head off.

"Stay back," I warned him.

"Or what?" He chuckled, and then another vampire appeared beside him.

"This one smells yummy."

"I get first bite," the big one said.

"No one is biting me!" I yelled out and pulled the charge of energy through my body. The light shot from my hand like a missile, smashing into the chest of the big guy. It danced across his body like a flame following a trail of fuel. He screamed and fell to his knees, ripping at his chest as the light chewed through him.

"What the hell was that?" The other vampire pulled a knife from his pocket and darted toward me. I shot another blast of the light energy but missed; instead, it hit another vampire fighting a hunter.

"Shit." I shook my hands as I tried to find the other vampire. "Where did he go?"

My answer came in the form of a hand around my throat.

"Ack!" I slapped his arm and struggled to break free.

"This is when you die." Honestly, his words might have been more impressive if I hadn't already charged my hand with more light and pressed it against his chest.

He looked down at my hand and then back at me. "Oh, shit."

Blast!

The power shot from my hand and tore right through his chest, leaving a hole big enough to put my head through. He dropped his hand from around my neck, and his fingers poked through the empty space. This wasn't a wound he could heal from. He pouted, actually poked his lip out, before he fell flat on the ground.

"Oh, my God. Did you do that?" Lena ran to my side. She kicked the vampire over and gagged at the sight of the hole in his chest. "I mean, you blew right through him! Whit! How?"

"It's too much to explain right now."

She looked around at the scene. "Right. Where is Jackie? It's time to go."

"I don't know." I pointed to the door. "She went inside."

"She should have come out by now." Lena looked worried.

"What?"

"Whitney." Domino appeared next to me, covered in blood. He glanced down at the body on the ground, and the corner of his lips lifted with pleasure.

"Domino." There was more blood covering him than before, which might have been a turn-on had it not been for what looked like a piece of ear stuck in his hair.

"Are you okay?" he asked.

"I'm not the one covered in blood." I pointed at his hair. "And body matter."

"You," he started then froze, looking up at the door to the plane. "No."

His expression made my stomach drop. "What is it?"

Lena and I looked back at the door just as Jackie flew out of it. Domino ran to catch her mid-air, and they slid back from the impact, but Domino remained on his feet. He sat Jackie down just as Lena and I made it to them.

"What happened?" I asked her trying to help her claim a steady footing.

"Damn, that bitch is strong." Jackie rubbed her side.

"What?" Lena asked. "Who is?"

"Reddick," Domino said his brother's name, and I followed his line of sight just as the vampire appeared at the door.

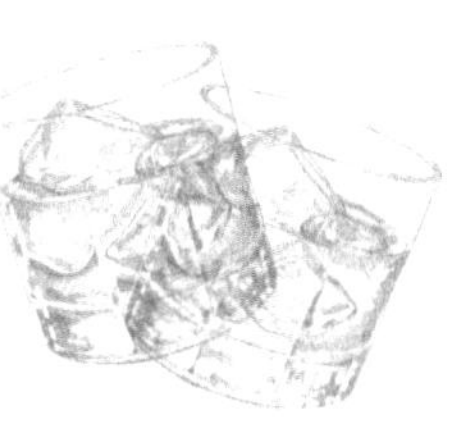

24

Brother's Play

Reddick walked down the steps like a man strutting the runway. He wasn't in the middle of a bloody battle between vampires and hunters—he was showing off his full suit and tie. When he reached the bottom, he gingerly stepped over the dead one I'd left there, refusing to get anything on his shoes.

We stood a good fifteen feet away from him, but he didn't approach any further. Instead, he waved his hand, and two other vampires appeared at his side. I only recognized one of them as the man who usually accompanied the woman with the purple afro and currently melting face.

Vance.

Vance looked at me like he wanted to rip my head from my shoulders. I assumed he knew about what I did to his partner. It wasn't as if the woman tried to bite me for the second time!

"Brother." Reddick kept his eyes locked on Domino.

"Reddick," Domino responded.

"What are you doing here?" Reddick asked as if he had no clue.

"You know what we're doing here." Domino stiffened beside me. "You can't have the girl."

"Are you planning to stop me?" he chuckled. "This pathetic group you've pulled together. You can't be serious."

"Oh, I am. And you're seriously underestimating us right now."

"Teaming up with hunters?" His face was painted with disgust as he turned his nose up at Jackie and then looked at Lena. "And a witch? Brother, you have lost your way." He looked down at the man with the hole in his chest. "Though, whoever did that, I applaud. That's impressive."

"I know how you operate, Reddick. You're stalling. You don't care who I spend my time with," Domino said. "And I sure as hell don't care if you're impressed. Cut the shit."

"Dammit." Reddick rolled his eyes. "I was really hoping we could drag this out a little more. You know how much I've missed playing with you!"

"This isn't a game," Jackie said.

"Oh, the hunter who keeps score of her vampire kills is telling me this isn't a game? Really?" He laughed. "It doesn't matter. We're done here. I have the girl, and there is nothing you can do to stop me."

As the smile spread across Reddick's face, another vampire appeared: a woman built like she spent hours lifting weights. She cradled Jai's limp body in her arms. She looked me dead in the eye and smiled, as if challenging me to try to take my sister from her. If I wasn't afraid of blasting through my little sister, I would have sent light through her ugly face.

"So, brother," Reddick pointed at Domino, "how do you plan to stop me?"

"I don't know about your brother, but I'm going to put my foot so far up your ass, you're going to regret hitting me!" Jackie threatened.

"Bring it on, little hunter!"

"Condescending piece of shit!" Jackie raged as she ran for Reddick. I expected him to defend himself, but he didn't have to. The vampire behind him stepped into Jackie's path, and the two collided. While Jackie fought his helper, Vance took the opportunity to make me his target.

The second he made his move, Domino pushed me behind him. He was my protector, but unfortunately, his brother took offense to his position and attacked before Vance could reach us. He flashed across the field and punched Domino so hard, my vampire guard flew away from me.

"Domino!" I called out, Reddick on top of him. The brothers fought against each other, throwing blows.

"Whitney, watch out!" Lena pushed me to the side and tossed a handful of glittering powder into the vampire's face.

Vance screamed and jumped back from us.

I moved closer to Lena, grabbing her arm. "What was that?"

"A special mix I made up." She handed me a pouch. "It won't kill them, but it will slow them down."

The sounds of Reddick and Domino's battle called every vampire and hunter to the area where we stood. Lena and I tossed the powder at the enemy vampires as we tried to push toward my sister. The woman holding her had retreated up the steps of the plane, now looking down on the battle below.

"I have to get Jai," I told Lena as another vampire dropped in front of us.

"I'll cover you." She blew the powder into the vampire's face, and he ran right into a hunter's stake.

Lena had my back, but even with her help, I made it no closer to my sister. It was like every step I took, I got pushed back three.

"How many of these damn things are there?" I called out in frustration.

"I don't know, but I'm running out of powder!" Lena called back.

I stopped to scan the scene. Jackie and Miguel fought back-to-back, taking out vampires. The other hunters worked through the battle. They were holding their own, but I could tell some of them were tiring.

How long could they keep it up? Even the vampires on our side looked like they were running out of steam. Every time we ended a wave, another would come. How many vampires had Reddick called?

"That's it," I muttered and then pulled the light into my hand. It was time for target practice. I shot a blast at a vampire's back, and it hit him perfectly.

He screamed and fell to his knees, clawing at his back, but nothing he did would put out the flame.

"Oh, so you're the one!" Reddick called out, and, as if Domino was no threat to him, he charged me.

His brother, however, wasn't allowing that. He was back on him, punching and fighting.

I continued blasting the vampires around me and leveling the playing field, but with each shot, I felt myself weaken. It helped, but I wasn't sure how long I could keep it up.

Suddenly, a strong hand gripped my throat and threw me down to the hard ground.

I turned over to see Nyesha standing above me. Her face was still partially melted, and her top lip looked like it might just fall off completely. She would not forgive me for that. I lifted my hand, hoping to blast her, but she kicked my hand to the side, and I felt the bone snap in my wrist.

"Ah!" I screamed as the pain shot up my arm.

"Whit!" Lena reached into her bag, but her face dropped when she realized she was out of her special powder.

"Enough of that!" Nyesha sneered and swatted Lena away. I watched my friend slide across the ground, her back knocked against the front tire of the plane. "I'm done playing games!"

Nyesha lifted me from the ground.

"Let me go!"

"Oh no, I don't think I will," she snapped. "I'm going to let you watch your lover die. And then, I'm going to rip your head from your shoulders."

Nyesha grabbed me by the throat again and held me back to her chest as she positioned me to watch what played out. Vance had recovered from Lena's attack, now fighting alongside Reddick. Though the rest of the vampires on their side had either died or fled in fear of my attack, they were still strong, and they were taking it out on Domino.

"No!" I cried out as they double-teamed him.

Reddick held him by the arms as Vance punched him repeatedly in the chest.

Blood spilled from Domino's lips, and I was sure it was his own.

"Oh, no," Nyesha teased me. "It looks like your lover is going to die. So sad. He was a great vampire but clearly flawed if he fell for you!"

"Fuck you," I said as I tried to look away from Domino's beating, but she grabbed my jaw and forced me to look back. "Domino!"

I called out his name, and he looked over at me. Something dark flashed in his eyes, and Domino kicked Vance in the chest, pushing him back into his brother. The brothers fell to the ground, and Domino prepared to defend himself against Vance, knowing the vampire would never relent. He didn't need to defend himself, though, because Jackie was on top of Vance in a flash.

My hunter bestie jumped through the air and planted her knee on the back of Vance's neck. She then raised the stake over her head, ready to plunge it into him, but Vance was quick. He knocked her away, but before he could attack, Miguel joined Jackie. The two of them took it to Vance, leaving Domino to deal with Reddick.

"Dammit," Nyesha complained just as Domino's back crashed into the side of the plane.

I looked back over to see Reddick standing triumphantly across from us. Domino's body lay limp on the ground.

"No!" I cried out, and Reddick turned his attention to me.

"Perfect." He smiled and ran for me. "You're mine."

In an instant, Reddick appeared, towering over me with a look like he wanted to bite me. But we both knew he wouldn't try it. How would it look to the other vampires if he couldn't do it?

"Get away from me," I warned him.

"Or what?" He frowned and then slapped me. My face stung from the contact with his palm, but I refused to cry. "You're mine now. I can have you both, and no one is going to stop me."

"Fuck you!" I cursed.

Reddick pulled his hand back, poised to slap me again, but his hand stopped mid-swing. Reddick's eyes bulged, and he gurgled the blood in his mouth as he tried to speak words I would never understand. I looked down to see the hand poking out of his chest.

The face staring back at me over Reddick's shoulder wasn't the one I expected. Instead of meeting the torn expression of his brother, the man I saw inspired a new fear in my gut. Vance, face covered in blood, peered back at me.

"Funny thing about that. I want her for myself," he said as he pulled his hand out of Reddick's chest and the vampire king fell to the ground, dead.

I gasped at the sight of Reddick's body.

"And now, it's your turn." Vance smiled at me.

"No!"

"Vance!" Domino crashed into Vance.

"Oh, now this is good," Nyesha said. I expected the bitch to be concerned about the dead king in front of us, but clearly, she knew Vance was going to turn on him. "He's been waiting years to do this. Vance and Dom. The battle of the ages! Everyone thought it was going to be Reddick, but no. Vance. It's always been Vance."

"Let me guess: you're his fan girl?"

She grabbed my wrist and squeezed it. I felt the bones crack under the pressure and cried out in pain.

"Show some damn respect!" she cursed.

"Whit!" Lena called out to me. I could see her out of the corner of my eye, still on the ground but pointing to where I knew the vampire had my sister.

That was it. I had to do something.

"Nothing said the power had to come out of my hand." I frowned.

"What?" Nyesha asked.

I pulled the energy into my core, just as always, but this time, instead of pushing it out of my hands, I pushed it to the top of my body. When it reached my head, I slammed it back into Nyesha. There was a bright flash of light, and then Nyesha let me go. I turned around, clutching my broken wrist to my chest as she fell to the ground, her entire face smashed in.

"Oh shit!" I gasped.

Nyesha wasn't done, though. The woman jumped back to her feet, face completely disfigured, and pulled out a knife. She charged at me. I tried to pull the power to my other hand; if I could pushed it through my damn brain, what was another hand? Only, I wasn't fast enough. Nyesha ran at me, and though I tried to sidestep her, her blade still cut into me. It tore through my arm.

I looked down at the flow of my blood and back up at the vampire who sneered through melted flesh.

"Whit!" Lena was by my side, pulling me further away from the vampire. "This isn't good."

That was when I noticed: every vampire, including the ones who were supposed to be on our side, stopped. Their eyes snapped toward me and my open wound.

"Shit." I tried to stop the flow of blood, but it was too much.

"She's mine!" Nyesha cried out and reached for me, hissing.

"No!" Domino ran and smashed into Nyesha, sending her flying into the trees.

The other vampires zeroed in on us.

That was when Maverick reemerged. My big ass cat ran out of the shadows, roaring like a lion. He leaped across the tarmac and landed in front of me. I saw his body shift and where once stood a massive cat, a dragon, exploded. He was far larger than any form that could wrap around me like he had before. He roared, and every vampire fled.

"Yes!" Lena jumped from the ground, cheering, but her celebration came too soon.

Vance hadn't run away like the others. He attacked. And as Vance made his move, Domino defended me once again. The two collided, and there was nothing I could do. The next thing I knew, Maverick used his mouth to snatch me up by the braids before he dropped me onto his back and took off running. I looked back to see my sister in the arms of the vampire. The muscled bitch smiled deviously and took off running in the opposite direction.

"No!" I cried out. "Jai!"

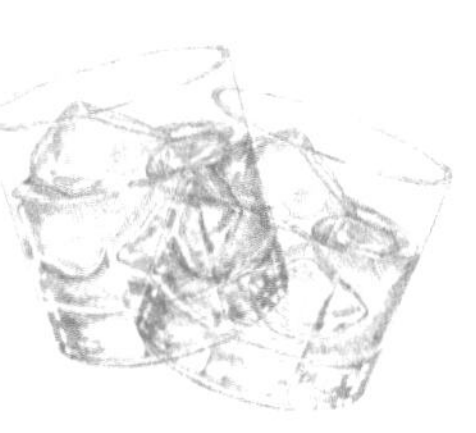

25

Dragon Cat

I clung to the back of my dragon cat with my one good hand as he ran through the night. I had no other fucking choice! If I let go, I would fly off and slam into a tree or something. A broken wrist was bad enough; I wanted to spare the rest of my bones. Lucky for me, there was a line of hair down his back, which I wrapped my hand in. My thighs clamped around him as best I could, but within minutes, they were burning. I knew I should have done those damn squats with Lena!

Maverick moved so fast, I had to shut my eyes against the rush of wind. I buried my face in his back and prayed I survived the ride. When the gushing air flow stopped, I opened my eyes to see the parking garage. Maverick had taken me home. How he'd managed to get there without anyone seeing him, I had no idea. Also, I didn't know if that was true, but immediately determined it wasn't my problem to deal with. Let the vampires solve it, since they were the reason all this was happening anyway.

He lowered himself to the ground so I could climb off, and once I was safely standing, he shrunk back to his cat form. I squinted at him; he wasn't the lion-sized beast that tore through vampires, but he wasn't exactly his normal size either.

"Maverick, you okay, buddy?" I observed him as he licked himself. The self-grooming did little to improve his appearance. He had blood in his hair, and his whiskers were stained pink.

Despite his unsettling appearance, the cat nodded as if he understood me, purred, and walked toward the door.

"I should go find the others." I turned in the opposite direction of the cat and found my parking spot empty. "Damnit. Domino took my car to Jackie's."

I patted my pockets and realized not only did I not have my phone, but I also didn't have my keys. That meant in order to get into my place, I would have to go down to the lobby and face the boy at the front desk.

"Oh, my God! Ms. Harris!" Cordell slammed the book in front of him closed and ran over to me as soon as I entered the lobby. "Are you okay? Did you get into a fight?"

"Something like that." I nodded. "I also lost my key. Can you help me out?"

Rawwar. Maverick fussed beside me.

Cordell looked down at the cat, and his eyes widened.

"What happened to Maverick?"

"He's a fighter too." I winked. "Key?"

"Oh yeah. Sorry," he said nervously before grabbing the key from behind the desk and leading me to the elevator.

We rode up the elevator in awkward silence. I could almost feel the questions spinning in Cordell's mind. Of course, he would have a hundred questions about why I looked the way I did and what the hell was all over my cat, but the kid kept his mouth closed. Clearly, he had a momma who taught him to mind his business. Nothing good could come of him learning about what I'd been up to. I told myself I just had to make it into my apartment. Once I was inside, he would go back to the front desk and eventually forget about me and my mess. Unfortunately, when the elevator door opened, all hope of him forgetting what he saw flew out the damn window.

"Holy shit!" Cordell cursed then looked at me with much more suspicion than before.

The hallway outside my apartment was completely fucked! There were holes in the walls, blood on the floor, and what looked like claw marks on the carpet. Those vampires had torn the shit up. I said nothing. I didn't want to incriminate myself, but considering I was the only one living on that level and I was coming home covered in blood, I was already the prime suspect. Still, I kept my mouth shut and followed him to my door. As soon as it was open, he stepped aside. I nodded at him and slid into my home, wondering how long it would take management to talk to me.

"Damn trying to pay a mortgage. They're going to kick my ass out of this building." I sighed and pressed my back against the door.

How the hell had things gotten so bad so quickly? A week prior, my biggest worry was finishing my pitch for a seaside artist and choosing the color pallet for my bathroom, then being scolded by Jackie for even mentioning the color mauve to her. Now, I was bleeding out, with a broken wrist and sore thighs, after riding a dragon home from a vampire fight.

Maverick slapped my leg with his paw and headed straight for his bowl. Damn my inner thoughts or self-loathing. The kings needed to be fed!

"Really? You're bugging me for food now?" I fussed. "No, no. Don't worry about it. We lost my sister to a bunch of vampires and my friends could all be dead. But you must eat!"

I marched down the hall and, despite wanting to scream, I didn't. Maverick had saved my life. Who knows what would have happened to me after being cut open while surrounded by vampires? After filling his bowl, I found the first aid kit. Nothing I had was good enough to handle the cut on my arm, but going to the hospital was not an option. How would I explain what happened? Instead, I poured peroxide into the wound, waited for the fizzling to stop, and wrapped it about a hundred times with gauze, using every roll I had.

Sitting at the kitchen counter, surrounded by the bloody mess, I looked at my custom couch. Funny how just a few days prior, that couch meant the world to me. It was the marker of my success. I'd made it to the top. But damn it if life didn't give me a swift kick in the ass. At that point, I felt lower than I ever had. It didn't matter how low I felt. Jai was out there—because of me, her life was in danger. I had to get her back.

I stood, a newfound determination making me forget about the blood loss, and marched over to the door. I could catch a cab or ask the front desk to call me a ride. There wasn't any point in trying to hide what happened. He would have already reported my mess to management anyway.

I had only made it halfway down the hall when I heard a sharp knock on the door.

I froze. Fear took over my body, and my mind raced with thoughts of attack. What if it was a vampire? What if it was Nyesha? She knew where I lived. She could have been there trying to finish what she started. The only thing I knew for sure was that if it was a vampire, I was safe.

And then, like a scene out of a horror movie, the damn doorknob turned. How the fuck did I forget to lock the damn door? Oh, sure, a city full of monsters chasing you down, no need to lock the fucking door! I don't know what my next move was. Panic told me to run, and I took one step, spun and slammed down so hard, the wall shook.

The door opened, and instinct took over. I lifted my good hand and forced whatever light I had left inside me to shoot out of my palm.

"Damnit!" the voice shouted.

I looked back to see Domino standing in the hall. Behind him, a hole burned in the wall.

"Domino?" I gasped.

"Are you okay?" he asked. "What happened?"

"I-I fell," I said as he ran over to me and lifted me from the floor. "My head."

I looked at the vampire whose glasses were now crooked on his nose, his face blurred.

Domino looked at my arm and saw the blood seeping through the bandage. He moved into action and carried me to my bed. Once there, he bit into his wrist and pressed the wound to my lips.

"Drink. Now!"

"Huh?" I muttered against his lips.

"Whitney, drink. Please," he begged. "You're losing too much blood."

It wasn't long before my own instincts kicked in. Soon, I was gripping his arm and drinking from him like an ice-cold beer on a hot summer day.

I felt the flow of healing through my body, and soon, the haze lifted from my mind as I saw Domino, looking weaker than I'd ever seen him. I dropped his arm from my lips.

"Domino!" The vampire looked ashen and weak, his eyes sunken and dark. "Oh, my God. What did you do?"

"I did what I had to." He smiled weakly. "You're okay now."

"Dummy, and now you're going to die! You already lost too much blood fighting!" I fussed at him.

"I'll be fine. The sun is coming up soon. I'll recover."

"Is that how it really works?"

He didn't respond.

"Damn it."

"Don't worry about me. You're okay now."

"Where is your phone?" I patted his pockets and found relief when I felt the device inside his pants.

"What are you doing?" He frowned as I lifted his finger to the scanner on the screen to unlock the phone.

"I'm calling Jackie." I dropped his hand once the phone accepted his fingerprint. "She got you blood once. Maybe she can do it again."

A quick search found Jackie's contact stored as, "Whitney's Big Mouth Hunter." After rolling my eyes, I dialed her number and waited. It went straight to voicemail.

"Damnit." I waited for her greeting to play. "Jackie, this is Whitney. I'm at my place. Domino is here, and he's hurt badly. He needs blood. Please call me back on his phone as soon as you get this."

I ended the call and set the phone beside me.

"You need to lie down." I pointed to the head of the bed. "Now."

"Yes, ma'am." He grinned.

"Now is not the time for jokes!" I fussed at him. "You're dying! Lena and Jackie are missing, and those vampires have Jai! I need you to be okay, Domino."

"I'm sorry. Whitney, I promise I'm not going to die. I've been through far worse than this. And we're going to get your sister back. They won't hurt her. They know how valuable she is." He promised me, but I didn't believe him. The man looked gray, not like the stone he was when he slept. This was more like the sickly gray of a man in his final moments.

"Just rest." I didn't want to think about what Vance and Nyesha would do to my sister. "Jackie will come through. She always does."

"I'm sure she will."

"Domino?"

"Yes."

"This is probably the wrong time to ask you this, but are you okay? Not physically. I can see you're not. But your brother died tonight. I know you two weren't the best of friends, but he was your brother."

"Yes, he was. And I don't know how I feel about it. I've imagined ending his life myself so many times." Domino looked out the window. "It's strange to say part of me is sad I wasn't the one to take his life. He took so much from me. It was the least I could do to pay him back for over a century of misery."

"Do you want to talk about it?"

"I'd love to, but the sun will be rising soon."

"Right." I reached over and hit the button on the side table. The curtain slid shut.

"Whitney, lay down," Domino said. "You still need to rest while your body finishes recovering."

"How do you expect me to sleep?"

"I don't. I expect you to lie next to me while I do. Because, unlike you, I don't have a choice in the matter."

"Fine."

I climbed into bed next to Domino and waited for the woodsy scent to feel my room as he slipped into his sleep state, but it never came. Domino's eyes closed, but it wasn't the same. Before, when he slept, I couldn't see him breathing. It was as if he had turned into a statue. That time was different. For hours, I watched his chest struggle to rise and fall. Then, as the day went on, a soft whistle came from his nose. I watched the hours pass and called Jackie three times before she answered.

"Did you get my message?"

"Yes, I'm waiting for the delivery," Jackie said. "Are you okay? What happened?"

"Maverick brought me home, and Domino showed up here. He lost too much blood, and then he gave me his. Now he's dying, Jackie. I can't let him die."

"Don't worry. That stubborn vampire won't die, Whitney. I don't like him, but he cares about you, so I'm going to do whatever I can to help. We'll be there in a couple of hours."

"Okay. Thank you, Jackie. Really." I stared at the phone a while longer after Jackie hung up.

I checked the time. It was already six o'clock. The sun would set soon. Would he make it that long? Time was slipping away, and with each tick of the clock, my desperation grew. Finally, unable to bear the weight of my fear any longer, I raced to the kitchen and snatched a knife from the counter. I returned to the bed where he lay, clearly struggling and clinging to life.

"I hope this doesn't kill you." I slid the blade across my wrist and held the wound to his lips.

Nothing happened. At first, I sat there, pressing my bloody wrist to his lips and just hoping he would take it. I almost gave up, but then his eyes opened, and he grabbed hold of my arm and accepted my blood. At first, he was careful, and it was almost like he didn't want it.

"Is my blood not good enough for you?" I pressed my wrist against his lips harder. "Drink, damn it! You promised me you wouldn't die."

He locked eyes with me, and when I nodded, eyes brimming with tears, Domino pressed his lips against my flesh and drank from me. This was the point when I thought he would turn into a ravishing monster. He would grip my arm so hard, I would lose feeling and be on the brink of death. That didn't happen. Domino was careful with me. Even though his pull was getting stronger, it was clear how much effort he was putting into keeping himself in check.

The vampire was careful, but that didn't eliminate all the risks. I felt the blood rushing through my arm to feed him. As nervous as I was that he might not stop, I was also relieved to see the life return to him. In minutes, his skin returned to normal, and he looked just as strong as the first day I met him.

"Domino," I said when my head started spinning. That couldn't be a good sign. I hadn't slept a wink and had barely recovered from my injuries.

When he looked up again and saw the worry in my expression, Domino gripped my arm and jerked away, pressing his back against the headboard.

"Whitney," he panted. "Why would you do that?"

"You were dying, and I had to sit here for hours watching you struggle. I wasn't about to let you die." I held my wrist to my chest. The blood still flowed from the wound.

Domino poked his finger with his tooth and rubbed his blood over the opening on my wrist. It quickly closed.

"That's new."

"Yeah, for small injuries, it comes in handy."

"Are you okay?" I peered at him. "My blood—it's not like toxic or anything, is it?"

"No, I mean, I'm fine." He paused, really considering my questions. "Actually, I feel great. Better than I have in years."

"Good. I was worried you would explode." I still watched him for any signs of a delayed reaction.

"You can stop looking at me like that."

"Oh, sorry." I hopped from the bed. "Now that you're up, I can open these curtains. I'm tired of sitting without a view of the sky."

I pressed the button next to the bed, and the curtains rolled open.

And sunlight spilled into the room!

"Oh, shit!" I ran, trying to pull the curtain back and failing against the mechanical system that opened them. "Hide!"

"Wait." Domino touched my shoulder, and I looked back at him. He stood in the sunlight—not fucking burning.

"Holy shit!" I gasped.

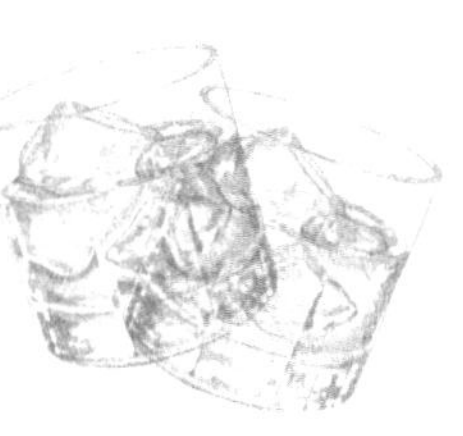

26

The L Word

"You're not burning up." I clung to the curtain, ready to swing it close if he suddenly went up in flames. "I mean, I don't really know if vampires burn up, but you're fine."

"We do burn, and no, I'm not." He held his hand up to the light and smiled as the warmth from the setting sun spread across his flesh. "I have not felt the sun on my skin in over a century."

"How is this possible?" I watched him closely. "I mean, are you still a vampire?"

Domino smiled, and his fangs appeared. "Yes. I'm still a vampire. I think it's your blood, Whitney. You did this by giving me your blood."

"Well, I'll be damned." I let go of the curtain to step closer to him. When I poked him in the arm, he frowned at me. "They were right about my blood being some magical cure for your kind?"

"It looks that way." Domino smiled, but as his joy grew, my relief that I hadn't barbecued his ass turned into a deep concern.

They were right. Inside my veins was the stuff every vampire wanted. By drinking my blood, they could be free to walk around at all times of the day, blending in with normal people. When would humans be safe if that happened? And what other rules did my blood bend for them? Would they be able to enter homes without an invitation?

"Whitney, what's wrong?" Domino asked. "I can tell by your expression your mind is racing. Talk to me."

"Huh?" The running list of questions drowned out everything else.

"You look worried." He put his hand on my shoulder. "I'm okay, I promise."

"Of course." I tried to shake off my fears, but instead, they just slipped right out of my big mouth. "Okay, so you're good now. And you can walk in the sun. There's nothing to worry about except other vampires finding out about this and wanting my blood. They're already after me with no confirmation, but as soon as they find out about you, it's going to give them even more cause to attack. And what about Jai? What will they do to her?"

"I understand your concern." He pulled me into his arms. "But you don't need to panic. We're going to keep you safe."

"Just like we kept my sister safe? No, I'm not. I, uh, we should go. Yes. I'll call Jackie and let her know you're good and we'll head over there." I pulled away from him to return to the bed and grabbed his phone then paused and handed it to him. "Actually, you do that. You call Jackie. I'm going to take a shower. I'll be fine."

"Are you sure?" Domino looked at me like he had just broken my heart. And maybe, in some way, that was how I felt—but it wasn't because of him. At least, I didn't think it was.

"No, Domino. I'm not, which is strange for me. I don't know what happens next. But what I do know is I need to scrub my skin clean of all the blood and dirt.

And after that, no matter what, I need to save my sister. That is all I can think about right now. The rest can wait."

"You're right." Domino took a step back. "I'm going to take a run while you do that."

"You're leaving?" The last thing I expected was for him to leave.

"Yes, is that okay?" he asked and held his hand out to me like he wanted to pull me back to him but didn't.

"I, uh…" I thought about what it meant to be home alone and realized I was letting fear control me. I refused to do that. "Yes. Of course. I won't go out, and I have Maverick here. I'll be okay."

"We really need to talk about him," Domino referred to my cat. "I mean, he turned into a damn dragon."

"Yes, we do." I shrugged. "But somehow, a cat dragon isn't the most outrageous thing in my life right now."

That should have broken the tension, but it didn't. The pause between us was so heavy, I felt like it could crush the entire building. That would be a great way to avoid talking to building management about what happened in the hallway. Eventually, Domino nodded and left and I went to shower.

In the bathroom, I realized the blood and dirt were also in my hair. The style was supposed to last a lot longer, but there was no way they would ever feel clean enough to stay in. The strands were matted with what I was pretty sure was flesh, and the sickening, pungent smell told me it was starting to rot.

After a long, painstaking hour of untangling my hair, which was made even more difficult by cutting the extensions a full six inches below my actual hair, I finally stepped into the shower. I mean, I couldn't be sure how much my hair had grown in the week since I put them in. Once I'd washed and deep conditioned my head, I scrubbed my body clean. Then, I carefully put in ten flat twists using my best conditioning twist custard and slapped on my bonnet. Maybe I should have dried it, but I was tired and ready to sleep.

When I came out of the bathroom with freshly brushed teeth, feeling like a new woman, I smiled. Domino had changed the bedding, and on the nightstand was a tray with a cup of tea and a note.

I hope this isn't cold by the time you get out.

I lifted the cup to my lips to sip. It was cold as ice, but it didn't matter. It was the thought that counted.

Exhausted, I climbed into bed, sinking into the soft sheets. The calming scent of tea filled my senses as I took a few more sips before eventually succumbing to sleep.

When I woke up, Domino was sitting in the bed next to me.

"You're awake," he spoke softly.

"How long did I sleep?" I rubbed my eyes and checked to make sure my bonnet hadn't run away in my sleep.

"Just a few hours." He nodded. "I just got back. Decided to clean up while I was gone."

"Oh." I noticed then the fresh clothes he wore. Simple. All black button-up and slacks. And he smelled amazing, that woodsy scent that usually filled the room when he slept. "You look nice."

"Whitney..." Domino held my gaze.

"Yes?" I inhaled; I could sense he was about to drop something heavy in my lap.

"I have to ask you this now, because if I don't, it will be a distraction," he began. "I need a clear head moving forward. I need to know where we stand."

"Okay..." I couldn't believe it. Was Domino giving me the 'what are we' speech?

"Do you regret giving me your blood?" he asked, and no. That was *not* what I expected.

"What? Why would you think that?" I sat up in the bed.

"You looked pretty regretful before," he explained. "I understand you did, what you had to do to save me. You weren't in your right mind, restless and upset about everything that happened. You may have acted rashly."

"No, Domino, I don't regret it. You were dying. I don't care what you say. The only thing I cared about was making sure that didn't happen." I paused for the confidence to continue. "I just never considered what it would do to you besides potentially killing you. Somehow, I forgot about the other side of it. And when I saw you standing in the sun, it terrified me that there could be others who be changed by my blood. What would that mean for the world if vampires could be free to roam, even during the day?"

"Oh." Domino's shoulders relaxed. "We won't let that happen."

"Just like we said we wouldn't let them get Jai. But they have her now." I inhaled slowly to stop myself from getting too upset. "Domino, seeing you in the sun, while amazing, made me realize that this is a level of responsibility I'm struggling to cope with. I didn't want this. It's no one's fault that it's in my blood, but I want someone to blame. A week ago, all my dreams were coming true, and now, I don't even know what I see for my future."

"Is there anything I can do?" He pulled my hand into his. "Whatever it is, just say the word. Whitney, I would do anything for you. If you want me to find that asshole who fired you and rip his throat out, I'll do it. I never liked him anyway."

I couldn't help but laugh at the thought of my former boss running from the vampire and falling on his uncoordinated ass.

"While that sounds appealing, murder isn't the solution for my unemploy-ment." I patted the bed beside me and repeated his earlier request. "Lay here with me."

Domino slid onto the bed beside me, and I put my head on his chest while he spoke.

"I talked to Jackie, and we're going to meet at her place tomorrow. I haven't told her about me yet. Figured it would be good to see the look on her face when she finds out." He chuckled. "I have eyes on your sister and, right now, she is safe. Lena's magic protects her from harm. Jackie and I agree we should let them think they have gotten away and then strike, give them a false sense of comfort while we recover. A few of her hunters were badly hurt, and one woman didn't make it. We also both agree that you need to rest. I told her you are okay. You'll sleep, eat, and then, we'll be on our way."

I sighed. "So I have another caretaker now."

"What?" He looked down at me.

"First Lena and Jackie, now you." I looked up at him. "I'm a lucky woman to have so many people who love me."

"Love?" he repeated the word.

"Oh, I-I didn't mean..." I stammered.

"You didn't mean what?" He narrowed his eyes.

"To imply you love me." I sat up, moving my head away from his chest.

"I see." He touched the spot on his chest where my head was.

"Yeah, I mean, I don't know how you feel about me, and it's only been a week. I just meant that you care for me, or at least you take care of me."

"Stop rambling." He smiled and grabbed my face. "Whitney, I do love you."

"You what?"

"I love you," he repeated and put his thumb over my mouth. "This is not the moment for you to ramble again. You don't have to tell me you love me. You're human, and love takes more time for you. I get that. But I've been around for over a century, and I'm a vampire. Love is different for us. It's instant, a product of the cursed magic that created us. When we find love, we know it from the first moment. I've loved you since I first laid eyes on you. I don't expect you to return that love just because that's how it works for me. I will earn your love because it is worth the effort, with or without the connection our blood has created between us."

My heart raced, and I tried not to hyperventilate beneath his thumb.

"I'm going to remove my hand. When I do, you will say nothing. And then, I'm going to kiss you, because I have craved your lips since I tasted your blood. I can't go without them a moment longer." He smiled. "Nod if you understand."

I nodded.

Domino slowly removed his hand, and then he kissed me. It was a gentle kiss, one that echoed the sentiments of his words. I felt it, his love, through his lips and his hand, which caressed my back as he pulled me closer. Our kiss lingered, and he waited for me to decide what happened next.

Despite all the things I had to worry about, despite the fear that my life could be at risk, I wanted one thing: I wanted Domino to make love to me. But I wouldn't dare say those words out loud. Instead, I fed more urgency into our kiss and tugged at the covers beneath him. Thankfully, he understood my intention without me having to give voice to them.

Moments later, he was undressed and under the covers with me. He slipped my nightgown off and tossed it to the floor before continuing our kiss.

I pulled him on top of me, our lips moving together until I was out of breath. And when I pulled away, gasping for air, Domino's kisses moved from my lips to my chin, then to my neck. He lingered there, one long kiss pressing against my pulse. I froze, expecting him to bite me—and in some ways wishing he would—but he didn't. In this moment, he wanted permission. He wanted me to say it, but I still couldn't bring the words to my lips.

When I didn't speak, his kisses continued down to my breast. He suckled on my nipple and slipped his fingers inside my pussy, hitting that sweet spot time and time again until he coaxed that first orgasm from me.

Then, he brought his fingers to his mouth and licked the taste of me from them before replacing his fingers with his dick. His lips returned to mine as he slipped inside me, inch by agonizing inch, until he could go no further.

I was never a fan of missionary sex, but with Domino, the weight of his body on me, the pressure of his hips, the scent of his neck, the taste of his flesh, it felt overwhelmingly wonderful. I lifted my hips to meet each thrust and moaned when he hit my limits. He moved with slow and powerful strokes, over and over, until once again, the vampire brought me to the edge.

"Domino!" I cried out his name as I came again.

With my release, Domino increased his pace. He slid his hands beneath me, gripping my ass and thrusting harder into me.

"Oh, shit." He buried his face in my neck. "Whitney, yes."

He pressed his lips against my throat, and then, without warning, he came. For five seconds, my head was in the clouds. I was floating, riding the wave of ecstasy, planning my next trip. That was, until I realized he hadn't used a condom.

"Fuck! Oh no." I pushed him off me and hopped out of bed. That was right—I just needed gravity to do its thing.

"What is it?" Domino breathed heavily as he watched me. "Did I hurt you?"

"We didn't use protection!" I pointed at his bare dick still dripping with cum.

"So?" He frowned like I was out of my mind.

"So? Don't look at me like that!" I put my hand on my hip. "Domino, I can't get pregnant right now! And diseases! There are so many damn diseases."

Domino grabbed my wrist and pulled me back to the bed, laughing.

"Calm down, woman." He kissed my forehead. "Vampires don't make babies. It has been tested. It doesn't work. And we've swapped blood. If there are any diseases here, we already share them."

"I—"

He stopped me. "There are no diseases. Fortunately for us, vampire blood filters out and eradicates any diseases a human may carry."

"Seriously?" I looked at him. "Wait, are you sure?"

"Yes, I'm sure. Vampires have existed for thousands of years. All your worries have been tested. You're not even the first of your bloodline to end up with a vampire, and no babies came from that. And from what I hear, they were real freaky!"

"Okay, I didn't need to hear that!" I slapped my hands over my ears. I don't know why, but suddenly, I was imagining my grandmother getting down and nasty with a vampire. That image would take years and a shit ton of whiskey to erase.

"Sorry." He chuckled.

"So you're like a walking cure for all diseases? They should package that."

"They tried," he admitted. "It would have been great for us, considering all the times mass diseases wiped out the human population. But there is no way to do it without turning the patient into a vampire, and no one wants that to happen."

"That's unfortunate."

"Are you done panicking? Can we rest now?"

"After we shower." I jumped back up from the bed. "Let's go."

"If I join you, we won't come out very clean."

I swayed my hips as I walked to the bathroom door, leaned against the doorframe, teasing my nipple between my fingers.

"Remember, I warned you." He stood from the bed to follow me.

Two hours and several orgasms later, we were finally clean and in bed, where we slept until the sun came up.

In the morning, I woke up to breakfast in bed. While he hadn't cooked, he *did* go out to buy food for me, and the man looked too damn pleased with himself.

"Did you have fun?" I popped a piece of the waffle into my mouth while Domino pulled the curtains back to let in more sunlight.

"Yes," he hummed. "You spend a hundred years without the sun and tell me how you feel when you finally get to enjoy it again."

"Is there anything else different about you?" I watched him closely as he peered out the window. "I mean, outside of the sunlight, what about food? Do you need regular food now too?"

"No." He frowned. "I tried, but I puked it right back up. Alcohol, I can drink, but food destroys something inside me."

"Interesting." I sighed. "Too bad, because these waffles are delicious!"

"It is." He returned to the bed. "Now, finish eating. I promised Jackie I'd make sure you did."

"Yes, sir!" I teased and promptly finished my meal.

My stomach full and satisfied, I dressed and walked out of the room, only to find Domino staring at me from the couch, his face pale with shock. I looked down, and there was Maverick, a fluffy ball of black, nestled on Domino's lap, his deep purrs rumbling like a tiny engine.

"What the hell?"

"I guess we've found something else different now that I've had your blood." He frowned. "Please get your cat."

"My cat?" I turned and walked away, shouting over my shoulder, "It looks like that's your cat now, buddy!"

"Whitney, please!" Domino begged.

I grabbed my things and headed for the door, where I waited for Domino. He came walking down the hall, cat in hand, a scowl on his face.

"Aren't you two just adorable together?" I poked him in the side as we left.

When we made it to Jackie's place, after making a few stops so Domino could shop in the daylight, I walked in first. Domino wanted to make a grand entrance, and to be honest, I wanted to see the look on Jackie's face as well. Inside, I found her sitting in the kitchen with Lena and Miguel, who I thought hadn't made it out of the battle, but he looked fine.

"You're alive!" Lena ran over to me, hugging me tightly before handing me my phone. "This thing has been blowing up, by the way."

"Oh, thanks." I slipped it into my pocket; whatever it was, it could wait.

"You look good." Jackie nodded. "I guess the vampire is good for something after all. He fed you, right?"

"Yes," I laughed. "I thought Lena was the mom of the group?"

"So did I!" Lena laughed.

"Yeah, well, when creatures of the night are involved, I take over that role!" Jackie crossed her arms. "And I'll kick his ass if he doesn't do right by you."

"About that…" I paused. "Creatures of the night, I mean."

"Yeah, what about it?" She frowned. "Did he die? Oh, Whit. I'm so sorry."

"Anyone want coffee?" Domino entered behind me, holding the coffees and pastries we'd picked up on the way.

"Son of a bitch!" Jackie stumbled back into the chair behind her.

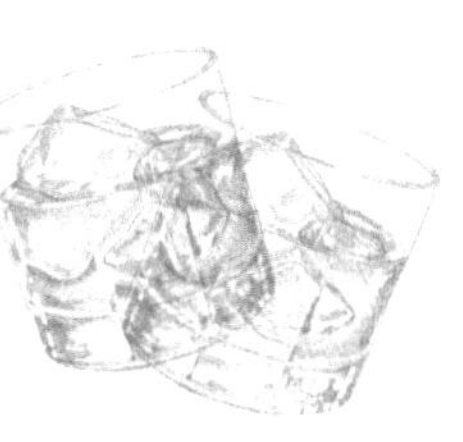

27

Day Walker

"Yep. That was worth the wait." Domino strolled over and placed the drinks and food on the table. "Look at her. I think she might pass out."

"She's not the only one." Lena stumbled back over to the table to sit down. "Damn near gave me a heart attack! How is this possible?"

"I gave him my blood." I didn't mean to blurt out the answer, but I panicked, and everyone looked at me like I had lost my mind.

"Your blood made him human?" Miguel asked, as if he'd heard the best news of his life. I could see the wheels turning in his mind. If he could, he'd have me hooked up to a mass production chamber, constantly pumping out blood to be used in their weapons.

"Human? No." Domino side-eyed the hunter. "Though I'm sure you wish that was the case."

"So you're still a vampire, but you're in the sun." Lena stood again, this time moving closer to Domino to examine him. "They were right. It wasn't just one of those legends that turns out to be a big pile of dookie."

"They were right." He frowned at her terminology. "Lucky for me, it didn't go the other way."

"What does this mean?" Jackie stood. "Is this permanent?"

"As far as I can tell, yes," Domino answered with a big grin on his face as Jackie rolled her eyes at him.

"We can test it!" Miguel said. "I'll just need a little of your blood."

"You're out of your mind, hunter." Domino tensed. "I'm not giving you any of my blood!"

"Wait, hear him out," Jackie said. "Miguel, how does that work? Exactly how much blood do you need? A bucket full?"

"Funny," Domino muttered.

"You have lab equipment here, right?" Miguel answered. "I can look at his blood on a microscopic level. I didn't get that medical degree for nothing. We've been studying vampire blood and its many mutations for years. If it's not permanent, I'll already be able to see it returning to its former state."

"Has something like this happened before?" I asked. "Have you seen this?"

"Not exactly this," Miguel narrowed his eyes and swung his finger at us, "but yeah. We've seen it before."

"How?" I asked.

"Witches perform backward spells that temporarily allow vampires to bend the rules, but those spells are never permanent," Domino summed up Jackie's 'everything is magic' response. "But there are very few witches who would dare play with that kind of magic."

"For good reason," Lena added. "It's dark stuff, and it messes with the mind of the vampire they perform it on, as well as themselves. I've seen witches go crazy for a lot less."

"Yeah, and typically, it's a one-and-done kind of thing," Miguel continued. "Their bodies don't like to be toyed with. I saw a vampire try to use a spell to battle the sun twice, and it turned his blood into battery acid, ate him up from the inside out."

"Damn." Jackie looked at Domino, and I swore, it was like she hoped that would be the outcome for him as well.

Miguel continued. "All we need is a small amount, and we can find out."

"Domino? Please," I urged him to consider it.

"Whitney." Domino wanted me to drop it, but I couldn't.

I grabbed his arm and pulled him away so we could discuss it privately.

"We should know what to expect," I said as soon as we were out of earshot. "I mean, you could accidentally get my blood on you and die. We can't risk that! I did this to save you, not to make it impossible for you to be around me."

"You're going to panic about this if I don't agree, aren't you?" He looked at me like he'd already given up the fight.

"Yes. And you said you would do anything for me, remember?" I poked him in the shoulder.

He glanced over his shoulder at the three, who pretended like they weren't trying to hear us. "Giving a hunter my blood wasn't what I had in mind."

"Domino," I said sternly. "Come on."

"Fine. I'll do it." He leaned closer to me and whispered, "Because I love you."

I froze.

"You know, your heart races and you turn beet red when I say that to you." He smiled. "I love you, Whitney."

"Seriously?" I whispered, and my fist landed against his shoulder. "Are you really messing with me right now?"

"I'm just having a little fun with you. Can't I have that much when you're asking me to willingly give a hunter my blood?" He kissed my cheek then turned to Miguel. "Fine. Let's do this."

Jackie took Miguel to retrieve the sterile materials he needed to collect Domino's blood. She wouldn't let Domino into the private areas of her house, no matter what.

"Bad enough there's a vampire all up in my house to begin with!" she fussed.

"Wait, how is it possible that he's in here?" I turned to Lena when I realized the point we'd all overlooked. "I thought you adjusted the barrier."

"I did, but he's not exactly a normal vampire anymore. You know as soon as this is over, she's going to have me come up with a new ward for this place so you can't come back in." Lena laughed and picked through the provided pastries. She smiled when she saw her favorite blueberry scone in the mix.

"What makes you think I would want to come back here if not forced?" Domino looked offended.

"I don't know. Jackie might grow on you like Maverick did." I nudged him.

"Don't remind me. The damn cat won't leave my car."

"What? Are you and Maverick buddies now?" Lena asked.

"Maverick has better taste than that!" Jackie returned with Miguel, who carried a tray of supplies.

"Let's do this!" he said eagerly.

Domino sat down at the kitchen counter, where Miguel set up his tray. It was quick and easy. He cleaned the skin, plunged the needle into his vein, and walked away with a vial of Domino's blood.

"I'll be outside trying to get your cat out of my car." Domino stood and walked over to me, giving me a quick kiss on the cheek before leaving us. This was clearly a move to give me time to talk to my friends, and as soon as he was gone, they pounced!

Jackie jumped from her seat and slapped my arm. "Bitch! What the hell happened? You were supposed to keep your blood to yourself!"

"Exactly what I said. You were running late with your blood supply. Jackie, I was sitting there watching him wither away!" I explained to myself. "I get it. You don't like him, but I do, and I need him to help me save my sister. There was no way I was going to just let him die, so I gave him my blood. I was afraid it would kill him, but I figured he was on his way out anyway, so I might as well try."

"And now he's a fucking day walker!" Jackie fussed. "That type of shit is supposed to stay in the comic books!"

"You mean alongside monster hunters, witches, and alien descendants?" I asked her.

"Yeah, and cats who shift into dragons!" Lena shouted. "Are we going to talk about that? Because that shit blew my mind!"

"Lena, you are not helping." Jackie held a finger up to hush her.

"How did it feel?" Lena lowered her voice, and both our heads snapped toward her. We knew what that whisper meant: Lena's gutter brain had slipped into the conversation.

"Excuse me?" Jackie asked.

"When he bit you." Lena looked at me. "Did it feel good? Did you like it?"

"You're a kinky bitch, I knew it!" Jackie gasped. "You have some kind of vamp fantasy, don't you? It's not just for the books!"

"I'm just curious." Lena shrugged. "I've never known anyone who had a vampire bite them!"

"And you still don't." I laughed. "Domino didn't bite me. I cut my arm and fed him the blood."

"And even with your blood in his mouth, he didn't bite?" Jackie squinted. "Swear!"

"I swear." I thought back to the moment his eyes opened and he accepted my blood. "It felt like he wanted to, but no. He drank from me and then used his blood to heal the wound."

"Damn. He does love her." Lena swooned.

My face warmed at the sound of that word again. "Love? Wh-who said anything about love?"

"Uh-uh, why are you getting all fidgety?" Jackie pointed at me. "What's that about?"

I took a deep breath and straightened myself. "I'm not."

"What happened? Spill." Lena grabbed my arm. "Tell us everything or I'll pinch you!"

"Keep those claws off me." I pulled away from her and took a deep breath. They were going to find out anyway. "Domino told me he loves me."

"Shit!" Lena hopped up. "And what did you say? Did you tell him you love him? Did you two promise to be together forever?"

"Lena, what the hell is wrong with you?" Jackie snapped her fingers in her face. "I swear, we've lost you to the bubble head community. Why would she say all that?"

"I didn't say anything," I answered.

"Yes!" Jackie cheered. "Let him eat on that! My girl got some damn sense!"

"It wasn't like that. He asked me not to say anything," I corrected her.

"What would you have said?" Lena leaned in, and Jackie paused, clearly the same question on her mind. "Do you? Do you love him?"

"I-uh—," I stared at my friends and decided to change the topic to avoid my building panic attack. "Jai. We need to find Jai. None of this is important."

"Damnit, she's right," Jackie said. "We're sitting here talking about a damn man when we need to be planning for this attack."

"Fine," Lena relented as well. "We'll save your sister, but then you're telling us the truth."

"How are you not beat up?" I joined them at the table. It was only after we sat down I realized neither had a single bruise on them. "After what happened back there, I expected you to be wrapped up in bandages."

"What did I tell you the answer to every *how* question was?" Jackie tapped her temple with her finger.

"Magic?" I frowned.

"Bingo!" she cheered.

"I have healing potions," Lena clarified; magic wasn't a good enough answer. "When we got back, I gave one to everyone."

"Oh, that's handy." I nodded.

"We don't all have a vampire in our back pockets," Jackie teased.

"Oh, shut up." Lena slapped her arm. "Drop it, girl."

"My sister?" I redirected the conversation. "Domino said he talked to you about her. She's safe and we're buying time?"

"Yes. The good thing is, we know exactly where she is." Jackie picked a pastry out of the bag Domino left on the table. "The bad thing is, Vance now has all of Reddick's power and then some. It seems he was planning to snatch the throne for himself all along. This just allowed him to push up his timeline, and he took it."

"So, he has all the resources of a king. That's not good." I wanted to be optimistic, but it was already sounding like the cards were stacked against us.

"King is just a political term they use in the vampire world. He's more like a mayor or a governor. Yes, he does have resources, but so do we," Jackie reminded me. "We're not out here just winging it. There are systems in place to deal with this, systems we will tap into if we need to. Right now, the goal is to keep this away from the officials. We don't want them finding out about you either."

"And now we have a secret weapon," Lena stated.

"What's that?" I asked.

"Domino!" Lena boasted. "None of the vampires know about him. They're all sleeping now."

"True." Jackie sucked her teeth. It was like she hated that Domino could possibly be part of the solution.

"I say we wait to attack until it's nearly dawn. Take the battle outside, and when the sun rises and the rest of them go running for cover, they'll realize he's not like them anymore," Lena explained. "Maybe some of them will even get caught outside and burn to bits."

"Are you sure she has a vampire fantasy?" I asked.

"Yes, but now I'm not so sure how twisted the fantasy gets." Jackie laughed. "When this is done, we're going to take you to see someone."

"I don't care what you two think." Lena lifted her nose in the air. "It's a brilliant idea."

"What is?" Miguel asked, returning with the vial of blood in his hand.

"That was fast." Jackie jumped from her seat.

"Yeah, and the results are in." Miguel smiled widely.

"What are they?" Domino reappeared, his gaze immediately shifting from mine, the silence speaking volumes.

That man was listening to our conversation, I just knew it. He couldn't read my mind, but I would tell him exactly what I thought about his eavesdropping later.

"Eager to find out if you're going to explode next time you try to bite my bestie?" Jackie teased.

"Jackie," Lena snapped at her like a parent scolding a child.

"Sorry." Jackie shrugged.

"What are the results?" I asked.

"The change is permanent," Miguel announced. "Domino's a day walker for good now."

"He is?" I looked at Domino, and the corner of his lips lifted just slightly. Even if he wouldn't express it in front of them, he was happy about it.

"Yes. Whatever you did, it's here to stay," Miguel said. "Not sure how I feel about that, but there it is."

"That's a good thing, right?" Lena asked. "I mean, we don't want Domino's blood turning into battery acid."

"Sure." Jackie rolled her eyes. "We just have one vampire who can walk in the daylight. That's not a problem until it's two or even three. Just another problem the hunters will eventually have to take care of."

"Jackie!" Lena slapped her arm and pointed at me. No, it wasn't like I was the reason the problem existed.

"My bad." Jackie rubbed my arm. "I'm sorry, it's just...I'm struggling with this."

"No, it's fine." I nodded. "I understand. I had the same thoughts when it first happened. The last thing I want is to be the reason someone gets hurt."

"It won't come to that," Domino reassured me.

"Yeah, we can find a way to protect you and make sure no other vampire gets your blood. I mean, you already said they can't bite you, right?" Lena offered.

"That's true, but Domino didn't bite me, remember?" I said. "There are other ways to get to my blood."

"We'll worry about that later," Jackie interjected. "Jai is the focus now, and I think Lena's plan, while freaky, is the best way for us to tackle this. We'll wait until it's close to daylight. Then, we'll attack. The goal will be to draw them outside, where we now have the advantage. While we fight, Lena and Whitney will get Jai."

"Okay," Miguel said. "We should start prepping the hunters."

"Right." Jackie headed out with Miguel.

"Uh…" Lena looked at us. "I'm going to go make some more potions and craft more vamp powder. Best to be prepared." She grabbed a cup of coffee and another scone before running out.

"They're obviously trying to give us time alone," Domino said.

"Why?" I asked.

"Maybe they think you should tell me you love me now," he poked at me.

"Hey, one more time, and I'm going to blast you." I brought sparks to my fingers and wiggled them in front of his face.

"I surrender!" A hearty laugh escaped his lips, and my phone started ringing.

My gaze darted from the screen to his face, my eyes widening in shock. "It's Jai."

His humor faded as he pointed at the phone in my hand. "Answer it."

I hit the answer button and put the call on speaker. "Hello?"

"Whitney? Whitney, please. It's me," Jai's frantic voice came over the phone. "They told me to tell you they won't wait. You have one hour after the sun sets. If you're not here, they will kill me."

Then, the call ended.

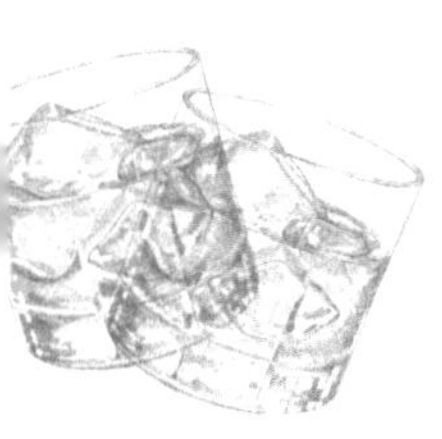

28

Rescue Mission Pt. 2

"**A**re you sure it was Jai?" Jackie sat across from me on the couch.

As soon as the call with my sister ended, I called my friends back to us. The plan we'd just laid out would never work. They wanted us to go right away.

"Yes. I know my sister's voice," I snipped at her before I held up my hand. "Sorry, I didn't mean for that to come off like that. I just can't believe this is happening."

"Maybe they think it will buy them some time," Miguel offered. "They think you'll have to leave before the vampires on your side wake up, which means fewer people to face off against."

"Damn it," Jackie cursed. "I'm really getting tired of these vampires trying to outsmart us."

"They must have had a familiar get her to make the call," Domino, who had been sitting beside me, flipping his phone on his leg, spoke. "It's the only way that call could have come during the day."

"Do you think they figured it out? That she isn't like me?" I looked at him. "Is it possible?"

"It would explain why they're suddenly calling to have you go there." He nodded. "They're using her as bait."

"How? I mean, I thought they couldn't touch her." I looked at Lena. "Isn't that what your protection spell is for?"

"Yes, but like Domino said, they have familiars. The magic works against vampires. I'm sorry, I didn't factor that in." Lena instantly looked like a woman beating herself up for a mistake anyone could have made.

"It's okay. We'll figure this out," Jackie comforted her.

"Is there any chance they already know about Domino?" Miguel asked.

"No. How could they?" I looked at Domino and then Miguel, who shrugged.

"He went out last night to run errands, right?" Jackie chimed in. "That's where you were when I talked to you."

"Yes." Domino nodded.

"Anyone see you? Maybe they could tell?" Miguel offered.

"How?" I frowned. "Did you get bitten and didn't notice?"

"I don't know. Maybe he smells different or something," Jackie said. "How else do you vampires keep up with each other?"

"Wouldn't you like to know?" Domino snipped at her. "No one smelled me or anything else. I was discreet because I had to be. I don't know who's on his side yet."

"Guys!" I snapped, sensing their taunting building again. "Please, not now."

"Seriously, you two need to get it together." Miguel was the one to agree with me this time, and he gave Jackie a look like he was both disappointed and jealous of their banter.

"What's the plan?" Lena asked. "Tell me what to do to help."

"We don't have a choice," Jackie said. "We have to go."

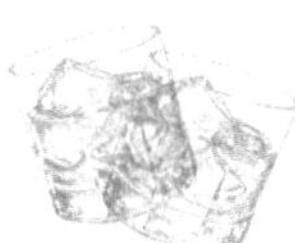

We stood together outside Reddick's former home. Apparently, whatever vampire took over the area also claimed the vampire king's residence. From our vantage point, we could see the familiars keeping watch. They lined the perimeter of the home and even stood at the entrance, where motorized gates held out any visitors.

"Alright. This is where we go ahead alone," Jackie said. "The other hunters are in place, and we were able to get a few more for reinforcements. Even though they're cloaked, the vamps will know they're here."

"Alone?" I asked.

"Yes, just the girls. Domino is with the hunters now. He's disguised as one and will come in with them. We're hoping it will help us out. It won't take long for them to realize who he is, but the shock value should knock them off their square long enough for us to make a move."

"They also had people watching Domino's place," Lena offered. "I had someone check out his home and they're definitely there. Looks like their plan was to ambush him the moment the sun went down."

"It's good for us. He isn't there." I couldn't imagine what I would do if Domino was also in trouble. I mean, of course, I would save my sister first—I mean, I only met the man a week ago, but I would really try to get to him after I knew she was safe. Odds were, I'd still be too late to do anything.

"Are you ready for this?" Jackie asked me. "This is your second vampire battle, but a lot has happened. How are you holding up?"

"Better than I thought I'd be. Granted, I thought this would be done by now, but I'm okay." I nodded. "Let's go get my sister back."

The three of us piled back into the jeep and drove straight up to the gate, Jackie at the wheel and Lena in the back. She was still working with magic I didn't understand, but she said it would help us. We needed all the protection we could get, so I didn't question it too much. We could dissect it all when my sister was safe and the vampire who threatened her was dead.

The gates were made of wide metal slats, positioned so you couldn't look through them. As we approached, I expected the familiars to stop us, imagined them grilling us for answers or even trying to attack. They did neither. Without as much as a glance in our direction, the gates opened, and Jackie drove right on in.

My heart stopped as soon as we pulled past the tall shrubbery lining the gates. Right in the center of the courtyard, strapped with thick leather to a pole and surrounded by blood-red flowers, was Jai, limp, her hands high above her head. Her eyes were closed, but her chest rose and fell with labored breaths.

"Oh, my God." I gripped the door handle, ready to hop out and run to her. "What the hell did they do to her?"

"Not yet." Lena put her hand on my shoulder. "Remember, we have to be smart about this. They want you to respond with emotions. I can tell Jai is okay; she's just in a deep sleep."

"How could they do this to her?" I looked back at Lena. "Is this magic?"

"Probably just a drug," Jackie said. "I know I said everything is answered with magic, but there are a lot of human inventions with the same effect."

"Okay, so what now?" I still hadn't let the handle go. My grip tightened around it until my fingers felt like they would burn through the material.

"We wait," Jackie answered. "It won't be long."

She was right. Moments later, two familiars, a man and a woman who both looked like they were sleepwalking, approached us. They said nothing, only nodded for us to get out of the car. It was after stepping out that I realized they were both holding weapons—small handguns. I wondered what kind of ammo they had and if it was strong enough to take down a vampire.

The two continued with their stoic appearances, and as they led us away from our ride, I realized why they were so at ease. Of course, they knew who my friends were and what they were capable of, but they also knew Lena and Jackie couldn't hurt them. It was in their oath. Lena had explained it to me. It happened after college, something all magic users had to agree to, and that included the hunters. They would harm no humans. Maybe that was why the vampires never turned them—they were human shields.

I, on the other hand, had no oath to stick to. No one would come down on me if I blew off their heads—except, of course, maybe the law, but I had a feeling that wouldn't be an issue. No magical network would let humans find out about what happened. If they hurt my sister, I was going to kill them. I'd deal with whatever psychological issues that left me with later.

"The sun will be setting soon." Lena pointed to the sky.

"Let the games begin." Jackie nodded.

Twenty minutes later, as I stood there wishing I could run to my sister, the sun fell beyond the horizon. As soon as the blanket of darkness covered us, Jackie tensed.

"Here we go," she muttered under her breath.

"It's going to be okay." Lena rubbed my arm.

I nodded because I didn't know what else to say. I had to believe she was right. We would all walk out of there alive and with my sister.

It wasn't five minutes after the sunset that Vance appeared in front of us. I figured he would have someone else do his bidding for him, wouldn't risk walking into a trap, but ego often led men to make foolish choices.

"Didn't even bother to brush your nasty ass teeth, did you?" Jackie laughed. "Disgusting."

"Jackie, don't taunt the vampires," Lena warned.

"You know me. This is how I play with them." Jackie winked at Vance. "You can take it, can't you, big boy?"

Suddenly, the wailing cry of a vampire rang out around us, and soon, a woman joined Vance. She wore a veil across her face, but her afro was still just as perfect as the first day I'd met her.

"I'm going to end your life," Nyesha spoke with her face still hidden.

"You talking to me?" I pointed at myself, stealing a little of that sass Jackie had.

"You ruined me!" Nyesha cried out and lifted her veil to show her face, still melting. Where my power touched her, she hadn't healed, and it looked like it was spreading, like a rash that even the strongest steroids couldn't fight. "Look at my face!"

"Damn, girl." Jackie looked at Lena. "Think you can do something for that?"

"I don't think the ancestors themselves could fix that." Lena pointed and frowned. "Maybe we can study it."

"Oh, you're all just so damn funny! Let's see you laugh after I rip your head off!" Nyesha took one step forward but stopped when Vance held up his hand.

"We won't end your life. We need you. Surrender, and your friends can take your sister," Vance spoke calmly. "I'm not here for another fight."

"No one came here to surrender to you," Jackie laughed. "If you think this is ending without a fight, you're really not cut out to be king."

"You hunters are always out for blood," Vance said.

"How ironic, coming from a literal bloodsucker," Jackie snipped back.

Lena and I let her continue poking at the bear; we knew what was happening. The longer Jackie kept Vance locked in their back and forth, the closer the other hunters got to us. We had to wait until they were in position.

"Are you going to let her talk for you?" Vance spoke to me. "This is your sister, and you can save her."

"I can also blast your face off," I threatened him.

"Hell yeah, she can!" Jackie cheered. "I mean, look at your friend over there. You're going to need a new name, girlfriend."

"That's it!" Nyesha screamed. "I may not be able to kill the one with the special blood, but a hunter, I can take out any day."

"I'd like to see you try it, patty melt!"

"Bitch!" Nyesha sneered at Jackie before she looked at Vance. "Let me kill her!"

"Fine." Vance sighed. "The hunter wants blood? Let her have it."

Nyesha grinned, though she didn't need to, as we could already see most of her teeth through the melted side of her face. "I'm going to enjoy ripping you apart."

Jackie lifted her hand and beckoned the vampire forward. Luckily, this gesture meant two things: Jackie was prepared to face the vampire, and the other hunters were right where they needed to be. But so were Vance's men. As the hunters came over the wall surrounding the home, the vampires met them with force.

The bloodsuckers poured out of the massive home and immediately went to battle with the hunters. As the others clashed, Nyesha went for Jackie, Vance for Jai. Before he made it to her, Lena, who had been silent, had already put her protective barrier around Jai. I pulled power to my hand and shot it at him, but he was ready for me. The new vampire leader leaped back away from my sister moments before my power slapped the ground where he once stood.

"I told you I would blow your face off!" I reminded him of my earlier threat.

Vance sneered at me. "If you won't come willingly, I'll have to take you by force."

"I dare you." Vance froze and slowly turned to find Domino, dressed in hunter's clothing. He stumbled back from him like he was seeing a ghost. "You know, I wasn't the biggest fan of my brother, but he was still my family, and you ripped his heart out. So, it's only fitting I return the favor."

I was so focused on the interaction between Vance and Domino while trying to keep an eye on Lena, who crept toward my sister, that I didn't see it when Nyesha knocked Jackie down. She didn't kill my friend, but she pushed her so far away, she couldn't stop her from coming at me.

"Whitney, watch out!" Jackie called out. I turned just in time to dodge Nyesha's hand, which was poised for my throat.

The vampire repeated the same action she had the first time we faced off. A woman of habit, she pulled a knife from one of her hidden pockets and stabbed me, this time in the thigh. I stumbled back, falling on my ass as the pain shot through my leg.

"Maybe your blood will fix what your magic did to me," she said with another wide grin.

"No!" I shouted as Nyesha lifted the blade coated in my blood to her lips. That was my biggest fear—my blood mutating another vampire—but there was nothing I could do to stop her as she licked the blade clean.

"There." She dropped the weapon to the ground. "That should fix me right on up. I already feel—"

Her words trailed off, and her gaze dropped to the rough skin of her hands. Nyesha stared at her fingers, twisting and flexing them before she looked at me. At first, her expression was one of wonder. Then, it became something else, something twisted with agony.

Slowly, the veins in her body lit up. Beneath her flesh, I could see a detailed map of where my blood spread through her, and then the light intensified. Everyone stopped to look at her as she cried out.

"What is this? What's wrong with your blood?" She pointed at me. "Why is this happening?"

I scooted back away from her as she started walking in circles, fanning her arms like a bird in heat.

"It burns!" Nyesha yelled. "Make it stop!"

She scratched at her arms and chest, but nothing she did stopped the spread of the stolen blood. And then, in the most disgusting showing I'd ever witnessed, Nyesha melted. Flesh dripped from her body like lava and fell to the ground. I thought we would have to watch her melt completely, but the show came to a sudden, explosive end when she burst into flames.

The crispy vampire body fell to the ground and quickly turned to ash. I looked up from the remnants of her body and the tuft of purple afro to see every vampire staring at me. Their expressions were a mixture of curiosity and fear. What did my blood, my existence, mean to them?

"Die!" A hunter with a short pixie cut jumped through the air and stabbed a vampire in the chest with a stake before they all went back to fighting. So much for the mourning period.

"Holy shit!" Miguel said as he ran over to help me up. He examined my leg, pulled out a tourniquet to wrap above my wound, and checked my pulse. "Are you okay?"

"Yes," I said and pointed to Lena, who had almost made it to a still-sleeping Jai. "Help her. Please."

"Are you sure?" He double-checked the bandage on my thigh.

"Yes, go!" I urged him.

Miguel took off for my sister, and Vance tried to stop him. I lifted my hand, prepared to blast the vampire, but Domino beat me to it. The two men became a blur of blood and fists. I kept my eye on their fight, as that was part of the plan, but I kept watching for Jackie. She had recovered and made a path to my sister.

Jackie made it to Lena and Miguel. Together, they worked to remove Jai from her restraints. When I saw her body slump forward into Miguel's arms, I felt relieved—though that only lasted a hot second as Vance slammed Domino into the ground so hard, he passed out. Then, the vampire who threatened to end my life ran for my sister.

"No!" I shouted, blasting the ground in front of him. He fell back with a growl and shifted his path. The new vampire king was coming right at me.

Before I knew it, he had my hands pinned behind my back, and he was out of head-butting range. The man clearly took notes from our last fight.

"Your vampire can't save you now," he growled. "If your blood is no good, then I'll just get rid of you!"

I looked over my shoulder at him. "Who said I needed a vampire to save me?"

One thing I'd learned from Nyesha was that every part of my body could be a focal point to release my energy. Fortunately for me, Vance wasn't as smart as he wanted to believe he was. I shifted the energy into my core and focused. This had to work. When the power built into a knot in my belly, I released the energy, letting it radiate across my flesh.

"Ow!" Vance pulled his hands back; already, my magic was eating away at him. "No!"

"Sorry, but you shouldn't put your hands on someone without their permission." I limped back. Energy or not, I still had a damn hole in my leg. Fortunately for me, no vampire would dare touch my blood after watching what happened to Nyesha.

"I'm going to kill you." Vance's sudden movement was met with Domino's swift reaction, his hand clamping down on his windpipe, cutting off his breath.

Vance struggled against Domino's iron grip, his eyes wide with a mix of fear and defiance as he peered at me. "I thought you said you didn't need a vampire to save you."

"I don't, but you killed his brother, and he kind of owes you one." I winked, and a moment later, Domino punched his hand through Vance's chest and ripped his heart out.

"Now we're even," Domino gritted, and Vance fell to the ground next to his scorched partner.

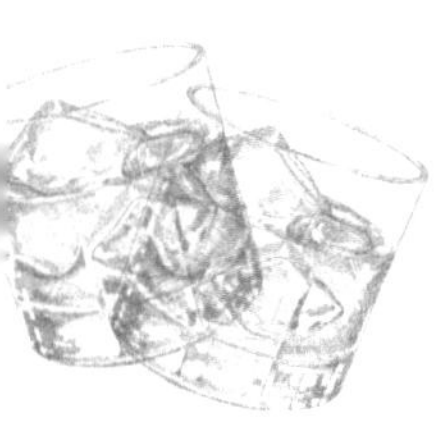

29

Custom Curtains

Don't ask me why, but I expected all the vampires to stop attacking. As soon as their vampire leader was down for the count, I thought they would sulk away into the shadows, but they didn't. The battle went on until Domino's allies arrived to even out the numbers. With Vance down, every eager vampire in the area wanted a chance to take his place.

When we finally left, the vampires were still fighting, but we realized they weren't coming after us anymore. This was a territorial battle that would end when one vampire displayed his dominance over the others.

"We need to get out of here," Domino urged. "If they don't sort this out by themselves, the council will intervene. If they send someone here, we don't want them finding us."

"He's right. We need to keep everything about Whitney hidden," Lena agreed as we piled into the Jeep.

"I'll drive." Domino took the keys.

Jackie sucked her teeth and held out her hand for the keys. "Excuse me?"

"Jackie..." Lena and I said her name at the same time.

"Not like it's his car!" she fussed as she climbed into the back seat with Lena.

"Do you ever think about taking over as king?" I asked Domino as we drove away from the chaos.

"I have, and I realized it's not for me," he admitted. "There is a lot that comes with the job. It's not as superficial as my brother made it look. I didn't ask for this life, but I try to make the best of it, and somehow, the idea of spending potentially hundreds, if not thousands, of years looking after annoying immortals doesn't sound appealing to me."

"I had to ask. I mean, if that's what you want, then I need to consider what that means for me. To be honest, I don't want to be involved with any more vampire stuff than I have to."

"Oh?" He raised a brow and looked at me from the corner of his eye. "You think about that?"

"We are stuck together now, right? There is a bond between us," I said nervously, ignoring the fact that my best friends were behind me and definitely listening to our conversation.

"Yes, we are." He smiled and pulled the car onto the open road.

As the car cruised on, I looked back at my sister, who was laid out across my best friends. Jackie rubbed her arms and Lena cradled Jai's head in her lap with a roll of herbs in her hand. She lit the end and drew circles of smoke above Jai's face.

"Is she going to be okay?" I asked. "What are you doing?"

"Yes, I think she will be just fine." Lena continued moving her hand in circles. "I'm weaving dreams for her. Just trying to take the edge off any anxiety she may be having. Even in her sleep state, this can be stressful. It's also starting the process to erase her memories of what happened. If I did it correctly, she should be dreaming of running through the clouds or something cozy like that."

"*If* you did it correctly?" I twisted in my seat. "What do you mean *if*?"

"Yes, I told you this isn't something I've done much of. I got instructions, though." Lena looked up at me. "I followed it perfectly, I promise."

"I swear, if you made this girl forget who she is!" Jackie fussed. "There is no coming back from that, Lena. You know that."

"She won't!" Lena rubbed her chin. "I mean, I don't think she will. Besides, this is only a temporary fix. Likosa is coming to help me perform the actual memory cleanse and make sure she's okay. It's not enough to erase a memory. We have to replace it with something else."

"Great, Likosa," I muttered.

"You don't like her, do you?" Lena asked.

"I'm just not sure I trust her, but if you believe she is the right person for this, then I'll go with it. Despite my feelings, I trust you." I smiled at her—I meant it. Even if I thought something was off about the woman, Lena had always been a good judge of character.

"Thank you." Lena smiled.

"In any case, it's better than her remembering the vampires who tried to kill her, right?" Domino tried to comfort me.

"You would think that." Jackie looked like she wanted to pop him on the back of the head, but she kept her hands to herself.

"Look, I'm just glad she's back and all this is over." I turned and relaxed back into my seat. "I hate that any of this ever affected her at all."

"Over?" Jackie laughed. "Girl, I hate to tell you, but this is just the beginning. I mean, there are vampires out there, running around talking about you, the woman with blood that destroys vampires from the inside out. If you think you're walking away from all this now, you are out of your mind."

"Yeah, you're kinda stuck with all this," Lena agreed. "And now that we have Jai back, I can also admit I'm happy you're in this now. Now we don't have to hide things or tiptoe around you anymore!"

"Focus on not destroying my sister's mind, please." I held my hand up to stop her cheery tone.

"I won't!" Lena fussed. "Hey, I'm a lot better at this than you're giving me credit for."

"Look, I'm supposed to be looking at art, not blowing up vampires!" I snapped.

"Whitney, please. You're special, and now you're a part of our monster ass-kicking team! It's a gift. Embrace it!" Jackie cheered. "I wonder what else you can do. I mean, you only just tapped into your power!"

"You're enjoying this way too much." I shook my head. "I don't want to think about any of that right now."

"Fine. You don't think about it, but I will. As soon as I get home, I'm making plans for us to work together to get you as strong as possible."

Jackie rambled on, but I couldn't be bothered to pay attention. I meant what I said. Jai was okay, and for the time being, the vampires weren't worried about us. Nothing else mattered to me, and I wasn't about to rush into thinking about a future joining my friends in the hunt for monsters.

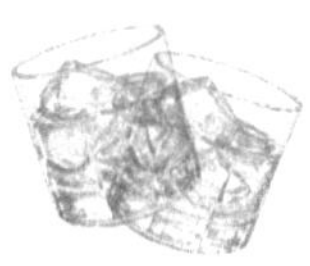

A few hours later, we had dropped Jackie and Lena off at Jackie's and were pulling into my parking garage. They were going to do more work and then meet us at my place. As much as I wanted to be there with my friends, I also needed to go home and deal with the mess. Besides, Jackie's place was still crawling with hunters, and her guesthouse had a hole in the wall. We didn't want to have to explain all of that to Jai when she woke up.

I held my breath as we rode the elevator up to my apartment. I wanted to get Jai past the devastation before she woke up. When the elevator doors slid open, I slapped my hand over my mouth.

The hall was perfect. The floors and walls had all been repaired, and there wasn't a hint of blood in the place.

"How is this possible?" I eased out into the hall like it was a mirage that would fade away.

"Money." Domino smirked. "Everything is possible with enough money."

"You paid to have this repaired?" I looked at him.

"Yes, I did. There are services that take care of these things. If you think chaos like this isn't happening every night, you're wrong. When it does, there are cleanup crews that erase the evidence of monsters who destroy custom carpets."

"I was preparing myself to get an eviction notice on my door." I sighed as I led him to the door. "Glad I don't have to worry about that now."

"Of course not. I wouldn't let that happen to you." Domino followed me inside. "You didn't ask for all this. You shouldn't have to lose everything because of it."

"Thank you." I closed the door behind him after he carried my sister inside.

Grrrrr! Maverick sat in the hallway and rolled his eyes at us.

"I should feed him. You can put her in my room," I instructed Domino.

After Maverick had his meal and Jai was tucked safely into my bed, we met in the kitchen. Watching my cat devour his meal reminded me I had had little to eat myself. My stomach growled as I searched through the kitchen for something to snack on.

"Would you like me to run out and get you something?" Domino asked.

"No, I'm good." I pulled out some kimchi, seaweed, and tuna. "This will do."

"Is that for you or the cat?"

"I know you aren't talking after the disaster you left in Jackie's kitchen!" I pointed at him.

He threw his hands up. "I'll shut up."

"Thank you."

Domino turned to look out the window while I inhaled the food. It wasn't enough, but I'd make it work.

"The sun will come up soon." He glanced back at me.

"What if he was wrong?" I asked.

"What?" Domino turned to me, quirking a brow.

"Miguel. What if the change wasn't permanent and you explode when the sun rises?"

"Remember me well?" he joked.

"Not funny," I fussed as I put the plate and fork in the sink. "We need to be serious about this."

"How about I just stick my toe out? If that lights up, then we know." Domino lifted his foot from the ground.

"Domino..." I fussed.

"The only thing we can do is try, Whitney." He walked over to me, his eyes filled with warmth, and gently pulled me into his arms. "I don't want to leave this world now, not after having finally found you. But what other choice is there?"

"That was mushy." I poked his chest. "We could just pretend it never happened and you can stay in the night."

"Seriously?" Domino shook his head. "What about your days on the beach? What about walking hand in hand under the sun? Don't you want that?"

"Yes, but I'd rather you stay alive."

"And what about the blood thing? Shouldn't we find out if your blood would hurt me?" he continued. "Or do you not care now that your sister is safe?"

"Ouch." I frowned. "Do you think I'm that selfish?"

"I didn't mean it that way." He sighed. "It was supposed to be a joke."

"I think your jokes only land when they're directed at monster hunters." I smirked.

"I'll keep that in mind."

"So we test it out and hope for the best." I looked out the window. "Is that what you really want to do?"

"Yes. I don't want to live with the mystery," he said resolutely.

"Okay. Then we'll do it."

Domino headed for the couch and stopped when I didn't follow him.

"You want me to sit alone?"

He shook his head. "No, but I can't sit there."

"Now that you mention it, I don't think I've ever seen you sit here. Why is that?"

"I can't." I stared at the special order symbol of my success. "It's like there's something holding me back."

"Okay, we can unpack that later." Domino grabbed two chairs from the kitchen table and pulled them to sit in front of the window.

We sat together, hand in hand, and waited for the sun to rise. I held my breath as the first rays of light touched my skin. When I turned to look at Domino, I could see the slight fear in his eyes.

"You're still here," I whispered.

"I am."

We sat together, smiling at the sun, until the doorbell snapped us out of our enjoyment.

"Who could that be at this time?" I pulled out my phone and looked at the camera. Standing there were my best friends.

As soon as I opened the door, Jackie skipped inside over to Domino.

"Oh, look, you're still alive."

He nodded. "Yes, and so are you."

"I'd say something about forcing a sharp piece of wood through your chest, but I'm actually glad you're alive." She pulled a brown envelope from her back pocket and handed it to him. "Here!"

"What is this?" Domino frowned at the envelope without opening it.

"A bill!" Jackie grinned.

"Excuse me?" Domino scoffed. "You're billing me? For what?"

"If you think I'm paying for the damage done to my home, you're out of your mind." Jackie looked over her shoulder at Lena and me and winked.

Domino opened the envelope and looked at the itemized list, his jaw tightening as his eyes lit up. "Fifteen thousand dollars for *curtains*?"

"Did you forget the one you set on fire after your nasty vampire sex?"

"You expect me to believe you paid fifteen thousand dollars for a single curtain?"

"No, but they were custom, and now, they all have to be replaced. I can't have curtains in my home that don't match!"

"You're out of your mind." Domino tossed the paper in her face.

The two bickered, and Lena lifted the coffee cup carrier.

"This is going to be the rest of our lives, you know?" She smirked.

I snatched up a cup of coffee and took a long drink. "That's starting to sink in."

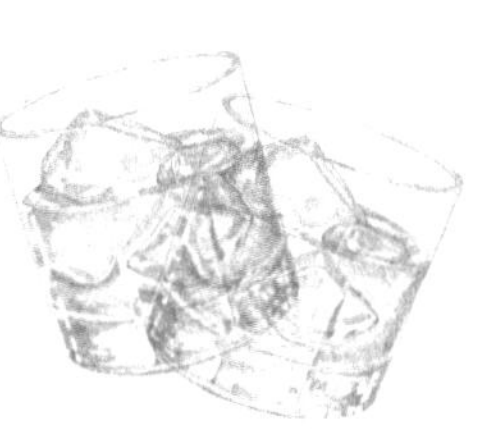

30

Bite Me, Vampire.

"Did she wake up?" Lena looked over at my sister from the open door.

"No, she's been like that since we got her back." I swallowed the lump in my throat as I watched my sister lay beside Maverick. Once he'd eaten, he joined her in the bed and hadn't left her side. "She will wake up, right? I mean, we didn't accidentally put her into a coma, did we?"

"The child will be fine." Likosa appeared behind us. "We must work quickly, though."

Lena and I stepped aside and let her enter the bedroom.

"Whitney, we need to do this alone," Lena said softly. She knew I didn't trust Likosa and didn't want me to protest.

"I can't watch?"

"No, especially with her energy powers," Likosa answered. "If you were to get emotional, it could interfere with our magic while we work in her mind."

"Right." I looked Lena in the eye, and she nodded. "Okay."

I joined Jackie and Domino, who sat in the front room, still bickering about paint colors and changes that needed to be made to her home. Domino questioned the cost of something labeled *chartreuse love*, and I rolled my eyes. There was no way I was going to sit and listen to them.

Instead of trying to convince them to cut out the noise, I went into my office. I had planned to spend so much time in the space, looking out at the water while I made deals for fresh artists. Instead, I hadn't been inside since setting up my new bookshelves.

"Might as well work on this," I muttered and went to complete the busy work of unpacking my office. I could feel the pushes and pulls of the energy Lena and Likosa worked with and tried everything I could to ignore it. Likosa's warning stayed in my mind. If I interfered, it could hurt my sister.

"You hiding in here?" Jackie slipped into my office, shutting the door behind her.

"Well, I wasn't about to sit out there with you two." I pointed through the glass door to the man sitting on my couch. "Are you done poking at the vampire?"

"Never." Jackie clapped her hands. "It's too fun."

"I think you like him more than you're letting on." I narrowed my eyes at her. "The hunter getting soft for her prey?"

"Miguel said the same, but I assumed he was just jealous." Jackie frowned as she considered my words. "No. He's a vampire. I'll always hate him."

"Why would Miguel be jealous?" I asked. "Is he the only person you're allowed to throw witty insults at?"

"Well..." she trailed off.

"Well, what? Are you two a thing?" I perked up. Finally, some tea that had nothing to do with me.

"Kind of." She sighed. "It's so cliché that I would end up with another hunter."

"What would be cliché is if you ended up with a monster," I corrected her. "Isn't that how the stories always go?"

"Don't give Lena any more story ideas." Jackie shook her finger in my face and laughed. "But seriously, are you okay?"

"Yes. I'll be better when Jai is awake and I know her mind isn't warped, though." I looked out the window. "I'm sure it will be okay, but the worry is still there."

"Lena is really good and with Likosa, so I don't think you have anything to worry about," Jackie reassured me.

"Thanks." I nodded. "I'm still shocked at how advanced Lena is. All these years, she's been practicing magic, and I never knew!"

"Okay, I need to know something. Aren't you excited now? I mean, your life is about to change." Jackie couldn't hide her enthusiasm even if she wanted to. Her eyes were so wide, I thought they might pop out of her head.

"Should I be?" I cocked my head to the side.

"Yes!" She grabbed my shoulders and shook me. "Come on, woman! Snap out of it. It wasn't long ago that you lost your job and didn't know what the future held. Now, you do."

"Maybe it looks that way to you, but not to me. At the end of the day, I'm still without a job and I still have bills to pay." I pushed her hands off me. "We aren't kids, Jackie, and unlike you, I wasn't born into a family with money. Hell, I wasn't even adopted into one."

"Sure, you don't have a rich father, but you now have a rich vampire. You telling me he won't pay your bills? Because if he's talking about going fifty-fifty with you, I'll stake him right now!"

"You'll look for any reason to kill him, won't you?" I laughed.

"Just say the word and he's outta here!" She mimed plunging a stake through his chest. "But seriously, listen to me, please. We're independent women, I get that, but let him help you until you work out the money thing. It won't be forever. In the meantime, we get to hunt monsters. I don't know if you know this, but it's a lucrative field!"

"Would I still get to be an art buyer?" I considered the thought. I could travel the world killing evil creatures and buying all the best pieces. That was close enough to being a spy, right?

"Monster-hunting art buyer with a vampire boo thang?" Jackie scratched her chin. "Lena is definitely putting that in a book! It will be her next bestseller! Who do you think they'll get to play you?"

Domino knocked on the door, interrupting Jackie's laughter, before he poked his head inside. "They're done."

I followed Jackie out of the office to find Likosa and Lena standing in the kitchen.

"How did it go?" I glanced at the bedroom door.

"She's fine. Still sleeping, but that will wear off when we're all gone." Likosa answered. "If she sees me, it might mess with her mind. I had to tiptoe into her head a bit there."

"Thank you," I paused, "I think."

"No problem. I have to get going now; other magical things need correcting." Likosa gave Lena a lingering hug then vanished from the room.

"I think that's our cue to get out of here as well." Lena picked up the bag she'd brought. "I have some things to do and a lot of people to apologize to. I missed a few tour dates."

"I'm sorry." I hugged her. "Thank you for making this a priority."

"Hey, it comes with the gig, right?" Jackie joined our embrace. "Now, I need to get those damn hunters out of my house and prepare for the contractors."

She said the last part loud enough to make sure Domino heard her. He muttered something I couldn't hear, and I ushered the ladies out of my place.

A half-hour after everyone left, Maverick strolled out of my bedroom, followed by a yawning Jai. She stretched her arms over her head and wiped the sleep out of her hazel eyes.

"I can't believe I slept that long, but I told you two a day on the beach would take it out of me." She lumbered over to the counter where we stood.

I hesitated to answer but ultimately decided to go along with whatever she said. "Yeah. We should have believed you."

"What time is it? I don't want to miss my flight." She squinted at the smart-watch on her wrist. "I have two new job interviews next week. I need to make sure I'm there to prepare for them."

"You have a few hours," Domino answered and nodded at me. Apparently, he knew more than I did.

"Domino, it was so good to meet you." Jai smiled at the vampire and then pointed at me. "I hope you do right by my sister. I would hate to have to set Jackie on you."

"Isn't this the part when you're supposed to threaten me yourself?" He chuckled. "Tell me you're going to kick my ass."

"Do you see me?" She waved her hands at her petite frame. "I can't do anything to a guy like you, but Jackie is a ball buster. She'll beat your ass, and I won't hesitate to call her. Trust me, I've done it before."

"Really?" Domino glanced at me.

"Yes, really." I shrugged; Jai had called my friend on exactly three of my ex-boyfriends. "Jackie, don't play about us."

"I'll keep that in mind." He nodded.

"My ride should be here soon," she said. "I'll go finish packing."

"We can drive you," I offered.

"No, you two need to be together. I'm a big girl. I can handle myself." Jai turned and headed for the bedroom to gather her things.

"Did I miss something?"

"The witch conjured a bag. I purchased a flight. A vampire I trust will drive her. He's waiting downstairs. Likosa said it's best to get her back to her normal routine as fast as possible. If she stays here too long, the story in her mind will unravel."

"Oh, okay." I nodded. "Thank you."

"As far as she knows. She came for the weekend to visit you and meet your new boyfriend."

"Boyfriend?" I raised a brow.

"Lena's words, not mine." He shrugged, but I could tell he wouldn't protest the idea.

Soon, we were standing on the curb outside my building, waving at the black car as it drove away with my sister inside. She looked perfectly fine and had the same bubbly energy that always annoyed me. I told her we would plan another trip, one where she could hang with Jackie and Lena, and that was it.

"Oh, Ms. Harris," Cordell addressed me as we entered the building. He hadn't been at his desk when we walked out. "Are you okay?"

"Yes, I'm fine." I nodded. "And about the hallway..."

"No, there's nothing to worry about." He winked. "But I want to apologize."

"For what?"

"Helping that vampire." Cordell's confession shocked me. "Reddick offered to pay my tuition if I did."

"Oh." I glanced at Domino, expecting some reaction, but he looked completely unphased.

"It was a shitty thing to do. You've been so nice to me, but I figured putting a letter in your car in exchange for all that money was worth it. I'm sorry, but I come from a poor family."

"It's okay. I understand." I nodded. "Thank you for telling me. Did you at least pass your exams?"

"Yes. I'm officially a licensed attorney," he said proudly. "This is my last week. I start my job next week."

"Congratulations. Now, stay out of this business, please." I pointed at him.

"Kind of impossible." He bit his lip.

"Why is that?" I asked.

"I hired him," Domino spoke up.

My eyes shot to the man beside me. "What?"

"He knows about us, he works on our schedule, and I'll need someone to handle all the shit my brother messed up. I may not be king, but I was related to him, so some of his crap fell on my lap now." Domino pulled me to his side. "Don't worry, he'll work with a team of lawyers who have been doing this stuff for years. He's just the face since the others can't be present during the day. "

"I don't like this." I shook my head. "He shouldn't be messing with vampires at all."

"I didn't think you would." Domino sighed. "But he's a big boy. He can handle himself."

"Are you okay with this?" I asked Cordell.

"I'm a first-year attorney making more than people who have been at this for well over a decade. Yes, I'm okay with it."

"Okay, but stay out of things as much as possible—and let me know if this one is mean to you." I poked Domino in the side.

"I will." Cordell nodded and smiled at us until the elevator doors closed.

"How do you feel?" I asked Domino as we walked back into my condo.

"Different." He looked at me. "But mostly the same. I'm stronger than I was before. I don't feel as thirsty."

"That's a good thing, right? It means my blood isn't doing anything bad to you." I examined him.

"I don't think it is."

"Good." I sighed. "And what about Reddick? I wasn't going to bring it up before, but I think we should talk about it, especially if you're responsible for tying up his loose ends."

"I thought I would feel worse about his death. Maybe if I had been the one to kill him, I would," Domino said honestly. "He was my brother, but the man hasn't felt like family to me since before we were vampires. Over a century of him tormenting me, and it's over. It's a strange sense of relief."

"And what about the vampire kingdom? Who will take over now?"

"That's not up to me to decide." Domino shrugged. "When it's all settled, they'll make sure every vampire knows about it. Right now, the biggest egos are still battling it out."

"The person who takes down the king doesn't automatically take his place?" I asked. "Isn't that why Vance was king after Reddick?"

"No, but I'll have to pay a hefty fine for doing so," Domino said. "Vance was king because he'd positioned himself to be king. He'd been planning that for years. I just hope they'll be a little lenient on me for killing him when they learn the circumstances."

"I hope so."

"Are you saying you won't be the queen of vampires?" He pulled me into his arms, and we stood in the hallway, hugging.

"Absolutely not!" I chuckled.

"Good. because I don't want to share you with them, and I don't want to spend all our time keeping your blood safe," Domino said honestly.

"You think the memo got out about what happens when you try to bite me without my consent?"

"If not, I'll make sure it does." Domino tightened his grip. "No one will dare come for you."

"What happens now?" I asked as Domino released his hold and led me through the apartment.

"I don't know." He sat on the couch, looked at the empty space beside him, and then glanced up at me. "What do you want to happen?"

I stared at the couch and then, with little hesitation, joined him. It felt just like I imagined it would—firm but soft, the cushions cupping my ass just right.

"I want to travel the world, collecting art," I answered Domino's question.

"Wait, you're sitting here now?" Domino smirked. "What changed?"

"I did." I nodded. "This couch was supposed to be a symbol of me stepping into a new version of my life. The promotion, the new job title, was all a symbol of a new me. Before I could even enjoy it, they snatched it away. I was left with this question of who I would be moving forward. I know it sounds crazy, but I didn't want to sit here until I had an answer to that question."

"Tell me, who do you want to be? What do you want to do?"

"I want to travel the world, collecting art," I answered Domino's question. "The new me isn't all that different from the old me. She just doesn't have a regular job tying her down right now. Maybe I can embrace that for a while. You know, while I figure all this magic stuff out."

"Then that's what we will do," he said confidently.

"Really?" I asked.

"Yes. I told you, it's my job to ensure all your dreams come true." He sighed. "And remember, I offered you a partnership before all this."

"I have another dream you can help me with." I raised a brow at him. "Actually, it's more like a fantasy."

"Tell me about it." He grinned. "I've run out of spy movies."

I grabbed his wrist and lifted it to his mouth. His lips curled up into a sinful grin before he dropped fang and punctured his vein. I drank from him, allowing the hypnotic effect to spread through me. Then, I wiped the blood from my chin with my finger and spread it across my neck.

I licked my lips as I watched Domino. His eyes were focused on my hand. When I dropped my finger from my neck, I ordered, "Bite me."

His eyes snapped up to me. "Are you sure?"

"Do you love me?" I asked, knowing exactly what his answer would be.

"Yes," he said with a heavy tone.

"Then bite me," I repeated my order and leaned my head back to further expose my neck.

Domino leaned forward, pressing his lips against my pulse, and then his teeth grazed my skin. As his tongue slid across my neck, cleaning away the blood, I shivered. The sensation of his warm breath on my skin made my pulse quicken before he finally sank his teeth into me.

As his sharp fangs sank into my skin, I felt a surge of terror, a fear it would end badly, that my blood would hurt him. The longest minute passed as he sipped from me, licking the blood from my neck, and then he pulled me into his lap.

I pulled away from him, my blood spilling down to my breast.

"Are you okay?" I asked.

He paused, the silence thick around him, waiting for something to happen. I could see the same concern in his slow, shallow breaths. His face remained stoic for a few moments, and then a wide grin spread across it, lighting up his features.

"Yes, I'm fine." He looked down at his hands. "No exploding."

"Good." My heart raced and my pussy tightened. "Do it again."

Domino leaned forward, but I pushed him back and jumped off his lap.

"Wait. Not here. I don't want to mess up my couch." I examined it to be sure we hadn't already gotten blood on it.

"Seriously?" he huffed.

"Hey, this cost a lot of money," I fussed. "I worked hard for that, and we aren't going to ruin it now."

"You're out of your mind." Domino laughed as he stood, picked me up, and carried me to the bedroom.

RAAWWARRR

As soon as Domino put me down, Maverick attacked him from behind, stabbing his claws into the vampire's back with a hiss.

"I thought we were cool now!" Domino yelled as he pulled Maverick from his back.

"Maybe he's still getting used to you!" I laughed.

"Yeah, right." Domino tossed Maverick out of the room, slammed the door, and returned to the bed. "I'm going to need more blood after that."

I licked my lips and dropped my head back to expose my neck. "Bite me, vampire."

The end.

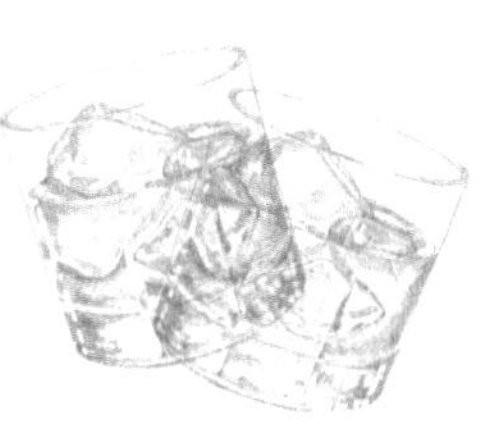

31

Who does that?

"Rayna, thank you for doing this." I greeted the woman as she appeared next to me on Jackie's porch.

"Of course. It makes sense that you would want me to meet them." She referred to my friends.

"Yeah. They convinced me to work with them on some things, and since you've agreed to help me continue developing my abilities." I nodded. "I figured your paths would cross at some point, so we might as well just do it now."

"Works for me. Besides, it gave me a reason to pop back to Earth."

"Missed it here?"

"I didn't think I would, but sometimes I do."

"Glad you could come back. Jackie is excited, but Lena is a little more hesitant than I thought she would be. You'd think she'd want to study you for her next book. The way you met Metice sounds a lot like what happened in her last novel."

"It does?" she chuckled. "Hard to imagine that."

"Yes, they're turning it into a movie now!" I boasted about my friend as I reached for the doorknob and glanced back at Rayna, who had a frown on her face.

"Oh?" The woman looked like she was trying to solve a quadratic equation.

"You might have read it. I remember you said you were a big book nerd." Just then, I pushed the door open. As I spoke the title of the book, Lena came into view and Rayna's voice echoed my own.

"To Conjure Love." Rayna gasped, then pointed her finger at Lena and shouted, "You!"

"Me?" Lena's startled eyes turned to me. "What did I do? Is this Rayna?"

"Why the hell would you put that spell in a book?" Rayna went on. "Do you know how dangerous that is? Do you know what happened to me?"

"Wait, that's how you summoned Metice?" I asked.

"Hold up, summoned?" Jackie popped into the room with a drink in her hand. "What's going on?"

"I read that spell from your book and ended up being dragged to hell a few days later!" Rayna continued her rant. "Come to find out you're an actual witch! How could you be so careless with your magic?"

"I changed the spell!" Lena fussed. "And I didn't think anyone would be dumb enough to try it."

"Who are you calling dumb?"

"I think that would be you." Jackie snorted.

"Hold on!" I jumped in between the three of them. "Everyone, please calm down. So what? Lena put a working spell in her book without considering how far dedicated readers might go. Rayna, things worked out well for you, right?"

A heavy sigh escaped Rayna's lips. "If you want to oversimplify things, yeah, they did."

"Okay, so there's no problem, right?"

Rayna took several deep breaths and launched another judgmental finger point at Lena. "You need to be a lot more careful with your work."

"I told her someone was going to try to conjure them a damn man. Look at what we have to work with. The dating pool is full of piss! It was bound to happen!" Jackie sipped her drink, then raised a brow at Rayna. "Wait, the spelled summoned a demon for you, right? What's that like? I heard demons are a lot of fun."

"Who told you that?" Lena asked.

"Hey, you're not the only witchy babe I know!" Jackie cackled. "One told me about a demon with two dicks! I'd like to meet him."

"My demon only has one dick," Rayna's expression turned devious. "But it rotates!"

"What?" Jackie cackled. "And you're yelling at her, girl, you owe her a damn gift basket!"

After a heavy pause, we all fell out laughing, and Rayna nodded at Lena. "Actually, hell yeah! Thanks. But don't do that again!"

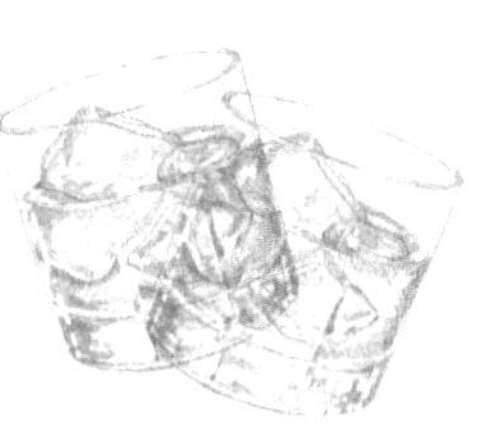

32

Hunting Party

Six months later, I stood with Domino by my side, watching my best friend fly on my cat dragon while shooting arrows at a group of rogue wolves. How the hell was this my life? I stepped back to give Maverick space as he came in for a quick landing in front of us.

"Now that's what I'm talking about!" Jackie jumped off Maverick's back, and he instantly returned to his cat form. "That is so much fun."

"Even more fun when you're shooting down monsters!" Lena clapped her hands as she appeared next to us. "I get to ride next!"

"You don't need a ride. Likosa taught you how to travel without one!" Jackie whined.

"You're both enjoying this too much," Domino grumbled.

"Oh, let it go, day walker!" Jackie teased. "I know you don't like taking out your monster brothers, but these are the worst of the worst, people even you wouldn't be friends with."

Domino said nothing as Jackie ran off to join the other hunters.

"She is never going to stop calling you that," I laughed, referring to Jackie's favorite new nickname for Domino.

"It's fine. I'll outlive her." I grinned as he pulled me into his arms. "Now kiss me and tell me you love me."

I lifted to my toes and pressed my lips against his. As always, his kiss made my stomach flutter and my pulse quicken. Before I lost my head, I pulled back from him and smiled.

"I really like you, Domino." I licked my lips.

"Like..." he groaned. "Still making me work for it?"

"It can't be that easy." I winked. Yes, I loved him, but I wasn't ready to tell him that. The man was immortal; he could wait for it. "Now, come on. There's a wolf to catch."

About the author

Jessica Cage is an International Award Winning, and USA Today Bestselling Author from Chicago, IL. As a girl, Jessica enjoyed reading tales of fantasy and mystery, but she always hoped to find characters that looked like her. Those characters came few and far in between. When they appeared they often played a minor role and were background figures. This is the inspiration for her independent publishing journey and the reason she focuses on writing **Characters of Color in Fantasy.** Representation matters in all mediums and Jessica is determined to give the young girl who looks like her, a story full of characters that she can relate to. Jessica has independently published over forty titles and has been featured in twenty different anthologies to date.

Thank you to our Kickstarter Supporters!

Ai'Asia Williams

Alanna Cole

Alecia Watkins

Alexis Myers

Alexis Washington

Alicia Hintzen

Allison Grier

Allyson Lindt

Alondra

Alonia Taylor

Alyssa

Alyssa

Amanda Balter

Amber Faye

Ash Raven

aylkaraemi

Britiney

C Malavasic

Carmen F

Caroline Coriell

Cerissa Howard

Chai PanDuh

Champrea

Chandra Lewis

Chanel Holm

Chelsie

Chemyeeka Lebrein Tumblin

Cherelle Hopper

Crowne

Destiny

Dorian Tobias

Elena

Erin Free

Famira

Fro Carducci

Gabrielle

Gata S

Gina Wohlgemuth

Golden Harshaw

Grace

Hamish Drummond

Hollie White

J Diggs

Jade Burns

Jasmyne

Jefferson

Jen (Fantasy girl)

Jennifer Milledge

Jessyka Muniz

Joanna Killigrew

Julie McAtee

Kalia W

Kandi Reid

Kaneka Tenia Jackson

Katee Robert

Kaysi

Keema Osborne

Kelli Eyres

Keyanni Mcclendon

Kira Brown

Kirstin Porter

Kristy Du'Gar

LaKevion Trotter-Clark

Larry Gochenouer

Lequeisha Sells

Maggie McAlister

Mal

Margaret

Marissa Krause

Midnight August Moon

Miles LaGree

Mysia N'yami Perry

Natasha Chisdes

Nese Gordon

Oles Dibrivniy

Olivia

Pluto

Rachel Walker

Raven McCandies

Rizing_1

Rochelle Lowe

ryinhah@icloud.com

Sangeetha

Sarah A. Macklin

Sasha M Fountain

Serena Sharber

Shalaunda

Shanique Hyde

Shenae

Shenita Wiggins

Shureice Dawn

Sierra Wanzer

Simo Muinonen

Sonya Bundschuh

Sophie Rich

Sophie Stern

Stephanie Williams

Stephleda

Susan S.

Tangela Williams

Tashanna Burton

Tenisha

Tianna Stubblefield

tongela

Tori Coke

Tyrisha H.

Xaviera

yunique

www.ingramcontent.com/pod-product-compliance
Lightning Source LLC
Chambersburg PA
CBHW021239190726
48289CB00005B/1398